Uncontrolled Burn (Covencraft #5)

by
Margarita Gakis

Print Edition, License Notes

UNCONTROLLED BURN
Book 5 of Covencraft

Cover by Steven Novak

To the Squee Gang - "When you find people who not only tolerate your quirks but celebrate them with glad cries of "Me too!" be sure to cherish them. Because those weirdos are your tribe."
— A.J. Downey, Cutter's Hope
I'm so lucky, happy and blessed to have you weirdos as my tribe

CHAPTER ONE

Staring at the freshly painted wall, Jade thought maybe Lily shouldn't be allowed to pick paint colors anymore.

"I like it!" Lily exclaimed and Jade did her best not to raise her eyebrows in surprise, because, really? Jade eyeballed it, trying to see what Lily saw. Lily stood next to her, hands on her hips, paint tray and roller at her feet. They'd cleared out the guest room and were redecorating, turning it into a bedroom for Lily. After pouring over Pinterest pages and YouTube videos, they'd finally made their way to the home improvement store and Jade had balked at Lily's paint choice, but said nothing. Lily seemed really gung-ho, but Jade figured once she saw the paint on the wall, she'd realize her mistake.

After taping and prepping and rolling on part of the first coat, Lily had a bright smile on her face. Not only did she radiate exuberance, Jade could feel her pleasure coming across their connection. Lily really did like it. It was a purple-grey-beige color that seemed flat and dismal. Like someone had thrown a glass of grape juice on a rain cloud. It was depressing.

"And I'm going to get some deep purple pillow cases," Lily continued, picking the roller back up. "And some soft grey sheets. Oh, and I might add in some burgundy accents. I really liked that one room I saw on Pinterest. I'm looking for a purple rug to cover most of the floor."

"That sounds… like a lot of purple," Jade managed.

"You hate it."

Lily didn't sound upset as she continued to paint. She mostly sounded amused. Jade picked up her trim brush and grabbed the back of the chair they'd brought upstairs, pulling it over to the window. She climbed up with her small can of purple-grey-beige and started working on the trim.

"It's not my room."

Lily snorted. "You really hate it."

She did. Jade shrugged one shoulder. Again, it wasn't her room. It was Lily's room. Separate from Jade's room. An idea Jade was still getting used to.

"We could redo your room too if you want," Lily offered. "What about blue? You like blue."

Jade did like blue. It was calm and clear. Made her feel cool and crisp.

"I bet we could even find the color of Paris' eyes," Lily teased. "Bring a photo to the paint store and have them match it with one of those fancy machines."

Jade scowled over her shoulder, seeing Lily purposefully ignoring Jade's sour look. "I'm not getting a paint color to match his eyes. That's one step away from him needing a restraining order."

It was Lily's turn to shrug. "He'd only know about it if he was in your bedroom. And if he *is* in your bedroom, I hope to god he's not looking at the paint."

Jade didn't reply, focusing on getting the paint as close to the ceiling as she could without it bleeding over to the ceiling. She shifted her weight, favoring the leg where Seth had dug one of his claws into the meaty part of her thigh while they'd been in the Dearth. It had only been about a week since she'd returned from Sakkara's errand. Gellar said it was healing well, but it bothered her. She'd bandaged it herself when she'd come home, but Lily had marched her to Gellar who'd promptly declared it needed stitches. Gellar claimed they'd gotten to it before it had a chance to get too infected. The skin around it was slightly hot and pulled tight. Jade had needed stitches on her arm as well from where Mnemosyne had bled her in payment for loaning out her car. That wound just itched. Both were likely to leave scars, though Gellar had done the best she could to minimize them; small, neat sutures all lined up in a row.

Jade's most striking scar was the patch of marble on her neck. A small expanse of skin that was hard to the touch, smooth under her fingertips, and cold, like stone. Her one wound from Medusa. The rest were a consequence of traveling through the Dearth, but her neck, that was from facing Medusa's stare. Bruce had a matching patch on his neck and he kicked at it often - his talons scraping against the stone, making a sound like nails on a chalkboard. He did it now as he sat in the corner watching Jade and Lily paint. Out of the corner of her eye, Jade saw Lily watch Bruce, and could see her contemplative expression. She wanted to ask Jade about the Dearth. She wanted to know what had happened.

Jade wanted to tell her. But... hadn't. Not yet. She didn't know if she was ready to. Or if she ever would be. In the week since she'd been back, Jade had returned to work, surprising herself with how easy it had been to fall back into the routine. Josef had been happy to see her and he'd hugged her tight. Uncomfortable tears had sprung to Jade's eyes at his warm embrace. She hadn't known how to respond other than to smile and say she was fine. His eyes had lingered on the patch of marble on her neck and she'd awkwardly raised a hand and placed it against her neck - as though by hiding it from view, she would keep it from people's minds. It was hard not to be self-conscious about a part of your skin turned to stone.

There'd been no further contact from Paris' mother, Sakkara. Paris had been forthcoming with what he knew, telling Jade about the conversations he'd had with his mother in Jade's absence. As if she'd expected anything else from him. It made her feel unbalanced. She wanted to be as honest and complete about her time in the Dearth and her face-off against Medusa, but she just... couldn't. Her feelings since coming home were a mess.

She'd been having nightmares about the assault again - something that hadn't happened in a long time. It was good that work was easy because her sleep was a disaster and she felt it taking more of a toll each day. She'd thought when she'd faced

Medusa, she'd started coming to terms with what had happened to her and Lily. But she felt sick every time she thought of it, and she was thinking of it more and more. She woke up in a cold sweat, feeling anxious and scared, even as Lily slept next to her soundly. Their connection wasn't strong enough anymore for Jade's feelings to wake Lily, which was just as well. They were worse than they had been in a long time and it made her angry and bitter. So much for dealing with things. So much for facing her past. Honestly, if this was what it meant to get *closure*, she felt pretty fucking justified in avoiding it all these years.

Then there'd been Seth and his information dump. Telling Jade that Sakkara had been the one to drown Jade when she was a child. For some reason, it was part of Sakkara's demon deal with Seth's sister. While Seth was forbidden from revealing the details of active details, he was able to allude to the details, or at least hint at enough that Jade could make some educated guesses. Jade didn't know if Sakkara's deal was still active because Sakkara was alive and still in service of a demon, or if there was something else, something maybe tied to Jade. She didn't know if she wanted to find out. She didn't know if she could afford not to.

Jade hadn't told Paris any of it. She didn't know how. *Remember that time? That time we were talking about all the crazy shit you found out your mother had done, like fake her death and make a demon deal? Guess what? She drowned me as a toddler too. Yeah, the demon in my pantry told me.* Paris already felt the need to apologize to Jade for his mother sending her to the demon realm. He'd probably feel responsible for her drowning Jade too.

He probably felt responsible for people crossing the street against the light half-way across town. He was no more responsible for his mother's actions than Jade was for her dad beating the shit out of her when she was a kid.

But knowing something and feeling it were two very separate things.

She went back to painting, focusing on the small section in front of her. This she could affect. This she could do. Paint a bit, get off the chair, move it over, and start a new section. Wash, rinse, repeat. The place where the strange patch on her neck transitioned from marble to skin itched, but she knew if she tried to scratch it, she'd get no relief. A lesson Bruce was yet to learn, if the kicking sound Jade still heard was anything to go by.

"I'm going to ask for my own job at the Coven."

Jade paused at Lily's words, the brush hovering millimeters from the wall before she placed it back down and wiggled it, getting the bristles into the junction where wall transitioned to ceiling. "Oh? You don't like Counter-Magic?" Okay, so Jade was no expert, but she thought she sounded pretty casual.

"It's not that I don't like it, but it's your job. How long am I supposed to sit next to you and work on spells?" Lily asked. Jade could tell by the tone it wasn't a question Lily expected her to answer. "I don't know as much magic as you-"

"Yet."

"Maybe ever. I don't have your memory for things. And I'm not as strong. I don't think Counter-Magic is a good fit for me."

Jade swallowed. There were a lot of things Lily felt weren't a good fit for her. It started when Lily said she was moving into the guest room. Then, the other day, she'd mentioned she was thinking about cutting or coloring her hair, for a change. Now she was talking about not working at Counter-Magic.

"Yeah, if you don't like it, you should look for something else," Jade managed, swallowing past the constriction in her throat. She didn't turn around as she stepped off the chair, moved it a few feet and then climbed back up.

"It's not that I don't like it. It's your thing. I want my own thing."

Jade nodded, not sure what she should say.

"I thought I'd talk to Paris, maybe Josef, Callie and Henri and see if they had any ideas. There must be a job posting board. I could check that out. Henri said when you showed up you got your power tested. I gotta get that done too so they know what my levels are. Henri said he'd help me get registered for my own Coven phone and email address."

"He knows all the boxes that need to be ticked."

"He is. He offered to read my aura, but I don't know how I feel about that."

Jade turned the brush in her hand, feeling the warm wood under her fingertips. "When was this?"

"Hmm? Oh, at yoga yesterday morning."

"Oh, I didn't know you went."

"You were still sleeping. Henri, Callie and I did yoga in the dungeon at the Coven and used the gym showers."

"Callie doesn't like to call it the dungeon," Jade said.

"God, I know, right? But it's so obviously a dungeon, no matter how many times she reminds us it's the library now." Lily continued to paint, using long up and down strokes on the wall. "But it's cozy down there with the low electricity and the lack of windows. But, yeah. By this time next week, I should have my own phone and email address. And hopefully my power level tested."

Jade remembered her own power testing when she came to the Coven. It had involved examining some items, working with others, and then Paris had tried to wash his magic over Jade - glamor her, they called it. She'd pushed him back, which she'd learned was incredibly rare. As Coven Leader, he had the most magic in the Coven. She'd been able to resist being overwhelmed by his power.

"Did Henri say if Paris was going to be there for your test?" Jade asked.

She felt, rather than saw, Lily shrug. "He didn't say. I remember your test. Someone more powerful than me has to be there, right?"

Jade hmmmm'd and kept working on painting.

"But it probably won't need to be Paris. Like I said, I'm not as powerful as you. Speaking of Paris though," Lily began, and Jade braced herself physically and mentally for what would come next. "Are you going to do anything about him?"

"About what?" Ugh, it was stupid to play dumb with Lily. She knew how Jade's mind worked and knew all her tricks, especially if the disgruntled snort she just let loose was anything to go by.

"About how you have feelings for him. *Feeling* feelings."

If it were anyone else, she'd play the, *I don't know what you mean* card, but she knew exactly what Lily meant and Lily knew it.

"I… don't know."

"You should. He likes you."

Jade bristled. "That's not all there is to it."

"Why not?"

Jade wanted to throw her paint brush down on the ground, see big splatters of grey-purple-beige hit the wall and window. She wanted to yell, suddenly, inexplicably. She wanted to shout at Lily that it was different, that she didn't normally feel an attraction to people, men, and now she did and didn't know what to do with it. She didn't know what it would mean to tell Paris. Or how to live with it if it turned out he didn't feel the same way. If he cared for her only as a Coven member, or a protégée. Jade thought of Seth needling her about her assault, trying to ply her for information only so he could use it to help Medusa. She thought of Medusa and the things she'd said. *You and I share a moment*. Medusa had seen into Jade's mind, into her heart, and known of Jade's assault. Even if she could talk to Paris and explain that she was hesitant and maybe scared, would she be able to articulate why?

"You know why," was all Jade said, focusing her eyes on the paint.

"Yeah," Lily said slowly and Jade felt the hairs on the back of her neck rise. "About that."

Jade turned to look at her, watching as Lily carefully set her paint roller down and then placed her hands on her hips. A serpent of fear curled in her stomach as she watched Lily and she knew what Lily would say before her mouth formed the words.

"When you were gone, with Seth, in the Dearth, I talked to Paris. He knows."

"Knows what?" Jade argued, knowing in her gut what Lily would say before she did, but somehow hoping if she pretended it wasn't true, then it wouldn't be.

"About what happened to us. He knows."

Jade set her paint brush down. Jesus, it was like none of her secrets were her own. Seth knew. Medusa knew. Now Paris. There were thousands of victim websites that would remind her it wasn't her fault, but all she could think in that second was, *he knows and it was her fault*. She had the sudden urge to go hide - curl up in the closet, pull the doors shut behind her and just… never come back out.

"Oh. I see." She stared at the line where the painted wall met the ceiling. She'd done a very good job of cutting it well and true - no overlap. That was easy to focus on. The perpendicularity where the two met. Clean lines. Straight angles. Don't think of anything else. Don't.

"I think it could help. Now that he knows. You don't have to worry he'll pressure you."

*No, now I'll worry that **he**, the monster who attacked us, will always be there. When I look at Paris, when I think about touching Paris, when he thinks about touching me, all we'll both be thinking of is **him**.*

Jade swallowed and nodded. "Sure."

Lily's shoulders sagged. "You wish he didn't know. You wish I hadn't told him."

"Jesus, either you're in my head or you're not, but pick a fucking side." Her tone was mean, cruel and she wanted to snatch the words back, but couldn't. Didn't.

Lily bristled. "You don't know what it was like. You weren't here."

"Well, you were gone for years and I managed not to tell everyone I met our entire history."

"Paris is not 'everyone you've met.'"

"No. He isn't."

"You weren't here," Lily repeated.

"No, I was trapped in the Dearth, with Seth, getting ready to face Medusa."

"And I was here, without you for the first time."

"Pretty shitty, isn't it? When the other half of you is gone." The full feeling of despair Jade felt when Lily died was pushed behind her words, adding weight and gravitas to them. Lily flinched, as though she'd been slapped.

"I didn't know… when I asked you to do that. To try and… I couldn't have known that it would be just you left."

Jade shook her head. Both sorry she'd let the force of her emotions out and not sorry at the same time. It took her a moment to feel in control of herself again. "I didn't mean to let you feel that. I don't mean it." Jade didn't know if it was true, but she hoped Lily believed it.

"No. No, you're right. I did that. To you. I asked you to do something I shouldn't have. And you did it. I knew you would. I trusted you to carry that burden," Lily said. "I asked you to cut our wrists, knowing you couldn't, wouldn't say no." Lily swallowed, toeing at the paint roller.

"It was a long time ago." It wasn't true. Jade didn't know why she said it. Maybe just for something to say.

"No, it wasn't."

"We don't have to talk about it."

"There's a lot we don't talk about. Like what happened while you were in the Dearth. Either for you or me."

Jade turned the paint brush over in her hand. "Not everything needs to be talked about."

"I want you to know you can tell me what happened. I won't judge you. I trust your decisions. I know whatever you did, it was right."

Jade nodded. At the moment she'd had to face Medusa, she'd turned away from Lily, from their connection. Sakkara had believed the key to facing Medusa, and surviving, was the dual connection that Jade and Lily shared. Their ability to see through each other's eyes. Sakkara and her demon mistress thought that meant Jade could face Medusa and survive. Lily thought it was true as well, at the time. Only it hadn't been about that. It had been about Jade being able to see Medusa for what she was. A woman who'd been violated and had chosen to become a monster, so that she would never be a victim again. It was Jade's ability to see her, to know her that had enabled Jade to face Medusa and not turn to stone.

Mostly not turn to stone. Except for the patch of marble on her neck, and the matching one on Bruce.

But Lily didn't know that. Paris didn't know that. No one but Jade, Medusa and Seth knew what happened in Medusa's home. Jade didn't have the words to explain it. She didn't know how to talk about what it was like to see Medusa and not see a monster. To only see a woman who'd been violated and had chosen to become a monster so that it would never happen again. Now, standing in Lily's new bedroom and staring at the paint drying on the wall, Jade keenly missed their intimate connection - where she could feel things and have Lily understand the full meaning behind all her emotions. With words necessary between them now, she didn't have the full lexicon she required.

She could open her mind to Lily - let Lily's mind merge with hers and share her consciousness, but to do so would likely lead to a migraine for Jade. She couldn't physically or emotionally handle one at the moment.

"It's not that I don't want to tell you," Jade began, dipping her paint brush into the can and wiping the excess off on the rim. "But when I think about it..."

She took in a sharp breath. She remembered seeing Medusa as both a Gorgon and a woman. Seeing her hair as serpentine creatures, writhing over one another. Seeing void eyes - bottomless and empty, waiting to drag Jade down. And then seeing just a woman. A young woman betrayed in a place she thought she would be safe. A young woman hurt so badly that she chose to become a monster so that it would never happen again. Jade realized as she thought, she'd been dipping her paint brush in the can and then dragging it along the edge to get rid of the excess, over and over and over again. She forced her hand to be still.

"You don't have to tell me," Lily said, directing her attention to her own painting, dragging the roller up and down the walls. "I don't want you to feel you have to share things with me. We're two different people. We're allowed to have secrets from one another."

"It's not a secret," Jade defended. Secret was too heavy a word. Secret implied willful concealment. It wasn't intentional or willful. It was simply Jade didn't know how to articulate it. And when she thought of it, her lungs went tight and hard - unable to pull in a deep breath.

"Maybe secret isn't the right word," Lily added, as if reading Jade's thoughts. Though they didn't share information so freely as they had, they still had a connection and were likely to know or understand what the other was thinking. "We're allowed not to tell each other everything. You're allowed not to tell me everything," Lily amended, running the roller through the paint tray and then back on the wall. "Just like I may not tell you everything."

The hairs on the back of Jade's neck rose. "What aren't you telling me?"

She saw Lily shake her head. "Nothing. It's just... we're our own people now. We're no longer two people sharing a consciousness. At best, we're like twins. Maybe we share some residual connections."

"And at worst?" Jade wished she hadn't asked. She didn't want to hear the answer.

Lily, ever the more pragmatic amongst them, answered nonetheless. "At worst, we're like estranged siblings. We share an upbringing and not much else."

Was that all she was to Lily now? An estranged sibling? Jade thought of the things they knew about each other, the things they shared. Who else could say that they'd lived inside someone else's mind - shared thoughts, feelings and beliefs? Who else could say they knew exactly how their father hit them - how his blows rained down, how you could feel the level of his anger in each one? Who else knew the exact feeling of being ignored by their mother? Of knowing that the woman you called mom knew your father was beating the shit out of you, but did nothing to stop it? Who else shared the exact emotion when a date turned horribly wrong, and a man turned to you with something in his eyes, something unfathomable and you knew, *you knew,* you could try to escape, but you wouldn't succeed?

Who else had someone with which they shared these exact, precise, emotions? And Lily so easily expressed it as a sort of estranged sibling relationship. Maybe it was, Jade didn't know. Lily was all she had.

"But if you do ever want to talk about it, you shouldn't feel like you have to talk to me."

"Who else would I talk to?"

"Callie. Henri." Lily shrugged. "Maybe a therapist."

She could feel her face curl up a bit at Lily's suggestion, but didn't say anything in response.

They worked in silence for a while, not speaking, the air between them only broken by the sound of Lily's paint roller going up and down the wall, and occasionally the sound of Jade getting off the chair and moving it over so she could continue on with the trim. The room, once a bland wheat color, took on the darker hue and started to feel like a cozy den - a haven.

"Maybe it's not too purple," Jade amended turning to see the wall that Lily had done.

"Like I said, we can do your room too, if you want."

"I don't know what I want," Jade replied, knowing she was talking about more than just her room.

Lily nodded, understanding. "Well, it's not like there's a rush, or an expiration date."

Jade swallowed, dipping her paint in the can again.

"But don't confuse not knowing what you want with being afraid to make a change."

"Oh my god, if we're going to turn this into a full on therapy session, I need to lie down and you should sit in a chair with a clipboard and a pair of wire-rimmed glasses."

Lily guffawed and gestured to place she'd spilled paint on the drop cloth. "Look at zis paint splotch and tell me vhat you see," she said in a horrible German accent.

"I see a plate of nachos and a bottle of wine," Jade replied, thinking of her stomach and not really looking at the paint.

"We should go for nachos tonight! I'll text Callie and Henri. And then we should see if they want to go shopping with us this weekend and we can get stuff for my room and see if we can find a running jacket to replace yours."

"And running shoes. I left them at Medusa's."

"There's a sentence you don't hear every day," Lily muttered, pulling out her cell phone. She'd taken over Jade's personal cell since Jade had a Coven one too. It made the most sense. But now, with

Lily getting her own Coven phone, Jade wondered what would happen to the personal one. What would happen to all the things of theirs they couldn't split? "Okay, texts sent. I told them we'll be at the pub at seven if they want to join us. If not, it'll be just us." Lily paused, setting down the phone and picking up the roller again. "I know you're not ready to talk about it, but do you realize you've never called her 'the Gorgon' since you've been back? You always call her Medusa."

"That's her name," Jade replied, going back to painting. "A gorgon may be what she is, but it's not all she is."

"Hmmm. I thought it was interesting," Lily continued. "I wasn't sure you knew."

Medusa was more than a monster, just as Jade was more than a victim. Some days it felt so obvious and other days it felt fresh and raw - something only recently exposed to air and light. It didn't feel right calling her the Gorgon any more. Not when she'd collapsed in front of Jade and Jade had held her as she cried.

"I knew."

CHAPTER TWO

Paris stood in the doorway to his home office, staring at the desk. It had been his mother's desk, originally, and then his. He'd planned on sitting down and getting a couple hours of work done, regardless it being the weekend, but looking at it now, his mind was stuck on his mother. Sakkara, as he preferred to call her in his mind now. On her lies. On her demon deal. On how she banished Jade to the Dearth to face Medusa. She'd felt entirely justified in her actions without remorse. Paris thought of what she'd said, about Jade, when Jade had returned from the Dearth.

"Jade could be a powerful tool for you, but you'll waste her if you coddle and cosset her. I knew she would be strong enough to survive both the journey and the errand. You should be thinking of what else she can do for your Coven, not be dropping everything here and rushing to her side."

Sakkara thought of Jade as an implement to be wielded - nothing more than a mindless, soulless thing, like a hammer or an axe. He didn't know if he could sit at that desk and not think of the ways Sakkara had lied to him. His eyes moved away from the desk to the floorboard, where underneath one of her demon grimoires was hidden. Jade had the other two. Paris knew she studied them and learned demon magic from them - demon magic at which she was quite proficient. Paris got a headache if he read any of Sakkara's grimoires for longer than a few minutes, something that didn't appear to affect Jade. He wondered if Jade suffered any unknown effects from the demon grimoires. Should he be worried? He wasn't sure who he would even ask. Perhaps Hannah. As the oldest witch of their Coven and certainly the wisest person he knew, she would either have the answer or know how to find it. Thinking of Sakkara's grimoires brought to mind some of what he'd seen in them: spells he couldn't decipher, languages he couldn't read, runes he didn't comprehend. Jade was figuring them out. With her sharp intellect and incredible memory for printed material, she was learning demon magic in a way no one else he knew did.

One of the runes in the grimoire still haunted Paris. The Resurrection Rune. Jade had recognized the rune, and left notes in a runeology book she had studied that Sakkara used a similar one in one of her grimoires - the grimoire still had Paris had under his floorboards. He'd confronted Sakkara about it. He recalled being quite ill as a child, being in hospital, and then suddenly getting well, his mother swooping in and smelling of her magic. Had she had the scent of black licorice on her then? The scent that clung to her when she used demon magic? He couldn't recall.

He'd been a child and the memory was hazy with time and became more clouded as he tried to recall it better. Could he have been mortally ill? Did his mother use some variation of the demon resurrection rune on him? Did he owe his life to her practice of demon magic? He could ask Dr. Gellar to request his childhood medical records, he supposed. They would detail what he'd been ill with and how sick he'd been, even if they didn't explicitly state that magic had cured him. He needed to know what that rune had been used for. He needed to know how far his mother had descended into darker magic. Sakkara had appeared horrified at Paris' suggestion she had used that rune on him, but he now knew her to be a very convincing liar. She had, after all, been dealing with demon magic for years and faked her death to the entire Coven. Including her own son.

Jade was already investigating Sakkara's grimoires, and the spells in them, but Paris didn't know how she focused her time. She had made some notes on the rune, but she made similar notes all over the grimoires - seemingly snatching bits and pieces of knowledge and information, working on compiling the whole. He could ask Jade to investigate the Resurrection Rune and he had no doubt that if he did, she would. He wasn't sure if he was comfortable asking. If he found out his mother had used demon rune magic to bring him back from death, would that change anything? Would he be better off not knowing?

Secondly, he thought of something Lily had said to him. When Jade had been in the Dearth. Her absence affected Lily keenly and she'd told Paris more of their past - their shared past with each other.

She'd told Paris things he unconsciously suspected, but never actually solidified. Things regarding Jade's reluctance to be touched, on her brisk behavior and defensive personality. Finding out Lily and Jade had been sexually assaulted was surprising and yet not. In some respects, he wished he could un-know. He felt strangely guilty for hearing it from Lily and not from Jade herself, as if he'd used nefarious means to gather the information. On the other hand, he was glad he knew. He felt in a better position to perhaps understand her.

Lily also told Paris how after the assault, after years of Lily and Jade living together, sharing a mind, a body, a consciousness, Lily had felt unable to continue and had asked Jade to end it for them both, to kill them. And Jade had done what Lily asked. Lily's words echoed in his mind now.

"Do you know what that's like? To have that kind of power over someone? To know you can ask them to do something, anything, and they'll say yes? You're not really asking them, are you? You're telling them. If they can't say no, it's not a question, is it?"

If Paris asked Jade to investigate the Resurrection Rune, he had no doubt she'd say yes. She had a curious mind and also, at times, appeared to have a desire to please. He wasn't sure she felt free enough to say no to him if she didn't want to look into that particular rune at this time.

How could he ask Jade in such a way to make it clear she was free to decline? And even if he managed to, would she still take him up on the offer?

Perhaps he was over thinking. She had a strong personality and had shown her ability to say no in other areas. Still, the worry lingered. The notion he could coerce her into doing something she may not have thought to do on her own, or may not want to do at all, weighed on him.

His mind was also tangled with other words of his mother's.

It's dangerous for a Coven Leader to become too attached to any of the witches in the Coven.

He was attached to Jade, though he wasn't sure what the extent of that was. Of course, he felt a fondness and a fealty toward all witches in the Coven. They were his kin and, as Coven Leader, he had a duty to protect them. Yet with Jade... he didn't worry about other Coven members like he did Jade. He didn't speak with them as he did with Jade, nor did they speak to him as she did - irreverently at times and brutally honest. She was not impressed nor cowed by his power or his position. He had always felt separate from the rest of the Coven himself. In his position, he never forgot that while he may be a witch like them, he was not one of them. And yet, with Jade, he had no notion of her being separate nor apart from him. She spoke her mind. She disagreed with him. She joked with him. That was something that struck him the most. She made him laugh. As well, though he felt a need to care for her, as he did the rest of the Coven, she was proving over and over again that she was more than capable of looking after herself. She'd been attacked by a demon, faced a rogue Coven Leader, battled her own personal trials and survived a trip to the Dearth, where she'd not only had a demon as her road-trip companion, but faced a gorgon and won. She hardly needed him to ensure her personal safety, however fleetingly his lizard brain may want to be able to guarantee it.

He thought of Bruce suddenly. Of his heavy, warm weight as he'd slept against Paris' leg while Jade was trapped in the Dearth. Familiars echoed their witch's feelings and Bruce had left Lily's side to be with Paris while Jade had been absent. Was Jade simply fond of Paris the way students were fond of their teachers? Some students became enamored with competent leaders, confusing admiration with affection. Bruce's behavior offered keen insight into Jade's feelings and thoughts, but perhaps Paris suffered from the Observer Effect; changing the very event he wished to observe by his observation.

All of his thoughts, while stemming from his initial one of the Resurrection Rune, were hardly germane to matter at hand. His mother's demon magic. Had she used it on Paris, as a child, to bring him back from the brink of death? And if so, did that affect any part of his magic now? What if... what if... there could potentially be a kernel of such magic still lingering upon him? Could it affect the Coven? Could he stop it? He could live with his mother practicing demon runeology upon him to save his life, he supposed, but he couldn't take the risk that it might affect the entire Coven. With that thought in mind, he pulled out his cell phone and called Jade.

And got her voice mail. He couldn't recall ever having to leave a message for her before.

"Hello. It's Paris. I... I assume you're still working on my mother's grimoires. Not that you have to or expect that of you. Well." He swallowed. "I've a request. You're free to say no, to be clear. You've no obligation to me, or to anyone for anything." Dear Goddess, he was babbling. "I wish to investigate... that is, ask for you to investigate the demon rune in my mother's books. The one for Resurrection. You've some notes. I saw them. When you were in the Dearth. Not before nor since. I'm not checking up on your work." He thought he might feel actual pain in his chest. "Please call me if you have questions. So. Yes. Goodbye."

Paris jabbed at the screen to end the call, wondering if he should take use of the disembodied voice's offer of deleting his message and re-recording it. It did not matter how he'd said what he'd said. His intent was clear. He would spend no longer thinking on it. He swore, staring one more time at the desk in his office. He would work from the Coven today. And perhaps ask his assistant to enquire into other options for a home office.

#

With the first coat of paint drying, Lily had taken the car hoping to track down the pillows she wanted. Jade cleaned her hands of paint and then checked her jeans to make sure she didn't have any on her ass before she sat down on the sofa. Bruce toddled over to her, sniffing her pant leg once and then letting out a mighty snort.

"Yeah," Jade said, pulling her phone out of her pocket. "Paint stinks. It's just for a little bit, bud, and then it won't smell so bad. If you really hate it, I can whip up a spell."

"Pffffffffttttt." Bruce waddled over to the fireplace, looking over at Jade expectantly. She immediately brought a fire to life in the hearth, the red and orange flames strong and bright. Bruce didn't so much lie down as throw himself on his side, wiggling a bit to get his belly closer to the heat.

Jade hadn't felt her phone vibrate when she was painting with Lily and was confused when she saw she had voice mail. She also sometimes had the opposite issue when she was sure that she'd felt or heard it go off only to check it and see that there were no notifications. Phantom phone vibrations. According to the internet, it was a thing in the world now. Checking her phone, her stomach fluttered when she heard Paris' voice, his tone measured and even.

As she listened, she absently sketched out parts of the Resurrection Rune he asked about, easily remembering its strange curves and lines. She could see Sakkara's grimoire in her mind - Sakkara's flowing, feminine script covering the top half of the page. Jade didn't know what language it was and hadn't done much research to find out yet. And then, at the bottom of the page, a little to the left, the rune. Jade had a post-it note on that page in the grimoire, noting that it reminded her of some demon runes, but that it wasn't quite similar enough. Possibly some kind of binding rune. She had no objection against researching it and probably would have even if Paris hadn't asked. She'd probably get around to researching everything Sakkara had in her grimoires eventually, and if Paris wanted her to focus on the rune, she could do that. She already had some books on order from Callie. She hung up the cell phone, staring down at the screen for a moment. Should she call him back? And say, what? *Got your message and totes can do that.*

Her gaze darted to the kitchen, beyond which lay her pantry. With her pantry came the demon portal and with the portal came Seth. Jade hadn't spoken to him since just after she'd returned from the

Dearth. He'd essentially told Jade that Paris' mother had drowned Jade as a child as part of her own demon deal. To what end, he either didn't know or couldn't say. Asking Seth about the demon rune might be the path of least resistance, but it also could be a path filled with poisonous vipers. The muscle in her thigh twitched where Seth's claws had dug into the meaty part of it. She still wasn't sure what he'd been trying to do at the time. Traveling through the Dearth with him as her only guide, she'd been pretty accepting of any information he'd had. Seeing how nervous he'd been approaching Demon Customs made her more keen to sit down and shut up. But when she'd been asked a direct question and when she answered, Seth had sunk his claw into her leg and kept it there, like she was a bug on an specimen tray. Then she'd had to give her talisman over as some kind of trade. Her fingers moved to where the salamander charm used to hang on her neck, against her clavicle. She had no idea where it was now. Still in the Dearth, she guessed, with the Customs Officer that took it. It was a powerful object, she'd been told, first by the Customs Officer and then by Seth. Paris had made it for her when she first joined the Coven, and though she remembered there had been some kind of spell or something when he'd placed it on her neck, and she was clearly well aware of magic, she'd thought it was more ceremonial than functional. Sakkara herself had also mentioned it, noting that she would have been better able to control Jade's dreams but the salamander charm made by Paris blocked her.

Jade missed it. She'd taken to fiddling with it while reading or thinking or when nervous about something. Now her fingers would drift to her neck and she would feel a moment of surprised loss, until she remembered that she didn't have it anymore. When she'd returned, she'd told Paris she'd had to trade it. Although it hadn't really been a choice, she still felt like she'd been given something precious and had neglected to take care of it. Shame and regret sat heavy in her gut. Paris said he'd make her another, but she didn't know if that was just something he said in the moment or if he meant it. She didn't know if she could ask.

Bruce sighed, long and drawn out, the side of his chest heaving up and then slowing sinking down as he exhaled. Jade stared at the phone again, thumb hovering over the redial button. Lily's words were in her head. *You have feelings for him. Feeling feelings.* She did. Jade knew she did. But she didn't know what those feelings were or what she wanted to do about them. She didn't normally feel attraction to men or women, even before she and Lily had been attacked. She could look at people and see how they were aesthetically attractive and how, intellectually, sex with them would be appealing. When she shared a body with Lily, she'd felt when Lily found someone attractive in a sexual manner, but it was never something Jade felt herself. She couldn't know if she wanted to be with someone until she got to *know* them. What if they were a raging asshole? What if they were the kind of person that grabbed into the bulk donuts without using the tongs, brushing against all the other donuts with their hands? What if they were like Dex? All smarmy charm and slick words, and talking to them was like talking to a mask with a snake writhing underneath the surface? Jade either didn't get that close to people to know them well enough, or if she did, once she knew them, she didn't like them.

Though she hadn't exactly traded histories with Paris, or sat around a fire pit sharing a bottle of wine, Jade did feel like she knew him. He was fair. He was loyal. He had great power, but didn't throw it around. He listened to Jade when she spoke. He didn't always like what she had to say, but he listened. And his eyes. Sometimes when she caught his gaze, she was surprised at how blue they were. Did they get more blue the longer she knew him or was it that they were so blue she couldn't remember the exact shade? Her stomach fluttered as she thought about it and she pursed her lips, feeling foolish. Taking a deep breath, she pressed redial before she could distract herself any further.

"Paris speaking."

Bruce's tail thumped on the ground a couple times, like a dog who wags his tail when his owner arrives, but is too lazy to get up.

"Hey, it's Jade. I got your message." Jade cringed at the way her words came out like it was a question she was asking. "About the Resurrection Rune," she continued. "And I can do that. I can research it."

"You don't have to. I want to be clear that you are free to say no if you like."

Jade frowned, confused. "Yeah, I know."

"I don't want you to feel if I ask you to do something, you are somehow obligated to accept. Either because I'm Coven Leader, or... or because."

"Okay." Jade had an odd sensation in her chest like she maybe almost knew why Paris was being so careful, but she didn't want to examine it closely. "I mean, I'm always looking into them, but if you'd like me to look into that rune, I don't mind. I can do that," she repeated.

"As long as you don't feel like I'm coercing you."

At his words, she swallowed, something in her chest sinking to her gut and wrapping around her insides, squeezing. Bruce got up from his place at the hearth and waddled over to her, pushing his snout against her knee. His tongue darted out and pressed against the inside of her wrist for a half a second before zipping back into his muzzle. Paris' word choice, *coerce*, made her immediately think of one of its synonyms. *Force.* She had a sudden urge to hang up and go upstairs and get in her closet, maybe with Bruce, and lie down with the door closed. Instead, she licked her lips, finding them dry.

"No. Not at all."

"Good. I'm glad."

Jade could hear the relief in his tone and she was relieved at the fact that he'd worried, but also slightly sick he felt it necessary to speak to her about it.

"Have you heard from her? Your mom."

"No," Paris answered sharply. "Wherever she slunk off to, she's been silent. Why? Have you?"

"Fuck no," she blurted. "If I had, you'd be the first person to know."

"Ah, well. Thank you."

"No problem." There was an moment of silence on the phone where Jade could hear him breathing. *Feeling feelings,* Lily's words echoed in her brain. People had feelings all the time. They didn't have to be acted upon. Maybe she'd be better off not doing or saying anything. Maybe not. She realized the silence on the phone was at critical mass, so to speak. Any longer and it would get wicked awkward. "So," she said quickly, "I'll look into the rune and I'll let you know what I find."

"Again, thank you."

"Yeah." She swallowed. "Okay, bye." She hung up the phone before she could embarrass herself further, pressing the device to her forehead and exhaling.

"Pfffffttt."

"Don't Monday morning quarterback me," Jade said, glaring at him.

Bruce flopped to his other side, leaving her wondering how he managed to show her his belly and make it seem like an insult at the same time.

"Pfffffffttt."

"I invite you to do better."

It's not like he could do worse, she thought, although she didn't say it out loud. She shook her head. Enough with the thinking about feelings. She had research to do. Research on the Resurrection Rune and possibly on demon magic to boot. Her eyes drifted toward the kitchen again. Bruce spat three times and Jade looked back at him to see him staring at her accusingly.

"I didn't say I was going to contact him," Jade defended herself. "But it would be foolish for me not to consider all my options."

Bruce gave a disgusted snort and walked away from the fireplace, trundling up the stairs with heavy steps. Jade had never seen him willingly walk away from a fire.

"You could save the judgey-mcjudgeypants until I actually fuck up!" she called after him.

"Pfffffftt."

"Right back at you," she muttered.

CHAPTER THREE

After seeing the strange landscape of the demon realm, being at the Coven, using a computer and going for coffee was odd in its mundaneness. Jade felt like people stared, but figured she was being ridiculous. No one knew the details of what happened to her. From Sakkara haunting her dreams, Lily appearing in the lake, to Jade and Seth being banished to the demon world and Jade facing Medusa - nothing was common knowledge.

Only a select few people knew the details: Jade, Lily, Josef, Callie, Henri. And of course, Paris. She was being overly sensitive. There was no reason for anyone to be staring at her. No reason at all. Except, of course, to them, she was still the only witch born outside a Coven and now she had a twin to boot. Yep. Nothing to see here, she thought as she squared her shoulders and made her way to Counter-Magic, feeling eyes on her the entire time.

She stuffed her purse under her desk and booted up her email, tapping her fingers on her desk and checking her watch. Ten after eight. It was a workday, like every other workday. She wasn't defeating demons, rogue Coven Leaders, having nightmares or finding herself stuck in the Dearth. Totally normal day. Except for how Lily was picked up early by Henri to have a quick coffee before Lily's power test. It was scheduled to start at eight-thirty. Without Jade. Which was fine. She didn't need to be there. Jade fully remembered her own power test and it's not like anything bad or painful had happened. It had just been her, Gellar and Paris.

Lily had been so excited, her face a mixture of determination and nerves. As Jade hovered on the doorstep, Henri had rolled his window down and heckled Jade for missing her run with Daniel that morning. She hadn't wanted to miss seeing Lily off for her test and maybe, possibly, hoping that at the last minute Lily would change her mind about doing it by herself and invite Jade along. But Lily had gotten in the car and waved happily at Jade before yanking out some lipstick and applying it as Henri drove away.

Jade's eyes scanned through her email. Cafeteria going nut-free, stained glass windows getting cleaned, Coven tax slips coming next week, a reminder that any new complex spells should be vetted by a senior witch in Counter-Magic, a notice that one of the middle schools was learning their first water spells this week so be on the lookout for random raindrops, puddles and water bombs, and a message about some natural disasters that were being watched by the Supernatural Council.

Eight-fifteen.

It was going to be a long morning if it was just email and paperwork. Not that she wanted people's magic to go wrong, but at least problem solving kept her busy. Maybe someone would bleach their hair and it would start failing out, or a teenager would get unusually high marks on a test and a teacher would want it audited for magic. Maybe someone's cat would go missing and they would need help with a locator spell. Although she hoped she wouldn't see any more eye color changing spells gone wrong.

Yesterday had featured a kid with bulging eyes and twisted optic nerves. She shuddered, remembering the young teen being led in by his mom. He'd wanted blue eyes. He'd gotten bulging sockets. Gross. With some guidance from Josef, Jade had managed to unwind the spell - using a bit of demon magic. Josef then made him some kind of eye poultice that smelled like lavender and cut grass. The mom had hustled her kid out of Counter-Magic, staring at Jade like she had a communicable disease.

"Not everyone is comfortable with demon magic," Josef had told her easily after the mother and son were gone. If it had been a cartoon, there would have been a hole in the exact shape of a middle-aged woman and a teenage boy punched through the door, given the speed they'd gone with.

"I could have done it with regular magic, but I couldn't be sure it wouldn't recur. With the demon magic, I feel more confident. It's precise. And those are his eyes. Pretty sure he wants to keep them."

"I'm not condemning you for your choice. You use the magic that is best for the case - that includes what you're most proficient with. I trust your judgment and that was a successful counter-hex."

"Tell that to his mom."

Josef sighed. "We've gotten complacent in our magic to some extent. It's good that you're able to branch out. Demon magic isn't negative or evil because of the source. Only the way magic is used that can determine that. There was nothing about that spell that was wrong or immoral."

Jade appreciated Josef saying that. She couldn't help but feel it meant something bad that she was good with demon magic. She liked it. It was structured and orderly. Given what Seth had told Jade about the demon world, the Dearth, Jade could see why. In a place where the normal rules of physics didn't apply, it would be even more important that any magic used was precise and specific, so the turnout could be predicted as much as possible.

"Paris wants me to do some research for him. On his mother's grimoires," she'd blurted.

Since getting the message from Paris she hadn't told anyone about it. Not even Lily. Lily tended to stay out of Jade's magic stuff - preferring to learn spells on her own and not just pick up what Jade already knew. Plus, she didn't have the aptitude for demon magic Jade had. That meant when Jade was nose deep in Sakkara's demon grimoires Lily was uninterested and Jade was usually by herself. While she'd already been researching the demon rune, she felt better knowing that Paris wanted her to do the same thing. Telling Josef kind of felt like asking for permission from him too.

Josef nodded. "Makes sense. I'm sure he's got a lot of unanswered questions about her. Problem is your research will lead to more."

"You don't think I should do it?"

"No, I think that you're the best person to look into Sakkara's books. Your judgment isn't clouded by sentimentality." He smiled suddenly. "And you're very smart."

Jade felt the urge to kick her toe at the ground and humbly deny his words, but she didn't. She *was* smart. She shouldn't be ashamed or shy about it.

Josef continued. "I just don't know what answers he's hoping to get. I don't know if there are any that would help him. That could be a tough burden on you. What you find out and how much you tell him about his mother."

Jade swallowed. She already felt the weight of that burden. Knowing that Sakkara was the one to drown her as a child and not telling Paris, or anyone, felt right and wrong simultaneously.

Jade brought herself back to the present as coffee was placed in front of her. She looked up to see Daniel, Henri's boyfriend, smirking at her, sipping his own beverage as he took a seat in his cubicle next to hers.

"Missed you running this morning."

Jade wrinkled her nose. "I know, I know. I have to get back in the swing of things." God, did she ever. She supposed that getting banished to the demon realm was a pretty good excuse, but she couldn't milk it forever.

Daniel glanced around, checking there was no one within hearing distance. "I don't mean that in a guilt-inducing way. With all the stuff that happened to you, it's understandable." He lifted one shoulder in a shrug. "But I still miss my running buddy. Even if you have horrible playlists."

She stuck her tongue out at him in mock annoyance. "Tomorrow," Jade vowed. "Or my waistline is going to make me regret it. I've still been running a bit, but the mornings are just blah." She took a sip of her coffee. Two cream, just as she liked. "God, that's good. If you weren't gay…"

Daniel laughed. "If I weren't gay, you'd probably avoid me."

Jade frowned. Was she that obvious? When she'd first come to the Coven, she'd felt immediately comfortable around Henri and Daniel because they were gay. They wouldn't want anything or expect anything from her that she wasn't prepared to give. Of course, she ended up liking them as people and as friends. They were kind, funny, supportive. She thought she kept her emotions and motivations well under wraps, but now she was starting to feel like everyone knew stuff about her. Sakkara. Seth. Medusa. Daniel. It was like being a bug on a microscope slide.

"Why so glum, chum?" Daniel's voice carried a dry tone as he booted up his computer, waiting for the desktop to load. He was only peripherally paying attention to Jade, the bulk of his attention focused on the screen. Jade was tongue tied. She thought about her conversations with Lily. She thought about the Dearth, about the things Seth had said about her past. The words that had been exchanged.

"Don't you want to heal?" Seth asked.
"Maybe this is as healed as I can get."

"Tell me why you're afraid of your feelings for your little English friend."

"I'm afraid he wants more than I know how to give. Or maybe he doesn't want anything."

Jade wanted to talk about it, but didn't. Maybe she'd tell Daniel everything and he'd respond with exactly what she wanted to hear. Or maybe she'd tell him and he'd respond that she was a fool - a broken, damaged fool - for wanting or wishing for anything. "Eh," she muttered finally, shrugging her shoulders. "Just thinking about stuff. Stuff and things."

Daniel turned away from his computer screen to look at her. "You wanna talk out loud? Bounce some ideas off me?"

Jade swallowed and looked away, shaking her head. "Nah. Maybe later. Thanks." Even as she said the words she wasn't sure if she meant them or if they were just something to say.

Daniel nodded. "Okay, well, let me know."

"You bet."

She checked her phone. Eight-thirty. Jade didn't know which witch was scheduled for Lily's tests. Dr. Gellar certainly was there running the tests, but Jade didn't know who would be there, trying to glamour Lily with their power. Would it be Paris? He'd been there for Jade's tests, both because she was a rarity being the only witch born outside a Coven, and because they suspected her power level would test high. They'd been right. But Lily wasn't as powerful as Jade. Yet. Maybe ever. Jade didn't know.

Lily had worried Jade's magic might spill over and affect her test. She was probably right. Jade didn't know if she could watch Lily take a test and not help out. She thought about tapping into their connection and trying to *see* through Lily's eyes, but held herself back. They were separate people now. Separate people with separate appointments. Lily wanted to do this on her own. Jade had to let her. She still checked her phone again for messages even though she hadn't felt it vibrate or heard it ping.

Lily wanted to do a lot on her own now. Get her own room, pick out her own stuff, get her testing done without Jade. Jade shook her head again. It was fine. That's what normal people did. They did things separately. Like maybe even went on dates separately with other people.

Maybe.

The morning was slow. She had a couple calls she was able to resolve over the phone. Both were young kids playing with magic when they shouldn't have been. Jade was supposed to log items from minors for Josef to review to see if he needed to follow up with any parents, but Jade didn't have the heart today. It felt like tattling. One was a younger girl trying to complete an anti-allergy spell so her family could get a dog. Her younger sister ended up with her nostrils sealed shut and Jade was able to work through the counter-hex over the phone. Poor kid. She just wanted a dog. It made Jade think of Bruce. Though she'd never really thought about having a pet, she'd become accustomed to him.

The other case was an older boy, a teen, hungover from drinking he shouldn't have been doing. He'd tried a hangover cure and ended up vomiting up quail eggs. Still with the shell on. Jade wasn't sure where the eggs were coming from or why that had been the effect of the spell gone wrong, but she also managed to counter-hex it over the phone, getting a grateful *thank you* whispered about four times in her ear. Jade traced the call and glanced at the number quickly, certain her memory would hold the digits securely.

"No problem, but do it again, and we'll have to call your parents." God, she sounded like such a narc.

The young man sighed. "I'm done. No more rye for me. Not only am I hungover, I think I might have done four rounds of karaoke. Possibly without the music."

"Yikes. Good songs at least?"

"Pretty sure it was 1970's love ballads."

Jade grimaced. "Ouch."

"I don't even know how I know the words to those songs."

"That shit is potent. Gets in your head like a bad fungus. Stay off the rye and you should be safe. But I'd avoid all hard liquor if I were you."

"I'm so embarrassed. I think I sang them to the girl I liked. I'm pretty sure she laughed."

"She might have thought it was cute." Maybe? Was that how dating and flirting worked? Jade didn't know, but the kid sounded *sad*. Like full on morose. "Go take a shower and have a friend bring you some greasy food."

"Yeah, I already texted. He's on the way, but said he'll make me sing 'MacArthur Park' again. And he might have posted some Vines from last night."

Jade couldn't help but laugh. He was miserable. Young and miserable. Despite what Jade was sure was a raging hangover, and the absolute grossness of vomiting, she wished her problems were so easily solved - a quick counter-hex and some fast food.

"As long as he brings you food, that's a good friend."

"Yeah," the young man drawled. "Thanks, man. For the help. And for not calling my parents. Ugh, I'm so gross. I'm disgusting."

"Go shower before your friend shows up. He'll appreciate it."

"'Kay. Thanks, dude."

He hung up before Jade could do anything more than snort at being called dude. She guessed it was pretty much gender-neutral now. She looked at her cell phone again. Ten a.m. No new messages. No missed calls. She put it face down on the desk, closing her eyes. Had her test taken this long? She didn't think it had. Her phone buzzed not two seconds later and she snatched it back up only it wasn't a message from Lily, it was from Callie.

Callie: *Come on down! One of your books is in :D*

Jade smiled at the emoticon. She could hear Callie's cheerful voice as she read the text. Jade had several books on order and she wondered which one had arrived. She grabbed her purse, spinning in her chair to face Daniel.

"Callie has a book for me. Are you good if I head down to the library?"

Daniel gave her a thumbs up as her phone buzzed again.

Callie: *If you haven't gone already, bring me coffee?*

The eight o'clock coffee was long gone and she could use another one herself. She ordered three coffees in the cafeteria - wondering if Henri would be free to join her and Callie for a quick break. On a whim, she ordered a fourth made up the way Lily took it - the same way Jade took hers. That hadn't changed at least. Not yet, anyway. She should be done her test soon, right? Jade bit at some loose skin on her lip as she sent a text to Lily indicating where she was and that she had coffee. She wished she could see one of those little notices when Lily read a message. Lily was using Jade's old personal cell phone until she got her own Coven phone and Jade had always kept that functionality turned off. She realized now how annoying it was.

Not seeing Henri at his desk, Jade only stopped long enough to leave a note on his chair telling him to meet them in the library. If he got there within the next ten minutes, there'd be hot coffee waiting. Any longer than ten minutes and they would ransom his coffee to the rats. She left a winky face next to her words and then kissed the paper leaving behind a mauve-ish smear of lipstick. It's not like anyone had ever seen rats in the dungeon, but that didn't mean they weren't there, waiting for coffee. Jade's gaze trailed up the grand staircase as she passed it on her way to the dungeon. MedLab was on the second floor. Where Lily was. She turned away. Lily would text when she was done. Right? Right.

Jade liked the dungeon, although Callie disliked it when they called it that. It was dark, cool and slightly damp. It smelled like old books and maybe a little bit of wet mold, but not in a gross way. Just like earth and nature. Jade could hear music coming from Callie's mp3 player as she traversed the staircase, hunching in on herself both to feel more comfortable in the narrow staircase and also to protect the coffee tray with her body. Precious cargo.

Callie sung along to the music, on-key, but softly. It wasn't a song that Jade recognized, but Callie tended to favorite the current top-40 more so than Jade, who got her recommendations based of her previous purchases, or if she heard something she liked on a TV show or movie.

"I come bearing gifts," Jade said as her feet landed on the cobblestone floor. She offered up the coffee tray like a sacrifice.

Callie looked up from behind the circulation desk, her fine blonde hair following her movements - a golden halo running on a slight delay.

"I thought people are supposed to be wary of those with gifts," Callie said, making gimme motions with her hands.

"That's only Greeks. Beware of Greeks bearing gifts."

Jade could see the exact moment Callie's brain went from "Greek" to "Medusa," her face going stiff and her smile not as natural. She knew about Jade's sojourn to the Dearth through Paris. It was like Jade could see each thought go across Callie's face: should she say something? Condolences? Make a joke? Or just ignore it?

Thankfully, Callie went with just ignore it.

"Right," she replied, taking her coffee and snapping off the lid. She took a wide gulp to get at the sweet whipping cream that was melting on top of her mocha. "Where's Lily?"

The thing about doing stuff solo was it wasn't just Jade who was used to them being a pair. Everyone they were intimate with - Callie, Henri and

Paris - tended to think of them as a matched set too. Jade pulled her own coffee out of the tray, squeezing it too tightly and causing liquid to spill up through the drinking hole.

"Getting her power tested," Jade answered, and then licked around the side of the lid and caught a stray drop on her hand.

"Without you?" Callie's eyes were wide and guileless. Cow eyes. Jade didn't mean that in a mean way. Callie's eyes were deep and soft as they stared at her.

"Yeah, you know, we're working on doing stuff separately." Some of us working on it more than others, Jade couldn't help but think.

She must have been convincing because Callie's face lit up. "I wondered if that was the case. You know, because she came to yoga with me and Henri and that just isn't your thing. But that's fine too. That it's not your thing. I know you like to run."

"Yeah, I find it hard to *be the tree*, and all that yoga stuff." Jade took another sip of her coffee. "So, one of my books is in?"

"Oh yeah." Callie flipped her hair over her shoulder as she went behind her desk. "One of those demon rune books you were looking for." She set her coffee down and then used a folded piece of paper to pick up the book.

Jade set her coffee down as well and reached for the book. "Slimy feeling?" she asked as she stretched her hand out. Her hand touched the exposed cover and she shivered. "Hmm. Not so much slimy as…"

"Cold."

"And sharp," Jade murmured, holding the book in both her hands. Like a blade left out in the snow, and then picked up by warm hands. Cold, sharp and slightly damp.

"Honestly, those books should come with warnings. I had no idea they were so…."

"Gross."

"I was going to say tactile, but yeah, gross works."

"Well, it's not like you've had a lot of experience in handling them. The ones in the dungeon hadn't been touched in who knows how long until I showed up. Probably the same with this one too."

"Yeah." Callie rubbed her fingertips together absently. "What are you looking for?"

Jade flipped the book open, getting a waft of something unpleasantly spicy as she did. Like a too-done meat dish that had spoiled before it had been cooked. "There's are some runes in Sakkara's grimoires. A Resurrection Rune in one and another one that's similar, but not quite right. I'm looking into it."

"Is that a good idea?" Callie asked.

"Paris asked me," Jade defended. Okay, so she was going to look into them anyway, but it definitely helped that he'd asked her too.

"Oh." Callie blinked. "Has he talked to you about his mom?"

"I mean, he's mentioned her. It's not like we had some deep heart-to-heart over it."

Callie nodded. "I worry about him, you know? He and his mom were close. Not, like, creepy close, but… he looked up to her and wanted to be as good of a leader as her."

"He's a better one." The reply was automatic. Jade hadn't needed to think about it to know it was true.

"Sakkara *was* a good leader. We all looked up to her."

"Until you found out she faked her death and was demon dealing."

Callie winced. "Yeah. It's different for you, I guess, because you weren't here when she was in charge."

I was until she drowned me, Jade thought. "You can understand, I'm not overly fond of her nor predisposed to give her the benefit of the doubt."

"No, I guess not. Why does Paris want to know about that rune anyway?"

"I dunno, but if he wants it researched, I can do that." Jade looked down at the book she had in her hands again, seeing a few runes that caught her eye. "It's not like I'll be using resurrection spells anytime soon."

Callie laughed. "No I don't suppose so." Her laughter trailed off an she frowned. "What do you think Sakkara used it for?"

Jade tapped the book, the sharp-cold feeling pinging her nerves, making her shoulder ache. The demon rune that Sakkara had burned into Jade to send her to the Dearth was still imprinted on Jade's skin. A tattoo commemorating her time in the Dearth. Awesome. Some people had their ex's name, some people had misspelled quotes. She had a demon transportation rune. Jade shifted her hand on the book. She'd likely have to spell a set of gloves to handle the book, like she had for other books she'd been using. It was like the demon magic was too powerful to be contained in the flimsy material of paper and binding; it leaked out like an oil stain spreading across cloth. "I don't know. Maybe nothing? I mean, you guys would probably remember if she was bringing people back from the dead."

"God, I hope so, but ever since Dex was able to cast that memory spell on the entire Coven..." Callie sighed. "I want to say I'd remember and yet, I'm not entirely sure I'd remember."

Jade's nose wrinkled at the mention of Dex. "Talk about slimy things." That fucker. She remembered what Seth had said, when Jade had mentioned that Dex got away via some kind of teleportation spell. *Fantastic if you're a demon, but practically turns you inside out if you're not.* She had a gruesome curiosity about what had happened to Dex. But curiosity killed the cat. It was probably better she didn't know.

"I hope wherever she went back to, she stays," Callie said.

"Yeah." Jade wasn't convinced that would happen. Something about that rune was still rattling in her brain. She drummed her fingers against the book. Her fingers made a sound like a rumble.

"I can't believe she's alive. I can't believe she's in service to a demon."

"I can't believe it's not butter," Jade murmured, not really paying attention to Callie. "Is Paris online right now?"

Callie blinked at Jade for a moment before jiggling her computer mouse, waking up her desktop. She checked the online messaging system. "Yes, why?"

"Can I?" Jade asked, pointing at Callie's keyboard. Callie nodded and handed the wireless keyboard and mouse over, swiveling the screen so that Jade could see it. Jade opened up a message window to Paris and typed quickly, the sound of her keystrokes loud in the stone-walled dungeon.

It's Jade on Callie's computer. When you're free, I've a question. Best asked in person. No real rush.

Jade was handing the keyboard and mouse back to Callie when a bing sounded from the computer.

No meetings at the moment. Stop by anytime between now and 11:30.

Jade checked her phone again. Still no messages from Lily.

"Should I tell him you're on your way?"

"Yeah," Jade pocketed her phone, juggling her coffee and the demon rune book.

"Is this extra coffee for Lily?" Callie asked, pointing at the tray where Henri and Lily's coffees still sat.

"Yeah. I don't know if she'll come get it. Or if she's busy. Or whatever."

"Okay. I'll hang onto it. I'll let you know if she stops by."

"Thanks."

#

Paris stared at the high-priority email in his inbox for longer than was necessary. *Forest Fire Alert - All Covens Asked to Report Witches Proficient in Fire.*

Jade immediately came to mind. She was by far the most proficient with fire in the entire Coven.

He had no doubt she would also be the most proficient across several Covens. The message itself wasn't unusual - natural disasters often prompted requests for magical assistance. The problem was his reaction to the thought of asking Jade to assist with a forest fire. He didn't want to. With what she'd been through of late - the return of Lily, his mother's machinations, and Jade's travels through the demon realm, he had a strong aversion to asking her for more. Not only that, but if witches were required for this, he was reluctant for her to leave the Coven. Not that he could or would stop her, but rather, he didn't want her far away from them. From him.

When she'd been in the Dearth, he'd feared for her safety and missed her presence. Her absence had been pervasive - a void felt everywhere. He'd felt it while he stayed at her cottage with Bruce and Lily, both of them subdued and melancholic without Jade. He'd also felt it at the Covenstead, which had surprised him. He often saw her while they were working, but Counter-Magic was an entire floor away from his office and he didn't necessarily run into her often. But while she'd been trapped in the Dearth, he found himself staring at the door to his office, as if waiting for her to appear.

Reading the message again, he knew as Coven Leader, if assistance was officially requested, he needed to offer help. He just didn't want it to be Jade.

A knock at his door finally drew his attention from the email.

"Yes?"

The door opened and as if conjured by his thoughts, Jade's head poked around the edge. "Your assistant isn't at her desk."

"She's gathering some files for me from HR."

"You know, I've never actually seen her in person. I don't think she really exists."

How did her brain work, he wondered. "I assure you, Suki is very real."

"Could be a ruse. Why do you even have paper files?" She had a large tome tucked under her arm and carried a coffee cup from the cafeteria in her other hand. She paused for a moment looking at her coffee cup as though she just realized she was holding it at the same time he saw it. "Sorry I didn't bring you one."

"I've had my morning limit already, I fear. We have electronic files, of course, but I'm looking into some older items that haven't yet been made digital."

Jade dropped into one of the chairs in front of his desk, pulling the book onto her lap. "Stuff about your mom?"

"It's unnerving how you seem to know things like that."

"I can put two and two together and I'm suspicious by nature. You'd be surprised what you can guess if you have that combination of attributes."

She set her coffee down on the carpeted floor next to her chair, watching it for a moment as if she expected it to tip over. When it didn't, she turned back to the book, flipping through the pages. While he waited for her to find what she was looking for, he glanced at the clock and frowned at the time.

"Is Lily's power test over already?"

Jade's lips pursed slightly and she shrugged one shoulder. "I guess you know about that since you're Coven Leader."

Her expression implied it might be a question, but her tone lacked the inflection.

"Yes, I'm aware of all tests for power levels."

"Oh. I wasn't sure if maybe you knew because you'd been there. You know, doing some of the testing."

"I don't expect Lily will test as powerful as you so I assigned another witch to that. Marcus from Supernatural Relations."

"I don't know him." Jade's tone was somewhat accusatory.

"He's of moderate power. Based on what I've seen and felt from Lily, I imagine he'll have enough power to push her magic back, but not so much that he'll overwhelm her."

Jade nodded at his words, her lips somewhat tight.

"I thought you'd be with her."

Jade fidgeted. "We're doing our own stuff now. You know. Separately."

From her slouched posture and brisk tone, it didn't seem like Jade was happy with that decision. He wondered if it had been Lily's idea. He thought again of talking with Lily about her relationship with Jade, while Jade was in the Dearth. Of Lily's struggle with what she perceived to be power over Jade.

"I'm sure that's difficult for you," Paris offered.

Jade picked up her coffee and took a swig. "It's for the best. I mean, we're separate people."

"Still, I imagine it will take some adjustment."

"Yeah." Jade shook her head, trying to shake off the dejected air that had descended upon her. "I'll hear from her as soon as she's finished. But until then, I wanted to talk to you about something else."

Paris didn't want to say, but he rather thought Lily should have finished her test already. If something had gone wrong, Dr. Gellar would have let him know. It was more likely that Lily had forgotten or been caught up in something else. "Of course. What can I do for you?"

Jade drummed her fingers on the top of the book. "Okay, so some of the books I ordered have come in and I'm looking into that rune for you. I mean, I'm looking at a bunch of your mom's magic, but that rune in particular."

"I'm aware. Although, I don't favor demon magic, I'm confident in your abilities. But please be careful."

"Totally careful."

"More careful than the time you cast a demon lie detector on your hand and then couldn't break it."

"One time. That was one time I did that and I told you about it. I haven't done it since."

"Hmm." Paris wondered at times what other magic Jade may have tried unsuccessfully and gotten herself out of without telling him. Or Goddess forbid, gone to the demon Seth to resolve. "Be careful," he iterated.

She made an X over her heart with her pointer finger, giving him a significant look. He supposed it was her way of promising. "So back to the Resurrection Rune. When your mom first came back from the dead, or not so dead, considering that she probably wasn't really six feet under, I asked you if people came back from the dead around here. Like on the regular. And you had said something like, 'not unless someone had necromancy.'"

"Yes. The magic of communicating and raising the dead. It's extraordinarily rare and quite a burden."

"If you say so. Anyway, you said there wasn't anyone currently at the Coven with that gift."

He remembered the conversation of which she spoke and nodded. "That's correct."

"I'm kind of stuck on the word 'currently.'"

"How so?"

"As in *currently* implies *not now*, but maybe you used to have someone?"

Paris paused, unsure for a moment how to respond. After weighing the options in his head, he pressed forward. "We did have a necromancer at the Coven, though she's not been here for many years."

"I thought that all witches had to live in a Coven. That's the spiel you gave me when you came and found me."

"Yes, and that's true. For the most part."

"The most part," Jade repeated. The stark grey of her eyes being rimmed in black made her gaze, at times, quite uncomfortable to bear. It was as though she could see directly into his mind, and didn't like what she saw.

"In some very particular cases, Covens have allowed witches to leave them."

"Do you break their magic?" Jade asked. When she had indicated she would leave the Coven, Paris had informed her if she did, he would be obligated to try to break her magic. He feared he would kill her in the attempt. Jade's magic was much too strong to be broken by him, or by anyone he knew.

"As I said, there are particular cases."

Jade's face was perfectly blank, but he had no doubt she was extremely vexed by his answer. "I see. And so this person, this necromancer, was one of those cases."

"Yes. She was allowed to leave the Coven with her magic intact."

"*Her* magic. It's a woman. The necromancer."

Paris nodded. "Yes. You've met her actually." Jade frowned. "Yvonne."

"From the hotel?"

When Jade had returned from the Dearth, she'd ended up miles away from the Covenstead. Paris hadn't asked how it happened and Jade had not offered. Fortunately, Jade had appeared in a town where a former Coven witch was located, Yvonne. Paris had been able to contact Yvonne and have her meet Jade, taking her to the hotel where Yvonne worked.

"Yes."

"She's a necromancer?"

"She was. Many years ago."

"What happened?"

"Necromancy is a terrible gift. It can seem like a blessing, but death is generally tied to strong emotions. Anger, betrayal, loss, grief. So much grief."

Jade swallowed. "This sounds like one of those *careful what you wish for* stories."

"It is. Yvonne manifested her power at a young age. Her family kept it a secret. Necromancy is not well understood and can have a stigma. Necromancers can be seen as unnatural, or something to be feared. No one in the Coven knew she'd exhibited those abilities but her parents."

"Okay," Jade said slowly. "What happened?"

"Yvonne had a sister. Kira. She died."

Jade's face was resigned and Paris knew she was ready for the words he would say before he uttered them.

"Her mother was grief stricken. In her grief, knowing of the powers of her other daughter, she…" Paris paused. "I wouldn't use the word 'ask.' Not technically."

"No, when you have power over someone, you never really ask them anything."

Jade's words, so eerily close to the words Lily spoke to Paris previously, made him hesitate. But the expression on Jade's face gave nothing away to indicate she was aware of the things of which Paris and Lily had spoken.

"No, you don't. I don't imagine she felt she had a choice. Her sister gone in an untimely fashion and her mother desperate. Later on, the Coven as a whole, my mother," Paris continued, "we could see how Yvonne's mother had… deteriorated. How she could have asked such a thing of her daughter. But for a time, no one was aware."

The silence in his office felt thick, like a dark, sticky syrup gone cold and forgotten.

"What happened to her? I mean, both Yvonne and her sister?"

"Necromancy is not well understood and as I said, it can have a stigma attached to it. Yvonne had natural ability and perhaps some innate sense as to how her gift should work, but she lacked any formal training. She wasn't particularly powerful either.

She... tried to bring her sister back and was... somewhat successful."

"Oh, Jesus. I'm thinking that necromancy is kind of an all or nothing thing and it sounds like she ended up more on the nothing side."

Paris nodded once. "Yes. Her sister was caught between two worlds. Unable to pass on, but Yvonne lacked the power to bring her all the way back to life. Yvonne's mother forced her daughter to continually cast the magic required to keep her sister alive. And when it failed, she simply made her daughter do it again. She wasn't abusive," Paris clarified. "It wasn't physical force."

"No, I get it," Jade said. "Like I said, when you have power over someone and you ask them to do something, you're not really asking them."

Paris knew of course of the context in which he and Lily had spoken of that notion. Lily had told Paris more of her history with Jade. Of how when they were younger, they were two people trapped in one body and when it became overwhelming for Lily, she'd asked Jade to end it. To end their lives. Lily had asked her because she knew Jade could never refuse a request from her. Paris wondered if Jade's understanding of power imbalance, of a person being asked something they could not refuse, stemmed from that incident. Had Jade known Lily asked her because she knew Jade wouldn't, couldn't say no? Or was there something else behind Jade's understanding that Paris didn't understand or may never comprehend? Though he felt he'd gotten to know Jade very well since she joined the Coven, she was in many ways unknown to him. How was she coping now that she and Lily were separate? With what had transpired in the Dearth with Seth? With the Gorgon? Did any part of her blame Paris for the things his mother had done?

Jade tapped her finger on the book in front of her, distracting Paris from his thoughts. "I've got this book on runes, and some of them are like your mother's. Similar like fonts can be similar to each other. This rune your mom has, on resurrection... she's got the Resurrection Rune itself in her grimoires, but more for reference. I don't think she was actually trying to resurrect anyone, if that makes you feel any better."

It did. Paris felt something unclench in his chest. "How can you know?"

"It's like there's a vibe with runes, an intent or essence. When I look at the ones your mom wrote, I don't get a *raising from the dead*, vibe. Then again, I don't know anything about necromancy. And it seems like it's not a real popular subject so there's not a lot out there. I thought if you knew a necromancer, which I guess we both do, actually," Jade said, a frown crossing her face as she thought. "I thought someone with that magic would know for sure. If they knew what necromancy felt like, they'd know if your mother's runes were used to raise the dead."

"You're probably right."

"Do you think..." Jade shifted forward in her chair and looked at him, her gaze seemingly sharper and more focused. "Do you think Yvonne would talk about her magic with me? Or is it really rude and insensitive to ask?"

"I don't know. She's not been part of the Coven for a long time. I do know that when I called on her for assistance with your return, she was very willing to help. But..."

"But you weren't exactly asking her to remember the time she raised her sister from the dead for her crazy mother."

"Precisely." Paris envied the way Jade was able to distill what he often found to be uncomfortable notions down to the bare bones of their existence. Though there were many things he didn't know about her, it wasn't due to direct subterfuge on her part. At times, she was the most direct and honest person he knew, and she certainly didn't sugarcoat things because he was Coven Leader. He knew if he needed honest words, he could ask her.

Jade's nose wrinkled as her gaze drifted off to the side, her face clearly indicating she was thinking. "Okay, I'll do some more digging and see what I find. If I come up empty, then maybe I'll ask you for Yvonne's number. I can always start off by thanking her for taking me in after the whole Dearth thing and suss out how she might feel about talking to me. I mean, I should probably thank her anyway. She was really nice to me."

Jade said it as though it were surprising that Yvonne had been kind to her. It made Paris sad to think she found it uncommon.

A notification sound rang from his computer speakers and though he was invested in his conversation with Jade, his attention was pulled to the screen.

"Lily's power tests are over and Dr. Gellar is processing them. Preliminary results indicate she's a low-moderate to moderate witch."

Jade pulled her phone from her pocket and frowned at the screen, pushing the device back into the folds of her clothes.

"Did she text you she was done?" Paris asked.

Jade's lips were thin and losing color from how tightly she had them pressed. "No, but I'm sure she's talking to Gellar or... doing some post-test stuff. Like I said, we're doing things separately now. She doesn't have to check in with me 24-7."

"Of course not," he said easily, noting how on-edge she seemed. "I imagine things are quite different for you now. For both of you."

Jade shrugged. "I guess. I thought she'd test higher."

"Because you did?"

"Yeah."

"You're not the same person. She was never truly a witch. You've always belonged to the Coven."

Jade frowned again.

"Does that bother you?"

She thought the question over, looking down at the book in her lap as she did. "No, I mean, I don't think so? I just have no memory of the Coven. Sometimes...." Her voice drifted off and he found himself nearly on the edge of his seat, wanting to know what she would say, what she thought, how she thought. "Sometimes, it's like all I know is Lily's life. And I thought it was mine, and now it's not."

"Your experiences are still yours, what you've lived through. What you've learned. I would hope you could see this as an opportunity."

"For what?"

"To find out what you truly want. To find out who you are. I don't mean to presume, but I imagine you've lived your life in counsel with Lily, without the autonomy to make many of your own decisions. You have that autonomy now."

There was a split second where the only emotion that flashed across her face was fear. Paris supposed he understood that. Being accountable for your own decisions could be terrifying.

"You have the chance now to explore whatever you wish. Aren't there things you think you may want?"

"Do you want to go for coffee with me?"

CHAPTER FOUR

Oh shit. For the most part, Jade thought she had a pretty good handle on her brain-to-mouth filter and didn't often make mistakes. But there she was, sitting there, in Paris' office. He told her Lily's tests were done, but Lily hadn't contacted Jade. She'd been hurt and confused, and then Paris looked at her with his too-blue eyes, asking Jade what she wanted. All Jade heard were Lily's earlier words in her head, teasing her, how she liked Paris. What did she want? The next thing she knew, she'd asked if Paris wanted to go for coffee.

Paris' gaze went from Jade to the floor where her current coffee cup sat and then back to her. His face seemed to say, *there's coffee there,* although she supposed he'd say it in a really formal way like, *it appears you've already obtained coffee a short while ago.*

Okay, so she could play it off that it was empty and she needed another, and that was on the tip of her tongue, but again it was like her mouth had suddenly seceded from her brain and decided it was going to run the show from now on.

"I mean, obviously I have coffee now, and I could get coffee by myself later, but I thought maybe you'd like to go for coffee with me, although you drink tea. So we could do that too. Tea for you. Not me, because no." Oh Jesus, it was just getting worse. If ever there was a time she wished she knew a spell to make the earth open up and swallow her whole, this was the time. "Or we could not go. Because it could be weird."

"Are you asking me on a date?"

Jade's entire face went hot and she was sure it was also red. She stood up, juggling the book in one hand and grabbing her half-full coffee in the other. "What are the chances of me casting a memory spell to make you forget the last five minutes?" As soon as she said the words, she immediately thought of Dex and the memory spell he'd cast on the entire Coven to make them believe they remembered him fondly and as a friendly witch. "Shit, I didn't mean that I would ever, you know, fuck with people's heads because that's wrong and bad and..." She needed to get out. Clearly, something critical to her higher-brain functions had snapped and she would continue word-vomiting if she didn't get out of Paris' office ASAP. "I have to leave." She turned and high-tailed it to the door.

"I would like to have coffee with you."

Jade stopped, turning back to Paris. "Seriously?"

"Yes, seriously."

"Even after…" She motioned with the hand that held her coffee cup. "The word vomit?"

He smiled and her stomach clenched in a pleasant way. "Yes."

"Oh." Was that it? Should she leave? "Okay."

"Did you have a time or date in mind?"

Shit, right. "Um, no." Ugh, she should have just picked something.

"I've a late meeting tonight, but how about tomorrow, after work?"

"Okay?" For someone who'd done the asking, she was making a real botched job of this.

"I'll come by Counter-Magic."

Jade nodded and hoped that the expression on her face was an approximation of a smile. "Okay," she related. "So I'll see you then. Unless I have to see you before then about the Resurrection Rune or your creepy mother." She should really shut up.

"All right." Paris nodded.

He looked all calm and relaxed and Jade thought she might throw up on the mostly-pristine carpet in his office. She bobbed her head once more and left, pulling the door shut behind her. She took one look at the coffee cup clutched in her white fingers and her stomach revolted at the thought of it. She tossed it in the wastebasket next to Paris' assistant's desk. Keeping her head down, she made her way out of the anterior office and into the hallway, watching the tiled floor beneath her feet as she headed down the grand staircase and back to Counter-Magic.

"You got your book," Daniel said as she entered their shared office space.

"What?" Jade asked, finally raising her eyes from the floor to look at him.

He gestured to the book in her hands. "Your book. You went to the library to get a book and you got said book."

Jade swallowed. "Yes."

She sat down and dropped the book and then let her head fall on top of it. A slippery, icy shock shot through the thin skin on her forehead and she jerked back, pulling a disinfecting wipe from the dispenser on her desk and wiping at her forehead. Damn demon books.

"Er, are you okay?"

Out of the corner of her eye, she could see Daniel eyeing her dubiously. "This day... this day is..." It wasn't exactly a wash because apparently she'd asked Paris out on a coffee date and he'd said yes. But also *she'd asked Paris out and he'd said yes*. "I might be sick."

Daniel pushed his chair further back and muttered some kind of spell, putting a barrier between them. "The sick stay home. So as not to infect the zombie plague on the rest of us."

Jade scowled at him. "I'm not infectious."

"That's what all the zombies say."

She opened her mouth to again proclaim herself healthy when the door to Counter-Magic opened and Lily came in, looking fresh and excited. Her smile was so wide it made Jade's own cheeks hurt. Henri was right behind Lily, his grin also ear-to-ear.

"Look! I got my own Coven phone!" Lily said, waving a smart phone up in the air. "I'm a real witch now."

"Yes, because the magic and the living in the Coven bit were all for show. It's the phone that sells it," Jade said, unable to keep her sarcasm to herself.

Lily stuck her tongue out at Jade playfully. "I'm serious. I'm registered. Thanks to Henri." She paused and turned to Henri, giving him a mock bow. Henri replied by mimicking the same gesture.

"She's all tested up, legitimately registered and maybe even has a job," Henri said. He was looking at Lily like she was some kind of protégé, his expression fond and proud.

"A job?" It was only half past eleven. How could so much have happened in only a few hours?

"Oh my gosh, yes! So I had my test and the witch who tested me, Marcus, he's from Supernatural Relations and I guess they have an opening and he heard that the werewolves really liked you," Lily said to Jade. "And so he thinks that my magic will also be a good fit for them, and if I do well with them, then I'll get to meet other Covens and also maybe some vampires!" Lily made a hooked-fang gesture with her fingers and waggled them.

"Vampires?" Jade looked sharply from Daniel to Henri and back to Lily. "I don't know any vampires."

"No?" asked Lily. She waved a hand. "It's probably months away anyway. But you liked the werewolves. I sort of remember." Lily made vague motions around her head with her fingers. "There was food. And masks. You had a good time."

"I did, but..." Jade trailed off, not sure what she wanted to say. "Your test went okay?"

Lily was staring down at her phone, pushing buttons and glanced back up at Jade. "What? Oh, yeah. I mean, I'm not very powerful, but I figured that already, so it wasn't a surprise. Well, the whole thing wasn't a surprise since I remembered your test. But Henri and Marcus said I did really well, especially since I don't have any training."

"I've helped you," Jade said, hating the way her voice came out somewhat plaintive and longingly.

"Well, yeah, but I never studied magic or spells formally."

"She handled her magic wonderfully," Henri said, rolling back and forth on his feet and bouncing on his toes. "You would have been proud."

Jade smiled, the skin of her face feeling tight and stretched. "I'm sure I would have been. I mean, I am."

Lily darted forward toward her and Jade instinctively stood from her chair and caught Lily as she darted forward and hugged Jade tightly. Jade could smell grapefruit and cinnamon - the essence of Lily's magic. The cinnamon was maybe a little like the scent of cloves, which Jade's magic favored. But there was no trace at all of the flowery scent Jade's magic gave off at times.

"It went really well," Lily said, her voice warm and close in Jade's ear.

"I'm glad." Jade was. It wasn't a lie. But she also couldn't help but feel a heavy, unhappy weight settle on her.

"Oh! And Hannah is back from the council to read my cards. We can go see her after work!"

Jade struggled to keep her face neutral. Her own tarot card reading had been... puzzling. Now, looking back on it, Jade could see why the cards had been confused - giving details for both Lily and Jade.

At the time, however, all Jade had known was that she didn't like what Hannah had to say about her cards. Jade wondered what Hannah would be able to see for Lily, now that she was separate. She wondered if Hannah would ask to read Jade's cards again. She didn't know if she would say yes. Lily, her emotions usually so in tune with Jade's, either didn't notice Jade's conflict, or chose not to. Jade wasn't sure which one hurt more.

"Henri said he'd take me down to Supernatural Relations for a bit of a tour."

"And we might go for lunch, depending on how long that takes," Henri added. "You'll come with us?"

Jade swallowed and, although she wanted to say yes, she found herself shaking her head. "No, I was down in the library today and then I had to see Paris about this book." She gestured at the runeology book on her desk. "So I should probably stick close to the office and get some work done."

"I'm sure Josef would give you the time off if you asked," Henri said.

Jade's eyes darted from him, to Lily's patient waiting expression and then to Daniel's more cautions, somewhat knowing one. "No, I know he would, but I don't want to take advantage or anything. You guys go without me. I'm sure Henri will have tons of gossip for you." Jade winked playfully at Henri. At least she hoped it was playful. Her insides were so mashed and twisted she couldn't be sure.

"It's not gossip if it's verified."

Daniel scoffed. "Oh, it's still gossip, it just makes you feel better when it's true."

"If people don't want to be talked about, they should be more discreet." Henri sniffed piously.

"I didn't even know you knew that word," Daniel replied. Henri lunged forward and dug his fingers into Daniel's love-handle area, making the other man let out an undignified giggling sound. "Fine, fine, stop."

"I'm very discreet!" Henri exclaimed.

Daniel sucked in huge breaths of air and nodded. "Yes, yes. Discreet." He grabbed Henri about the neck and planted a kiss on his forehead. The gesture was easy and intimate and Jade felt like a voyeur seeing it.

"Okay, call us if you change your mind," Henri said. He grabbed one of Lily's hands and led her out of Counter- Magic. Lily gave a grand wave, her face still bright and happy. Jade raised her own hand and waved back, staring at the doorway long after they'd left.

"You okay?" Daniel asked.

Jade nodded. "Yeah, why wouldn't I be?" She sat back down in her chair, rubbing her shoulder. Sakkara's Binding Rune, the one that sent her to the Dearth, ached. Jade rotated her neck, trying to get at the pain to no avail.

"No reason. Must be strange seeing Lily out and about. Getting tested on her own. Getting a job."

"I'm happy for her."

"I never said you weren't," Daniel replied. He swiveled his chair, ending up facing his computer screen.

Jade continued to stare at the doorway. She wanted to call Lily back. To ask her more about her test, to question her about the position at Supernatural

Relations. To tell Lily about Jade's meeting with Paris. Instead, she opened up the runeology text and read, trying to focus her mind on the words in front of her. Resurrection. What did it mean, and what had Paris' mother done?

#

Jade felt weird driving Lily to Hannah's place, still remembering too easily what it was like to be a passenger on the journey. Hannah's looked as ominous now as it had then. Maybe it was because she was rarely there and it had an uninhabited look. Hannah spent the majority of her time with the Supernatural Council. There were a myriad of youngsters she employed to keep her place well-manicured. It was impeccably kept - nary a stray leaf to be seen. But there was still something missing, as if the trees, hedges and building itself knew they were long absent from human company. Maybe the place had looked spooky and haunted long before Hannah moved in; Jade didn't know. All she knew was Hannah's place was an enigma to her. Wider than it was deep, it was like an old ranch house that had been forgotten. The hedges were bare, but beautiful in a winterish way. The empty garden beds and stark winter tree left Jade with the impression of abandonment instead of hibernation. A place forgotten instead of gone to sleep.

Lily was a bundle of nerves next to her. Her excitement and anticipation were tactile - suspended in air and nearly suffocating Jade. Jade grit her teeth.

"I remember your card reading," Lily said, her voice trembling. "You were so nervous. I wonder what she'll see for me now."

Hannah was supposed to be able to pick up pieces of the past, present and future, as well as get a general sense of a witch's magic. At her own reading, fear had been coiled in Jade's gut. Fear at the thought of someone knowing about her, about Lily. About the things they kept secret.

However, it had mostly been a bust. Although Hannah had seen water - murky water - she'd not been able to say what it meant. Jade realized now it must have been the lake and her connection to it. Her memories of being drowned by Sakkara. Had Hannah sensed any part of Sakkara's involvement? And if she had, would she have mentioned it? At the time, Jade had only known she had a deep fear of water. She supposed drowning as a child would do that to a person.

Jade didn't remember the day she died clearly. She remembered water. Hands holding her down. Images of a dark figure looming over her. Sakkara, Paris' mother. Holding Jade's four-year-old body under the water until it went slack and limp.

Lily turned to her, eyes narrowing.

"Should I not get my cards read?"

"What?" Jade asked, not looking at Lily as she turned the key in the ignition to stop the engine.

"You've got this… feeling about you. Regret or… remorse or something else. I'm not sure."

Jade hadn't told Lily what she'd learned from Seth. About Sakkara. She didn't know how to say the words. And to be frank, she didn't want to deal with the deluge of questions that would come afterward. Why did Sakkara do it? For what purpose? How did Jade's essence come to reside in Lily? Was there still more that Sakkara would or could do to them? Would

Jade tell Paris? They were all questions Jade couldn't answer. Not yet. Maybe ever.

Jade paused, both hands resting on the wheel. "It's not... you should have your cards read. That's for you."

"You're keeping something from me," Lily murmured.

Jade's hand tightened on the wheel. She wanted to protest; she wanted to agree. "I'm... there are things I can't..."

Lily's lips pursed together and she stared out the windshield at Hannah's ranch house. "I told you. We don't have to share everything. We're separate now. We have our own feelings and thoughts." Lily's breath caught and she sighed.

Jade nodded, feeling hollow, her own thoughts swirling. *I don't want to drag you down with me. You can be who you were meant to be. I don't know how to say out loud the things we always shared in our minds.*

Lily smiled, bright and fake, the expression not meeting her eyes. Jade knew that look. She often wore it herself. "Let's go get my cards read."

The engine of the car ticked as it cooled as she and Lily climbed the worn, slightly-sagging steps of Hannah's house. The front door swung open and Hannah stood before them in the doorway, slightly shadowed. Her eyes, a peculiar and beautiful shade of violet, flickered between Jade and Lily for a moment before resting on Jade.

"Hello, Jade. It's good to see you again," Hannah said, her voice even and measured. Her gaze moved to Lily. "And it's lovely to meet you, Lily."

Lily raised her eyebrows and eyeballed Jade quickly before turning to Hannah. "You know, most people at the Coven can't tell us apart."

"They aren't looking close enough."

Lily nodded. "Our eyes. Mine are green. Jade's are grey."

Jade had the feeling she knew what Hannah would say before she spoke.

"That's one of the differences. Please, come in."

Hannah turned from the door, leaving it open for Jade and Lily to follow. The inside was as well-kept as the exterior, although slightly dim and dreary. Jade had the urge to swap out all the light bulbs for 100 watt ones, and maybe add some track lighting on the floor, like they did in airplanes to help you find the way to an exit.

"I'm so glad you were able to come on short notice. I'm not able to take many breaks from the Council, but I found some time to steal away to come home."

Jade snorted. "Well, it's not like people say no when you ask."

Hannah turned around, gesturing for Lily and Jade to enter the small parlor as she did. "You are always free to say no. No one is at my beck and call. Certainly not a witch who has faced a Gorgon and survived."

Jade bristled. Hannah's forehead creased slightly in a frown, like she knew she'd said something wrong, but wasn't sure what. Jade wasn't sure either. She just… didn't like how Hannah talked like she knew about what Jade had been through. She hadn't been around, she hadn't been there. Jade wondered if everyone in the Coven knew more about her than she was willing to share.

"I've made tea and brought some cookies. They're from some elves I know."

Again Jade snorted, thinking of little cartoon elves, their bodies squat and fat, living in small, comical tree. She grabbed a cookie and wanted to sigh at the taste: soft, creamy and buttery. It fell apart in her mouth, melting on her tongue.

"The elves are quite gifted," Hannah said.

Jade took a seat and slid the lone, empty tea cup closer to her. "Is this Paris' tea, or something else?"

Lily sat down as well, looking slightly lost at only seeing one tea cup.

"Paris prefers orange pekoe. This is a jasmine blend I favor."

The hot liquid let off steam as Hannah poured, the pale grey tendrils disappearing into the air. Jade sniffed. It smelled faintly of perfume, but not in a bad way. It was delicate and light. "This smells nice."

Hannah smiled. "I'm glad you like it." She set the pot down. "Now," she said, turning to Lily. "It's time for your cards."

"That's it? No tea?" Lily asked, in the middle of sneaking a cookie.

"There will be time afterward."

"Isn't Jade coming?" Lily looked frantically toward Jade and Jade felt ashamed at the smug satisfaction that rolled through her. It was hard doing stuff alone. She pushed the feeling down.

"If you prefer, and if Jade agrees, she could sit in. But I find it works best with just me and the witch."

"Oh, I…" Lily looked torn.

Jade waved her off. "I have tea, cookies and my phone." She swallowed a bit of dry shortbread. "You'll do great."

Lily nodded, her throat working slightly as she swallowed. "No, you're right. Of course you are. Okay." She nodded. "Okay."

Lily gave Jade one last quick glance before she followed Hannah into the smaller room and Hannah slid the double doors shut behind them. Jade remembered at her tarot card reading Hannah had set out three decks of cards and Jade had reached for the set she found the prettiest. It was a choosing of a sort. Jade never did find out what it meant, only that she'd had to choose the cards and then shuffle them. Hannah'd had a hard time from the start, asking Jade what she'd thought about as she shuffled, asking to hold Jade's hand. She said Jade felt apart from the Coven. Like maybe she didn't belong. In retrospect, not much had changed. It was hard to feel like she belonged when she felt like she was always still learning. About magic, about the Coven, about herself.

Jade remembered one card in particular. The White Knight, the card of salvation. Jade had been offended when Hannah had told her what it meant. She didn't need to be saved. She could handle life. Mostly. She paid her bills on time and ate vegetables. But Hannah had said that the card could also be interpreted as Jade saving someone. Jade picked up another cookie and let it melt in her mouth, savoring the salty-sweet taste of butter and sugar. Could that have been when she stopped Dex? Or maybe when

Lily came back? Could either of those things be seen as a salvation of sorts?

Jade hadn't had the chance to ask because it was then Hannah realized her magic wasn't working correctly and that had led to the entire Dex debacle. Jade stared at the closed doors. What would her cards have said if Hannah had read them without the influence of Lily? Did Jade really want to know?

Thinky-thoughts weren't her strong suit. It's not like she could change the past, or even the present, by sitting around thinking about it. The future, however, she might be able to change. Or affect. Things like if she went for a run tomorrow or studied demon magic more. Or how her date would go with Paris.

Jesus, what would they talk about? They usually talked about magic, or crazy shit that was happening at the Coven. Or most recently, his not so dead mother. Not exactly date material. What did people talk about on a date? Current events? Shit. She better Google some news. Likes and dislikes? What would she say? That she really hated being dragged into the Dearth, but it kind of all worked out?

She was so screwed. She pulled up the browser on her phone and started reading up on current events. Ugh. She was better off not knowing. Paleo diets were all the rage, twins separated at birth reunited, global warming would kill the earth…. *Forest Fires Force Evacuation of Surrounding Towns. Witches to be on Standby.*

Hmmm. That was interesting. She remembered an email about the Supernatural Council watching some natural disasters. A fire, a tsunami, and some aftershocks from an earthquake. She wondered if these fires were any of the same events. She knew pretty much zilch about the Supernatural Council. She supposed she should be more informed, but honestly, just trying to stay alive in the Coven was kind of taking up a lot of time.

She clicked on some links, read some articles on the situation. Saw some crazy videos. People preparing to evacuate and filming from their cell phones as they packed. Smoke in the distance; the sky having turned orange and grey.

As was the way of the internet, she clicked on a link that went to another link that went to another link and before she knew it, she was on Wikipedia, reading up on controlled burns and the Global Fire Initiative. Damn internet. She'd be here all night.

The sound of the twin doors sliding open caught her attention and she looked up to see Lily emerging from the room, a tight smile on her face. Hannah followed behind, looking calm and serene.

"What's the verdict? World domination by next Tuesday?" Jade asked.

"Not… quite," Lily replied. Jade frowned, her gaze darting back and forth between Hannah and Lily. Had something upset Lily? If so, what? Not really thinking about it, Jade stood, ready to do something. Fight? Yell? Eat another cookie?

Lily held up a hand. "It's fine. Nothing is set in stone." Lily's eyes darted over to Hannah as she spoke, as if seeking confirmation.

Jade narrowed her eyes. "That sounds ominous."

Lily hesitated and Jade realized it was because she didn't want to tell Jade what her cards had said.

"Oh." Jade couldn't help as the word slipped out of her lips. "Oh, you don't..." She exhaled. "That's fine. You don't have to tell me." She didn't. And Jade just had to keep repeating that to herself until she believed it.

Lily winced. "It's just..."

Jade held up a hand. "It's okay. Really." She made an extra effort to ensure her own feelings were bottled up tight as she smiled. When Lily's shoulders relaxed, Jade knew she'd been successful.

"Jade, I was wondering if you'd let me read your cards again," Hannah said.

Jade blinked. "Why?"

"Well, as you recall, I had a poor reading of you. Both because of your ties to Lily and because of Dex's meddling with our magic."

Jade snapped her teeth together. It's not that she didn't want her cards read, except for how she didn't want her cards read. "Do you read other people in the Coven more than once?"

"Other people in the Coven aren't you," Hannah countered.

"Lucky them," Jade said, her lips curling in a bit of a smirk.

"Are you afraid of what the cards might tell you?"

"Are you?" The best defense was a good offense. Answer a question with a question.

"Should I wait in the car for this?" Lily asked, taking small steps sideways toward the exit.

Jade didn't want to know what the future would bring. In some respects, she supposed it could be a warning: if she knew something bad would happen, then she could prepare for it. But on the other side, ignorance was bliss.

"One card." She didn't know if this was a negotiation, but if it were, she would start low. To her surprise, Hannah nodded.

"One card." Hannah tipped her head toward the small side room. Jade pocketed her phone and followed. Lily stepped toward the small table still filled with biscuits and Jade's lukewarm tea.

"I'm eating these cookies and finishing your tea."

"There's more in the kitchen, of both, if you like," Hannah called over her shoulder. As Jade followed her into the parlor, Hannah whispered a word of magic and the doors slid shut.

Jade remembered well the small table upon which sat three decks of tarot cards. She eyeballed them like she would a venomous snake. Hannah took a seat and gestured for Jade to do the same. Jade tapped her fingers against her thigh and then slowly, carefully, sat down.

"You seem like you're about to be attacked," Hannah said.

A sudden thought popped into Jade's mind. "Why didn't Paris want to touch the tarot cards? When I had my reading?"

Hannah paused. "I don't recall."

"I do," Jade said confidently. "You thought there was something wrong with your magic. We left my card reading and you asked Paris to shuffle the cards and draw three. He said he didn't deal with tarot cards."

Hannah pursed her lips together, but said nothing.

"You said you wouldn't ask if it wasn't important."

"I thought your memory was for printed material. I didn't realize you had such incredible recall."

"I probably couldn't tell you what socks I'm wearing right now, but when something seems important, I pay attention. You said you wouldn't read his future. It was only then he agreed and flipped three cards."

"Tarot cards are not an exact science. It's part mysticism, part intuition and part divination." Hannah inclined her head toward the three decks on the small table. "You said you'd pick a card."

Jade pursed her lips and then reached forward, toward a lovely floral deck. She paused and then moved her hand to the plain deck next to it. There was no ornamentation on the backs of the cards. Just a simple matte dark grey finish. Hannah's expression didn't change. Jade picked up the deck and started shuffling.

"So Paris doesn't like having his cards read?" she asked, watching Hannah's face. There was nothing. "Maybe he doesn't like tarot cards. Maybe he's one of those free will kind of people, or maybe..." Jade stopped shuffling, watching Hannah carefully. Her face was too still, too expressionless. "Maybe he had his cards read once and didn't like what they said."

Hannah's eyes shifted from the cards in Jade's hands to Jade's own eyes. "I'm not sure if you've a talent for divination and prognostication or if you're just exceptionally gifted at reading people."

"What did Paris' cards say?" Jade asked, a heavy, thick feeling settling uncomfortably in her belly.

Hannah shifted slightly in her chair. "They say children of abusive parents tend to be quite empathic. Extraordinary at reading people and situations. It's a learned skill in an attempt to protect themselves. If they can read and predict their abuser, they may be safe."

"Is this a tarot card reading or a therapy session?"

Hannah's lips twitched. "Maybe they are the same thing."

Jade shuffled the cards a few more times, her fingers itching to lay them down and fan them out - like a soft, worn poker deck. Instead, she flipped a few cards and slipped them back in the deck, losing them in the shuffle. Her hands stilled and she took out one card, setting it down on the table face down.

"What did Paris' cards say?" Jade asked, her voice quiet and soft. Two of her fingertips remained on the card.

Hannah reached forward and touched two of her own fingers on the card, but she didn't flip it over. "I read Paris' cards when he was seven. I read all the witches in our Coven. Either when they turn thirteen, or when they move here from another place."

"Paris was born here, wasn't he?"

"Yes. He was."

Neither one of them moved, both still touching the card on the table.

"Why did you read his cards so young?"

"His mother asked. She was Coven Leader. I thought I was doing her a favor," Hannah replied.

"But you weren't," Jade deduced from Hannah's words and her expression. "His cards were... bad."

"Good and bad are quite flexible terms. The future is fluid. It can change."

Jade tapped her pointer finger on the card in front of her. "What did his cards say?" She felt a roiling in her stomach. A storm of dark liquid.

"That is between Paris and myself."

"And his mother," Jade added.

Hannah swallowed. "And his mother."

Something inside Jade clicked, like the pieces of a puzzle fitting together. "If a woman like Sakkara, a mother, a powerful witch, thought her child was in danger, there's no limit to what she would do to prevent that."

Hannah was surprised by Jade's words, but thought them over. "No, I suppose not."

"She probably wouldn't balk at a demon deal. She probably would have sought one out. No matter what she had to do for her end of it."

Hannah pulled her hand away from the card, her fingers hovering over the table in the air. "You know something. What do you think Sakkara did?"

"If she called upon a demon for assistance, and that demon told her... told her to kill someone, she'd do it."

Hannah shook her head. "No, it's not only anathema to our nature to deal with demons, but to kill as well..." Hannah swallowed, her fingers twitching slightly. "It's unconscionable."

"If Sakkara was asked to kill a child. To drown a child. A sacrifice to save her son, she'd do it," Jade finished, not breaking Hannah's gaze.

Hannah shook her head, her violet eyes bright and watery. She knew what Jade meant. "She couldn't have."

Jade pursed her lips together. "She did."

"No. You… someone has told you this and it's a lie."

"Someone did tell me. Seth."

"There you have it. A demon. They lie, dear. They lie for many reasons."

"I remember. I remember being held underwater. I remember her face. Her hands." Jade's breath hitched as she felt ghostly hands pinning her. The same hands had pinioned her down when Sakkara sent her to the Dearth. "And then…" Jade shook her head. "Nothing. There's nothing else."

Hannah pressed her fingertips to her mouth, her expression horrified. "No. No, she wouldn't have. The cards… I made it clear that his cards were fluid. They don't always tell the truth."

"But they tell enough that people rely on them. People believe them. They come here to get them read. I did. Lily did. Paris did." Jade paused. "What did his cards say?"

Hannah hesitated and then spoke quickly, the words rushing out of her like a river. "He dies. He dies young. A Coven Leader is a strong witch and with magic, can outlive our mortal counterparts, but… Paris dies younger than any other Coven Leader before. A betrayal."

Jade went cold. In her mind, she imagined a small child, Paris, hearing those words. "You told a seven year old that?"

Hannah shook her head. "I didn't know what I was saying until it was said. The cards…" She gestured before her to the solitary card Jade had pulled. It still sat, face down on the table. "It was the cards, not me."

"Bull shit. Are you saying you have no free will? You couldn't have told him it was all-" she waved her hands around "-undetermined and wow, it looks like he'd get the latest Pokémon for his birthday?"

"The cards are not like that. I am only a conduit."

Jade narrowed her eyes. "You could have lied."

"No, not with the cards. I cannot."

"What else did you tell him?"

"I told you, the cards are fluid. There are interpretations-"

"You tell me what you told him."

"Turn your card over," Hannah countered.

Jade did. It was a woman with some kind of beast next to her. A lion's head, a horse's body, taloned feet and some kind of tail. The woman had her arms wrapped around the beast and its head was tilted slightly downward. It meant nothing to her.

Hannah seemed relived or maybe vindicated. "Strength. Fortitude. Endurance." Her gaze darted up to Jade. Hannah's eyes were electrical, almost brimming with their own light. "You were the unknown variable."

Jade pushed back slightly from the table. "I don't know what that means. And I don't care. I flipped your card, so you tell me. What else did you tell Paris? Tell his mom?"

Hannah shook her head and then shrugged. "Nothing. There was nothing. Only that... the cards seemed to indicate there would be a betrayal. But don't you see, don't you realize? You changed that. If what you say is true, about Sakkara... I don't know the deal she made, but if one was constructed and you were involved, then you are a new variable."

"You and Sakkara both talk about me like I'm some kind of tool. A hammer or wrench," Jade said. She didn't like it. It made her feel less. Like a bolt or a cog. A mindless object in a machine.

"But you're not, that's the point. You have feelings and you act on them. The things you choose... If Paris would let me read his cards again... If you could talk..."

Jade pushed back from the table, her chair tipped over with the force of her standing. "If you think I'll be recommending your services or endorsing your voodoo after this..." Jade broke off, shaking her head. "You fucked with my head. And based on Lily's face when she came out of her reading, you fucked with hers too. And Paris. Jesus. He was seven and you told him the boogeyman was real and waiting for him under his bed. Who does that?"

"Jade, this is... you're from the mortal world. You don't understand."

"No, I don't and I don't want to. Demons. Deals. Death omens. Lying and trickery." She shook her head again. "It's shitty because I kind of liked you. You seemed nice with your cookies and tea and your cards. But shame on me. Like you said, abused kids are good at reading other people. It just took me a while to read you."

Hannah blanched, her face going even more pale; the violet of her eyes stark against the white of her skin. "I mean you no harm. I read the cards. Nothing more. Nothing less.

"Yeah. I guess the cards are a bitch that way." Jade leaned forward. "You can consider this one free." She flipped the top card of the deck over. "Nine of Wands. I bet you can make that fit whatever you want to say about me."

Hannah's eyes moved over Jade's two cards; the card of Fortitude and the Nine of Wands. "These cards... Pull one more. One more and I can read them as a set.

Jade thought of Paris' words and took pleasure in repeating them. "I don't deal with tarot cards, Hannah." She pulled open the sliding doors. Lily looked up expectantly from where she sat, dusting cookie crumbs off her lap.

"That was quick."

"We're leaving," Jade said.

"If you could just pull one more card," Hannah said from behind Jade, following her closely. "This is important."

Jade turned on her. "I'm not pulling any more cards for you. I can't believe I thought..." Jade paused, taking a breath. "I wanted to trust you. I think I did trust you. Paris trusts you and you don't deserve it.

Hannah drew herself up straight, the thin skin of her neck looking as old and haggard as she did, stretched thin over her veins and bones. "I've always told him the truth."

"You don't tell seven year olds truths like that," Jade replied. "I know what it's like to be a child that sees too much. Knows too much about the adult world. It sucks. It's not right."

"Paris has always been older than his years."

Jade stared at her. "Jesus, you think you're right."

"So, tarot card reading was a bust, I'm guessing." Lily stood behind Jade, her fingertips brushing against the small of Jade's back - a touchstone.

"Tarot card reading was a bust," Jade confirmed. She turned to Lily. "You don't have to tell me what she said, but... you should... you shouldn't..." Jade didn't know how to say what she meant to say. "If you think that what she told you is the truth, don't." She leveled Hannah with her gaze. "We control our own lives."

"Of course you do. But your decisions may be predestined. They affect others in your life." Hannah moved forward as though to touch Jade. "One more card, Jade. For me. For Paris."

Jade moved back, out of her reach. "We're leaving. We won't be back." She moved toward the front door of the house. Lily snatched one more cookie before following her.

"You have the ability to change his future," Hannah called after her. "I think you already have. Isn't that worth knowing?"

"You'll only say what you want to say," Jade called over her shoulder. "What the cards say. I'd rather..." she paused, not sure how to finish her sentence.

"We make our own futures," Lily finished. As Jade exited the front door, she felt Lily's fingers intertwine with her own and squeeze hers tight. She squeezed back.

"Please. Just one card."

Hannah's voice carried across like the space between them - thin and stretched. Like a bad batch of taffy pulled too far.

Jade turned, walking backwards as she spoke. "You pull one for me. I guarantee I don't care which one it is. It doesn't matter."

Hannah nodded sharply and went back in her house. Jade got into the driver's seat of the car, Lily taking the passenger side.

"What happened in there?"

Jade twisted the key in the ignition. "You tell me. She read your cards too."

"She said... What if she tells the truth? What if what she says comes true?"

"I don't believe that." Jade didn't know if she was telling the truth or only saying what she wanted to believe. But what Hannah said about Paris... he couldn't... he'd only been in her life a short time, but when she thought of what it would be like without him, she felt cold and anxious.

"She knew about us. She couldn't read your cards because of me. Because of our relationship."

Jade pulled out of Hannah's driveway, the wheels of the car spitting gravel. "If you think what she says is real, you'll make it real. I could read anyone's horoscope tomorrow and make it fit if I want."

"Maybe."

Jade didn't like Lily's tone. It sounded narrow and sparse. "If you tell me what she said, I'll tell you a thousand ways I'll stop it." She hoped her words were true. Thinking of what Hannah told Paris when he was a boy, Jade's words *had* to be true.

Lily was silent beside her. Jade clutched the steering wheel.

"It doesn't matter, I suppose."

Tell me, tell me, Jade thought. *I can't fix what I don't know.*

"If… If what she says isn't set in stone then I suppose it doesn't matter," Lily repeated.

Jade's knuckles were white as her fingers clenched the steering wheel. Her hands were talons - sharp and brittle, joints of bone pressing against the skin, eager to escape.

Lily's words made Jade think of Medusa. One of her hands drifted from the steering wheel to touch her neck and feel the patch of marble there. She could have been turned to stone, but she wasn't. She chose to face Medusa and see who she was, who she is. Even though it meant Jade had to think about her own past. That meant something, right? That meant she controlled her own fate, didn't it?

"Nothing's set in stone," Jade said, pulling her hand from her neck and putting it back on the wheel. "Not even us."

CHAPTER FIVE

Jade stared at her closet and wondered what someone wore on a coffee date. It's not like she had a lot of variety in her clothes. Black pants for work. A lot of solid neutrals so everything kind of matched and she didn't have to think about it. She stared longingly at her favorite jeans, crumpled on the floor. The Coven was pretty lax in its dress code. Business casual, and Jade did her best to live up to the casual side of that expression. She ended up wearing either slacks or her darker jeans with a slightly work-ish top most days. On the weekends it was yoga pants and a sweater or jeans and Henley.

She pursed her lips. Should she even attempt to dress different? Would that be some kind of a message? And if so, a good one or bad one? She should have gone running today. Not that she would look better after one day of running, but she could pretend she did. She'd begged off once she remembered that she only had her old, mile'd out trainers, her good ones lost forever in the Dearth. Bruce sighed loudly from his snoozing place in the closet.

"Yes, yes, terribly inconvenient for me to be standing here with the light on, I know."

She heard Lily knock on the door.

"You don't to have knock," Jade called out by way of a greeting.

Lily came in already dressed for work. She looked great, like always. She wore a dark grey skirt with some kind of long-sleeved pink blouse and had on really sparkly necklace on that hung low. Her earrings matched the necklace. Jade figured she'd probably wear their grey boots with the skirt. Jade recognized the clothes; they'd been at the back of her closet and not worn for ages. She never wore skirts. Any they had could firmly be considered Lily's, and never hers.

"I can feel you emoting from across the hall. What's up?"

Jade ducked her head low and mumbled.

"I'm sorry, what?"

Bruce poked his head out of the closet. "Pffffffffft."

"I'm telling her!" Jade said to him and then turned back to Lily. "I might have asked Paris for coffee and we're going after work and I don't know what to wear."

"Holy shit." Lily blinked and Jade swore to god if Lily had been wearing pearls, she would have clutched them. "When?"

"I told you. After work."

"No, I mean, when did you ask him?

"Yesterday."

"And you're telling me now?" Lily's tone was a screech and Jade flinched, opening her mouth to apologize, but Lily was already pushing Jade out of the way and grabbing a top from Jade's closet. She prodded Jade toward the bathroom.

"I already showered."

"Well, get back in there and wet your hair because the pony tail is being retired for today."

"No, I don't..." Jade squirmed away from Lily. "I like the pony tail. It keeps everything neat and out of the way."

Lily crossed her arms, careful of top she was holding. She narrowed her eyes as she studied Jade. "You did a great job on your makeup."

Jade shifted slightly. She thought so too. She used dark grays and silvers which complimented her eye color and then lined her eyes in black. She wore wearing her favorite matte lipstick - a deep fig-plum that didn't dry out her lips.

"I'm even wearing highlighter." Bruce thumped his tail on the floor from the closet.

"It looks good." Lily paused. "Do you want to look special or different? Or is that too much pressure?"

Jade had never been so grateful to have someone know her so well. Lily's question cut down to the crux of the matter. "I don't know," Jade admitted. "I like the stuff I wear. It's why I wear it. But..." She shrugged.

Lily nodded. "Okay, this top." She held out a soft black turtleneck that Jade liked. "And your dark jeans. And then I've got a plum colored scarf that will look good with your lipstick. It's not flashy, but it *is* ombre. A little outside your comfort zone."

"I can do that. And I was thinking the heeled booties."

"The suede ones? Definitely. But those are going to suck to work in all day."

Jade wrinkled her nose. "Ugh, yeah. But they look good."

"You don't have to sell me on those boots. I love them. Okay, get dressed and I'll see what earrings I can torture you with."

Jade stripped out of her robe while Lily rummaged around in their small jewelry box. Or maybe it was Jade's now since Lily seemed to have other stuff in her room. She shimmied into her dark jeans. They were made of the kind of fabric that stretched as you wore it and was comfy, but always left you wondering if you'd gained weight since the last time you put them on. She had to suck in to get the zipper up. She kind of hoped Lily wouldn't notice Jade was wearing her favorite pretty bra as opposed to one of her more functional ones. She wasn't ready to answer any questions about it. She wasn't even sure why she put it on. She had zero intentions of it being seen, but it was pretty and she liked it. Lily left the room for a moment, coming back with a gauzy plum colored scarf and making a beeline for Jade.

Before Jade could even attempt to fumble with it, Lily draped it around Jade's neck and tied it in a swirly kind of knot. Jade felt like a child as she tilted her chin up out of Lily's way.

"Okay, the earrings are some fake sparkly things I got. I know you don't like the flash, but these are small and tasteful."

"You said that about the four-carat pink ring you wanted to buy."

"That was tasteful! And it was costume so it wasn't like I was spending a gagillion dollars." Lily fluffed the knot and then motioned for Jade to hold out her hand where she dropped some earrings and a couple of stackable rings into it.

"When did you get these?"

"Henri and I went shopping yesterday after lunch."

"I don't want to wear your new stuff for the first time. You should get to do that."

Lily rolled her eyes. "Oh my god, just put them on."

Jade followed her instructions and then stood still while Lily examined her. Lily leaned forward and sniffed.

"Are you wearing perfume."

"No."

"You should. Where's that vanilla one we had? It has some anise in it too, I think?"

"Oh, um…" Jade went to her dresser and rifled through the drawers until she found it and gave herself a spritz.

"Do one more spritz an hour before you go."

Jade nodded, tucking the small travel-sized vial in her pocket. "Well?" she asked, turning in a small circle.

"You look great."

"I think you have to say that. We have the same body."

From the closet, Jade heard, "Pfffffft."

"Thanks, Bruce," she called out.

Lily stuck her tongue out and Jade imagined that, in the closet, Bruce was doing the same thing. "Weirdo. But seriously. You look nice."

Jade swallowed. "Thanks." She raised a hand and fiddled with the fringe of the scarf. "You don't think… I mean it's not… I really like him."

"I know you do."

"I mean as a person, not just…" Jade sighed. "I don't want to fuck that up."

"I know. You won't."

Jade wished she knew how Lily sounded so confident about it.

"So!" Lily clapped her hands together. "Coffee after work. Where?"

Jade paused.

"Go to Crema. You like it there," Lily instructed.

"They have that tea he likes," Jade agreed. "Orange pekoe."

"Aw! You remember his tea."

"Shut up." Jade face grew hot.

"Do you need the car or is he driving?"

Again, Jade paused, unsure.

"I'll ask Henri for a ride home after work and you can have the car. If you don't need it, it can stay at the Coven overnight," Lily said easily. She pursed her lips and then added, "Do you want me gone from the house for a while tonight?"

Jade frowned. "Why?"

"In case, you know…" Lily did a sort of shimmy with her hips and Jade frowned harder.

"In case there's a random rumba?"

"Jesus. Sometimes I can't believe we shared a brain." Lily squared her shoulders in a gesture Jade recognized as something she also did when wanted to be clear and precise. "In case you invite him back here. For some fun times. Or sex," Lily added at Jade's continued frown.

Jade felt a shock of panic flood through her veins like an electrical charge down a wire. "I'm not... We're not... It's coffee."

"It is. But you like him and he likes you." Lily took a step closer to Jade. "You've known each other for a while. It's up to you what happens or doesn't happen tonight. What do you want?"

"I'm... I don't..." Jade blinked, panic squeezing her heart. Bruce shuffled restlessly in the closet and let out a whining sound.

"Okay, so you're not ready for that. That's fine," Lily said easily. "Maybe you'd just like to have him back here for coffee."

"After we've gone for coffee," Jade said, her tone flat.

Lily's lips quirked. "Yeah, that could sound weird. So ask him back here to look at some spell books or something."

"I don't want to make it seem like a work or magic thing."

Lily nodded. "Fair enough. Go for coffee and see how it goes. If you do decide you want me out of here, for any reason," she said quickly when Jade opened her mouth to protest, "text me. I can drive around the preserve or go see Callie or wait in the car in the driveway like a creeper."

"I don't think it will be necessary."

"Well, the offer stands."

They headed downstairs, Bruce's feet heavy on the steps behind them. Jade made a beeline for the coffee pot, pouring them both cups while Lily got the creamer out and added it to both mugs. Lily tapped her fingertips against her mug and Jade gave her a questioning glance.

"Listen, it's probably not a great time to bring this up, but it's been on my mind."

"Okay. What?"

"I think I want…" Lily stopped and licked her lips, her gaze going toward her mug. "I'm going to go see Mom and Dad."

Jade paused mid-motion, mug halfway to her lips. She set the cup back on the counter.

"Why?" Jade blurted.

Lily shrugged one shoulder. "They're our parents."

Jade's eyes narrowed. "Is this about your tarot cards last night? What did she say to you? You know, I used to think Hannah was like the Coven's Fairy Godmother, but I'm starting to wonder if she's more like the Evil Step-Mom. Comes around to give people shit and stuff to angst over and then fucks off for the rest of the story."

"It's not about my cards. Not really."

"I told you yesterday - don't believe her. If she told you something you don't like, it's not real." It couldn't be real, Jade thought. Not if that meant Paris…She pushed the thought aside, focusing on Lily.

"You don't know that." Lily fiddled with her coffee mug, running her fingertips over the handle.

"I do know that. I'm not a sit back and wait kind of person. If there's something that Hannah thinks might happen or *predicted*," Jade made harsh air-quotes with her fingers, "I'll find a way to stop it."

Lily's eyes focused on her, bright green and sharp. "You're not a superhero."

Jade snorted, feigning bravado and hoping that Lily wouldn't see through the facade. "I beg to differ. I've defeated a demon, stopped a rogue Coven leader and most recently travelled the Dearth and faced Medusa. All I'm missing is the cape."

"Capes are impractical. They would get caught in things."

"So does long hair, hence the ponytail," Jade said, pointing at her hairstyle. She licked her lips. "But seriously. If Hannah told you something…"

Lily sat back in her chair, waving her hand dismissively. "I know, I know. But like I said, it's not about that. I can't help but feel… you know, they weren't always horrible."

"They don't give a fuck about us. Dad liked to beat the shit out of us and Mom liked to pretend it wasn't happening."

Although they tried not to intrude in each other's minds anymore, Jade could still feel when Lily didn't want to tell her something or was holding something back. Right now, Lily's mind was like a high, barbed wire fence with an obnoxious **KEEP OUT** sign.

"It wasn't always like that," Lily said quietly.

Jade felt the rest of Lily's unspoken words. "Before I showed up, you mean."

"I don't think it was you. I think it was something else. It was connected to you, but it wasn't something you did."

Jade looked away. Lily's assurance didn't make her feel better. She took a deep breath and tried to use her words. "I don't see how that can be true. If you're saying that it wasn't like that before I came, then it must have been me." Jade swallowed, the ghostly feeling of her father's fists and her mother's indifference still tattooed on her skin. She rolled out her neck, liking the way it sounded and felt when her vertebrae cracked.

"It could be related to you, but not caused by you."

"I don't think the different matters."

"It does. You know it does."

Jade sighed. "It's up to you."

"Don't be like that."

"Like what?" Jade asked.

"Like you don't care. Like it doesn't matter to you."

Jade shrugged. "I don't care. And it doesn't matter to me."

Lily pursed her lips. That was the problem. When you knew someone the way Jade and Lily knew each other, there were no such things as lies.

"I feel like I have to do this."

"They'll let you down," Jade continued. "You'll go there expecting something and you won't get it."

Lily nodded. "Maybe."

Jade ground her jaw.

"I have to try," Lily added.

Jade nodded, but didn't understand why Lily would even want to *look* at their parents again let alone visit them. Jade didn't even know if they were still alive. She'd had no contact over the last few years. They could be dead for all she knew. She hoped they were dead.

She would keep repeating it to herself until there wasn't a sick weight on her shoulders when she said it. Talking about them made Jade think of her mother - her biological mother - and the picture Josef had given her. Adeline. Petite. Blonde. Grey eyes. Just like Jade's. She didn't like to wonder about what her life might have been if things had been different. It hurt. A bone-deep ache that lingered.

"When were you thinking of going?"

"Soon."

The word felt like lemon juice on a paper cut - stinging and sharp. "Oh."

"I just think it would be easiest. I might have a job in Supernatural Relations quickly. Henri said my papers had to be reviewed by Marcus and Paris. So I should go before I get too involved in anything."

"Well, I… I'm…" *Busy, emotionally traumatized, unavailable.* "I can't go with you."

Lily nodded. "I didn't expect you to."

That made Jade angry and relieved all at once. Angry that Lily would go anyway. Relieved she didn't expect Jade to go with her.

"If it's all right with you, I thought I would take the car when I do go."

Jade shrugged. "Sure. I don't need it. And you'll probably want a quick way out of it when it all turns to shit."

"You don't know it will."

Jade stood up, turning her back to Lily. She fiddled with her pony tail, tightening it. "It's nice to have a pony tail now. I've always liked the way they look. Bouncy. Easy."

"Don't." Lily's voice was tired. Resentful.

Jade couldn't stop. Or rather, she didn't want to. "I remember Dad grabbing us by our ponytail once and yanking us back to him. And he was so angry about… something. Whatever it was that made him angry. Who knows?"

"I'm going, Jade."

"And the next day," Jade continued. "You cried and asked me to cut our ponytail off so he couldn't grab it next time. And I did. With Mom's pinking shears because I couldn't find anything else. It looked ugly. It was awful. But it worked."

"That was a long time ago."

"Not that long."

"Long enough."

Jade looked at Lily. For a moment, she thought of Seth. And his words about Medusa - how she couldn't get over what happened to her. About her own words back that maybe Medusa didn't have to, shouldn't have to *get over* what happened. Jade thought, at the time, maybe she couldn't get over her own assault. Now Lily was talking about more things from their past. Sometimes it was like the whole world was moving on and Jade was stuck, standing still. A heavy stone in the middle of a raging river.

"Well, I can't stop you." Jade poured out the rest of her coffee down the drain. A near sacrilege, but her stomach revolted at the thought of drinking it. She looked out the small window above the sink. The sun wasn't all the way up yet - too deep into winter. But the sky looked clear and she thought it would be a bright winter day.

"I need to do this."

Jade recognized the tone of Lily's voice. She used it herself. It meant *you can't talk me out of this* or *you don't get to tell me what to do*.

"You'll call when you get there? Or text? Something?"

"Yes. Of course."

Jade reached for her talisman, forgetting she no longer had it. She pressed her fingers against her collarbone where it used to rest, missing its warm, simple weight. She wondered if she could make one for Lily, or if someone in the Coven would make one for her, the way Paris did for Jade. Protection for her trip.

She wasn't sure what kind of magic worked on ghosts of the past.

#

There was another high priority alert in his inbox when Paris arrived early at the Coven. He'd already read it once on his smart phone before even coming into the office, and now, at his desk, he read it over again once more.

Forest Fire Alert Update - All Covens Asked to Report Witches Able to Assist.

Paris knew of three witches in his Coven who would be able to help other than Jade. However, those witches combined wouldn't be able to offer a quarter of the assistance Jade could. She simply had a gift for fire he didn't understand. He would be remiss if he didn't consider her abilities. He needed to discuss it with her first. With any other Coven witch, he felt comfortable offering their assistance without consultation - they were raised by a Coven, either this one or another, and understood that in times of crisis or natural disaster, they could be called upon. Paris didn't know if Jade knew that, nor was he willing to offer her assistance so quickly after all she'd recently been through. A quiet, deep part of him darkly hoped that if he asked her to help, she'd say no. She would stay at the Coven and continue her work at Counter-

Magic, close by and safe. Or as safe as she'd ever been here.

He checked the online messaging system and saw Jade's status was still set to *out of office,* indicating she hadn't yet come in. He was just about to set an alert to notify him when her status was *available* when his office door opened.

"Hannah, I wasn't expecting you." Paris had known she was in town, as she kept him generally apprised of her comings and goings, and he certainly expected to see her at some point during her visit, but hadn't thought it would be at seven in the morning at the Coven.

"I knew you'd be here early. I would have called last night, but I thought…" She cut herself off, her gaze drifting away for a moment. "I thought I could get the answers I need from the cards. But they've been unhelpful."

Paris frowned. "All right. What can I do for you? You seem upset."

Hannah came forward and set a deck of tarot cards on his desk. Paris sat back, moving away from them.

"I need you to shuffle the cards," she said.

"You know I don't deal with tarot cards."

"Yes, but this is important."

"No, Hannah. I won't have my cards read again. You know why."

"Please. You don't understand. I think… you know the future is malleable. Changeable. You need to have your cards read again."

"I need nothing of the sort. The future *is* changeable and malleable, as you've noted. Which is why tarot cards are unimportant. I am in command of my own fate."

Hannah's lips pursed. "Yes, of course, but there are also other factors. I know what I told you when you were a boy-"

"Yes, and after that reading surely you can understand why I'm not keen for another. I know you were only doing as my-" The word *mother* still hovered over his tongue, distasteful now when he thought of her. "As Sakkara asked. But I was too young for a reading and too young for what you told me." He felt traitorous saying the words to Hannah. She'd been a large part of his life. He saw by her expression his words cut her deeply, but that didn't make them any less true.

"I know. At the time, I didn't realize... of course I couldn't have known what the cards would say."

"Of course not. And as I said, I recognize Sakkara asked for a reading when I was too young. I don't know why. But I will not shuffle those cards again."

"Lily came for a reading last night."

Paris was surprised by the non-sequitur but nodded. "I hope it went well for her."

"She has an... interesting journey ahead."

Paris wondered what that meant and to his mind, unbidden, came the Chinese curse: *May you live in interesting times.*

"Jade's initial reading was unclear. Murky. All due to her relationship with Lily. When she shuffled, even though at the time it was only Jade in control in their mind, Lily's presence confused the cards. I never did get a good reading on Jade."

Paris hadn't known that. Jade's reading had been between Hannah and Jade. He'd never asked and neither Jade nor Hannah had offered anything.

"I asked Jade if I could read her cards again, but she refused."

Paris wondered what Hannah had told Jade when she'd read her cards if Jade refused to have them read again. Though he knew he shouldn't, he couldn't help but ask, "What did you tell her before?" Dread coiled in his stomach as he wondered if Jade had a reading far too similar to his own.

"Nothing. There had been nothing to see, nothing to tell."

Paris felt a tension he hadn't known he was holding melt out of his body. "Is that why you wanted to read her cards again?"

"Yes. No. I…" Hannah paused and then looked directly at him again. "Your future and hers are intertwined. I haven't seen it in the cards, but I know it to be true. I need to see your cards again. Yours and hers."

"I'll not have my cards read again and, given that, I certainly cannot force Jade to have hers read. Nor would I wish to do so. If she chooses not to have them read, then that is the decision."

"I feel, or rather, I fear that some of the things your mother has done may be tied to this. Please, Paris."

"The inclusion of my mother is hardly an incentive, Hannah. If anything, it's a deterrent. I don't know why she faked her death, why she dealt with a demon, why or how she continues to serve that demon. And I suspect I'm better off not knowing."

"Your mother was... is very intelligent. She always had the Coven and your best interests at heart. Surely you must have considered that when thinking about why she would have made a deal? Why she would deceive us all in such a fashion?"

Hannah hit upon the crux of his rumination of late. Of course he'd wondered why his mother had made the deal she did - what it meant, what she could have gotten in return. He'd wondered if her own deal was the reason she'd cautioned him so many times in his youth on the evils of dealing with demons. Often times she'd warned him how they lie, how they deceive. And, naturally, he'd wondered if anything about his own life had any part in her deal. Of course he'd wondered. His mother had been an exceptional leader. He could think of very few things that could have compelled her to make a deal. If she still remained, at her core, the person he thought she was, she must have had powerful and irresistible reasons for her deal. However, he also saw her through the lens of being her son, and her protégé. He knew he was afraid to look too closely at her reasons in case they altered too much of his own paradigm.

"I could spend the rest of my life, I suppose, trying to untangle the reasons Sakkara has done what she has. But I've a Coven to lead and a business to run, and I don't know that the truth will assuage any feelings I have on the matter."

Hannah swallowed, watching him closely. For what, he wasn't sure.

"Let me read your cards."

"No."

"Please. I rarely ask you for anything."

"That does not mean I'm obligated to say yes when you do. I'm sorry. I cannot, I will not have my cards read."

Hannah exhaled sharply, the sound loud in his office. "Then I need to read Jade's."

"If she agrees."

"She won't. But as Coven leader, as yourself, if you ask her, she will do it."

Paris huffed. "If you think I've that kind of power over her, you're mistaken."

"If you ask her," Hannah repeated, "she'll do it."

"I will not ask."

"Paris," Hannah began.

"No," Paris reiterated. "You're asking me to force her to do something she does not wish to do." He shifted in his chair, all too aware with what his words may be associated. All too conscious of Jade's past, thanks to his conversations with Lily. "If she does not want her cards read, that is the end of it."

"I feel the future of our Coven may be at stake. Surely that is enough?" Hannah implored.

Paris swallowed. "I cannot be a leader that forces his will upon someone. My answer is no."

Hannah appeared to straighten her spine, appeared to try to make her self taller. "There are things a Coven Leader must do. I do not understand the decisions your mother made, but I believe she always acted in the best interest of the Coven. You must be that kind of leader."

"I am not my mother." Paris felt a sense of relief and release at his own words. "I cannot be the Coven Leader she was. Nor do I wish to be."

"Let me read your cards. I fear you may be lost."

The weight of her words was dense and absolute. In that moment, he was seven years old, hearing her voice tell him he would die young. He felt the same awful reverberence in his bones now as he felt then. The same hopelessness and terror. Only now, he was an adult, and better suited to shoulder the load.

"As long as I serve the Coven, I am never lost."

"When I told you of what I saw in the cards, when you were young, I..." Hannah stopped and could not meet his eyes. "It was a mistake. You were too young and my words were too brutal."

"It is in the past."

"But it needn't be. If you let me read your cards, or if you tell Jade to have hers done, I feel the cards can tell us the truth. A new truth."

Paris looked at the tarot cards on his desk. Stiff paper with pretty pictures and images imprinted on them. "That way lies madness, Hannah." He held up a hand to forestall her immediate response. "And if you read my cards tonight and they do not tell you what you want, will you return tomorrow? And the day after that and the day after that?"

"This is not a blind hunt. Things are at work here. There must have been a change."

"And if there has not?" Paris questioned. Hannah looked away, unable to answer him. "I cannot be a leader if I'm constantly second guessing my actions and then consulting tarot cards for the outcome. I make decisions. Perhaps they are right, perhaps they are wrong. But they are mine. I will not yield that. I will not ask Jade to yield that either. If she refuses to have her cards read, that is her right. Her choice. I have no authority to take that from her."

"I could read them without your knowledge. Leave a deck in your presence and then read the cards later."

"You could. I hope you would not."

"When I heard your mother was alive, I thought... I thought at first it must be some kind of dark magic. In a sense, I suppose it was. Demon deals area always dark. I wondered what could have driven her to such lengths." Hannah's violet eyes bored into Paris'. "I know of no greater power than that of a mother who wishes to protect her child."

Paris' stomach dropped, the sensation leaving him ill. "Are you suggesting my mother's deal had something to do with my cards? With what you prophesied?"

Hannah licked her lips, her tongue darting out quick across her skin. "I don't know for certain. But I knew your mother. I worked with her for many years. I cannot imagine anything else that could have compelled her to follow such a path. If I read your cards, we may know the truth."

It was the first time in years he was remotely tempted to pick up the deck of tarot cards and shuffle. He stared at the cards on his desk and could almost feel the weight of them in his hands. The cards were worn, slightly frayed at the edges. They were surely a favorite set of Hannah's. If he changed his mind, he could not only learn his future, and perhaps clear the heavy, immutable weight of Hannah's long-ago prophecy, but he could also understand his mother's actions. Would learning she dealt with demons to secure his future free him from her machinations or ensnare him further?

Hannah moved forward, one of her hands stretched out. "Let me read your cards. Shuffle them, Paris. We are at an unknown crossing here. You. Your mother. Jade. There are connections that I sense, but cannot name or define." She rested two fingertips on the cards. "Shuffle these cards, and we may know."

"And if you read them, Hannah, and they do not tell you anything, or at least, anything new, what then?"

"I don't think that will happen."

"But it could." He shook his head and pushed himself further back from his desk, from the cards. "No, I will not have my cards read."

"Please."

"No."

Hannah pursed her lips and then leaned forward and took the deck of cards off his deck. He breathed out a sigh of relief as she worked an old elastic around the deck and slid them back in her purse.

"Will you stop me from asking Jade again?"

"You have your own will, as does Jade. If you ask her and she says yes, that is her choice. But if you ask her again, and she says no, I wish, as Coven Leader," he couldn't help but stress his title, "that you will not ask her again."

"Very well. I abide by the Coven Leader's wishes, and seek to do no harm."

The words were old and practiced - spoken a thousand times before by a thousand different witches. They left him feeling slightly hollow and old.

"Thank you."

Hannah seemed to consider her next words, and he dreaded them slightly. "I noticed Jade was missing her talisman when she visited."

Paris let out a breath - this he could do something about. "Yes. A consequence of her trip to the Dearth."

"The Dearth?"

"That is what they call the demon landscape. The Dearth. She indicated she had to trade it. I'm not sure why or for what."

"I wondered when I saw it missing from her neck. It was quite powerful and she seemed fond of it."

"I believe she was. I'll have to make a new one."

"Will you?"

"Yes. Of course. All witches have a talisman."

"Yes, all witches have a talisman made for them by a mentor. Once. But after that, well…" Hannah waved a hand. "Talismans are lost or misplaced or used up. You've no obligation to make her another." Her violet eyes seemed to bore into him. "Unless you wish to."

"I do."

She nodded and her lips curved in a bit of a smile. "Then I wish you luck. And may I suggest hematite. For protection."

"Thank you. I was somewhat at a loss." Choosing a salamander the first time had been a natural fit for Jade - a mythical creature that could endure fire. But now, knowing more about her, he didn't want to simply re-create what she'd already had. He wanted to forge something new and different.

"And possibly, red jade."

Paris had to think for a moment, recalling his stone and crystals knowledge. "That's the stone of a warrior."

"It is. It suits her."

"I don't wish to make her a warrior."

Hannah smiled ruefully. "I don't know that you have a choice. I think she already is one."

CHAPTER SIX

Another day, another set of emails. Like yesterday, she read in her inbox a notification about a forest fire. It was now dangerously close to being out of control. The email proclaimed all witches proficient with fire needed to identify themselves to their Coven Leader, if not already known and/or done.

Did Jade need to identify herself? She was good with fire. She felt comfortable with it. It was the only magic she didn't need words or spells for. She willed something to happen and it did. Small sparks for the fireplace, a constant flame for Bruce, a light when she was stumbling in the dark. She didn't know how she did it. It was just easy. Effortless. In comparison, her earth spells sucked dishwater. She couldn't make rocks move or dirt shift, a key component in one of the dusting spells she was desperate to make work in her cottage. It didn't matter how much she tried, and that shit was tied to housecleaning so it wasn't like she didn't feel motivated. Her water spells were okay-ish. Except for that time she caused a rainstorm in the Preserve. That probably happened to a lot of witches, right? Then there was wind. Wind she thought she could be better at if she tried, but it seemed like a lot of work, and there was also demon magic to learn. How valuable could wind be? What would she do? Huff and puff and blow a house down? She didn't have a lot of spare time to work on other spells.

Paris knew she was good with fire, didn't he? He probably got the same emails, only more important and official. She didn't need to say anything, right?

But she wondered if volunteering would help her *fit in,* whatever that meant. Lily was getting a job with Supernatural Relations. She'd be meeting new people and would no doubt be a good fit. She had already made fast friends with Callie and Henri. Lily fit in wherever she went and Jade... just didn't.

Maybe this is what fitting in meant. Maybe it meant when you saw a place you could help, you did. Or had she already done that? Didn't she prove herself with the whole Dex thing? She'd stopped a raging, insane Coven Leader. That should earn her some street cred.

People-ing was *hard*. There should be a manual or a pamphlet. Jade could probably help out with the fire stuff. She was comfortable as long as it was just about fire. She opened up a new email message and stared at the empty window for five minutes. Finally, she decided not to think about it and just type.

To: Paris, Coven Leader.

Message: *I saw the email about needing witches were good with fire. I'm good with fire. You probably knew that. I'm available. You probably knew that too.*

J

She hit send without waiting spell check to review. There. Done. She tabbed quickly over to the incoming Counter-Magic Log, looking for things she could help with. Email sent. Problem solved, right? Right.

People-ing wasn't just hard, it sucked.

She gave herself a shake. On to problems she *could* solve! As usual, there were things on the log she could help with. House spells gone wrong, location spells not working - that sort of thing. She saw something that made her want to hide under her desk. Problem in the sewers. Not that she wasn't grateful for finding Bruce, but the sewers were gross. She had zero desire to go down there. She wondered if that was something Bruce could do? On his own? If he wanted. She wouldn't send him down there if he didn't want to go. But she had this feeling, like if he could do it and wanted to go, she could ask him. She fired an email off to Josef asking him if such a thing would be a) covered by Coven insurance and b) generally allowable even *if* covered by insurance. Business, man. Sometimes it was harder than people-ing.

There were several empty calls noted on the log - times when people called in and then hung up before speaking. Maybe people-ing was hard because most people were weird. Why call the Counter-Magic line if you didn't want to talk to Counter-Magic? Bizarre.

"You look good today."

Jade immediately turned to Daniel, her eyes narrowing. "Why would you say that? Did you hear something?"

"What are you talking about?"

"Why do you feel the need to say I look good today?" So help her, if Lily had told people about her date with Paris, Jade would... well, she didn't know what she would do, but it would be something.

"Because I thought you looked good!" Daniel exclaimed. "Jesus, I take it back. You don't look good. You look horrible. I'm surprised they let you walk around looking like that without a bag over your head."

Jade pursed her lips, taking the coffee he offered her.

"Sorry," she offered as he sat down at his desk. "I'm... sensitive today."

"No shit."

Jade laughed and wished she could scrub her face with her hands, but it would mess up her makeup. "So, I look okay?" she hedged.

"Is this a trick question? Will I get my face bit off if I answer?"

"No, I'm serious."

"Yeah, you look nice today." Daniel paused. "Care to tell me why it's such a contentious issue?"

It was on the tip of her tongue to tell him about her date with Paris when Hannah walked in to Counter-Magic. Her heart sank.

"Great," Jade muttered, cracking the lid on her coffee and taking a sip.

"Hannah!" Daniel exclaimed, sitting up straighter and sounding more professional than Jade had ever heard him. "Josef isn't here right now. He's resolving an issue with a younger witch and a growth spell."

"Thank you, dear, but I'm here to see Jade." She smiled at Daniel and then turned her violet eyes to Jade.

"Lucky me," Jade intoned. "What do you want?" The way she slurred her words together, it sounded more like a single multisyllabic word, rather than a set of individual ones.

"Jade," Daniel said, his tone low. "R-E-S-P-E-C-T," he sang slightly.

"I have plenty of respect," Jade countered, flicking her eyes from Daniel to Hannah and back again. "When people deserve it."

Daniel swallowed, making a loud sound. Jade thought he might be about to have a brain aneurysm.

"It's all right, dear," Hannah said, directed toward Daniel. Jade wondered if she actually remembered his name or if she chose to use an endearment because she didn't. It didn't matter, she guessed. "Jade and I are working through some things."

Jade snorted, the sound out before she could stop it. "Sure. Let's call it that."

"Dear," Hannah said, this time directing it toward Jade. "Even after our discussion yesterday, I wanted to ask you if you've reconsidered. Perhaps now that you've had some time to think on it, you can see the benefit. Would you have your cards read?"

"Nope."

Hannah took a breath. "Although, it is your right to decline-"

"It is. So I did. And continue to do. Decline."

"I implore you to think of the larger picture. There are things... there may be events... your arrival at the Coven changed so much."

"Yeah. Your annual coffee consumption will never be the same again."

"This is important. If we could speak in private-"

"No," Jade snapped, thinking of Medusa as she did - of the clear, concise, and complete way she said, *no*. Like it was an entire sentence without need of further clarification.

"Oh, look at that, there's a meeting I'm late for," Daniel said awkwardly, getting up from his desk. Jade flicked her eyes to the clock. 8:47. There was no way he had any kind of meeting that started at 8:45. He wanted to make an escape.

"You don't need to leave," Jade said, "Hannah was just about to go."

Hannah paused and smiled, the skin around her lips tight and dry. "Please think about what I've said. It's not just *your* cards I'm interested in."

"Maybe if I find out you told Lily something upsetting, like you've been known to do," Jade said meaningfully, "then I'll stop by."

"I wish you would, dear. There are so many things I could teach you, or learn from you."

"I have work to do." Jade hoped that would be the end of the conversation.

Hannah nodded, tipping her head forward gracefully. "Take care, dear. You're a valuable member of the Coven."

"I feel all warm and tingly about that." Jade pressed a hand to her sternum. "Or maybe that's heartburn. Tough to say."

"Jesus, Jade." Daniel's voice was thin and high-pitched. He had the look of a skittish animal, ready to bolt.

"I hope you'll change your mind," Hannah said.

"I hope you'll stay away from me. And Lily and Paris. Have a good one!" Jade waved cheerily as Hannah left Counter-Magic, moving slow and gracefully. Jade felt Daniel's eyes on her. "Don't look at me like that," she said, spinning her chair to face her computer again. "She's not some fairy godmother."

"No, she's the oldest and most respected member of this Coven."

"I'll give you oldest, but I'll fight you on respected."

"She sits on the Supernatural Council."

"So what?" Jade shrugged.

"It's a very respected position."

"If you say so. I don't know anything about it."

"How can you not know anything about it? It's like our UN."

Jade looked at him. "I've been a little busy since I got here. Demon-dealing, power-hungry witches, bat-shit crazy witches back from-" she cut herself off, not wanting to reveal the truth about Sakkara. Did Daniel know? Jesus, she couldn't keep it all straight. "Whatever. I haven't exactly had time for the extended, in-depth tour."

"I'll find you some articles to read on it." Daniel hurriedly typed on his keyboard.

"You can send me all the articles you want. It's not going to change my mind about Hannah."

"Was there something bad in your cards? You know, she doesn't make the future, she just relays what the cards tell her. It's not her fault."

Jade rolled her eyes. "Yes, she's completely innocent." *Except for the time she told a seven year old he would die young. And god only knew what she told Lily.*

"You didn't grow up here," Daniel continued.

"And at first I was kind of bitter because my childhood sucked, but now I'm starting to think I had the better end of the deal, and that's including the fact that I got the shit kicked out of me regularly."

"Josef respects Hannah. Paris respects Hannah."

Jade swallowed. "That doesn't mean I have to."

"But you respect them. Their opinions. Don't you?"

"Jesus, why are you the cheer-leader of the love-and-respect-Hannah-train?" Jade exclaimed. "I don't like walnuts either. Are you going to start waxing poetic about those too?"

"A Coven is built upon the relationships of its witches. We're a community. A family."

"A lot of families don't all get along."

"I just..." He exhaled, nostrils flaring. Jade could tell he wanted to say something but wasn't sure if he should.

"Say it. Whatever it is, you should say it."

"You already have a hard time fitting in."

"I have no idea what that has to do with Hannah."

Daniel exhaled again. "Just... didn't you notice after you helped us with Dex that people were starting to warm up to you?"

She had. It wasn't like they were throwing parades in her honor and the kid at the liquor store still ID'd her every week, but her latte was always made just how she liked it at Crema - with the thick, creamy foam. And they put a coffee sleeve on it for her. The grocery cashier let her know automatically when stuff in the flyer applied to her order, and Jade saved six bucks last week and got bonus trip miles on her card. She also noticed the spot where she liked to park tended to be free, even if she was running late. "Yeah, maybe."

"It's not that people *want* to find a reason to dislike you..."

"Stop. I can't take the flattery."

"But if you go around making a big deal about how you don't like Hannah, for whatever reason," Daniel continued before Jade could interrupt, "their current level of trust is..."

"Fickle?"

"Tenuous."

"Well. I lived a long time on my own without Coven approval. I guess I'll survive again without it."

"Just... don't make your life harder than it has to be."

Daniel turned back to his screen and went back to work while Jade wondered if she knew anything other than making her life harder than it had to be.

#

The Universe or the Goddess must be testing me, Paris thought, as he stared at the two emails that had arrived back to back in his inbox.

Update: Witches Proficient in Fire to be on Standby.

It was followed almost immediately by Jade's email, indicating she was available to assist.

The forest fire reported earlier was quickly moving beyond the ability of the mortal responders. Wind shifts and an unseasonably dry summer, combined with partially dry winter, were enabling the fire to burn out of control. While it had been seemingly contained to an uninhabited area, a recent wind change caused it to turn its course, a small town now in its path. Citizens of the town were placed on alert; an evacuation notice hanging over their heads like a heavy guillotine. Some had already chosen to evacuate. Paris clicked on an interactive map showing the current path of the fire and its possible projected path if weather patterns remained unchanged. It was like watching one of those science fiction moves wherein a world-wide epidemic was released. The small red center on his screen expanded farther and farther, then farther still, until it devoured not only the small town, but the neighboring hamlets and a national park.

And Jade had expressed a willingness to help. He could not ignore that. Not only would she be the most powerful fire-witch they had, she'd *offered*. He didn't want to deny her that.

And yet, and yet.

Fire work was dangerous. Fire was unpredictable and fast. Faster than humans, potentially faster than magic. It also tended to work best from a close proximity. If Jade wanted to assist, she'd have to be close to the flames. Maybe right in the middle. Paris didn't want to put her in that kind of danger. As a Coven Leader, he could caution her to be careful, and ensure that regular safety protocols were followed, but that was it. If she wanted to help, if she agreed to assist, then her decisions on what to do and where to go were her own. He could not take that autonomy from her, no matter how much he feared for her safety.

With any luck, the weather would shift, or they would be able to force a small, controlled change of the wind and Jade would not be needed.

Paris found throughout the rest of the day, he had to continually push the thought of the forest fire and the potential need for Jade to assist to the back of his mind. A meeting with Finance and Budgeting went over the allotted time, and although it was important, he kept checking his watch, so much so that one of the meeting presenters apologized for it running late twice. After the second apology, he resolved not to check the time, but still keenly felt each slow, laborious reading of the presentation. He wondered if there were any way to send out a Coven-wide email that if you put words on a screen, you needn't read those exact same words verbatim as part of the presentation. Not only that, but there should be some sort of maximum allowable words per slide. He swore one was at least a thousand words long and the presenter read every, single word.

Every one.

Finally freed from spreadsheets, pie charts and bar graphs, Paris took a moment to check his email once more (no further requests regarding witches and fire) and then headed down to Counter-Magic. He was surprised to find Jade wasn't at her desk.

"She's with Josef in MedLab," Daniel explained.

"Did something happen?" Paris asked, immediately concerned at Daniel's words.

Daniel exhaled, puffing out his cheeks as she did. "Love spell gone awry."

Paris winced. "Caster or castee?"

"Caster. I think there was a backlash and they called us. Jade took the call and flipped the fuck, I mean, er... It didn't go well."

"What happened?" Paris checked his phone again. It couldn't have been too serious or Josef or Dr. Gellar would have emailed him.

"I only know what I overheard," Daniel hedged.

"I won't take it as written in stone. Go on."

"Jade took the call, it sounded like the spell went bad and the caster was eating every food they had ever declared they loved and Jade found out what kind of spell they'd been trying to do and went ballistic." Daniel paused. "I didn't know her voice could get that high-pitched. I would have guessed her to be an alto, but she's got the pipes of a soprano."

"What did she say?"

Daniel exhaled again. "Stuff about consent and forcing people to do things they didn't want and criminal charges. There may have also been some threats of bodily harm. Really creative and painful threats." Daniel looked a little pale.

"I see," Paris said quietly. He imagined he knew quite well the direction the call had taken at that point given Jade's history. "I don't think we've ever addressed that aspect of love spells before. They're usually just dismantled."

"Yeah. Well, I think the guy on the phone ate himself sick while Jade was yelling at him, and I don't think she feels sorry about that. Josef called MedLab pickup to go pick up the caster and then headed up there to wait for him."

"And brought Jade with him."

"Yep, and that's where it goes beyond my pay-grade." Daniel licked his lips nervously. "She was pretty upset."

Paris nodded. "Thank you. I'll head to MedLab directly."

"Good luck. You're gonna need it."

Paris found Jade and Josef arguing outside MedLab upon his arrival. Their voices were low and hushed, but there was no mistaking their body language. Jade's arms were crossed over her chest and she was hunched over herself, her face pale, her expression stark and angry. Josef was more relaxed, but was gesturing tightly with his hands. While they hadn't attracted much attention yet, it was only a matter of time. It was nearing the end of the work day for a lot of witches and more of them would start passing by. Paris approached them slowly, able to hear their words as he did.

"I don't care if he vomits out his entire stomach," Jade hissed. "Why should I help him? *Do what you will though it harm none*, I thought that was our motto."

"It is, but-"

"No! There are **no** buts. He was planning on harming someone. Making someone feel things they don't feel. Do things they didn't want to do."

"That probably wouldn't have happened. Most love spells don't work and those that do are generally harmless."

"Are you shitting me right now?" Jade stamped one of her feet. Now that he was closer, Paris could see she was on the verge of tears - her irises sharp and bright against her reddening sclera.

"Love spells are so complex that they don't often work. As you can see." Josef gestured back toward MedLab. He must have caught Paris' motion because he turned, looking somewhat relieved to see him. "Paris."

"Josef. Jade."

Jade immediately rounded on Paris. "I can't believe I have to fucking explain to you people why love spells are criminal."

Paris wasn't quite comfortable with being lumped in with "you people," but recognized this wasn't the time for him to address that. "They can be quite disturbing."

"Can be? Can be?" Jade's voice, though hushed, went up several octaves. He suddenly understood Daniel's comment about Jade potentially being a soprano. For a moment, she seemed to nearly vibrate and then she cursed and let out a rather large, perfectly round fireball. It burned hot and bright, a flash flame in the middle of the hallway.

If their argument hadn't already drawn attention, Jade's use of magic on Coven grounds just did. Paris noted a number of stares and tried to angle himself so that he would block Jade from their view.

"Perhaps we could discuss this somewhere private." Paris hoped to move them to a quieter, less public place where he could calm the situation down.

Seemingly agreeing with him, Josef placed a hand on Jade's arm in an attempt to lead her away and Paris winced in automatic response. Jade didn't like to be touched and Pars could well imagine that any reaction she would have normally had would be only magnified.

Jade batted Josef's hand away quite forcibly, an audible *smack* from the motion. "Don't you fucking touch me."

"I'm sorry," Josef said automatically, looking completely bewildered at Jade's harsh reaction.

Jade crossed her arms over her chest, even tighter than they had been before, her hands tucked deep into her arm pits. "If I wasn't here, causing a ruckus, he'd probably get counter-hexed and then be on his merry fucking way and that would be the end of it, wouldn't it?" She blinked, clearly trying not to cry, but failing. She swiped angrily at her tears and let out a mighty sniffle that echoed throughout the entire corridor.

"I'm afraid our measures for dealing with this type of spell aren't what they need to be," Paris intoned.

Jade laughed, a broken and wet kind of sound. She wouldn't meet Paris' eyes. "Oh my god, English. You sound so political right now. I might be a fucking basket case at the moment, but I can still tell you're trying to *handle* me."

"I'm not. I swear I'm not," Paris replied quickly, and he meant it. His eyes flicked to Josef and thank Goddess he seemed to understand and slowly backed up, away from both Paris and Jade. Paris turned back to Jade and tried to focus only on her. She refused to meet his eyes, staring off to the side, looking as though she could set fire to the entire Coven in that moment and not feel a second of remorse. "I want to understand the full implications of what you're saying, and I want to change the way we respond to these types of spells because... because I can see now how incomplete our understanding of it all is."

Jade swallowed, her jaw working, and he waited for her to speak. "That still sounds like a lot of bullshit." She swiped at her new tears. "And you're only saying it because you... because Lily told you." She exhaled, the breath coming out of her lungs sharp and short.

Paris nodded, knowing what Jade meant. He only felt this way now because Lily had told him about their history. Their assault. "Yes. You're right."

Jade's eyes finally darted to his, quick and assessing. He wished he could flinch or look away from them, so sharp and keen was her gaze.

"I wouldn't have thought of a love spell as a form of coercion the way I do now. Now that I've learned of your past. Now that I've thought of it. But I want to learn and understand and change the way we do things if that's necessary."

"Well, it is."

He nodded again. "All right. I believe you and trust your judgment. What should we do?"

She gnawed at the skin of her lower lip, gaze darting back toward the door of MedLab. "Someone needs to talk to that kid and explain to him *why* what he did was wrong. And not just because he used really shitty and sloppy magic. Because that's a mess too."

"Okay," Paris replied, wondering who would be able to take a task like that on. "Normally someone from Counter-Magic deals with bad spell work, but in this case, we may need someone with skills and authority outside of magical use to highlight that this isn't about the spell work; it's about what he was trying to do with it."

Jade nodded. "Yeah. And maybe some kind of punishment. I mean, I'm not stupid, I know you can't walk in there and throw him in, like, magic jail because of what he did, but he has to learn it's not okay. Do you have something like that? Something for punishment like you did with Matthew when you broke his magic?"

"We do have fines and restrictions for people using magic. Older, antiquated things we don't use anymore for death spells, or illegal hexes. But I'm sure something can be agreed upon. This may entail more than simply assigning a consequence."

"What do you mean?"

"As you said, he has to learn it's not okay, and I'd prefer others learn that before they commit an offence."

"Oh." Jade blinked, her mind processing his words. "Like public service announcements?"

"Perhaps. Or we need to talk to the schools, or we need to form a committee or a branch of Counter-Magic. I don't know."

"That's your stuff." Jade held up her hands defensively. "Running things and dealing with people."

"It is. It could be yours as well. Would you want to work on something like that?"

He could see she was considering his words and not dismissing them out of hand, but she was still apprehensive.

"Think on it. We can address this instance and decide where to go from here later." He raised his hand to the height of her elbow and waited for her to pull away. When she didn't, he rested his hand there, cupping the joint of her bones in his palm. "I'm sorry this has upset you, but I'm equally glad you're here to assist in its resolution."

Jade lips curved, a wry smile. "You might not be so glad when you get Josef's report on this incident. I knew that kid would make himself sick and I let him. Twice." Her words were defiant, but also testing: she wanted to know how he would react to her statement.

Paris smiled in return. "I'm sure I won't be able to tell that from the official report. Though it may not be evident to others, I've no doubt you're subtle when it suits you."

Jade laughed again, and this time it didn't sound so awful and broken. "Yeah. That's the word that people use to describe me. Subtle."

"Did you still want to go for coffee tonight?" he asked. He wondered if the day's events had colored her mind on the matter.

She looked confused. "Did you? I mean, if you don't want to, that's fine." Jade shrugged one shoulder. "It's fine."

Paris had the sudden notion it would decidedly be not fine if they cancelled and hoped his expression accurately conveyed he did still want to go. "No, I've been looking forward to it."

"Really?" Jade asked and then seemed to school her face, her expression going somewhat bland and neutral. "I mean, sure. Okay. We can go to Crema. Because I like it. I assume you like it too, but if you don't-"

"Crema is fine. However, I would like to check on this witch first." He tipped his head slightly toward the door of MedLab.

Jade's eyes, always a cool shade of grey, grew somewhat colder. "Better you than me. I'd probably make him barf for three more days. I have to... get my purse or check my email or something. Anything that's not here right now," she said honestly.

"I'll come back to Counter-Magic when I'm done."

Jade nodded and then her hand came to rest on his forearm. Given her disinclination for touch, he found himself staring at her fingertips, pale and stark against the dark knit of his sweater.

"Thank you," she said. "For..." Her voice trailed off and she shook her head. "Thanks."

"I remain your most humble and obedient servant." He recalled her saying once that he sounded like the closing of an old, historical letter when he said such things. At the moment, he could think of nothing else to say that encompassed the mood. To his surprise, her cheeks flushed, turning slightly pink.

"Careful or I'll hold you to it," she teased, pulling away slightly. He took a chance and increased his hold on her slightly. She paused, staring down at his hands and then raising her eyes up to him. At first, he was concerned he'd overstepped and he thought he might be on the receiving end of one of her harsh glares. The pale grey of her irises contributed well with her ire when she was angered. But it wasn't a challenging look she wore; it was more contemplative. Thoughtful.

"I hope you will," he added.

Her fair skin flushed further and he was momentarily stymied by a flush of heat in his own face until he realized it was a rush of her magic, flaring out from her core and enveloping him in a quick sphere of heat.

"Oh, wow. I'm sorry, I should..."

"I will see you downstairs," he finished for her, knowing he said the correct thing when she ducked her head and nodded. She turned, pulling free from his grasp.

"I know I'm not the best person to ask about this, but if he keeps barfing, it's probably not the worst thing that could have happened. He's kind of an asshole. And I know that doesn't sound impartial, but trust me, after you talk to him, you'll agree."

Paris watched her go and then schooled his expression for what could meet him on the other side of the door to MedLab.

After three minutes, he understood what Jade meant. This boy, this child, was an asshole. While he was no longer actively eating himself sick, he still suffered bouts of nausea and had vomited an additional three times and wanted to know why "the outsider witch" hadn't cured him.

"You're lucky that 'outsider witch,'" Paris repeated, his tone as even as he could make it, "didn't leave you to vomit up all of your viscera. I dare say she wanted to and I'm wondering if I should have authorized it."

The young man paled. He'd been petulant and combative and clearly expected Paris to take his side. Although Paris hadn't anticipated being the one to give the boy an explanation on consent and permission, he found himself gearing up for an extraordinary lecture when his smart phone buzzed three times in succession - a high priority email. Although he was loathe to interrupt dealing with the miscreant witch, he couldn't ignore a priority message.

Call to Action - Witches Proficient in Fire Called to Report for Immediate Assignment.

"Josef. Please bind this young man's magic for a period of two weeks." He paused for a moment, not quite sure what he would say next until the words were out of his mouth. "I'm afraid Jade and I have just been called away on the matter of an uncontrolled forest fire."

Josef nodded, ignoring the young man's protests even as Paris tucked his phone back into his pocket and turned to leave MedLab.

Well. He supposed that settled that. If Jade were still willing, they were on their way to a forest fire.

CHAPTER SEVEN

Daniel had left for the day by the time Jade got back to Counter-Magic. His chair was empty and his computer screens black. She was kind of glad because it meant she didn't have to talk to anyone. She sat at her desk and reached for her purse, noticing only then her hands were shaking slightly. She took a deep breath and pulled out her phone, wondering if she could, if she should, text Lily. To tell her what? That something else had come up that reminded her too much of their assault? What more could she say about it? Especially given that she didn't think there'd be anything Lily could say in return that would help?

Jade slipped her phone back into her purse and took out one of her lipsticks and compact mirror instead, finding comfort in the ritual of putting on makeup. Her hands may be shaky, but their muscle memory was good enough for a smooth, even application of the shade with only minor touchups required with her fingers at the corners and her cupid's bow. She took another deep breath and tried to remember what had just gone right instead of what had gone wrong.

It had been hard fighting with Josef. She hadn't been able to articulate what she wanted to say and got too angry. It had been more and more difficult to find the words she wanted. Then Paris arrived and she'd been ready to fight him too. But Paris *listened* to her. Paris saw she was upset and asked for her thoughts and opinions. He even asked if she wanted to help in an official capacity. Did she? Would that mean she'd be even more entrenched in what had happened to her? She had made it her unspoken goal - to get over her past. Getting over something meant you didn't dwell on it and think about it all the time, didn't it?

Jade didn't know. She might be interested in finding out more about what she could do to help. She sighed and unlocked her computer. If she was waiting for Paris, she may as well work. Or shop online. The internet was a tempting place, and she was starting to realize that things were missing from her closet. Well, not so much missing as taken by Lily. Not that those things didn't belong to Lily as well. Jade suspected with Lily wanting her own room, and her own job and now to go see Mom and Dad, more things needed to be split. Almost all of Jade's things were Lily's things - purchased while they were "together." Even if they hadn't been, Jade didn't feel right about calling dibs on anything. Jade didn't own anything, if she really thought about it. Everything she bought, she'd bought while feeling like the lesser half of Lily. Even the things she'd purchased while they were apart. Maybe that should make her happy given that she'd had to put three band-aids on her feet today because of the boots she was wearing. Maybe it was a good thing she didn't really own such ill-fitting boots. They were shared. She fiddled with the fringe of the somewhat-borrowed scarf as she stared down at the heeled booties. *Neither a borrower nor a lender be*, she thought. Maybe she shouldn't keep anything. Give it all to Lily - Lily's car, Lily's parents, Lily's past.

She had her own people now. Her gaze drifted to Josef's office, the door open, his desk empty. He was probably still upstairs dealing with the love-spell caster. Now that she'd calmed down, maybe she could explain better to him why she felt how she did about the love spell. It was coercion. It was the same to Jade as if someone had used rohypnol or another drug. If a someone was unable to say no and forced to do something they didn't want to do…

She hunched in on herself, missing Bruce suddenly and keenly. She felt exposed and vulnerable. When Bruce was around, she had another pair of eyes.

Bruce liked Josef, Jade thought. Was it because he was family? He *was* family, right? Was shared DNA still shared when Jade didn't have her original body anymore? She thought of the picture Josef had given her, of Jade and her mother, both blonde and fair. When Jade had seen herself in her dreams, dreams haunted by Sakkara, she'd been a chubby child. Round and soft at the middle. Thinking of herself as a child while also thinking of Sakkara made Jade angry and sick and… impotent. She couldn't fight back against Sakkara. Not then and not now. She'd tried when Sakkara banished Jade to the Dearth. It had been a dismal failure. The most Jade could do to hurt Sakkara would be to tell Paris the truth - tell Paris that his mother had drowned Jade as a child, and then let Sakkara deal with the fallout. She seemed to care about Paris. As much as any mother, or sociopath could. But that would destroy Paris. It was obvious he was devastated by his mother's actions. As much as Jade would love to twist a knife in Sakkara's heart, she didn't want to do it by twisting it through Paris' heart first.

Sakkara. Lily. What on earth would she possibly have to talk about with Paris on a date if the thoughts usually in her head were about betrayal, demons, and magic?

A sound behind her caused Jade to jump and automatically alt-tab out of the website where she was half-heartedly shopping and back to her work email. Out of the corner of her eye, she saw Paris in the doorway to Counter-Magic at the same time as she saw she had a new email message. Her eyes were drawn in two directions.

"I'm afraid we must cancel our date."

Her knee-jerk reaction was, *fine, whatever, I didn't want to go anyway*, followed immediately by, *you fucker, I wore these boots all day*.

"Oh, um, that's okay. I mean. You can change your mind or whatever. Things… change." She swore to god she could speak English that made a modicum of sense and wasn't only capable of spewing half sentences and jumbled words.

"Pardon? No, that's not… I still very much would like to go on a date, that is, if you are still amenable."

"I'm… amenable." Jesus, what did that word really mean? She should Google it. Or thesaurus it. It sounded weak and floppy. Like a lace glove. "But you can cancel. Or back out. If that's what you want," she added. She couldn't talk about consent with one half of her brain and then turn around and imply that Paris couldn't change his mind.

"No," Paris repeated. He held his smartphone in his hand and regarded it like it contained answers to the mystical questions of the world. "The fires. You've seen the correspondence, yes?"

Jade nodded slowly.

"And you've indicated you're willing to help."

Jade shrugged one shoulder. "Yeah."

"It's been requested. Officially."

She had no idea what that meant. "Okay."

"Witches proficient in fire are asked to report for immediate assignment."

Again, she had no idea what that meant. She decided to go for broke. "That means nothing to me."

"It means I need to give your name to the Council, officially. As I've not yet. I was… I hadn't… well. At any rate, we'll likely have to leave post-haste."

"Do people really say post-haste?"

"Pardon?"

"I thought people only said that in Jane Austen movies and historical fiction."

"It means immediately."

"No, I know what it means, I just didn't know people used it." She grabbed her purse and took her coat out of the small cabinet next to her desk. "I'm ready."

"You'll have time to pack a bag."

"You said immediately."

"I have to contact the Council first."

Jade looked down at his phone and then back at Paris. He appeared befuddled for a moment as he did the same.

"Are you contacting them, or…"

"You're sure? You're sure you want to help?"

"Yes," she hedged. "I'm good with fire, I think. And they said that's what they wanted."

"No, you're perfectly correct. You're fantastic with fire and will be incredibly useful. I've no doubt. You were the only witch in the Coven I considered. I want to ensure you're comfortable with helping."

Jade shifted on her feet. "I'm getting mixed messages. Do you want me to help or not?"

"Do you want to help?"

"Jesus, I offered!"

"You did. And that is your right, but not your obligation."

"Okay. Well, I do. Want to help," she added, searching his face. Normally, she was excellent at reading people, but his face was perplexing. His expression was more confused than anything else. Was he happy she was offering or not?

Paris nodded. "I'll contact the Council."

"So you said."

He nodded again, and began typing on his phone. "Very well."

Was that British for *this conversation is ended*? She couldn't tell. "I don't have a car," she blurted.

"Sorry?"

"A car. Lily wanted it. She needs it to go… ugh, it's complicated. But I don't have one. I don't know if that's important. And Bruce. I have to see if

Lily can take him." She thought of Bruce at her parents' house. The house she grew up in. She didn't like it. "Or maybe Callie. He feeds himself, but he needs a friend."

"We'll have time to make arrangements," Paris said, raising the phone to his ear, presumably for a phone call.

"You said post-haste!" she protested.

"I'm aware, but-" He paused, clearly listening on the phone.

She felt a dry hangnail on her thumb and raised the digit to her mouth, trying to grasp the offender with her teeth even as her mind screamed at her it was a bad idea. She had a moment of satisfaction in ripping it off before sharp pain set in and she regretted it. Dammit. Paris was identifying himself on the phone and indicating he had someone "extraordinarily proficient in fire." Jade wanted to puff her chest out at that, even though she was nervous. Translating from British-speak, she was pretty sure it meant she was hot shit.

There was some agreeing, some non-verbals and several *I see*s. He checked his watch and it automatically made her check hers as well, although she didn't know what for. Then, his eyes met hers and though she wasn't inclined toward fairy-tale notions, she thought her heart lost its rhythm for a moment, beating erratically out of time. She had to look away.

She busied herself faux-tidying her desk - straightening her notebook, putting a stray pen back in its holder, wondering if she needed more staples - until she heard him sign off the call.

"The Fae will transport us."

"You're wearing a wickedly unhappy face about that. Did you think we would drive? Or fly?"

"It's more time-sensitive than I thought. I had assumed we would fly and then drive, but the latest wind shift was quite unexpected and there is some farmland and domesticated animals currently at risk."

"Don't they have witches for rain or wind?"

"Weather work is dangerous and quite complex work, as there are many interconnected systems. We have meteorologists in our supernatural network as well as in the human realm but there are too many unknowns. Why do you think the weather is so often incorrect?"

Jade shrugged. "I dunno. I thought we were all just used to those guys being wrong and still getting paid."

"Unfortunately, no. If we introduce magical rain in one area, it could lead to hurricanes in another. Send the wind too harshly here, and suffer the consequences there. As I said, we have meteorologists and they're working with the data models at the moment and engaging witches proficient in air and water, but it's difficult. The witches can't predict exactly how their magic will manifest and it makes it extremely difficult to run meteorological simulations."

"Yeah, you guys aren't really big on empirical and precise data." Jade felt that since being at the Coven, a lot of things were about feeling and sensing. She wanted some hard numbers and measurable statistics. It was part of the reason she gravitated toward demon magic. It was precise. After experiencing the randomness of the Dearth, she could appreciate why that was so.

Paris' lips curved slightly. "Just so. If they can accurately predict the fallout and ensure it won't adversely affect the area, nor any other areas, they may try to affect the air and water, but we can't hope on it."

"What about razing the forest?" Jade asked. "Like when the forest fighters cut down the trees to take away a fire's fuel."

Paris paused and Jade could see him choosing his words. "Earth magic is... extremely reluctant to be used in a destructive manner. Even though it's for the greater good, the Earth doesn't necessarily know that. That sort of destructive magic... the Earth is resistant to it. It's almost akin to dark or demon magic. And because we are so intimately tied to nature, there could be magical consequences. As well, the control that would be required, to only raze certain trees along a certain latitude or longitude... there aren't many witches with that kind of power and control of Earth."

Jade thought about Paris' magic. The way it felt. She remembered when he'd taught her to cast a circle. She'd lost control, overwhelmed by the lake nearby. The lake where she'd died. At the time, and even now, her water magic was thick, jiggly and cold - like slimy Jell-O trapped inside her. She'd thought if she just used more power, she could control it and she'd reached out, grappling for something, her magic hitting Paris'. It had felt like a rock, sharp and solid. She'd been surprised at the ferocity of it. She'd expected something quiet and tame - a lazy house cat. Instead, it had felt like a wild animal leashed. A lion held captive by a confident man with a chair. Vicious. Paris' power felt like how Jade imagined a caged hurricane would: pulsing, pushing, pressing at the edges, but lashed down. Tethered, but not tamed.

"Could you do it?" she asked. "If there wasn't any kind of magical backlash."

Paris paused. "Perhaps."

"But?" Jade heard the hesitation in his voice.

"But I don't know how much power that would take."

"Okay. And that's a problem because?"

"I've never... My mother's teachings... and my own studies... I've been cautioned many times about using so much power."

"Is it bad?" Jade shifted a bit on her feet. She really liked having a lot of power. She might not be in control of it, but if she were, she wouldn't feel bad about using it.

"It can be dangerous."

"Dangerous like...?" Sometimes talking to Paris was like trying to lead a drunk cat through a maze filled with rabid dogs.

Paris' fingers twitched, still wrapped around his phone. "It's not good for a Coven leader to have that much power. We should be stronger than most of the Coven, yes, but it's not power that's to be used."

"Why do you have it if you're not going to use it?"

Paris thought for a moment, his eyes drifting upward as he did. "It's rather like... It's more akin to..."

Sudden insight hit Jade. "Are you like a weapon of mass destruction?"

"Excuse me?"

"Everyone knows big countries have them, but no one really thinks they're going to be used.

Because, you know. Ka-boom." She made an explosion sound effect and billowed her hands like a cloud expanding. "But people think everyone needs to know they're there. Just in case."

"That's… quite appropriate, actually."

Jade nodded. "So, you have all this power, but you don't think you can or should use it, because that's like pulling a nuke out of your back pocket. Makes people twitchy. And maybe the Earth unhappy?" Jade wasn't sure of the last bit, but when Paris nodded, she realized it was true. "Your job sucks."

A laugh forced its way out of Paris. Jade got the impression it surprised him more than her.

"It does!" Jade added. "You have all this authority, but you have to use it for 'good.'" She made air quotes around the word. "And you've got this power too, but you're not supposed to show it off. You're old money that has to pretend it's just doing okay when new money is going around throwing dollar-dollar bills and buying cubic zirconias for everyone at the party." When he smiled at her, her heart stuttered. She felt a couple of stray hairs brushing her face and she tucked them sharply against her skull, behind her ear. "So, transport via the Fae. I'm guessing that means we're not going economy class."

"No. I'll fill you in and we can make arrangements for Bruce and gather some things."

#

"Why don't you have your car?" Paris asked as they drove to Jade's cottage.

Jade shifted in the passenger seat, the takeout bag they'd stopped for crinkling in her lap. With the timeline the Council had given them, they'd not have time for much. When Jade suggested take-away, Paris had cringed inwardly. He remembered when Jade first arrived at the Coven and they'd shared a meal; she'd chosen fast food. She was either more discerning in her tastes now, or had tried some places in the area since then, because this time she suggested a well-loved Indian-Persian take out restaurant. The fragrant curry filled the car along with a hint of sugar from raisins and a touch of cinnamon. The cinnamon reminded him of Lily's magic. Jade's tended to favor the sharper scent of cloves.

"Lily wants to go see our parents. Well, her parents."

Jade didn't often talk about her past, but she'd referenced it before. Paris knew she was from an abusive home: her father physically assaultive and her mother disinterested and absent. When Jade had been in the Dearth, Lily had also spoken of their upbringing and something she'd said niggled at Paris' brain. She'd said that their parents, *her* parents, hadn't always been that way. Their behavior - their father's abuse and their mother's distance - had only started when Jade arrived. Lily had been quite clear she didn't think Jade was responsible; something had shifted upon Jade's arrival and remained irrevocably altered. Jade's tone when she spoke of Lily going to visit her parents clearly indicated her feelings on the matter.

"You don't think she should go?"

"I think she wants something that won't happen. Dad was..." Jade paused and Paris heard the takeout bag crinkle. He glanced over to see her unclenching her fingers from the paper sack. "I know more about the way he likes to hit than I do about him as a person. And Mom…" A disgusted grunt escaped Jade. "I don't know if she was on booze or drugs or just didn't give a shit, but she wasn't there. Her body was there, but she wasn't. So, no, I don't think Lily should go. I don't know why she gives a shit. I don't."

"They're her parents."

"They were mine too," Jade said hotly and Paris thought he was getting to the actual heart of the matter. "I know that that my mother, my birth mother, was part of the Coven. That I was part of the Coven. But I don't remember that. I only remember *them*. And maybe I didn't originally have their DNA, but I do now. I'm in a carbon copy of their daughter's body. They're the only parents I remember. And they sucked."

Paris realized Jade and Lily had the same body, obviously. He struggled at times to tell them apart if he wasn't close enough to see their eyes, or if he hadn't heard them speak. But until now, he'd not quite understood that meant Jade's appearance wasn't what it was meant to be. He'd seen pictures of her as a young child but hadn't put it together in his mind she didn't look different because she'd aged, or she outgrew her looks.

Her mortal body died; it was dead. Buried somewhere. She was living in some kind of magical copy.

Something clenched inside him as he thought of her tiny, delicate body, buried in the ground, encased in Mother Earth. He wanted to look up the burial details now, something he hadn't thought of before. Perhaps Jade's younger self was buried with her mother. He hoped so. Had Jade already thought of this? Had she already found where her bones lay in the Earth?

Paris wondered what Jade would have looked like, if the past had been different. He recalled images of her mother in clippings after Jade's "death." She'd been a petite, blonde, fragile-looking woman. The fragility may have only appeared after the death of her daughter; Paris didn't know. If he remembered correctly, she looked nothing like Jade at all. Except for her eyes. Jade's sharp, grey eyes were exactly like her mother's.

"I'm sorry," he said simply.

"For what?"

"I can see it's difficult for you. That you struggle. And I'm sorry."

"It's not your fault."

Something in her tone made him glance her way again. She was uncomfortable, holding herself rigidly.

"No, but I'm sorry just the same. Additionally, it can't be easy to deal with this and your trip to the Dearth."

Her hollow laugh rang out in the car. "You know, the Dearth really sucked, but was easier in some ways. I knew what I had to do. Find Medusa and face her. And not piss off Seth doing it." Out of corner of his eye, Paris saw Jade's face wrinkle slightly with distaste as she spoke of the demon. "Easy peasy, right? But now... I don't think there's a roadmap for this."

Unable to help her with her situation with Lily, Paris resolved to find something with which he could assist. Bruce. Jade was worried about what to do with Bruce. "So, if Lily may not be able to watch Bruce, who would you prefer? Callie? Henri? I'm sure either one would be happy to help."

"Yeah," she agreed, though Jade's voice sad, full of melancholy. "I don't like leaving him."

"He did all right while you were in the Dearth."

He could see Jade nod, out of the corner of his eye.

"I know. I just... I like to see him. I thought maybe he'd be able to do some Counter-Magic work. If he wanted. He'd be really good at going into the sewer if we needed. He lived down there."

"Have you spoken to Josef?"

"Not yet."

"I think it's a great idea."

"Only if Bruce wanted."

"Of course. But, as your familiar, he's extraordinarily tied to you. If you think it's a good idea, he probably will too. And I agree, he'll likely be good at it."

Again, Jade nodded. "So," she said finally. "We eat, we pack and then, we're on the move. Give me the rundown."

Although Paris was far more interested in continuing their conversation, finding it intimate and informative, he realized the necessity of imparting information to Jade.

"We'll be transported by the Fae. They use portals to travel. I'm afraid I don't know much about them."

"I know a little about them. Because of the Dearth."

"What do you know?" Paris asked, intrigued. Inter-dimensional travel was the purview of demons, Fae, and dark magic.

"Seth told me some things," Jade replied and Paris schooled his face to not show his feelings about the demon. "He told me…" Jade paused, thinking. When she continued, her voice seemed somewhat distant, as though she was recalling the information from far away. "He told me there are fixed and unfixed portals. Fixed means both places are set: Leaving Place A, going to Place B and neither can be changed. But you can also leave a fixed place to an unknown place, and leave an unknown place to a fixed place, and leave an unknown place to an unknown destination." Jade paused again and bobbed her head, as though she were counting sums.

"Yeah, that was the gist of it. So when Sakkara sent me to the Dearth, she was using an unfixed to unfixed portal. She was sending me from some place on this side that wasn't a known portal and she had no way of knowing exactly where she was sending me. It's why we had to travel to find Medusa. Or maybe Sakkara couldn't used a fixed portal. Maybe there isn't one near Medusa's place, or even if there were, Sakkara didn't know about it.

"And then, when I came home, Seth said we could travel to a fixed portal with a fixed entry point on this side. But that would take time and I didn't want to wait. I wanted to be gone. So he pushed me through - unfixed entry portal to an unfixed destination. He used a shit ton of my power. I think he could have gotten me closer, but I made him stop because it hurt."

"You didn't know where you would end up?"

She shook her head. "No. I guess I'm lucky. I could have ended up in Antarctica or in the middle of an ocean. At that point..." She sighed. "I was done. I didn't care. I couldn't be in the Dearth anymore and Seth was pulling a lot of magic from me to power the trip. It hurt. I told him to stop and I ended up where I did."

Paris was flummoxed. He had no knowledge of portals himself. They were demon and Fae notions - unknown to him or the Coven in general. The thought of his mother forcing Jade through a portal while not knowing where she was sending her was... difficult to fathom. He also wondered, again, what had happened to Jade in the Dearth. For her to risk being transported with no notion of where she would end up... his mind boggled. She could have died upon her return to their world simply because she ended up in the middle of a nuclear reactor, or an iceberg, if such things were possible.

"And also," Jade added, breaking him out of his thoughts, "Dex."

"Dex? What about him?" Paris was confused.

"When he got away, he used teleportation. It's like portal transportation but not, according to Seth."

"What did he say?" Paris was unable to stop the question from leaving his mouth when she paused.

"It didn't go well. For Dex. I think he survived, but it didn't go well," she repeated. "Seth said he was disfigured."

"How?"

"I didn't ask. I don't ask him stuff if he doesn't offer." He heard the crinkling of the takeout bag as she fidgeted. "I know you don't like me talking to Seth, but I'm careful. I know he's a demon. I know he's not my friend. I know he only talks to me because he wants something from me. I'm careful," she repeated. "Not only with what I ask, but how and why I ask it. If I don't need to know something, I don't ask. He would see answering as doing me a favor and then I would owe him."

"I'm sure you are careful. And I know you're smart. But that doesn't mean it's not dangerous. Bomb squad personnel are careful and intelligent. It doesn't mean they aren't in danger."

They reached Jade's cottage and Paris parked on the street, seeing Jade's car wasn't in the little driveway. "Do you think has Lily already left? To see your parents?"

"Uh, no, she said she would be late tonight." For some reason, the words made Jade blush and she hurried out of the car, taking the food with her. Once inside, they headed directly for her kitchen. Paris turned toward the sound when he heard the familiar tick-tack of Bruce's claws on the floor as he joined them.

"Hello, Bruce."

Bruce came up to Paris and pressed his snout against Paris' calf, pausing for a moment until Paris crouched down and pet him on the head. Bruce ambled out of the kitchen, throwing a look over his shoulder at Paris as he threw himself down in front of the fireplace.

"I think Bruce is looking for a fire," he surmised.

Jade rolled her eyes as she pulled plates out of the cupboard. "He's always looking for a fire." She made a motion to snap her fingers and Paris held a hand up to stop her.

"You should probably save your fire magic."

Jade frowned. "It's literally a finger snap."

"Humor me."

"You face the wrath of Bruce, then."

"I'll conjure him some flames," Paris said, calling up a simple fire spell. As the flames hissed to life, Bruce let out a satisfied huff and shuffled his body closer to the grate.

"Back to Seth, I don't think he means me any harm. Not really." Jade brought the plates and some serving spoons to the table. Paris pulled containers out of the takeout bag and set them down. "I'm sure that sounds naive or something. That's not to say I don't think he wouldn't hurt me just for shits and giggles or if I suddenly became inconvenient. But I don't think he's actively looking to harm me, if that makes sense?"

"It does. I don't feel better about it, but it makes sense."

"I talk to him because I learn things. About magic, about portals." She paused as they sat at the table. He could see she was struggling with something; he had the impression she had more to say, but wasn't sure she should. He remained quiet, spooning some curry and rice on his plate and then doing the same for her. She pushed her food around a bit, and then said, "Sometimes Seth gives me information."

Paris reached for a bottle of water slowly, unsure how to respond. "Information about what?"

"He knows things," Jade said, unnecessarily, for of course the demon knew things; he was an ancient magical creature. Again, Paris waited for her to continue. "About me," she clarified. "He knows things about my past. Things I don't know."

In that moment, it was as though each hair on his neck and arms stood up and shivered independently. "What sort of things?" What could a demon know about Jade? What could there be to know?

Jade tilted her head, her eyes remaining focused on her plate as she picked up a small amount of food with her fork. "Stuff about me and Lily."

"Like what?"

Again, she inclined her head. "Just stuff. It might not be true."

He examined her face but looked down when he felt something press against his leg. Bruce was back, having abandoned his precious fireplace. He sat on the kitchen floor next to Paris, his side pressed against Paris'. Bruce turned his head and Paris would have sworn his eyes said, *don't you fuck this up.*

"But you think what he told you is true?" Paris asked, his tone neutral. He wanted to ask what Seth told her, he wanted to keep asking until she told him. But if she wanted him to know, she would tell him. She wasn't a riddle maker or game player. She said what she wanted to say. If she wasn't telling him something, it was because she wasn't ready to speak of it. Not yet. He hoped it meant that she would eventually tell him.

"Yeah. Yeah, I think it's true." Jade didn't seem happy about it, her face grave and serious.

"I hope you know... That is, I hope you understand, whatever he's told you, I won't judge, if you share it with me."

Jade looked up at him then, her cool grey eyes rimmed in black, stark and assessing. "I know."

"Do you? You needn't worry I'd hold something against you. I feel I know you. I may not know all the details of your past, or what you're thinking at any given moment, but you're a good person. You're good for the Coven. You're good for me as well." He hadn't been aware he would say the words until they were out of his mouth. Now they were and he felt he had to continue. "I've spent my life being separate and apart from the very Coven I now lead. It's difficult to find people who will be honest and challenge me. You're one of them. You're also very powerful and though I... though at times...."

He wasn't usually at a loss for words, but he didn't know how to articulate what he wanted to say. He wanted to say that although he felt the need to protect her, he recognized she could protect herself. Though he wished he could keep her safe, he knew it wasn't his place. As Coven Leader, he wanted to keep safe each and every member, and while he wished the same thing for Jade, he was well aware she was powerful enough to challenge him and protect herself. She lacked control and focus, but if she were to learn those things, he had no doubt her power would be a match for his own. Perhaps even supersede it.

"You are a part of this Coven. Though your position with us is unique and singular, I trust you. I value you. Whatever Seth has told you, true or not, that won't change."

Jade looked like she was about to reply when she suddenly froze then turned sharply toward the pantry, where the door swung open on its own.

"Oh, shit."

"What?" Paris looked toward the pantry as well, but wasn't sure what he was supposed to be expecting.

"Seth."

CHAPTER EIGHT

Seth materialized in her pantry, leaning against the door jamb like he'd been casually waiting there for eons. His dark eyes glittered and when he smiled, his teeth were white and sharp. Perfect.

"Possum!" He held his arms wide, as though he expected Jade to run into them. "And her tedious Englishman." His nose wrinkled. "Well, you can't always get what you want."

Since the Dearth, whenever Jade saw Seth, she still saw his demon ears and tail; she wondered if Paris saw them too, or if it was a remnant of her time on the other side. Seth's tail swished behind him like a cat watching a mouse it wanted to pounce on. Swish, swish, swish.

"Go away, Seth."

"It's so amusing to me, dear Possum, that you continually try to order me around."

"It wasn't so amusing when I called you to me and you ended up trapped in the Dearth," Jade countered.

Seth's eyes darkened and a wash of vertigo rushed over Jade as he let his power pour unfiltered. Out of the corner of her eye, Jade saw Paris brace himself on the table. No doubt he felt the same effect from Seth's gaze. "No, it wasn't. Take care not to do something like that again."

"Absence makes the heart grow fonder," Jade replied. "And familiarity breeds contempt. Maybe if you were gone more often…"

Seth reigned his power back in and the vertigo faded. He held a hand to his heart and pretended to wipe a tear from his eye with the other. "Sniff. You sound so grownup right now."

"What do you want, Seth?"

He hurled a pair of shoes through the portal and both she and Paris flinched back. The shoes were well-worn, covered in sand and filth. They had seen better days. Bruce, finally noticing Seth was present, flipped around to face the pantry and gave a mighty huff, spitting three times.

"You left these with Medusa."

Jade scrunched up her face. While she'd been missing her shoes, she didn't expect or want them back. Bruce toddled over to them and sniffed, batting them with his tail. They careened across the floor and hit the back door with a thud. "Thanks. I'll be sure to burn them."

"So, tell me," Seth said, ignoring Jade's tone, "here you have your Englishman, and I see takeout on the table. Dare I hope this may be a date?"

Jade's cheeks went hot and the tips of her ears itched. Bruce hissed. Maybe it was a date, Jade wasn't sure. They'd planned for a date and then had to cancel, sort of, but had ended up being with each other anyway. No matter what it was, it wasn't something she was willing, wanting, or ready to discuss with Seth.

"You came all this way to return a pair of ratty old shoes and comment on my social life? Times must be tough in the Dearth."

"Times are always tough in the Dearth." Seth made a show of looking around, almost comically so. "No wine? You always have wine when I arrive, Possum."

Jade didn't want to face Paris after Seth's comments. It was true. She did keep wine on hand for Seth, but how to explain that? Okay, she could bravado her way through this. Maybe. Hopefully. "No wine. I only need it to stomach the company. Or bribe you."

Seth laughed, deep and rich, like warm honey over toast. "Touché, Possum, touché. Tell me," Seth added, turning his gaze toward Paris, "is she as witty and charming with you as she is with me?"

"I'll not be baited into an inane debate with a demon," Paris replied.

Seth raised his eyebrows and mouthed the word, *inane*. "He's so stuffy, Possum. I can't imagine what you see in him."

She'd thought the blush she'd had earlier was fading. It roared back to full intensity at Seth's taunting. "Again, you came all this way to toss a pair of shoes at me and tease me?"

Seth's eyes flicked back from Paris to her, his gaze calculating and thoughtful. "No."

When he didn't continue, Jade gestured with her hands. "And so?"

"It's a private matter."

If she didn't know better, she'd swear Seth's only goal was to bait her and piss her off. Or Paris. "We don't have any private matters, Seth."

"Don't we, Possum? Should I take that to mean that everything we've discussed, you've discussed with the drab Englishman? Everything?"

Jade stiffened. God, don't let Seth mention anything about Sakkara and how she drowned Jade as a child. If this was a date, that would kill it dead. Even if it wasn't, Jade didn't want Paris to learn about it this way. Or ever, really. It would never be a good time for Paris to learn what his mother had done. She swallowed, the takeout she'd eaten sitting heavy and hard in her stomach. "Be careful, Seth."

"Why?"

Yeah, why? Jade's subconscious repeated. She crossed her hands over her chest. Bruce hissed and it reminded Jade her best defense was a good offense. "How's Medusa?"

Seth paused, a flicker of confusion passing over his face. "What?"

"Medusa, how is she doing? It seemed like you were hoping to… rekindle something. How's that working for you?"

Seth smiled, his expression getting slightly harsher as he worked his jaw. His eyes grew even darker. "You tell me."

Jade fidgeted as Seth tossed the ball back in her court. "How would I know?"

"Indeed. How would you? It's not as though you two have anything in common. Or share some kind of understanding."

Bruce's tongue flicked out and hit Jade on the ankle before he waddled away and tucked himself behind Paris' legs. Jade wondered what it was like for Paris - silent in the face of her conversation with Seth.

Taking a chance, she replied. "I guess that means it's going bad."

"Badly, Possum. Check your grammar," Seth snapped.

In that moment, with him reduced to correcting her grammar, she actually felt sorry for him. "Badly, then. I told you in the Dearth, your thing with Medusa, with the way you push things, it's complicated."

"Is it?" Seth's tone was sharp, cutting.

Jade deflated. She didn't want to fight with Seth. She didn't want to be his friend, but she didn't actively want to hurt him either. "Yeah, it is."

Seth paused, eyeing her up and down, his eyes flicking to Bruce and Paris. Jade stiffened, wondering if she'd made a huge mistake and he was about to flay her alive; instead, he nodded.

"Well. Look at us. Conversing. Oh, don't make that face, Possum. It could freeze that way. Think of how horrid it would look - your scrunched-up face and marble-patched neck."

She resisted the urge to reach up and touch the cool stone of her neck, but she couldn't stop her hand from drifting to the spot on her collarbone where her talisman used to rest. She missed her little silver salamander.

"I see you haven't got a new trinket yet."

Jade dropped her hand. "Nope. Not since I had to trade mine to get your ass through Demon Customs."

"*Our* asses, Possum. Yours and mine. They were a package deal at the time. What a road trip," he deadpanned.

"Yeah, I think about how much I don't miss it every day."

"Speaking of…"

"Okay, here we go." Jade made a waving *gimme* motion with her hand.

"How is Mother Dearest?"

Seth directed his question at Paris, and Jade turned to him as well, surprised by Seth.

"I've not seen Sakkara since she retrieved the Osiris box," replied Paris.

"Really? No visits? No tête-à-têtes?"

"None," replied Paris.

"Soooo." Seth ran a fingertip down the length of the door jamb. "You haven't heard anything from my sister either, then?"

"Oh my god, are you here just to ask about her? Are you dragging us into your sibling rivalry?"

Seth pointed at Jade, his fingernail long and sharp. "You were dragged in by his mother. Don't put this on me."

"We haven't heard from Sakkara. Go home, Seth. Or don't. But get out of my pantry."

"Nothing from my sister?" Seth prodded.

"Beat it." Jade made a jerking motion with her thumb.

Seth nodded. "Lovely as always, Possum. If you do hear from Mother Dearest or my wretched sister, you let me know." His gaze held hers and, after pausing for a moment, she nodded once. He smiled, his white razor-edged white teeth crowding his mouth. "I enjoy working with you." He turned back to Paris. "You, not at all."

Bruce hissed.

"Ugh, horrid thing. You neither."

The air around him shimmered and he vanished. Jade took a can of Lysol out from under her sink and sprayed the doorway of her pantry, making a demon-hex with the aerosol. "What?" she asked at Paris' look.

"I don't think I've ever known anyone to combine disinfectant with magic."

"Better safe than sorry. It's not like the Dearth was dirty, but it felt dirty." She sighed as she saw her shoes. "You know, even though I missed those shoes, I really am going to burn them." She sprayed them liberally, then whispered a few words of magic, setting them alight in a hot, quick fire that burned bright.

"You're meant to be saving your fire magic."

Both Bruce and Jade made the same *pfffffft* response. "That hardly took any magic at all." The flames were already dying down and Jade could feel the remnants of them slipping away into ether. She grabbed a small-handled brush from under the sink and opened her back door, hunkering down as she swept the ashes of the shoes out into the winter air. Bruce came behind her, his snout pressed low the ground, going over the area. She stayed crouched while he worked. He stopped and thumped his tail once on the ground. "All good, bud?"

Bruce sneezed, his pink tongue darting out as he did.

"Is that a yes?" Paris asked, amused.

"About as close as we'll get," Jade said, pushing her hands against her knees to stand.

"The demon hasn't been by since you've returned, I gather."

"No. I would have told you."

"I didn't mean to accuse or imply. I was only clarifying." Jade swore she could see the wheels of his brain turning for a moment - large, steam punk cogs rotating. "You are good at dealing with him. I don't think I could be so casual about it. And I don't mean that in an offhand way. You're quick and I think it surprises him. But he also seems partial to you."

Jade snorted. "He's about as partial to me as you are to a map or a wrench - something you use to get what you want, but then don't really think about as you stuff it back in a drawer. In the Dearth," she started but second-guessed herself, wondering if she should say anything.

She stole a glance at Paris' face and found it careful, so careful. A look of interest with raw curiosity simmering underneath. She looked away, not sure she could keep eye contact and make it through what she was trying to say.

"A long time ago, Medusa and Seth had a... thing. I don't know if you can call it a relationship or if they were boyfriend-girlfriend or maybe they just tore people's faces off and turned them to stone for funsies. But there's something there. Definitely on his side and on hers …"

Jade thought back on Medusa, the things she'd said, how she'd spoken to Seth - her words, her tone. She also thought about her own feelings; how she knew when she wanted something, but not always what that was, or what to do about it. Or what she would do with it if she got it.

"Medusa feels something too, but…" Jade had to clear her throat, finding it tight and thick. "But it's hard for her, I think. Because of her past." She made herself look at Paris again and tried to understand his expression. Still curious, interested. Intensely invested in what she was saying, with maybe a small bit of understanding. "Seth wants her to get over it. He wanted to know how to make her get over it."

"What did you tell him?"

She put the handled brush away, back under the sink and turned her back to Paris, washing her hands even though she hadn't touched any of the ash. "That he can't make her do anything she doesn't want to do. And if he tries, he's just another person forcing her into she something she doesn't want."

He was silent for a moment, digesting her words. She listened to the sound of the water running out of the faucet and down the drain for a few seconds before shutting it off.

"If she wanted to, could she? Get over her past?"

It was dark enough outside that, as Jade dried her hands, she could see both their reflections in the kitchen window. Paris stood about two feet behind her. As if he felt her eyes on him, his gaze shifted to meet hers in the darkened glass. Jade swallowed. She had the sudden, jittery notion she should throw the dishtowel down and just… run. Run out the back door to the fence of the Preserve, hop over it and keep running until her chest burned and her eyes watered and she coughed from the exertion and the cold.

She forced herself to carefully hang the towel on its hook as she turned to face Paris. She crossed her arms over her chest, holding them tightly.

"I don't know if she could. I don't know if I can," she said, being brutally honest. They'd pretty much been talking about her as much as Medusa. "I'm trying."

Paris took a step closer to her, then another, and one more until he was intimately in her space. He was so close she could feel the heat coming off his body. She couldn't look him in the eye, so instead she focused her gaze somewhere around his collarbone. He raised a hand slowly and paused.

"May I?"

Jade wasn't sure what he meant, but she nodded. She didn't feel scared. Or at least, she didn't feel scared in a bad, awful, horrible way. She *was* scared. But it was exciting and nerve-wracking in a good way.

Paris' hand moved closer until she felt the press of his fingertips against her neck. They were on the soft skin where she thought her jugular might be. She moved her head to the side slightly, tipping her chin down, trying to give him better access. His thumb pressed lightly into her skin as it moved up to the marble patch. It was a odd sensation. The stone area on her neck was like a limb gone to sleep. She got pressure indications from the surrounding tissue, but nothing from the nerve endings that should be there.

"Does it hurt?"

Paris' voice was so quiet and low, Jade wondered if she only imagined him speaking.

"No. It pulls sometimes. Like new scar tissue that formed too tightly. Sometimes..." She sucked in a sharp breath as she felt the pressurized sensation of him running his thumb over the area. "Sometimes I'm afraid it might tear. Like if I turn my head the wrong way, it'll stretch too far and then..." She didn't know how to finish her sentence. All she could think about was his thumb on her neck. She stared over his shoulder, seeing the wall behind him but not really *seeing* it.

"Will you tell me what happened?"

He didn't need to clarify; she knew what he meant. He wanted to know what happened to make this small area turn to stone. What happened when Jade saw Medusa.

"I was blindfolded. She was talking to me, but I was blindfolded. She talked about what she'd been through. About what I'd been through. Not in specifics, but..." Jade swallowed, feeling where her throat pulsed out slightly and Paris' thumb moved along with the undulating motion. His fingers rested against the back of her neck, his hand nearly encasing her throat, but she didn't feel trapped. "But I understood what she said. What she meant. Seth told me she asked to be a Gorgon. When she was hurt. It happened and then she asked for... I don't know what the word is. She asked for something in return."

"Recompense," Paris murmured. "Restitution."

"Yeah. She wanted to be a monster. She asked to be a monster. So that no one could hurt her again."

His thumb brushed past the barrier where flesh met stone on her neck and back again. A sensation of pressure, then warmth with pressure, then only pressure again.

"She said we shared a moment and maybe if I'd been offered the kind of power she'd been given, I would have taken it. And I thought..." Her vision clouded and her throat tightened again. "She was right. If I could have become a Gorgon, then, in that moment, I would have."

"And now?"

Jade exhaled, controlling her breath so it came out in one, long, shaky stream instead of a bunch of quick huffs.

"I don't know."

Already close, Paris moved closer and for a moment, his hip brushed against hers and she couldn't stop her breath from hitching. He paused, keeping a hairsbreadth of space between them.

"She's beautiful," Jade said, not knowing why she was still talking. "Medusa. She's beautiful. And lonely." When Paris didn't say anything, she continued. "I don't know if she knows she's lonely. I don't know if she'd admit it."

"Are you lonely?"

She wanted to say no. She wanted to scoff at the idea and shake her head. "Sometimes," she said instead.

When Paris moved in closer, she had an instinctive urge to move away, to twist out of his proximity. But she held fast, feeling like a timid winter rabbit, hiding under a tree in the heart of the season, praying her lack of movement would grant her safety. As he leaned in closer still, one of her hands came up and cupped his elbow, feeling the sharpness of the joint underneath her palm. He pressed his lips against hers, warm and firm. Her eyes were closed, and she breathed in through her nose, inhaling cedar and mint, along with the faint scent of clean laundry - all the things she associated with Paris. The heat from his body radiated against her - constant and steady. He tipped his head and she started slightly at the touch of his tongue against her lips. She was about to open her mouth when his hips pressed against hers. Her heart stuttered and she needed to escape, get out, get away. She pulled back, pushing against him with one hand. She was breathing hard, like she did when she ran, only now a little from fear and maybe… want.

"I'm sorry," Paris whispered, moving away. She clutched his elbow, keeping him still.

"Wait. Just…." She didn't know how to finish her sentence, but she felt him relax where he stood. He didn't pull farther away, but didn't move closer either. She kept her eyes closed, and breathed in and out. She was safe. Nothing would happen to her. She heard Bruce's nails on the linoleum and then felt his tail press against the arch of her foot. "I'm okay, I just…"

"You don't have to explain yourself to me."

"I want to. I just don't know what I want to say." Jade opened her eyes and found Paris' already open as well and staring at her. Not in an accusatory or panic-inducing way. He was merely observing. His thumbs brushed against the sides of her face and she had the sudden, irrational worry she hadn't moisturized that morning.

He nodded, then shifted forward a bit. She was scared for a moment that he would kiss her again and she wasn't sure she was ready for it, but instead, he pressed his lips against her forehead. She burrowed against him, relieved and disappointed all at once.

A loud buzzing rang out in the room. Without pulling away from their embrace, Paris pulled his phone out of his pocket.

"The Fae are ready for us."

\#

It's not like hearing the Fae were coming over was a mood killer, except it was. Jade cleaned up the takeout, leaving it in the fridge for Lily, and checked the living room. It was one thing to have Paris over, but having the Fae over felt like having "company" and she didn't want there to be dusty lizard footprints on the tile of the fireplace.

"I know you said post-haste, but this is fast. I have to, I mean, Lily might not make it home."

"We can ask the Fae if they will wait. However…" He paused and the look on his face, the way his eyebrows twisted slightly made her take pity on him.

"I'll call her." Jade pulled her cell phone out and dialed, hoping Lily was still using her old phone and not the new one the Coven would have issued her. She cursed inwardly when she got her own clipped voicemail greeting back at herself.

"Hey, um, so, I have to leave town for work stuff and I don't know if you're going to see Mom and Dad right away or what. But Bruce…"

"I'll call Callie, I'm sure she can take Bruce if Lily's not able."

"Okay, so Paris thinks Callie can take Bruce," Jade continued. God, she hated leaving messages. She always wished she'd written down what she wanted

to say first. "I don't know how long I'll be gone."
Jade looked at Paris and raised her eyebrows. He
uncharacteristically shrugged, his phone pressed
against his ear. The gesture was completely foreign
on him. Like watching a fish ride a bicycle. He turned
away and spoke lowly, his voice unintelligible to her.
She turned her own back, feeling like it afforded her
some privacy. "Our date got mostly cancelled because
of this work thing, but things went well anyway. I
think. I'll talk to you about it. I hope. If you do go
before I get back and you see Mom and Dad, be…"
Careful? Spiteful? As hurtful to them as they were to
us? "Just call or text me. And don't forget to throw
out the yogurt in the back of the fridge." She
grimaced thinking about its expiration date. "And the
bagged salad. It won't last." She really ought to have
something more momentous to say than random shit
about expired groceries. "I'll text you when I get
where I'm going and let you know what's up. I'm
about to meet the Fae, I think. Wish me luck."

She hung up before she started gushing about
the kiss with Paris. While in many people's lives, she
was sure a chaste kiss such as the one they shared
wasn't news, it had been her first since… well, since
the attack. For a long time afterward, she'd wondered
if she would be capable of being close to someone, if
it would even be possible. Not only had it been, but it
had been heart-poundingly fantastic. Her face flushed
and she hoped it wasn't flaming red. Damn fair skin.
Bruce was in front of the fireplace, sacked out once
more, and his eyes watched her as she refolded an
already well-folded blanket and set it on the back of
the couch.

"Company's coming, Bruce," Jade said, moving a lamp half an inch to the right, then moving right it back. She whispered a quick dusting spell that coalesced all particles into a dime-sized spot; she brushed the dust off the table and onto the floor with her finger. It would have to do.

"Try not to ask the Fae any questions. An exchange of information can sometimes be seen as 'services rendered' and they may expect payment in return," Paris said, fluffing the pillows on the couch. Great, so he was nervous too. That didn't bode well.

"Got it. No questions."

"Do not offer anything. No coffee, no water, nothing. Do not take or give anything. An exchange with the Fae can be extremely dangerous. They do not think the same way we do. Something we consider banal or harmless may carry a great offense. Similarly, the things they consider to be a gifts are not always seen by humans to be favorable."

Okay, that wasn't a statement Jade could leave alone. "Like?" she prompted.

Paris' lips thinned. "Hannah once told me of a man who asked a Fae to make him rich."

"Okay. Seems pretty harmless."

"The Fae used their magic and he had a workplace accident. He lost both legs from the knees down, and suffered extensive scaring of the face and chest."

"Jesus," Jade blurted. "What the fuck? How does that make sense?"

"He received significant compensation from his employer through their insurance since they appeared to be at fault."

"And now he's rich," Jade finished, understanding.

"Now he's rich," Paris agreed.

"Okay, so keep my mouth shut and don't ask for anything. I can do that. Anything else?"

"Try not to stare. Or invade their space unnecessarily."

Jade gave him a thumb's up. Those were things she disliked herself and was pretty sure she could avoid. "Is Bruce going to be okay?" she asked. What if he went over to them and sniffed them and they took offense? What if he hit them with his tail and it wasn't allowed?

"Bruce should be immune to their laws. He's a magical creature, like they are."

"I'm magical," Jade said defensively.

"Not like Bruce. Bruce is… His magic is…" Paris struggled for the right word even as he gestured toward Bruce.

"Pfffffttt." Bruce stuck his tongue out and flopped on his side, smacking his chops.

"A special snowflake?" Jade hedged.

"That's about the size of it."

"Should I pack? I mean, is there time?"

Just off the main foyer was a small mudroom and without waiting for an answer, Jade went in there and grabbed her gym bag, rooting around and finding Lily had left some clothes and a slightly damp towel that really should have made its way directly into the laundry machine. She lifted the lid and found it already full with partially-washed things. She dumped the gym clothes and towel on the floor, bringing the bag back out with her into the foyer. She upended her purse into it, chasing after a lip gloss that went astray and rolled across the floor. It wasn't perfect, but the contents of her gym bag and purse would do in a pinch.

"Okay, I've got the basic essentials in here and probably enough lipstick to get me through a zombie apocalypse."

"How many do you have in there?" Paris asked, peering at her bag.

She held it shut as best she could, given how full it was. "Best not to ask."

There was a knock at the door.

"Okay," said Jade, slinging the bag onto her shoulder and making her way to the door. "No beverages, no offerings, no questions. They're like a street-harassing asshole. Do not engage. Y'know. As much as I can avoid it."

Paris put his hand on hers as she reached for the door handle. "I would answer for you, but the Fae are quite particular about ownership of dwellings. This is your house. You must answer the door."

"Well, I'm kind of the middle of doing that," she replied, her gaze darting down to where his hand covered hers and then back up to his eyes. His lips quirked.

"Yes, I suppose you are."

Jade twisted the handle and opened the door.

Before her stood extraordinary… creatures. It didn't feel right to call them people. One was female, if the fine bone structure and long hair could be used as indicators. She was tall. Six-foot-five, maybe six-foot-six. Her long, dark brown hair fell perfectly straight to her waist - not a split end nor wayward curl in sight. Her eyes were amber, like a bottle of whiskey hit by sunlight. Her skin was a lovely brown-butter color - soft, creamy and uniform. The other Fae stood slightly behind her. Male, Jade thought. His hair only fell to his shoulders and his features were slightly more angular. He had the same amber eyes, the same buttery skin. Jade expected them to be wearing robes or gowns, but instead, they looked like they shopped at Eddie Bauer. Puffy vests, khaki corduroys, and long-sleeved knit sweaters.

The female looked her up and down. "Your body is not the one given to you at your birth."

Jade flinched before she could school her emotions. She thought about Paris' warnings - no questions, no offerings. She figured she could answer without either. "No, it's not."

The female Fae looked her up and down. "It will add another layer to the transport."

Jade's eyes darted toward Paris but without turning her head, she couldn't see if he had a reaction to the female's words.

"If you say so." Jade thought that was a pretty neutral answer. Jade stepped backward, leaving room for the two Fae to enter her cottage. As they passed over the threshold, she felt a shock of electricity shimmy up her spine.

"There are demon locks on this establishment.

Jade paused before answering, thinking of her words, not wanting to break any of Paris' rules. "There are."

The female nodded. "They are quite well constructed. Although I sense some gaps."

"Where?" Jade said, and when the female's eyes darted to her, dark and gold, she flinched backward. "That was not a question. That was an uncontrollable response from my mouth."

The female's lips twitched, so subtly that if Jade hadn't been scrutinizing her, she would have missed it. "They are of little consequence. They are detectable to us, but would not be to other creatures."

Bruce toddled into the foyer, examining the Fae and spitting three times.

"A familiar." It was the male that spoke this time, but his voice was eerily similar to the woman's.

"That's Bruce."

The male Fae crouched down and after a moment's pause, Bruce waddled over, his forked tongue darting out quickly to touch the male's outstretched hand.

"He's interesting."

"Pfffffttt," Bruce hissed.

"He's a loyal and steadfast companion," the male said.

"He is," Jade agreed.

Both the female and the male looked at Jade, then Paris and then back to Jade again.

"We will construct transport to the required area."

Jade took a step back. "Is it a demon portal?" She knew it was a question, but she needed to know.

The female looked her up and down again. "You've gone through demon portals. You've traveled to and spent time in the Dearth."

Although her words formed a question, her intonation didn't indicate she was asking. Jade willed herself to remain silent. Maybe this was part of how they interacted all the time. If questions carried expectations, maybe everything was a statement. The male stepped forward and sniffed the air around Jade.

"Yes, this one has travelled to the Dearth and returned, though not through a method of her own devising. Both ways she was forced."

The female nodded. "That is acceptable. Please come closer to us."

"I'm traveling with her," Paris said, taking a step closer to Jade.

"You are a Coven Leader."

"I am."

"Other leaders have not travelled with their witches."

"I will accompany this witch."

"Transport was for the witch alone." She looked at Jade accusingly and Jade fought to stay still. Hey, she wasn't going to argue with Paris if he wanted to come, but she also didn't need any grief from the Fae.

"Jade is extraordinarily proficient in fire magic and will be vital to the efforts; however, she is still new to the ways of magic and I will accompany her." Paris leaned closer to Jade.

The male sniffed Jade again. "He is correct. This one is powerful with fire. If her skill were equal to her power, she alone would be sufficient."

"Hey," Jade said, feeling affronted. "I'm still learning."

"And much learning you still require."

Ouch.

The female sighed. "Let us not quibble, Pheredon." She turned to Jade. "Step closer to your Coven Leader."

Jade glanced at Paris and then took a step into his space. The female looked them up and down again. "You are a good match for this witch. There are... spaces in his being that you may fill."

"Okay," Jade replied, not sure what she should say. If she said, *thanks*, was that like accepting something? "Acknowledged." All those years watching Star Trek were totally paying off.

The female turned her eyes on Paris. "Betrayal of this one will end in catastrophe, potentially for all."

Even though she didn't articulate the words herself, Jade was embarrassed by them. Was that a compliment or some shade? She felt Paris' body stand straighter next to her. "I'm aware."

"Her loyalty, once earned, will never be forsaken, even at the altar of her life. It is a burden."

Jade wanted to hide. This was worse than having your parents meet a boyfriend.

"It is no burden to me. The weight of this responsibility is welcome."

The female paused, seeming to inhale and exhale, the motion attributed to her entire being, not only her lungs. She turned her amber eyes to Jade again.

"To be... intertwined with this one will cost you greatly. Is this acceptable to you?"

"I don't know what you mean," Jade said honestly. "But..." She felt Paris' fingers touch her own and then slip in between the gaps until they were interlocked. "Yes. It is acceptable to me." She felt the press of his fingers against her own as he squeezed.

"Very well." The female turned to the male and they spoke quickly back and forth in a language Jade didn't recognize. It reminded her of the demon tongue, only opposite. The demon language was all consonants and hard letters - *K*s and *T*s, but this was all vowels and soft sounds - long *A*s and *O*s coupled with *sh* and *th* sounds, like rushing water.

"You will be transported as close as possible to the site. From there, you will arrange you own transport."

Paris nodded and Jade was glad she didn't have to answer. "That is acceptable."

"Step closer to one another."

Jade paused and shuffled an inch closer to Paris, their shoulders and arms touching.

"As though you were one," the male Fae said.

Jade turned to Paris and found him staring at her. She raised her arms at the same time he did, as though to embrace. The entire thing struck her as comical and she laughed, catching Paris' eye. He slipped his arms around her waist and one of his legs stepped between hers. She laughed again, her hands resting on his shoulders, nervous at his proximity.

"Be silent. Your vocal sounds may affect the vibrations of our magic."

Jade pressed her lips together, unable to meet Paris' eye. His hips pressed against her own. In fact, his lower torso was cradled in her hips, his arms around her. She rested her chin on his shoulder. If they weren't clothed... She stiffened. She couldn't think about that. A thrill paired with a shock of anxiety ran through her veins. It was work. *Work, work, work.* She was working.

"Pffffft."

Bruce waddled out of the foyer and back toward the fireplace. She didn't know how long Paris' fire would last without him there. Hopefully long enough for either Lily to come home or Callie to come by. There was a hand at the nape of her neck, cold and sharp. The female Fae. She leaned forward and spoke so closely into Jade's ear, Jade felt the press of her cold lips against the warm shell of her skin. It was still the foreign tongue - the Fae language, Jade supposed.

Then, as with her transport to and from the Dearth, there was a tugging, pulling sensation. Travel to the Dearth had felt like vertigo, the world disappearing in front of her. Travel back from the Dearth had been painful; she'd thought something inside her had been about to rent in two. The Fae magic was like being drunk and having a friend yank on an arm to follow them: a dizzying, but almost fun sensation; although one that could quickly cross over into nausea if said friend pulled any harder. The cottage went dark around her and her eyes moved from the doorway, through which she'd just seen Bruce leave, to the one solid thing currently in her world. Paris.

He was watching her , his eyes so sharp and blue. She had the thought that if telepathy could be forced through sheer force of will, his gaze could do it. She couldn't look away but wanted to squirm and shift under the intensity of his gaze. It was as though he was strangely lit - from above or underneath, she couldn't tell. His features shifted and for a moment, his eyes seemed hollow - dark shadows underneath, empty sockets, as though he wasn't there at all.

Hannah's words echoed in her mind. *He dies. He dies young. A Coven Leader is a strong witch and with magic, we can outlive our mortal counterparts, but... Paris dies younger than any other Coven Leader before. A betrayal.*

Her heart stuttered. She was looking upon his lifeless face. No crisp blue irises, only shadows where they had been. She clenched her fingers, feeling the press of his flesh under her hands and it felt stiff and cold. She clutched him harder, trying press her body closer to his, as if by her presence she could change what she saw.

She blinked and the vision was gone. She was again looking at his eyes, as blue as they'd been before.

In the color of his irises, she could make out her own reflection. The skin around the corners of his eyes crinkled as he narrowed his eyes, concern etching the lines deep. She felt an ache in her ears, like how they sometimes got when she was out in a harsh winter windstorm. The pain penetrated deep into her skull and she couldn't meet Paris' gaze any longer. She closed her eyes and dropped her head against his shoulder and then turned to press one of her ears against the fabric of his shirt. It made the ache lessen, at least on one side of her head. Her nose brushed his throat, but when she inhaled she couldn't find the scent of cedar chips she normally associated with him. She clapped a hand over her exposed ear and then felt one of Paris' hands close over top of it. The ache in both ears lessened slightly. There was a loud *pop* and then nothing.

CHAPTER NINE

The sky was orange. Or rather, a part of the sky was. And it was warm, for which Jade was grateful. She hadn't thought to grab her jacket and neither had Paris. She raised her head from Paris' shoulder, but keep her arms around him. Looking around, she realized the sky was only orange in one direction. It took her a moment to understand.

The forest fire.

They were still entwined in each other's space and although she was loathe to pull away, she had no reason to stay pressed up against him. Before she moved, she searched his face, looking for any trace of what she'd seen while they'd been... in between, she guessed. She didn't know how else to describe it. They were at her cottage, now they were here. But somewhere, in between, she'd looked at him and seen something awful on his face. Something like death.

"Are you all right? You look like you've seen a ghost."

Jade exhaled shakily and then swallowed. She had. Paris' ghost. Maybe. Or something else. She didn't know. Hannah's words echoed in her mind. She shook her head. "Trick of the portal. Or something," she said. She reminded herself she could feel the strength of him under her arms, the heat of his body against hers. She pressed her fingers into his shoulders, feeling the soft give of living flesh.

"What did you see?"

She shook her head again. "Nothing." A nervous laugh bubbled up her esophagus and escaped her lips, high-pitched and out of character to her own ears. "That was way better than when your mom sent me to the Dearth. Or when Seth sent me back." She cleared her throat hoping to shake out the wobble in her voice.

"Are you joking?" Paris asked.

She couldn't stop staring at the orange of the sky. By the rest of the horizon, she guessed it was late afternoon. But where the fire began, pale blue melted into orange with no gradient lines. If she had to pick the exact point where blue slipped into orange, she couldn't do it.

"No," she replied, turning back to him.

He looked vaguely ill. His hair was stark and harsh against his skin, which had paled slightly. "That was horrid. I thought someone was yanking on my viscera. It protested vehemently. And you say it was better?"

She hadn't thought it was that bad. She hadn't felt like she would vomit this time and she said as much. "I mean, last time, I thought I was going to barf. And this time, not so much."

"What did it feel like? To travel to and from the Dearth?"

Jade thought about it. "I felt like a sea cucumber." At his look she continued, "You know, they vomit up their guts when they're being hunted and then they swim away and grow new ones while predators eat their insides. I watch a lot of the nature and learning channels," she added, seeing his eyebrows twist up as she explained. "It hurt. And I was scared," she finished honestly. "Really fucking scared."

"And this time?"

"Not scared." She hitched her gym bag up higher on her shoulder. "I was with you." At his smile, she felt suddenly dangerous and feminine. "I mean, don't get all arrogant or anything. You're the Coven Leader. I'm probably safer with you than anywhere else on the planet. Maybe even the Dearth." Her cheeks hurt from her own grin, which got wider when he laughed at her words. Was this flirting? Was she flirting with him?

"I won't let it go to my head."

She looked away, too embarrassed and self-conscious to hold his gaze. Her eyes were drawn again to the orange sky. The smoke, spicy and woodsy, was thick in the air. A bitter, harsh smell lingered underneath it and she wondered if it was the smell of destruction. Jade wondered if she could feel the fire from here. She'd felt the lake, the one she drowned in, from far away. It pulled on her, calling her name across the Nature Preserve. It still might; she stayed away from it now. She didn't like how it pulled at her. An undertow. A thick, sucking sensation. How much of that was actual sensation and how much was her hind-brain remembering being drowned, she wasn't sure.

But fire she liked. Fire was fun. An excitable puppy with too much energy and not enough toys and playmates. She let her magic unfurl, looking for it.

It was like she was magnetized and suddenly too close to another large magnet. There was a tugging sensation deep in her chest, wanting to yank and pull away. She gasped and stumbled backwards. She jerked at her magic, reeling it in as quickly as she could.

"What, what is it?" Paris asked.

"The fire. I didn't mean to… I mean, I guess I did. I thought I would look for it. It's…" She searched for the right word, not sure what she wanted to say. "Ravenous."

Brows furrowing deeper, Paris pulled his phone from his pocket. "Let's check in. Someone from the main site will come out and get us. Then we'll find out what their plans are. Until then, please don't try to use your magic. I don't mean that as an order. It's a request."

Jade nodded. Given the way the firestorm had felt, it was easy to agree. "Okay."

She watched the orange sky as Paris spoke on his phone, arranging for someone to drive out and pick them up. From the way he spoke, it sounded like this was a typical occurrence; Fae drop people off close, but not exactly at the site.

"They're about a two hour drive away."

Jade scanned the sky again. She'd thought it was closer, given how much smoke she smelled and how orange the sky was. "No shit. That's one hell of a fire. We could start walking. I mean, I'm guessing we follow the fire."

"Yes." Paris indicated the way with his head. "We go north."

Jade looked down at her shoes. "Ugh. I picked the wrong shoes for today. I think my blisters will have blisters." Her feet were killing her. She'd been dressed for a date, not for highway hiking and if she'd been thinking with all cylinders firing she would have changed shoes before the Fae transported them.

"Goddess save you, I hadn't actually seen them. What on earth are you wearing?"

"Date shoes," she blurted without thinking. "Shoes to make my feet look good."

"I don't think I've once thought about how your feet look."

"Well, thanks for telling me now! You couldn't have mentioned this before I picked these shoes? They're completely inappropriate for a forest fire!"

"I didn't know you'd pick special shoes for our date. Nor can I be blamed for a raging forest fire."

"Okay, I feel like you should get a pass on the fire, but of course I'm going to pick shoes for a date. You're best friends with a woman. Don't you pick up anything from Callie?" She looked at the highway in front of her. She could take her shoes off. It seemed well paved. Gravel would be a bitch though since her socks were thin. Hmmm.

"I could carry you."

She hoped her expression conveyed her full incredulity and horror at the thought. "Are you insane? I'm…" Well, she wasn't about to tell him how much she weighed, but it was more than anyone would be comfortable carrying. "And you're…" She didn't want to say he was about her height, which he was, but some people were touchy about that shit. Plus, it would be all kinds of awkward. Did you make conversation while someone carried you? Would he try to carry her bridal style? She might agree to a piggy-back, but he didn't seem the piggy-back type. "Let's just start walking and if I start bleeding from the feet, I'll let you know. Probably."

"We can wait here, if you'd like."

She shifted her gym bag on her shoulder again. "I'd feel better moving, you know?"

He nodded. "May I carry your bag?"

She clutched the bottom of it. "Um, that's okay. I got it." It was her gym bag. It had all her shit. She didn't want to hand it over.

"What have you got in there, anyway?" he asked as they started walking.

"Stuff. And things. Like getting ready stuff." Hair brush, flat iron, makeup, perfume, extra socks and underwear. "You probably have a comb and some deodorant and that's it."

"That would be a fair assessment."

"It takes a little more to get me ready for primetime."

"I'm sure you'd look lovely without any accoutrements."

She laughed, honestly and unabashedly. "You say that to be charming, but you don't know the horror." She thought of how she looked when she woke up. Pale skin, dark eye circles, blotchy complexion.

"I'm not trying to be charming."

"But you are," she blurted, feeling her face heat. "Charming. Anyway." She adjusted her pony tail. "I wear makeup for me. I like how I look with it. It's my shield."

"Your shield against the world."

"One of them."

The road was paved well. There were some uneven spots, maybe frost bumps or bad asphalt, she didn't know. It was easy enough to keep a steady pace. Still, her feet throbbed. She couldn't decide if it was worse when her foot was in contact with the road, or when it hovered in the air and got a glimpse of potential freedom. Without thinking, she paused. Paris stopped immediately next to her. She reached out and grabbed his arm for support while she pried one bootie off, then the other, putting them in her gym bag. The asphalt was warm under her thinly socked feet, but still felt even. No gravel. It must not get icy or snowy enough for sanding and salting. Just in case, she pulled out her extra gym socks and tugged them on. So fashionable. White socks with her dark jeans. Classy.

"You cannot mean to walk without shoes."

"Er, I do?" She stood upright, socks finally how she liked them. "It's way better than the boots. They look good, but feel like cement braces."

"I cannot. That is, you should not have to..." He made a gesture like he wanted to pick her up and then stopped.

"I feel like I should thank you for your chivalry, but also remind you that it's dead."

"It might be on its last legs, but it's not quite dead yet."

#

"I had to walk a lot. In the Dearth."

"Oh?" Paris was surprised to hear Jade mention it.

She'd not spoke much of her time on the other side. The things she'd shared with him, in her pantry after the demon had visited and left, had been the first time he'd heard her speak of her time there. He'd been humbled by her honesty; by the way she'd spoken of what had transpired. She wasn't an open person by nature. Indeed, since he'd met Lily, he often felt Lily offered more in five minutes than Jade had her entire time at the Coven. Not that he censured Jade for her nature. He rather liked her the way she was.

He'd wondered about the patch of marble on her neck since she'd returned. It had been cool to the touch under his fingers, and the way she'd easily bared her jugular to him was burned in his mind. No doubt a near Herculean feat for her. When she'd stepped into his space for transport by the Fae, he'd caught the scent of her magic - cloves and linden blossom. Underneath, he'd caught a hint of vanilla. He'd never known her magic to have that scent before and he wondered if she'd worn perfume for their date. He was unsure where they went from here. He didn't want to rush, but at the same time, he didn't want to insult or offer an offense by not appearing invested.

"I know you and Lily want to know what happened there, but honestly, most of it was just…" She flapped a hand around. "There was walking. And then driving."

"From where did you get a car?" Did the demon world work like the mortal one? Had they rented?

"From Mnemosyne. She runs the demon tiki bar."

Her tone was casual. As though she'd been at the local coffee shop meeting an old friend. "You met the physical manifestation of Memory? At a demon tiki bar."

"Well, I don't know if that's what they call it, but that's what it looked like. It was dark and weird. And there were these blowfish hanging from the ceiling, but I think they were still alive. They puffed out and then shrank." She mimicked the gesture with her hands, a vague look of disgust on her face. "I drank this stuff that was like paint thinner." She shuddered. "I barfed it up as soon as I was on this side again. Involuntarily. My insides were not pleased. Gross." She sighed. "Anyway, Seth worked out this deal with Mnemosyne and she gave us her car. Hey, I don't know if this is relevant, but she took some of my blood in exchange for it."

"What?"

"Memory. She gave us the car in exchange for some of my blood. I'm not going to get yanked back there when I don't want to be, or turned into a sand worm or something, am I?"

"I don't know." He was genuinely flummoxed. "Why did she want it?"

Jade shrugged. "I dunno. And I didn't ask. Shit was going down and I… couldn't care about that then. I guess it can't be helped. She's got it now."

Something she'd mentioned when the demon had been in her pantry tickled his brain. "You said you had to trade your talisman?" Paris asked. "As part of a demon custom?"

"It was *at* Demon Customs. It's like a border crossing, I guess. Seth didn't say much about it, but he was pretty shifty when we got there. There was this... thing. Like a man-shaped thing, but also he reminded me of bugs. He ran the booth and he and Seth talked for a bit. It felt like going to a communist or fascist country. Do you have papers, oh shit, we don't have papers, but we're not staying. Well, what's your business. Oh, you know, just visiting. I don't know if I need to get this form, no, you really don't need to get that form." She reached down with one of her hands as she walked and pressed against the meaty part of her thigh. He recalled she'd had a puncture wound there when she'd returned. It must be related somehow to the trip through customs if she was thinking of it now. "I didn't mean to, but I fiddled with it. The charm. And the man-bug-thing saw and he said wanted it and Seth said..." She paused, as though recalling his words exactly. "He said because you made it, as Coven Leader, it was strong. But also, it had protected me when Sakkara was in my dreams. And when she sent me to the Dearth, it kept me alive. Some people don't survive the trip. He said it was like a solar panel, rebounding the magic back and getting stronger. It made it more powerful than it already was."

Of course he'd used a rather powerful protection and guarding spell when he'd made it, but certainly not something that he thought would ever need to be used in such fashions. "He said it protected you during your trip to the Dearth?"

Jade nodded. "Yep. And from your mom before that. Your mom mentioned it once too."

"Sakkara spoke of it?"

"When she was still screwing around with my dreams. Before we saw her in real life. She said the talisman you made had a lot of magic in it and it had been hard to get around. It was why she ended up needing to put a hex under my bed to get me to come to the lake. She couldn't get to me otherwise."

Though he disliked hearing of the things Sakkara had done, he was proud and happy his talisman for Jade had offered her some protection. "I wish it had been enough to stop her. Both from your dreams and from sending you to the Dearth."

"I didn't like being in the Dearth, or hanging out with Seth, but... I'm not sorry it happened, if that makes sense." As they walked he looked over at her. She was studiously looking ahead, or so it seemed. Perhaps she was merely keeping an eye on where she was going. "I was scared and it was bizarre, but when I met Medusa, when I saw her, I could see her both as she was and is."

"How so?"

"I saw the Gorgon and the woman, and I don't... I had to think about myself too and I'd been... not doing that. For a long time. Lily tried to make me think about things, but I wouldn't and in the Dearth, I had to. But now..." She trailed off, sighing.

"Now what?"

"I thought if you faced shit, it was supposed to get better. You see those self-help books and those fake celebrity doctors on TV and they talk about 'closure' and facing your demons." She snorted. "I've legit got a demon living in my pantry. I'm facing him more than I'd like. I don't know how much more I can 'come to terms' with my past." She made air-quotes around the words.

"Have you ever tried talking to a professional?"

She looked at him like he'd asked her to swallow a live goldfish. "I'm not going to talk to someone I don't know. I can't even talk to Lily. What would I say? My dad, who wasn't really my dad, beat the shit out of me. But that's over now. My mom was so emotionally detached, I'm pretty sure she was a mannequin and some strange elves came over every night and changed her clothes and pretended to make her move. That's over now too. When I was in university, Lily met some guy and he... and we..." She swallowed. "It happened, and I'm here. I'm still here." She touched her chest and he wondered if she was telling him or telling herself. "I can't *say* those things to someone."

"You said them to me."

Jade stopped in the middle of the highway. Her skin took on some of the orange light, making her look otherworldly. Her pony-tail swayed, moved by the former momentum of her body. "I don't suppose you have a degree in psychiatry or a counseling certificate or something?"

"No. I'm afraid I was too busy learning to be a Coven Leader."

She laughed, a wry, somewhat sad sound. "Slacker." She shook her head and started walking again and he winced at her socked feet. "You know what, English? Your accent lets you say a lot of shit other people couldn't get away with. I probably would have sucker punched someone else who said that."

"Is it only the accent?" he hedged.

"No. No, it isn't." She dipped her chin down, her eyes darting up to meet his.

"Lucky me."

Jade snorted again. "Yeah, 'cause lucky you is on some highway walking toward a forest fire right now."

"I can't think of anywhere else I'd rather be."

She blushed and tucked her chin tighter to her collarbone. To spare her any further perceived embarrassment, he turned his gaze back toward the sky. It seemed more red now. Still orange, but a deeper tone. The smoke burned his nostrils and lungs. A few days of this would no doubt leave them both with bad coughs and blurry vision. Once they were picked up, they would likely be issued personal protective equipment. If not, he'd see about some kind of a spell to protect them. It would have to be very precise, focusing on their immediate personal space. It would be difficult, but possible. Thinking of magic reminded him of Jade's earlier attempt to touch the fire. He wondered if he could reach out and feel it himself. Though she'd indicated the fire was powerful, he had far more experience with magic and a higher level of control. He uncurled his magic, sending it through the Earth, toward the darkened sky. Earth was by far his best power and he felt more comfortable approaching the fire through it than through the air.

Heat, vehemence, destruction. What word had Jade used? *Ravenous*.

It was a living thing; chewing, gnawing through the earth, devouring everything in its midst.

It scared him. He hadn't expected so much. So much power and destruction. They should turn back.

Jade's power was strong, but this, this fire, was a thing unleashed: a wild, hungry thing destroying anything in its path. He feared it would not stop until Mother Nature herself stopped it or it ran out of fodder.

"Are you okay? You don't look good. Are you sick from the Fae transport?"

Jade's voice broke him out of his reverie and he pulled his power back. He stared at her. Though she was tall, nearly as tall as him, and not a frail thing, she seemed breakable to him at the moment, with the echo of the fire's power in his mind. He thought again of the small body that had been hers as a child, drowning in the Preserve's lake, interred somewhere back at the Coven.

"I'm fine."

Her face indicated she didn't believe him, but she respected his lie. She stopped suddenly and snapped her fingers. "Oh, shit. I don't have my phone charger."

He hoped it would be the least of her worries.

#

"Hey! Civilization!"

The truck was still far away, but was a growing speck on the narrowed strip of highway stretching out before them. Jade raised her hand in a salute and the high-beams of the truck flashed twice in response, indicating they'd been seen.

"I hope that's our ride. If not, we're probably going to end up slaughtered, our bodies never found, like one of those low-budget horror flicks."

"What sort of movies do you watch?"

"Hey, it's hard to sleep sometimes," Jade defended. "I watch a lot of late night cable."

"Watching that drivel cannot be good for you," Paris intoned.

"It's an acquired taste."

They'd been walking for about an hour and either the original estimate of two hours until they were picked up was wrong, or they'd gone farther than Jade'd thought.

Paris squinted into the distance. "Looks like the lights on top of the vehicle are that of a regional fire marshal or first responder."

"Safe from a backwoods killer or the zombie apocalypse yet again."

God, Jade was happy to see that truck. Her feet were killing her and pretending they weren't was getting harder and harder. She wasn't ready to take Paris up on his offer of carrying her, but she had been ready to ask if he knew any spells for sore feet. She'd been afraid to ask in case the answer was no and her question inspired his misplaced chivalry again. She could *not* be carried. That would be awkward as fuck.

Happily, the truck caught up to them. It pulled to a stop and two men exited the cab.

"Paris and Jade? Magical fire support?" one of them asked, checking his smartphone. He was a younger guy, around Jade's age. Jade wondered what he'd do if she said they weren't 'Paris and Jade.' Maybe she should pretend they were random hobos in street clothing in the middle of a highway. Would they still get a lift?

She let Paris handle the meet and greet. She hated small talk. These guys were helpers - part of the regional fire-fighting crew, not currently off active shift, but required to work given the immense scope of the fire. Jade and Paris got in the back of the truck

- a spacious beast that probably cost more than the mortgage on her tiny cottage back at the Coven. The men handed them face masks, the kind doctors wore during surgery.

"It'll help with the smoke," the driver said.

Jade put hers on and felt foolish. It was like she expected some kind of plague outbreak. The elastics were cheap and pulled at loose hairs, but the air was less smokey with it on. Paris did the social thing he probably had to do a million times over as Coven Leader. He asked their names - Philip "(call me 'Lip")" and Joey. Jade wondered about guys named Joey. When did they make the switch to Joe? Was there a deadline? And how did it feel to miss it and be perpetually called Joey?

"How many other witches are helping you?" Paris asked.

"Two were picked up this morning and another two this afternoon. You guys make five and six."

"Just five," Paris clarified. "Jade is proficient in fire and I'm here to support her."

Jade was surprised by his words. She knew Paris came along to accompany her, but she also thought that maybe he'd use his own mojo on the fire as well.

"You any good with fire?" Joey asked. He turned around in the passenger seat and faced Jade and Paris while Lip drove. Joey had a bad brush cut that was probably efficient, but damn, it did not suit his face. His face was young, but had a fatigue written on it that Jade sympathized with. He'd probably been working round the clock since the fires started.

"I am tolerable in all elements."

"That means he could probably kick some ass, but prefers not to," Jade added, smirking at Paris' expression. How much of her smirk made it past the mask of doom, she didn't know. "What? It's true."

"We might need you," Joey said to Paris. "This fire is bad. It was a dry winter last year. Not a lot of snow here or in the mountains. Then we had a dry spring and no run off. Summer was hot and, you guessed it, dry. We had a fire ban all summer long and while campers were pissed, they followed it. Fall wasn't any better. We hoped to get snow this winter, but we're still waiting."

"What started it?" Jade asked.

"Don't know," Lip answered from the driver's seat, eyes forward on the road. "No time to find out at this point. We're just trying to slow it down."

Jade watched the landscape pass by as they drove. She was familiar with the Nature Preserve back at the Coven since it was her running path, but this was different. The Preserve was thicker and denser. Here, there were thin trees at the edge of the road, with white-barked trunks. Not a lot of brush, it seemed. Further beyond the road were trees she was more familiar with - pine and fir. But everything was brown. Even the fir and pine trees which should be a lush dark green, had a sickly brown cast to them. Dry. Just like Lip had said.

They passed the limits for a town and she saw the requisite landmarks. A burger joint, a coffee shop, a couple of motels. As they made their way deeper into the small city, more motels and hotels sprung up. It was a transitory place, she guessed. Maybe there was some industry here. Maybe not. She didn't know. Should she? Should she learn these things to fit in?

Before she could ask, they pulled into a hotel parking lot and Lip stopped the car. The lot was crammed with cars and trailers, even tents. Some guy was boiling water on a small camp stove in the middle of the concrete pad. Did he live here? Work here?

"This is where we've set up a headquarters. Fire marshal's inside. Me and Joey are off-duty for the next eight catching some sleep before we head back out. We'll be cutting a line to the southeast. I'm sure the marshal will tell you about it."

Jade hefted her gym bag back on her shoulder. She'd forgotten how heavy it was while she'd had her reprieve in the car. It was mostly makeup, but the weight of it made her feel safe. Secure.

"We'll get you jumpsuits and boots." Joey looked down at Jade's sock feet. "Looks like you need boots the most."

She curled her toes in. She had a good reason for not wearing shoes, but it felt really fucking frivolous now. "Thanks," she managed.

"See you around. Stay safe." With Lip's parting greeting, he and Joey left Jade and Paris in parking lot of the hotel. Paris walked directly to the hotel and Jade envied him in that moment. She wanted to stop and look around, get her bearings, but he seemed unbothered by the foreign surroundings. This was his job, she realized. He'd been doing this his whole life.

Paris kept a steady, even pace once inside the hotel, but twice, Jade caught his gaze darting down to her sock-clad feet.

"English, we're on carpet now. You can relax."

"Relaxing will not be an option while we're here, I'm afraid."

"How do you know where you're going?" He seemed to just know which direction to head. She wanted to stop and read some signs, maybe watch people for a few minutes. Paris just moved.

He pointed to the signs for the main conference room. "I'm sure if this is their main headquarters, they've allocated the largest space for their central operations."

It made sense once he said it out loud. Sure enough, they entered the main ballroom and it was a riot of movement, sound and people. She inched closer to him. She wasn't shy, but this was a lot of people all in one room. Paris easily stopped a young man passing by and asked where they could find the fire marshal. He pointed out an older gentleman in the center of a cluster of people, all focused on a table. Jade watched for a moment, as the man spoke while gesturing. He paused, listening while another person, a man again, answered back. He nodded sagely, making eye contact with everyone at the table. He reminded Jade of an older American actor, Sidney Poitier. His face was composed and serious. His body language was careful and precise.

"May I?" Paris asked.

Jade pulled her eyes away from the marshal and didn't know what Paris meant until she looked down at his outstretched hand. For a second, she thought they were fighting about carrying her gym bag, but then she realized he wanted to hold her hand to get through the crowd. She slipped her hand in his, wishing she'd taken a second to wipe it off on her jeans first. It was sweaty from being balled into a fist.

Paris easily cut through the crowd and Jade wondered if he was really good at dodging people or if openings were made for him by the way he moved. She realized she was surrounded by men and it was jarring. Before the Coven, she often noticed she was part of a minority. She was the only woman in the elevator at work, or she looked down the coffee shop line and didn't see any other women. But, since joining the Coven, she'd gotten used to seeing a more even gender split. Sometimes, she'd been around more women than men. Counter Magic was kind of guy-heavy, but when she'd looked at the listings for Supernatural Relations, where Lily was going, it had favored women over men. She guessed it made sense there'd be more guys here. Firefighting was a physical job. But Jade hadn't been prepared for it. She counted only three women as they crossed the room. She wondered if any of them were witches or if the other witches brought in would end up being male as well.

When they reached the main table, Paris didn't interrupt the current conversation. He had an easy confidence about him that Jade envied. He existed in a space: didn't puff his chest, make huffing sounds, or bully his way in. Yet he had a presence. Each person at the table took notice of him in some fashion. Jade wasn't sure how Paris did it. Sure enough, when the marshal was done speaking, he turned immediately to Paris.

"Marshal Nate Danvers. How can I help you?"

"I'm Paris, this is Jade. We're from one of the Covens."

Danvers nodded as they shook hands, then he held his hand out for Jade to shake as well. He had a steady, firm grip that she appreciated. He didn't try to break her fingers, nor did he insult her with a dead-fish handshake.

"You're just in time. Three other witches are here. We're meeting in two hours to go over where we'd like you to work. Have you been settled yet?"

"No, we came directly here after the Fae transported us."

Danvers grunted. "I bet that was fun. We tried to get the Fae to help too, but they're twitchy SOBs. Won't help with the fire directly. I suppose they brought you here, so that's something."

"The Fae are peculiar and particular about their magic. As well, assistance from them is not always a good thing."

"So I hear from the other magical folk," Danvers said to Paris.

There was a loud buzzing and six people in the general area stopped and grabbed at their smart phones only to pocket them again when they realized it wasn't theirs alerting. Danvers reached for his as well, and won the cell-phone lottery, so to speak; his was the one buzzing. He read something on his phone and grunted again.

"The wind is shifting. We'll meet in an hour instead. I'll send the word out to the other witches. Get settled and suited up. Check in at the main desk, they'll give you a room and get you situated for gear."

"I won't need gear. I'm only here to accompany Jade," Paris said.

"We'll suit you up at any rate. An able body is a deployed body. If you've got magic, I'll take it."

It was awkward for Jade standing there while they spoke, but she didn't know what else she could offer. Sarcastic jokes? It wasn't the time or place. People moved and worked around them intensely. She could feel their effort, their worry, their motion as they threaded in and amongst each other. They hummed. Like a hive of bees, only it wasn't so much audible as tactile. It moved through the air and pressing against her skin. A Morse code, feeding her information through the shell of her flesh.

"Be back here in an hour. If you're hungry, we co-opted the pub on the main floor. You can get food there. The gift shop is where we stock up: toiletries, power cords, clean underwear," said Danvers.

Paris nodded. "Thank you. We'll return in an hour."

Danvers finally turned to Jade. "You must be good with fire if you're here."

"I do all right."

"I'm glad you didn't say you're hot shit, no pun intended, or tell me what a marvel you are. That thing out there is a beast and it needs respect."

"I felt it." Jade hoped she wasn't speaking out of turn. "It's... hungry."

Danvers nodded, something in his eyes shifting as he realized she wasn't going to peacock or posture. "It certainly is. It won't give up easy."

Jade nodded. "Neither do I."

Danvers smiled. "Fair enough. See you in an hour."

CHAPTER TEN

"We're heavily booked due to all the fire personnel we have. I have single rooms with a king sized bed. Is that acceptable?"

Paris' pressed his lips together tightly at the concierge's words and Jade got the impression that no, it wasn't acceptable to him, but if that was all they had, it was all they had.

"That's fine," she answered, jumping in when it felt like Paris had paused for too long. King sized beds were huge. Paris could sleep on one side and Jade on the other and it would feel like he was an ocean away. Probably.

The young clerk's face relaxed and Jade got the feeling it hadn't been acceptable for a few people ahead of them, but it had been necessary nonetheless. He handed them two cards and then went through his script. "Breakfast is in the pub from six am to eleven. You can get food all day long, but the menu is set. We also serve lunch and dinner. The lobby gift shop should have anything else you require. If not, we can get items shipped in. The fire crews usually work in eight hour shifts, but with the escalation of the fire, they now run in twelve hour shifts that overlap. Have you been assigned a shift?"

"We're magical support," Paris offered. "I'm not sure where they'll place us."

The clerk nodded. "The front desk is staffed 24-7, even in non-emergency times, but we've made our rotations full so we don't have a skeleton crew. If you need something, call us. We can get it for you. The elevators are to your left. You're on the fourth floor, to your right as you exit the elevator."

Jade took her card and slipped it in her makeup case. Paris pocketed his.

"Where can we get boots and gear for Jade?"

"If you tell me your sizes, I can have it sent up."

Paris looked at Jade expectantly. "Um, I wear a ladies size 10 for my feet, the same for clothing." God, she hoped they didn't size shit like an ancient communist country. If they had a true size 10, she'd be okay. If not, she'd end up wearing a skin-tight contraption or a rucksack. Tough to say.

"I wear a thirty-four, thirty-six."

Hearing Paris order, she was outraged. At the sound she made, Paris turned to her.

"What?"

"If your pants are perfect and mine will only fit a hobbit, I'll let this fire burn."

"We're unisex," the clerk offered, not appearing fazed by her comment.

"And by that you mean you size everything for men?"

The clerk looked confused at Jade's question.

She rolled her eyes "Okay. Give me a thirty-six waist and thirty-six long and a belt."

He made a note in his computer as they moved to the elevators. Again, she was surrounded by men. Three younger guys smelling like smoke and covered in soot rode the elevator with them. They were a quiet, somber bunch. If they closed their eyes and leaned against the elevator, or each other, they'd probably fall asleep on their feet.

The hotel room was like all hotel rooms she'd been in: beige and kind of bland. But it had a lock on the door and everything looked and smelled clean. Jade had no complaints. She tossed her gym bag down on the little suitcase tray and riffled through it until she found her hair brush. She pulled out her ponytail and brushed her hair before yanking it back into its holder and securing it once more. She found a spare Chapstick in her makeup case, thank god, and applied liberally, inhaling the minty-vanilla scent. She smoothed her hands over her hair, checking for any strays. Ritual complete.

She turned and caught Paris staring at her. "What?"

"I don't want to tell you what to do," he began.

"But you want to tell me what to do?" At his horrified look, she added, "I'm kidding! I'm teasing you. If you want to tell me something, I'm listening. That doesn't mean I'll do anything about it, but I'm listening."

He nodded, seemingly placated by her response. "I know you're powerful. And you're quite unique; not only in our Coven, but across other Covens as well."

"Okay." His eyes were quite blue at the moment. She wondered if it was the blandness of the hotel room contrasting against them or if he was just very focused.

"In the past, when you've used too much magic, there have been physical consequences for you."

"My nosebleeds."

"And your migraines."

"The migraines might be because of Lily." When they *shared* too much, or Lily tried to retrieve memories from Jade's mind, Jade either got a migraine or felt the echoes of a previous one. She hadn't had one since coming back from the Dearth, but it hadn't been very long.

Jade also hadn't used much magic since coming back. She hadn't had to. She thought about when she first arrived at the Coven, when Matthew, a jealous Coven witch, had tried to force a demon to pull Jade through a portal. She'd *pushed* at Matthew and had somehow been able to force her will onto his. He'd had a magical obelisk he used to control a spell and she'd made him drive it through his eye, blinding him. In that moment, that act of forceful magic had made something in her brain feel loose and slippery. She'd bled from the nose. Then there was Dex. She'd been about to bind his magic, using a considerable amount of her own, when he'd teleported out. It had made her ears bleed.

"They might be caused by both," Paris said, eyebrows raising slightly. "We don't know. You might trigger one if you use too much magic.

Obviously, I know you're proficient with fire. And you're exceptionally gifted. But, please, be careful."

It was on the tip of her tongue to say something automatic, rote and glib, like of course she would, she always did, blah blah blah. She paused and then nodded instead, hoping he saw she took his words seriously.

"I will. Those things aren't fun for me either. Migraines and nosebleeds. I just... don't always know the limit until I hit it, if that makes sense? Or go past it? I know there's a limit there, but it's like I come around the corner and *pow*!" She punched a closed fist into her open palm, making a loud smack. "There it is."

"It does make sense. You've only used your magic for a short time. Most witches have a lifetime to learn their limits."

"And also," she added, not wanting to sound combative, but feeling like she was, "it's not like I'm doing frivolous things. Matthew was actively trying to kill me. Or rip out my heart at the time. And Dex... I don't know what he thought his spell would do, but when it didn't work, he was pissed. I thought I could bind him. I think Lily was starting to surface then. I think it was her voice in my head I heard telling me to do it. I know we have the same voice, obviously. Same voice, same body. But it was different when it was *her* speaking. The way your subconscious can work on problems when you're not; I think she was doing that for me. So when she told me to bind him, I tried." Jade rubbed at one of her ears, remembering the odd feeling of blood coming out of them. "I don't know how much magic I'll use here. I don't know how much I'll be able to do. It's my first rodeo." She twisted her lips in what she hoped was an approximation of a smile. "I think I can help. I'm good with fire. But I'll think about what you said. I'll be careful."

"Thank you."

A knock at the door broke the comfortable silence that fell between them. Their gear had arrived and taking one look at the utilitarian beige fabric Paris handed her and the military-style boots, Jade had one thought on her mind and couldn't help blurting it out.

"I'm totally gonna be a ghost buster in this."

#

A ghost buster she was. A shapeless, sexless ghost buster. The jumpsuit fit over her jeans and turtleneck, and she tried to see her butt in the mirror by twisting and looking over her shoulder. She swiveled, checking herself from the front again. She could hear Paris only a few feet away, putting his own jumpsuit on; the rustle of the flame-retardant fabric loud in the quiet room. Okay, yes, she was here to fight some fires, and it didn't matter what she looked like while she did it, but damn. Yuck. In the suit, she had the same relative dimensions as a Twinkie - one size fits everywhere. She was a cylinder. Ugh. At least the boots felt okay.

She was happy to find a zippered pocket on the side of her leg that could hold her phone. A deep pocket on the other leg looked like it could carry a bottle of water. She tucked the hotel key card and some Chapstick into the chest pocket, and felt a absence of stuff given the remaining number of pockets the suit had. Unless she started randomly shoving shit from her gym bag into her pockets, she'd just have to leave them empty.

She turned back to Paris and even though his jumpsuit was shapeless, he looked good in it. She didn't know what he did to stay fit, if anything. Maybe he was one of those guys who was perpetually and inexplicably in shape. She frowned. He could be one of those CrossFit people. Or fencing. Or equestrian sports. Did the Coven have horses? Had she seen horses ever?

"Are you alright?"

"Do you ride horses?"

"No. Why would you ask that?"

"It's just… are we dating? We were going to go on a date, but it was cancelled. But we had dinner together anyway and we had… a moment." She could feel her face flushing as she thought about the press of his lips against hers. About what could have happened if the Fae hadn't been ready to bring them to the fire. She thought about Lily making arrangements to be out of the cottage in case something more happened between Paris and Jade. It wasn't something Jade was ready for. Yet. "But I don't know what you do in your spare time. Or if you have spare time. And you know about Bruce and my past and Lily and you've met the demon in my pantry. But I don't know if you work out or if you're just naturally fit and you eat takeout six times a week." She was a little breathless at the end of her speech.

Paris blinked and then said, "I row. At the gym. It's rhythmic and it helps me solve problems. When the weather's nice, I row at a reservoir."

"What about the lake?" she asked, meaning the lake where she died, where Sakkara drowned her.

Paris shook his head. "Never the lake on the Preserve. It's always felt off to most people in the Coven. Myself included."

"Still?"

"I don't know. Do you think it's changed?"

She shrugged and made a sound that approximated, "I don't know," but lacked any actual consonants.

"I like to row. I have a rowing machine at my house, but it doesn't get as much use as I like. The gym is more structured. I get more done there. I've tried a skiing machine that's similar and I like it as well."

She couldn't imagine a more horrible workout. Trapped on a machine, going back and forth, and back and forth. "I run. I don't like it, but it's doable and effective."

He nodded. "You run with Daniel a lot, correct?"

"Yeah. Henri and Callie always say they'll join us, but they hate it. They like yoga. And going for smoothies."

Paris laughed. "That sounds like Callie. She's been trying to lose the same ten pounds since I've known her."

Jade laughed too and shuffled her feet a bit. "Okay. So you row. You're a rower."

"What prompted the question?"

Jeez. She couldn't exactly say she was thinking he cut a fine figure in his regulation fireproof jumpsuit. Or she *could* but there was no way in hell she would. She shrugged to buy herself some time. "I just... was curious. That's all."

"To answer your other question, I'd like to think of us as dating. Unless that makes you uncomfortable or it's unwanted."

It did make her uncomfortable but not in a bad way. More like a rollercoaster. Sharp turns tugging at her stomach, making her want to laugh or shriek out loud.

"I'd like that." Each word was hard to say, but she managed to get them out.

"Then we're dating. And when we're back at the Coven, we'll make up for our missed date and actually have a meal outside of your house. And not at a fast food establishment."

"I like fast food."

"I recall. But I'd like to take you to dinner."

"Okay, but nothing too fancy. Sometimes at those places they only give you, like, two bites of food, and one of them is some kind of weird egg from some bird you've never heard of topped off with something unidentifiable and green. I don't like that stuff."

"Nothing too fancy," he agreed and then checked his watch. "We should head back down to meet the fire marshal and other witches. We only had an hour."

Jade nodded. "Okay, so forest fire and then back to the Coven."

He gestured with his arm for her to precede him out of the room. She patted her leg where her cell phone was, and her chest pocket for her key card and Chapstick and deemed herself ready.

She heard Paris' phone buzz at the same time she felt the vibration of her own phone. While they were riding down in the elevator, they checked their devices.

"Callie says she can take Bruce if Lily goes anywhere."

"Lily says she's home from dinner with Callie and has Bruce," Jade replied, reading her own phone. "I guess we've a pretty small social circle." She responded back quickly that the Fae had transported them and she'd provide details later. She also added that they were checked into a hotel, likely for the duration.

Lily: *The no-tell motel?*

Jade smiled even as she rolled her eyes at the lewd emoticon Lily sent.

Jade: *I'm here to work :P*

Lily: *To work it, you mean. JK. Stay safe. Text me when you know more. I expect updates.*

Jade: *Me too. On Bruce, I mean.*

Lily: *Update 1. I can't make fire in the fireplace. He's pissed. Or sleeping. Hard to say.*

She laughed when she got a picture of Bruce with his eyes partially shut in front of the now cold fireplace. It *was* hard to tell if he was pissed or sleeping.

"Bruce is coping," she said, holding her phone up for Paris to see the pic.

The elevator hit the ground level and she pocketed her phone again. "I know he took care of himself for years in the sewer, but I like knowing he's okay."

"He's your familiar. You share a bond. He's quite attached to you."

"The big lug."

The main ballroom was as crowded as when they left. She didn't know why she thought it would be different, but it made sense that it would remain a constant hub of energy and people for as long as the fire raged. The high ceilings helped keep the sound from bouncing so much, but it was still a loud and crowded place that aggravated her nerves.

"May I?"

Paris was holding his hand out again for hers, asking permission and it hit her suddenly that she didn't know if that was the way he was or if he was doing it because of her *thing*. Her past. The sexual assault in her past. Jesus, if she was going to deal with it, she supposed she couldn't keep thinking about it in italics.

"Why do you do that?" she asked, the question blurting from her lips.

"Do what?"

"Ask permission?"

He seemed flummoxed. It wasn't a word she normally used, but it was so perfect for him in that moment, she could think of no other.

"You don't like to be touched, and I don't want to grab at you."

"Is it... do you do it because... I don't want everything about me to be about what happened to me." She thought about Medusa, and her words in the Dearth. *Don't you want to be something other than that moment?* "I'm... more than that moment," she said, repeating her words to Medusa.

"All right. What do you suggest?"

Well, shit. She wasn't sure.

"You don't have to ask permission."

"For what exactly?"

She thought about what she wanted, what she would be okay with. She didn't want to be all, *it's all fine! Go ahead!* then he'd do something she hadn't thought of and she'd whip off a fire spell and singe off his eyebrows by accident. If she wanted to be fair to him and to herself, she had to really think about it. "To hold my hand. I'm okay with that."

"And for anything else?"

She didn't want to lie, but the truth was hard to articulate. She opened her mouth to say that anything was fine, but it wasn't. "I might need warning, or asking."

"Asking sounds good. I can do that."

This was ridiculous. She couldn't expect someone to follow the inexplicable and complex rules she needed. He'd forget or she'd freak out and that would be the end of that. If she were smart she'd say *fuck it all* and go back to living with her lizard and the woman who used to share a brain with her and it would be fine, it would be all fine. It would be enough.

The shock of his hand against hers jolted her and she looked down to see his fingers had slipped between hers.

"All right? You seem out of sorts."

She blinked, staring at their hands intertwined. She wanted to pull back and run away, but she also liked how it felt.

"I don't know. Can we go find out about the fire now?" *Fire I can do,* Jade thought. Even though it was hungry and ravenous and powerful, she felt like it was safe. Safer than human interaction.

"Of course."

Paris moved toward the table and she moved with him. She hesitated to say he led her because she knew where she was going, and yet, he did move a step ahead of her and the crowd moved out of their way at his presence, like he was an NFL linebacker clearing the field. She tried to figure out if it was the way he moved, or maybe the way she moved as well, that made people inclined to get out of their way.

Danvers was still at the main table, drinking something from a paper cup, listening to three people crowded around him. The two women and a man, each holding a laptop that was still open, spoke Greek Chorus style - sometimes their words overlapped, and sometimes they took turns, but it all had a flow and style to it.

"We just don't have enough data-"

"-To complete the models. Not without at least-"

"-Tapping into several satellites that we've been told are off limits. Even if we could get that data-"

"-Or more data, we'd need stronger modeling software than what we currently have. And more processors. Our simulations are approximations-"

"-At best. And only if the weather stays the same which it probably won't because-"

This time Danvers finished the round, "Because a fire of this size creates its own weather."

"Yes!" One of the techs, a small-statured woman cheered, typing with one hand while balancing her laptop. "We don't even have enough precision on the current weather, never mind trying to extrapolate the weather pattern shifts the fire is creating itself."

Danvers looked up from the techs and caught Jade's eyes, then Paris', with his own. "So you're saying the weather witches can't help."

"We don't know what to tell them. We can't push the model out far enough to determine if we'd be helping or just pushing the fire into another direction." It was the petite woman again. Her hair was dark and spiked in a way Jade envied. When she and Lily had cut their hair short, it had just gone limp. That woman's hair was a work of art: precisely chopped and styled.

The woman's eyes darted over to Jade and scanned the area behind Jade. Jade turned and found three other men standing behind her.

"Are you the weather witches?" the woman asked.

"Fire," Jade answered.

"Oh good. If I understood what they told me, you don't create or affect weather; you work on the fire itself." She clutched her computer closer to her and Jade winced, wondering if she was cracking the hinges of it. She probably needed a laptop for her work, but dang. She should get a tablet or she'd crack the lid right off that thing.

Jade didn't know who "they" were, but she nodded anyway. "Yeah."

"Us too."

Jade turned and realized the three men behind her were the other fire witches.

"Problem?" Paris asked.

She must have been making a face. Jade leaned in closer to Paris. "I kind of thought there'd be more women than just me."

He seemed surprised and it occurred to her, he probably hadn't thought about it. His brow furrowed. "I think R&D is working on a study at the moment, actually, checking the dispersion rates of elemental power across our Coven. We tend to have more women proficient in water and earth, rather than fire and air. I think the neighboring university is doing a gender study on it as well, inquiring if that's because water and earth tend to be more life-giving powers."

"Do you have to read about those kinds of things all the time because you're Coven Leader? Or do you just read them because you like it?"

Paris laughed, the corner of his eyes crinkling. "Yes, to both."

"Fire witches, gather 'round the map."

Danvers voice cut through the crowd and Jade moved closer to the table, Paris moving in tandem with her.

"Round of introductions. Let's keep this short and sweet. Danvers, fire marshal."

"Paris, Coven Leader. Here as support."

Jade didn't know what to say when he turned to her. "Er, Jade. Good with fire. I guess."

"Adam, this is my fourth assist."

"Michael. My third assist. I've worked with Adam twice."

They exchanged some kind of bro-code nod at one another. The third guy cleared his throat and was softer-spoken than the others.

"I'm Clay, I've helped one other time."

Great. Not only was she the only woman, she was the newbie as well.

Danvers sucked on his coffee cup lid, drinking it like it was a cigarette with a tough filter. Was it the nature of the coffee or how he drank in general? He didn't waste any time, spreading out a paper map.

"The fire's calmer tonight, but that's due to an inversion. It cools at night along with the surface of the earth. It'll likely stay that way till tomorrow, but then we're in for another hot day. When the inversion breaks, the winds will kick up and help the fire along."

"Any pyrocumulous clouds?" asked Adam. Jade had to say the word to herself a few times slowly so she'd remember. She didn't know what he meant.

"Not yet, but we're on the lookout. If that happens, we'll let you know ASAP."

"We can't do anything about them," Michael said, somewhat accusatorially. "Our magic is for fire, and those clouds are wind, water, and electricity."

"I don't expect you to do anything but get the hell out of its way," replied Danvers.

If she hadn't been nervous before, she was now. Her fingers itched to pull out her smartphone and start Googling everything she was hearing.

"But what do you want us to do? Just stop it?" she blurted.

Michael rolled his eyes and Adam made a *tsk*ing sound. Jade resisted the urge to flip them both the bird. Honestly, if they were here to be posers, they could do it on their own time.

"I just need it stopped," Danvers agreed. "How you do that is up to you."

Jade nodded and if she was any judge of character, her simple agreement went over well with him. Paris' fingers twitched where they were intertwined with hers. She wasn't sure if it was a show of solidarity or an involuntary muscle spasm.

"What happens from here?" Paris asked.

He asked Danvers, but it was Adam that responded. "We usually go up in the 'copters and get a look. From there, I'll tell them where I can do the most work."

"And?" Jade prompted.

"And we work. If necessary, they'll drop me there."

Oh. So, maybe in the forest. Wow. Okay. She was glad she had boots. She took a deep breath. Clearly Adam and Michael were kind of douchebags, but knowledgeable douchebags, so she needed to walk the fine line between asking their help and keeping the fuck away from them.

"What do you think of the fire so far?" Jade asked, recalling the ravenous feeling she'd gotten from it earlier.

"What do you mean?" Michael asked. He had a pristinely coiffed hair style that looked like he hadn't spent the actual twenty minutes it took to make it artfully disarrayed.

"I mean when you touched it already. Is this like other fires you've felt or what?"

"I can't possibly get a reading from here. It's too far out." His tone implied she was an idiot for asking.

Jade turned to Adam. "And you?"

"It's like Michael says, we're too far out."

"Oh."

"You said it felt hungry," said Danvers, cutting in, echoing Jade's words from earlier.

Michael started to roll his eyes, but paused when she caught him. Jade recognized the gesture, having done it many times in her lifetime.

"Yes," she answered. "It's like... like a wild thing. I mean, I know fire is generally thought to be wild, but this was... feral and ravenous."

"First of all, you couldn't possibly have felt it. As I said, we're too far out. Secondly, fire doesn't have emotions."

Jade turned to Adam, reading the patronizing expression on his face all to easily. "First of all," she said, echoing his words perfectly, "I can and I did. Secondly, yes, it does."

"It's energy. Learn how to control it and it will obey the laws of physics. It doesn't have feelings."

"I feel like you've probably said the same thing about some of the ex-girlfriends in your life and that's why they're your exes."

His face flushed and he tipped his body toward her as though he was about to take a step closer. He seemed to realize at the last moment that she was nearly as tall as him. Paris' fingers tightened around hers and she had this sense like he wanted to pull her back, out of Adam's reach, but managed to keep himself still.

Adam scoffed, the tension leaving his body. "This is why men are better at fire and wind. Women tend to get emotional about it."

"Wow, there is so much patriarchy and entitlement in that statement, I'm legit not sure where to start."

His eyes narrowed as he studied her. "Aren't you that witch? That just showed up one day? Not from a Coven? You are, aren't you?" He nodded to himself. "So you've been practicing magic for all of five minutes and think you can help, is that it?"

"Jade is a highly valued member of our Coven and is extraordinarily proficient with magic."

It seemed like Paris was trying to keep the trash talking classy. Jade wanted to stick her tongue out at Adam after Paris was done speaking and say, *So there. Extraordinarily proficient.*

"Hey, if you can help, I'm all for it. But start making it worse, and I'll bind you."

Jade laughed. She couldn't help it. She thought of Matthew and Dex. Of Seth and the Dearth. Medusa.

"Threatening to bind someone's magic isn't the sort of thing you joke about." There was definitely a "young man," implied at the end of that sentence, but Jade figured Paris knew it would be a tough sell when he and Adam looked about the same age.

"It's fine." Jade waved a hand. "You know, Adam, if you think I'm making it worse, you're welcome to try."

"If you two are done with your magical pissing contest, I've got a fire I'm trying to stop."

Jade's cheeks flushed hot at Danvers' words. He was right. They were here to work. But it was hard not to want to grind someone's nose into the ground when they were being a dick. She still wanted to flip him off. She resolved to be the bigger person.

Or at least she meant to until Adam gestured at her the *I'm watching you* - using two fingers to point at his own eyes and then rotating his hand to point them at her. She pulled her hand from Paris' and double flipped him off. Asshole.

They leaned over the table as Danvers gestured at the large map covered with clear plastic. He used a couple of dry erase markers to show them where the fire had started, where it had spread and the current projections for it based on the upcoming weather.

"Shit," Jade said, not meaning to speak aloud. Right now, the fire was eating its way through an unpopulated area, filling its belly, but if the weather patterns held, it was set to turn and drive its way toward the town.

"Shit is right. We already evacuated some neighboring hamlets. We announced a voluntary evacuation an hour ago for the town and anyone that can leave without too much trouble is already packing up."

"And a forced evacuation?" Paris asked.

"Probably noon tomorrow unless you guys are able to push it back."

"Is that the goal? To push it back? Or do you want it stopped?" Jade asked.

"You don't stop a fire of this size," replied Michael. "We can only push it back to an area that's already burned and let it…"

"Starve?" Jade added. She could tell he was hesitant to use food related words given her argument with Adam minutes ago.

"Yeah. Starve."

Clay looked nervous, but didn't add anything. Jade felt bad for him. He didn't seem as cocky and brash as Adam and Michael, and she wondered if, looking at the scope of the fire in front of them, he was scared.

"What if it could be stopped?" Jade asked. "Wouldn't that be better?"

"As Michael said, you don't stop a fire of this size. You can't." Ugh, Adam again.

"Has anyone tried?" Jade pushed.

Adam dismissed her with a snort. "Well, you're welcome to. And when it starts to eat you alive, I'll be sure to pull you out."

"It's difficult to find a place for the power of the fire to *go*," Paris said to Jade, breaking some of the tension.

Jade turned to him, interested in his word choice. "So, the goal is the drive it back to a place it's already burned, and it will burn itself out, because if you try to stop it, you need someplace else to put that kind of power?"

She heard another derisive sound from Adam. He'd probably never had an unexpressed thought. "You're not going to last ten minutes out there if you don't know the basics."

"You worry about yourself and let me worry about me," Jade fired at Adam and then returned her gaze to Paris. "What if I found someplace for that power to go?"

Paris paused. "I don't know. I don't know if anyone's tried. Where would you put it?"

Jade shrugged. Could she eat power like that herself? Or could she pull it in and channel it out somewhere? She turned to Danvers. "If it could be stopped, that would preferable?"

Danvers nodded. "Of course. It would shorten the lifespan and we wouldn't have to push it back and then do recalculations for wind, weather, and fire patterns. But it sounds like it's not possible." He glanced at Adam, Matthew and the silent Clay, and back at Jade.

"I don't know if it is. I just like to have all the info I can get." She tapped her finger on the map, upon which a clear view of the city in jeopardy was spread out. "You have a hospital, an old folk's home, and an animal shelter all near the outskirts of town."

Danvers grimaced. "Yeah. New buildings. Commissioned within the last couple years. Land out there is cheap compared to land downtown."

"And they have evacuation plans?"

"They do."

Jade wondered where the animals would go. She should be worried about the people first, she guessed, but when she saw the animal shelter, she thought of Bruce. What if he was in a place like that and she couldn't get to him? What if Lily and Callie hadn't been around to look after him? He could probably survive in the sewers again if he had to, but she didn't want him to.

"So what now?" Jade asked.

Adam snorted. "Now you get to put your shiny new powers to the test. We go to work."

CHAPTER ELEVEN

Sure, Jade heard Adam when he said they flew in helicopters, but when the time came for her to get in one, she hesitated.

"I'll be in the main headquarters," Paris said. "I'm sure I can get a radio set connected to yours." He gestured toward her gear. She'd been outfitted with both a radio and helmet. The helmet made her feel like a lollipop - all top heavy and awkward. The radio was strapped across her shoulders along with some kind of vest unit. Again, she had way too many pockets and not enough stuff. She nodded, and the weight of the helmet made her neck bob uncomfortably. She knew her expression was that of a worried poodle - tight and anxious. She glanced from Paris to the helicopter and back again.

"Okay."

"I don't know if our cell phones will be affected by the fire. I can find out. But radio will probably be best."

"Sounds good."

It sounded horrible, in fact, but Jade wasn't about to blurt that out. Although dinner had been hours ago, she regretted it as she eyeballed the helicopter. She didn't get airsick, but had only ever flown commercially. For once, she was glad she'd skipped the coffee, not sure how the sludge they'd been serving in the ballroom would've done in her stomach.

"If you've changed your mind, we can leave. Though you're proficient in fire, you don't have to do this."

Jade could see Adam getting into another helicopter a short distance away. He had a causal, easy grace as he stepped up and in. She didn't need to prove anything to herself or him, but seeing him get in the helicopter made her angry. If a douchebag like him could do this, so could she.

"No, I'm okay. I got this."

Paris' hand was on her forearm, his grip strong. "You are very powerful. I've no doubt you can help. Please be careful."

Jade swallowed thickly. "I will. I probably won't do much. I'm new. But I'll be careful."

Paris moved forward slowly, giving her time to pull away or sucker punch him. She wasn't sure which he thought more likely. Although she had ample warning, when his lips finally pressed against hers, it still surprised her. She wasn't sure what else she expected since his intent had been clearly broadcast through his posture and expression.

He pulled back. "I'll be listening."

She felt shaky in her knees and elbows, still feeling a ghostly impression of his lips against hers.

They'd been warm and dry. It hadn't been a passionate kiss, but her lips tingled nonetheless. "In any other context, that would be super creepy. But right now, it works."

Paris smiled, his eyes tight. "Stay safe."

She thought she should have something super cool and nonchalant to say, but all she managed was to nod and move her lips in the hopeful approximation of a smile. She wanted to absurdly ask, *is this a smile? Am I doing it right?*, but Paris was already several steps away from her.

Someone grabbed her hip to help her into the helicopter. She stiffened before she recognized the touch as completely anonymous and sterile, allowing them to help her. It was just someone boosting her weight, not trying to cop a feel or harass her in any way. Once seated in the helicopter, the pilot and co-pilot introduced themselves and their names flowed over her grey matter like water over a river rock - completely forgotten in the rush.

It was so loud. She knew it would be and had expected it, and yet she was still unprepared for how loud the helicopter actually was. She was equally unprepared for the sudden jerks in motion. They were proficient pilots, but her body wasn't accustomed to being moved in such a fashion.

"We'll circle around the area we need you to help in," one of them said. He'd shouted, so she heard it through her ears and broadcast over the radio.

"Okay. And then what?"

"Then you can do your magical stuff."

Though she had no idea what he meant, she nodded and smiled. "Sure." She was yelling. Was she too loud? She didn't know. Everyone else was yelling, so she gave it a shot. So she was expected to use magic right away? The whole time? For how long? Ugh, she should have asked more questions.

From this high up, she could see the smoke and flames stretching out across the landscape. Night was starting to fall. It had already been quite dark and dismal with the smoke blocking the sun, but with it coming on night, she realized how much sunlight had been making it through before. The orange, red, and yellow of the fire was easier to pick out against the dark smoke. It didn't look like anything fancy. Like a snake undulating or any other kind of imagery she'd ever heard about fire. It just looked like fire. Bright. Hot.

Unlike when they'd first arrived and she had to seek the fire out to test its edges, she was close enough now that it tugged at her without her having to send her magic out. It was a relentless pull against her guts. She didn't like it. Coupled with the way her stomach reacted as the craft dipped and swirled, she really hoped she wouldn't puke. She didn't see any plastic bags and didn't know what would happen if she tried to open a window and lean out.

She did okay with spatial relations and was able to orient where they were based on the map Danvers had shown them down back at the hotel. The town was to their back, the fire to their front and stretching out along one of their sides. There was a river to the other side, but unless the fire shifted, it wouldn't head in that direction. Too bad. The water would have been a natural fire wall. She could see the area where they wanted to contain it or drive it back. Already there was a small line cut into one side - a swatch of felled trees and brush - the firefighters efforts to keep the fire from spreading in that direction. She didn't know a lot about firefighting other than the basics - starve it out or put it out. But magic, magic she could do.

Jade reached out with her power, opening herself up. The fire was sharp and in her mind, she had the sudden image of claws, snapping at her. She pushed back in her seat, feeling the solidity of it against her back. It was hot in the craft. No doubt it was hot everywhere, but wasn't the pleasant, sunny feeling of being in a patch of sunlight or the cozy feeling of laying down next to a fireplace with a good book. It was the sickly, cloying feeing of being somewhere too hot without escape.

"That area is the one we're hoping you can cut off and turn back. Are you able to give a go from here or do you need to be closer?"

"I don't need to be closer," Jade said quickly, eyeballing the area the co-pilot pointed to. Again, she recognized the general landscape from the overview with Danvers.

Okay, so push the fire back. Turn it. Direct it. Just like creating fire in her hands, but slightly different. No big deal.

She reached up to her neck, forgetting again she didn't have her little salamander. It wasn't like she needed it, but she really missed it. For lack of anything better to do with her hands, she curled them into fists and pressed them into her lap, staring at the area. She pushed out with her magic, reaching for the fire.

It was like banging her head into a brick wall. A hungry, angry, hot, sharp brick wall. She flinched back.

"You okay?"

Jade nodded, not taking her eyes off the fire. This time, when she reached out with her power, instead of pushing at the fire, she tried to grab at it, pulling it toward her for a moment. A bright flare went up from the area she was focused on, blue in color.

"Shit, is that you? If that's not you, we gotta get out of here."

"That's me. Hang on."

She pulled more fire toward her, the blue flame spreading out, going indigo and then violet.

"Uh, like, I'm not magic, but I think you're making it worse."

"Hang on," she repeated.

He wasn't totally wrong. Instead of containing it, she'd fueled it, making it stronger, but with her own magic instead of the fuel of the forest. It wasn't just burning bark and wood and trees, it was burning magic, and *that* she could control. She wanted it hotter, she needed it hotter. It would burn out all the natural fuel in that one little pocket and then the only thing it would have left would be magic. Her magic. She poured power into it, and the fire gleefully chomped it up - like a child's game where hungry hippopotamuses gobbled up shiny marbles. It ate and ate and ate until the trees were ash, and the grass was ash and even the dirt below wanted to surrender and become ash. And suddenly, it had nothing but magic to feed on. Magic she controlled.

Jade unclenched her fists and mimed crunching a sheet of paper into a ball, or crushing an empty bag. The flame shrieked and the pilots yelled at each other, something she didn't catch. All she could focus on was collapsing the fire. The helicopter lurched sharply sideways as she brought her hands together again and imagined crushing a tin can between them. There was sucking, a kind of cracking sound that made her ears pop hard and she winced, but kept her hands clasped together, feeling a section of the fire die between them.

The helicopter swung in a lazy circle around the section she'd just worked on. There was only a charred, white mess of ash. She'd forced it to burn out that area and then starved it. She felt proud, fierce, and scared all at once. Her eyes stretched out over the enormity of the area. One small patch down, thousands of acres to go.

"Holy shit. Can you do that again?"

Jade pulled her gaze from the ground to meet the co-pilot's eyes.

"Isn't that why I'm here?"

He made a whooping sound, pointing to the next area for her to work on.

#

Back at the main conference room, it took some doing to get a radio and be connected on the same channel as Jade. Luckily, all his years as Coven Leader made him well-versed in navigating endless red tape and minutiae. The concierge directed him to one person, who directed him to another, who directed him to a firefighter crew, who then directed him to a middle-aged man who was able to get Paris a chest harness set and patch him in. Unfortunately, he took his time setting Paris up and explaining in great detail most of his entire work history. By the time Paris was connected to the radio traffic from Jade and the pilots, she was about to start working with the fire. He wondered if she needed any pep talk or reassurance.

Before he could tell her he was listening, and available if she needed, he felt a sharp pull of magic in the air. It took him a moment to realize it was Jade's magic. She was working the fire. He could feel her, attacking it with power, akin to throwing gasoline on it, forcing it hotter, higher, before crashing her own power into it and making it bend to her will. It was forcefully frightening. He knew she had power; to feel the raw state of it was always surprising. So much for needing a pep talk.

The chatter on the radio was turned down low, becoming a constant and almost soothing background noise to him. He could direct his hearing to it and tune in, catching what was being said, but it was low enough that he could tune it out if he was having another conversation.

Danvers was working with a set of young but tired-looking firefighters, all getting ready to go back out. They were heading out to cut another line, felling trees further out from town, hoping to keep the fire from progressing any closer. The small woman with the choppy hair and laptop from earlier rushed up to them and thrust her laptop in front of Danvers.

"Look at these pictures!"

The firefighters continued their plod through the room and out the door while Danvers stopped to look at her screen. She was one of the data scientists, Paris had learned. In the time since he'd left Jade at the helicopter, he'd familiarized himself with the motley crew in the hotel ballroom. There was Danvers, of course, the city mayor and some councilpersons, the head of the emergency response team, and several members of the press. Notably, there was also one member of the Fae - likely the liaison for the supernatural and how the call for magical assistance went out in the first place. Paris had made eye contact with him and he nodded, but Paris wasn't sure if the Fae's expression indicated he should know him, or he knew him, or if she was merely acknowledging him as another magical entity. He opted to keep a discrete distance. Adding to the bustle, there was always several contingents of firefighters coming and going.

The data scientist slapped her laptop down on the main table with such force Paris winced in sympathy for the device, which appeared to be one small collision away from a life of being held together with duct tape.

Danvers gazed down at the screen intently before he looked up, looking for someone. Paris, it turned out. As soon as he made eye contact, he motioned him over. Paris came beside him and Danvers angled the laptop toward him.

Violent indigo flames shot up from the ground, completely incongruent with the surrounding orange fire, grey smoke, and green underbrush. The scientist reached over and pressed a key.

"And look at this one! I didn't even know you could make fire that color. Of course, I've not had a chance to study magical fire myself. Just natural disasters. But wow!"

She pressed another key and another picture came up of the deep, dark flames reaching to the sky, looking as though they were trying to claw their way up. The next photo showed a barren area that had been completely scorched. He didn't have to be told it was Jade's work. He wasn't sure how to articulate it, but he thought he could sense her through the pictures, burning the fire hotter and hotter, and crushing it with her will. It was a ghost of what he'd felt earlier. He wondered if he stepped outside if he would smell cloves and linden blossom on the air, mixed in with the fire and smoke.

"The area's still hot, but I don't think it's burning," the scientist continued. "Which is incredible. I can't wait for winter."

Paris frowned. "Why winter?"

"When a fire burns long and hot, sometimes it can smolder underground. It eats dead grass, root systems, and peat. During the winter, we get awesome pictures and data because we know none of the heat is coming from the weather itself, not usually. We're also keeping an eye on it case it comes back in the spring. Some fires sleep," she made a quick motion with her hands, resting her cheek against them, like a perfect portrait of a child sleeping, "but come back when the weather turns again."

"But you don't think this one will?"

"I don't know. We watch them all. But this," she waved a hand at the computer, "is giving us so much data on magical intervention. Usually witches head out, we see some movement of the fire through the satellite, but nothing like this. This is awesome!" She pulled her laptop close again, holding it like a book in front of her, the screen and keyboard resting against her chest. "I mean, the destruction is bad. Horrible and bad, but the data is going to be spectacular." She glanced down at her laptop. "And the pictures are cool."

"Pardon me," Paris said and she paused in the middle of moving away. "Could you send me those pictures?" He held out one of his cards.

She took it and shrugged. "Sure. You want the data too?"

"Yes," he said on the spur of the moment. Perhaps Josef knew of someone at Counter-Magic who would like it, or even Jade herself.

She nodded and went back to a smaller table where her cohorts, several laptops, and a personal coffee maker had taken up residence.

"How much fire work can Jade do?" Danvers asked.

Paris turned back to the man. "I don't know. This is her first time in the field."

"If she can clear more areas like that and we don't have to worry about spread, we'll be in a much better position."

A sense of dread coiled in his stomach. He knew Jade was powerful, and she was here to help, but at the same time, Danvers words made recall how his mother spoke about Jade. As though Jade were only an asset or tool to be used and nothing more. She was more than that, but with the amount of power she had, it often eclipsed how people saw her.

"She came to help. As long as she's able and it's safe to do so, I'm sure she will."

"I've never had a Coven Leader accompany any of their witches before."

"Jade's rather new to Coven life. Her background is unique."

Danvers glanced over at the data science table, where heads were bowed and keyboards clicking. "I look forward for what that means for this fire."

It took Paris a moment to find the word he wanted to attribute to Danvers' tone. Avarice. Directed toward Jade's magic and what it could do. "When will you know the affect it's having on the whole?"

"The next data pull and resource roundtable is in two hours. The witches should be back by then and we can figure out where to deploy them next."

"How long will she get to rest?" Paris checked his watch. It was almost ten at night. They'd been up all day, transported by the Fae and she'd been thrust right out into work. Jade would need time to sleep.

"Depends on what the numbers tell us. She seems powerful."

"She is, but her magic's not like everyone else's."

"Yeah, I'm starting to see that."

"As I said, as long as she's able and it's *safe*," he stressed the word, "I'm sure she will help."

Danvers continued to stare at him. No stranger to scrutiny, Paris stared back.

"All right," Danvers finally said. "I guess we'll know more at the next data pull."

"I should arrange for a change of clothing and some other supplies." He handed Danvers a business card. "If something arises, I'm on the same radio channel as Jade." Without waiting for a response, Paris turned his back and left the ballroom. He felt his phone vibrate once and checked it quickly, seeing it was the pictures of the fire he'd asked the data scientist to send. A fondness swelled in him as he stared down at the sharply colored image. Jade's magic certainly was unique.

He occupied himself gathering things for them both at the gift shop, and then checking his Coven email, and finally checking in with Callie. Lily was back at the cottage and Callie hadn't been required to check in on Bruce, but remained at the ready should such services be required. Her enormously fat cat, Stuart, walked in front of her face several times as they Skype'd, each time Callie batting at his fur and huffing indignantly.

"Stu, still on the phone."

"He doesn't care, Callie. He never has and he never will."

Stu sat down in the small space between Callie's laptop and the end of the table. "Honestly, Stu. I'm trying to have a conversation here. Anyway," she continued, pushing his fluffy tail off to the side. "Things are going okay? No major crises?"

"Except for a massive forest fire, no, nothing."

She rolled his eyes at him. "You know what I mean. No demons or Gorgons or weird shit."

"No, nothing weird."

"Then why do you have that face on?"

"What face?" He could see himself in the small box on his screen. He looked normal.

"Do you remember when we were kids at camp and you fell off the rope course and the fabric of your pants was actually stuck in the wounds on your legs, but you didn't want to tell anyone because we'd snuck out and weren't supposed to do it?"

"Vaguely. Why are you bringing this up?"

"You've kind of got that same look on your face now. Like you're annoyed or hiding something, but you don't really think you should talk about it."

He could deny it, but clearly Callie knew him well enough there would be little point. "The fire marshal is very interested in Jade."

"He hit on her?"

"What? No."

"Oh. What do you mean?"

"I mean, he's interested in her power. She's quite good at this. It was a shock to him, I think. I don't think the other witches are as good."

"Well, she's good at stuff like this. I mean, not that she's done exactly this before, but if you think about what she's done at the Coven, she's good at getting shit done. That's a good skill to have."

"Of course it is. I'm happy she has it."

"You just wish other people didn't get to know it so much?"

He took a deep breath. "After a fashion."

"Soooooo," Callie drawled, pretending to sketch something on the table with her finger. "A little bird told me something today. Ugh, Stu!" Stuart swished his tail back and forth, whipping Callie in the face. She pushed it away again. "Something about a date?" She looked at him expectantly.

"You talked to Lily." Paris surmised. Of course Lily would know about his date with Jade.

"She's a lot more *share-y share-y* than Jade. Not in a bad way, I mean, she wasn't gossiping. She wondered if I knew anything and we thought, as besties of the new couple, we should collaborate."

"Well, unfortunately, our impending transport from the Fae precluded our date."

"What? But I heard there were special shoes picked out."

"Yes, apparently, I should have known about the special shoes; however, I've no idea why anyone would think special shoes are a requirement for a date."

"I can't believe we're best friends. You've seen me pick shoes to wear out with Nick."

"No, I haven't."

"Yes. You have. You've helped!"

"I've no recollection of this."

"Clearly. Shoes can be a big deal. Not for everyone, but didn't you see the shoes Jade wore to the Coven ball? The ones Henri picked out?"

"Er?"

"Ugh!" Callie exclaimed. Stuart hissed at the loud sound and sauntered off. "They were completely impractical, but stunning. Anyone that wears shoes like that cares about shoes."

"I'll endeavor to be more mindful of shoes in general."

"So, no date?"

"We grabbed takeaway and ate her in kitchen."

"So, kind of like a date," Callie mused, her brown eyes big and hopeful.

"Until the demon showed up."

Callie grimaced. "She's really got to do something about that pantry."

"I get the impression he's the devil she knows. She's... oddly good at dealing with him."

"Is that like if someone is a really good bug killer? Sure, it's good they have a skill, but really, they probably wish they were doing something else." Callie sagged in her chair, her shoulders slumped. "What a bust."

Paris thought back to Jade's kitchen and their conversation. The feel of the skin of her neck under his fingers and the hard patch of marble from her time with the Gorgon.

"It wasn't. A bust, as you say," he added when Callie looked confused.

Her face lit up. "Oh, really?"

"I thought it went rather well."

Callie fanned her face comically. "Luckily I speak Paris fluently and know that means you may as well be gushing right now."

He smiled, feeling light and happy. His phone buzzed and the banner flashed that it was an incoming phone call from a number he didn't recognize, although it had a Coven prefix. Normally he would just answer, but it was late, he was tired, and preoccupied thinking about Jade.

"Do you recognize this number?" he asked, rattling it off to Callie.

"Oh! That's Lily's new Coven phone! She might be calling you if she can't get a hold of Jade. Okay, I'll let you go, but I expect to hear more details about the exact nature of 'rather well' later on!"

He wasn't sure what more she wanted to know that he'd be willing to share, but in the interest of expediency, he simply agreed. "All right." She disconnected their call and he immediately answered Lily's call. The screen went dark and it took him a moment to realize she'd actually called him and not initiated a face-to-face call.

"Pairs here."

"Hey, it's Lily, I can't get a hold of Jade. Is she with you?" Lily's voice came out sharp and clipped - no social niceties attached.

"She's out with the fire crews at the moment. She appears to be doing well."

"Oh." Lily sounded unsure or perhaps confused. "I just… I thought she'd be able to talk to me. Does she have cell phone coverage?"

"I don't know."

"Oh," Lily repeated. "But you think she's okay?"

"Yes, I've got a radio set and I'm connected." He paused, listening and also checking in with his magic. "She's not currently talking, but I can feel her magic working. Why do you ask? Do you feel something?"

"I just…" Lily huffed. "We're separate people and I know I've been pushing her to be separate…"

She had? Paris didn't realize. He knew Jade had been unhappy as of late and she'd seemed somewhat displeased about not being at Lily's power tests, but he hadn't known it was something they were actively pursuing.

"But I kind of thought that… I mean, I guess I didn't know…" Lily exhaled. "So, she's out with the fire crews?"

"Yes, and from the data I've seen, she's doing quite well. There are photos, if you'd like."

"Can you send them?" She laughed, but it wasn't an amusing sound. It made him feel hollow and empty inside. "I thought I was okay with all this. But she's not here. Again. She just got back from the Dearth, you know?"

He did know and so he stayed silent, leaving her room to speak.

"She couldn't contact me then, but now, she could, but hasn't and it feels different and…

Goddamn it, Bruce, I know my fire is shit and it's not Jade's, but it's all you have!" Lily cleared her throat. "That last part wasn't for you."

"So I gathered. Bruce doing all right?"

"I managed a pathetic little fire, not even worth the fireplace. More like a candle and he's kind of pissed. Or depressed. Or both." Lily paused again. "But she's okay?"

"Yes, she's doing well. I think you'll enjoy the pictures."

"Okay. Well. When you talk to her, if she doesn't notice the thousand messages I've sent to her phone, tell her to call me. I don't care what time it is."

"I will.

Lily exhaled and Paris swore he heard Bruce make his customary *pfffffttt* sound in the background. "Okay. Keep me posted. I'm going to lie down and pretend I'm sleeping comfortably for eight hours."

"Try to get some actual rest. I'll let you know if anything is amiss."

"You know, I actually feel better hearing that from you. 'Kay. Talk to you later."

She disconnected and Paris was left staring at his blank screen. Truth be told, he was rather forlorn at the moment himself, but couldn't imagine indulging that emotion. He had gathered supplies, checked in with Callie, Lily, and the Coven (by way of email), and now was bereft of tasks. It was far easier being Coven Leader than it was sitting on the sidelines while people worked.

Paris went back to their shared hotel room and laid out the extra supplies he'd gathered - change of clothes for Jade (another fire suit and undergarments), extra charging cables, some protein bars and bottles of sports drinks. His gaze was drawn toward Jade's gym bag and he wondered if it would be an invasion of privacy for him to unpack and sort the contents. Deciding that was a *yes*, he turned his back on it and left the room, heading back to the main conference room.

He passed time listening in on various conversations. The data scientists argued over some kind of modeling software , a couple of younger men were discussing the tools they had for cutting a line. Another group of men were discussing the food and lack of variation in it.

Paris found himself back at the head table he'd begun to think of as Danvers'. The fire marshal was across the room at the data scientists' table, nodding along to something the woman with the spiky hair was telling him. On the table in front of Paris, the most recent maps were laid out with harsh marker lines carved into them. His eyes were drawn to the area where he knew Jade was working. Digitized red flames marked out where the fire was. Written over top in darker marker were circles around the small bits Jade was working to contain. The was a long, harsh dark line demarcating something, he wasn't sure what but he suspected it was the fail-safe zone for the highway. He could see how if the fire approached the area the long line bisected, it could jump the asphalt. From there, there was a wildlife sanctuary, a small satellite community, then the town. He pulled his phone out and stared at the picture of Jade's fire, the one the scientist had sent him. He glanced back down at the map. If Jade was successful, and he had no doubt she would be, he could easily guess where she'd be going next.

Wherever the fire was the worst.

CHAPTER TWELVE

Paris was waiting at the landing spot for the helicopter when it came back. He resisted the urge to move forward as the copilot helped Jade out of the craft. She laughed as she stumbled, but with the sounds of the blades still turning, he didn't hear it. He could only see the motion of her shoulders and the shape of her mouth. She spotted him immediately and lurched toward him, her gait sloppy and ungraceful. She was exhausted. She more or less ran into him and he caught her, wrapping an arm around her shoulders. She turned and waved at the pilots and they gave jaunty salutes back.

"You smell like smoke," he said inanely. Of course the entire area smelled of smoke and ash, but it was particularly strong on her, mixed in with the scent of her magic, cloves and linden blossom.

"And victory!" she crowed, pumping one of her fists. "They said I did really well. I did a lot of areas."

"I saw and heard." He guided her away from the helicopter to a car he had waiting to take her back to the hotel. It was dark now, late night or early morning - depending on how you thought of it.

"How?"

"I was listening on radio. I didn't get a chance to tell you but then I didn't want to interrupt. For seeing, I had satellite photos. Of your magic. The data scientists sent them to me. I can show you back in the hotel room."

"Oh, cool! I wonder if they'd send the data too."

"Already asked for and granted."

"I love nerds," she said dreamily. She sounded loopy. Punch drunk. He wondered how tired she was.

"How is your magic holding up?"

Jade swayed as she walked, knocking into him with the full force of her weight. He managed to keep them in a straight line as he took her around to the passenger side of the car.

"Oh my god, it's so awesome. At first, I was like, I don't know how to do this, then I did it and it was like **CRUNCH**." She clapped her hands together. "And then poof!" She blew her hands apart. "And it worked and looked kinda pretty."

"The pictures are quite lovely." He opened the passenger door and she folded in on herself, like a strange origami flower collapsing. She fumbled with the seatbelt and he finally took it from her grasp and buckled her in, like a wayward or errant toddler.

"Josh and Chuck, the pilots, they were super nice and they helped point out where I should work exactly, and Josh has a three year old. Can you believe that? I didn't even think he was old enough to drink, but he's someone's *dad*. And he talked and talked and talked 'bout his kid, but it was cute you know? He eats dirt, the kid, not Josh, but Josh thinks it's funny. Thinks it's great. But dirt. Kids are messy."

She was quite overtired, he decided. Rambling and babbling everything about her day. He'd been able to hear snatches of their conversation on the radio. Hearing her repeat it was like he'd watched a movie he'd only been partially paying attention to and then have someone tell you all about it. He didn't mind. He made agreeing sounds in counterpoint to her chatter as he slipped into the driver's seat. It was a short drive back to the hotel and he hoped she didn't fall asleep. He could carry her if she did, but she had expressed several times she wasn't comfortable with that.

She had her fingers pressed against the glass of the passenger window and stared out at the glowing sky. "It's so different from down here. It's almost like it could just be lights. But up there, it's fire and hot. So hot. But pretty too."

"Do they know if you're going back out?"

"Hmm? Oh, I'll have to. It's huge. It's huge. Like… Huge."

"Huge," he repeated fondly. "Got it. I know you're tired-"

"I am," she interrupted.

"But if you're up to it, Lily would like to hear from you."

"Oh." She dug into some of the pockets of her fire suit, finding her phone and pulling it out. He could make out the frown of her eyebrows in the light from the device. She punched some buttons and held it up to her ear. "Hey, you called?" Paris could hear the similar tones of Lily's voice on the other line. "Yeah, I'm good." Pause. "I got to ride a helicopter! And then it was just magic shit." Pause. "No, his woobie is in the wash. He dragged it outside and it got muddy."

She was talking about Bruce, Paris guessed. There was a long string of talking from Lily and Jade sort of turned her body away from him.

"Well, no, cause the Fae were coming. And then Seth showed up." Pause. "I don't know, he likes to check in. He's not that bad, except for how he's amoral and scary as fuck." Pause. "I can't ward the pantry. Then I won't know where he'll show up. Are you worried? Because you can close the door, and he can't open it from his side. Plus Bruce is there and he can tell if Seth's about to show up, so… just leave the kitchen." Pause. He could hear the tone of Lily's voice as she went through a series of questions. Jade breathed deep and exhaled long and loud out her nose. "I'm kind of in the middle of a fire thing here so it's not like there's been time for dating or whatever." She paused and her voice went more quiet. "Jesus, can this wait? Because he's right *here*. And I'm tired as fuck and stupid in the head."

Paris surmised that Jade was getting the same questions from Lily that he got from Callie. He snorted, amused.

"Yes, I was careful. No. No migraines or nose bleeds."

Paris supposed he wouldn't have to ask now since Lily had. He'd worried about Jade using too much power when he'd seen the photos. They'd been spectacular, but distressing. How much power had she used and was she suffering ill-effects? From her answer to Lily, it appeared she was okay. He pulled into the parking lot of hotel. Though it was three in the morning, the place was a hubbub of activity with buses pulling in and out, people milling about, news cameras and lights illuminating the dark.

"Could you tell when I was doing magic? No, eh? Hmm. No, I don't know, I thought maybe you'd have known because it was a lot." Pause. "Yes. I'm careful. I'll check in when I know what's happening next. Oh, we're back at the hotel now. I need a shower, a liter of water and maybe some food and a nap." Pause. "Yeah, of course I will. And tell Bruce I miss him." Pause. "Okay. You too." Jade hung up and frowned at her phone.

"Problem?" Paris asked as he parked and turned the car off.

"I have, like, fifteen percent battery left, which means the entire thing might shut off at any moment. Ugh."

"I have charging cables." She turned to face him and he was surprised by the sharpness of her eyes in the moment, their grey almost silver.

"You're my hero."

"I'm also your Coven Leader."

"And not just a pretty face." Though buckling her seatbelt had been an issue, undoing it wasn't and she managed to extricate herself from the car with a few jerky movements and some stumbling. He raced around the side to catch up and pull her close again to keep her from falling.

"Is your magic cedar chips or is that you?"

"Pardon?"

"You always smell like cedar chips. And mint. Laundry too. But I don't know if it's your magic or you. I mean, I guess the laundry is your clothes."

"I... don't know either." He'd never taken note of what his own magic smelled like. He certainly took catalogue of others, but never his own.

The concierge came up to them immediately as they entered in the hotel.

"Fire Marshal Danvers would like you to see him."

"Are you all right to go, or do you need to rest?" Paris asked.

"No, it's fine. I'm good," Jade replied, drifting out of his arm reach and toward the ballroom. She pulled Chapstick out of one of her pockets and applied liberally. He smiled at the gesture. Apparently, fighting fires magically didn't make one immune to old habits. A vaguely vanilla-mint smell trailed behind her, intermixed with the scent of her magic as they made their way through the ballroom.

As though he had them on internal radar, Danvers raised his head from where it was bent in conversation with several men in suits when they entered. He waved them over, still listening to what the men were saying. From the snippets Paris heard as they approached, it was the city's mayor, chief of police, and emergency response.

"Gentlemen, this is our new fire witch, Jade and her Coven Leader," Danvers said.

Paris bristled at the word *our* - as though Danvers somehow thought Jade belonged to him.

"Well, I'm one of the fire witches. You've got Clay, What's-his-face and the other asshole."

Paris wasn't sure if Jade's fatigue made her snappish, or if she also bristled against Danvers' word choice.

"You were able to clear a large area. The data scientists say it's unlikely the fire will spread that way now that you've blocked it."

"If by block you mean incinerated it, then I guess so. Yeah." Jade crossed her arms over her chest and moved slightly closer to Paris.

"When can you go back out?"

"She only just returned," Paris interrupted.

"And we need her out again," the city mayor replied. "If she can clear the area toward the town, we won't have to evacuate."

"Okay, well, *she* is standing right here and doesn't know. When were you thinking?" Jade asked.

"I'd like to send you back out right now if you think you're able."

Paris shook his head. "No, absolutely not." He winced as he realized he'd not given her the chance to answer for herself, but then realized she was nodding along with his words.

"Yeah, what he said." She jerked a thumb at him. "I need to eat. And sleep." She checked her smartphone. "And my phone is dead." She turned to Paris. "What time is it?"

"Quarter to four."

She made a face. "Gross. Okay, give me six hours."

"How about four?" Danvers replied.

Paris wasn't a physical person, but the urge to step forward and sock him in the jaw was strong.

"Why only four?" Jade asked. "What's the difference two hours will make?"

"We don't know. That's the issue," said the chief of police. "Every minute counts."

"I get that, but I just…" She sighed and reached up, tightening her ponytail, the smell of smoke and ash stronger when she moved. "I need to sleep."

"I think that settles it," Paris said. "I appreciate the undue stress you're all under, but if Jade doesn't have time to rest and recharge, her magic won't be as effective."

"Again, what he said," Jade said, tipping her head toward him. "I mean, I'm stupid right now. I don't even…" She exhaled. "If you put me out there, I don't think I'll be able to do much. Besides, don't you have the other guys? How did they do?"

It was something Paris wondered as well. He'd been so focused on Jade's work, he'd not even thought to ask after the other witches.

"They're not as effective as you."

"Okay, well, super flattering, but I still need to eat a hamburger and sleep."

The men didn't look happy, exchanging looks and slight nods.

"Great, you've all done that weird dude-nod thing which means you're good. I'll see you in six hours."

Her exit, he supposed, would have been a lot more profound and theatrical if she hadn't stumbled and fallen into his side as she did it.

"Ugh, tripping totally ruins that mic drop."

He took the opportunity to put his arm around her shoulder and pull her close to him. She was pliant under his arm, leaning against him.

"I've no idea what that means."

Jade laughed and it turned into a coughing fit. "Sorry. Smoke." She took a breath and then had to hold off another coughing fit. "It's like... a way to epically end something. It's kind of ruined if you stagger out."

"Your point was still made."

"But was it Snapchat worthy? Probably not."

"I've no idea what that means either."

As they got on the hotel elevator, she turned her face to him. "You still think your phone's for making calls, don't you?"

"For what else would it be?"

She smiled, the grey of her eyes sparkling. He thought he might be a little enchanted with her.

Once back in the hotel room, she put her hands on her hips and looked at the bed and then her gym bag, as though both were offensive.

"Are you all right?"

She sighed. "Yeah. I'm just having a debate. Shower and wash versus faceplate in bed." She breathed out with her lips loose, making a flapping kind of noise, like a horse neighing.

"How about you shower and I'll order you some food," he asked, picking up the phone.

She rubbed at one of her eyes, smearing mascara and her left-over eyeshadow everywhere. "'Kay."

"A hamburger and fries, you said?" he asked, already dialing.

"Yes. And tell them to kill it. I've no interest in trying to cook my own food or resurrect it." She grabbed her gym bag and then rooted around in it for a moment.

"There are extra supplies in the bathroom, should you require," he intoned, not sure what she was looking for. "Including shampoo and hair conditioner."

"Fancy." She closed the door to the bathroom and he became distracted by the person on the other end of the phone, ordering food for them both. He'd not eaten either and found the idea of a hamburger strangely compelling.

Jade stumbled out of the washroom ten minutes later and he marveled at her speed. He'd barely had time to order their food, set their devices to charge and set an alarm for tomorrow, or later today, depending on how he looked at it. He'd also managed to change into a pair of soft cotton pants and a t-shirt. Jade stared at him as though she didn't recognize him.

"Are you all right?"

"You're in… not dress pants or jeans."

"Correct. I gathered supplies from the gift shop."

"And you're not wearing socks."

"No, I'm not." She stared at his bare feet for a moment before giving her head a shake, water droplets falling from her hair as she did. She'd changed as well into workout leggings and a t-shirt. There were damp patches from where her hair hung loose and wet.

"D'you remember that hair thing you did, when I came back from the Dearth?"

"Do you mean when I dried your hair for you?"

"Yeah." It was all she offered as she sat on the edge of the bed and tipped her head forward. He guessed it was a cue to step up. As he'd done before, he raised his hands above her head and spoke the words of the spell. Water steamed off and she shivered. He passed his hands over the area a few more times, steam dissipating out into the air. She sighed, her eyes closed. He gathered her hair into his hands, the strands of it soft, like baby hair. Frizzy and somewhat dry.

"I hate doing my hair. It takes so long and then I still need to flatiron or curl it."

He made a low sound of agreement, though he wasn't sure why she felt the need to do more to her hair. It was what it was. There was a knock at the door and he was surprised the food was ready so quickly. He supposed the entire staff of the hotel was engaged keeping everyone fighting the fire happy and satiated. No doubt the newest witch proficient in fire scored high on their list. He set the food tray down on the bed in front of Jade. Her eyes opened halfway and she lifted the lid, grabbing the burger and the side of ketchup. She dipped her burger in the condiment and haphazardly aimed the concoction toward her mouth. A pickle slice squeezed out and fell onto the plate. He tried to focus on his own meal, but watching her eat was like watching a trainwreck in slow motion. She was obviously exhausted, but stubbornly determined. She ate a few more bites in a similar fashion, a bit of tomato falling off at one point and landing on the plate with a loud thunk. She placed the remainder of her burger on the plate and pushed it away, closing her eyes and leaning back against the headboard. Dinner, it seemed, was over.

Paris leaned forward and chanced taking the plate from her, not sure if she would slap at him or not. She remained motionless, eyes closed. He set the plate on the dresser.

"You should lie down."

"Ugh, my tummy will not be happy with that," she replied, but stretched out on her side of the king-sized bed. She sighed. "I miss Bruce. He presses against my back. It's warm."

"I recall," Paris said wryly setting their food containers on the armoire.

"Yeah?"

"Yes, when you were gone," he replied, lying down on the far side of the bed, attempting to keep his distance, "Bruce came to my room. He's quite persistent."

"Yeah," Jade said, her voice dreamy and somewhat distant as she rolled to her back. "Lucky bastard."

Paris wasn't sure what Jade meant by her words. He shuffled a bit and turned off the bedside lamps, using magic to capture the one on her side. Out of the corner of his eye, he could see her sleeping as Lily had. Arms crossed over her chest, as though she were lying in a coffin. The thought chilled him.

"It's cold."

"You're not under the covers," he replied.

"Hmmm." She didn't move, remaining as she was with her arms crossed and hands clasped over her heart.

"Jade. You should get under the covers before you fall asleep."

She grumbled, but took his advice, shuffling down a bit further in the bed and scrunching up her pillow. "I didn't set my alarm."

"I've set one."

"I didn't plug my phone in." She moved to get out of bed.

"I did it."

She sagged back into the mattress. "Are you taking applications?"

"For what?"

"To be my butler. Getting me dinner. Charging my devices. If you could tell me where I put my keys when I don't leave them in my coat pocket, and make sure my Chapstick never runs out, the job is yours."

"I assume you'll need some kind of references."

"Bruce will vouch for you." Her voice was drifting off, getting quieter and a bit more slurred. "You shouldn't trust Hannah like you do," she said apropos of nothing.

"Pardon me?"

"Hannah," she said, her voice coming out like a sigh. "She read Lily's cards and I don't think they were good. But she wouldn't tell me. Lily or Hannah. And then she wanted to read mine again."

"Yes, she told me you declined."

Jade snorted and bed moved slightly from the force of her exhale. "Yeah. To put it mildly." Though it was quiet, Paris could sense the weight of words Jade hadn't yet said, the expectation of them on the air. He waited and before long, she spoke again. "But it wouldn't matter if she read them or not. They're just cards."

"Tarot magic is quite powerful. Many cultures use something similar as a form of divination. It's a way to tap into Mother Nature and the magic of the universe."

He heard the rustle of the bedclothes and then a second later, the lamp on her side of the bed flicked on. "Is it? Or is it a bunch of crap?" Though only moments before he'd thought she'd been about to drift off to sleep, she seemed wide awake now.

"Tarot is another part of the magic that we use. Some people are better at it than others. Hannah is an expert."

"Says who?"

"I don't know what you mean."

"Says who?" Jade repeated. "Like has she got some kind of degree from Tarot University or a special decoder ring?"

"No, of course not, but she's been reading cards for years. For more years than I know, actually. Is this about Lily? Are you upset about what her cards said? Did you ask her?"

"No, I didn't because I don't have to. Inputs and outputs, action and reaction. That's how my magic works, and that's how the universe works too. And if I don't like the output, I'll change the input."

"And what if all inputs lead to the same output?"

"I won't say it's impossible because, hey, everything is possible to some degree. But it's statistically improbable."

"You should talk to Lily and see if she'll tell you what her cards said." Paris wasn't sure he could help Jade with this if she didn't even know what it was that upset Lily.

"Oh, I intend to, but..." She paused, her lips pressing together firmly for a moment. "But this is about your cards too."

"Mine? How?" He was honestly flummoxed at how the two were related. He'd not had his cards read in years.

"Hannah told me what your cards said. What she told you."

"When?"

"When you were a kid."

He'd only had his cards read the one time, and to be sure, when someone tells you, as a child, that you will die young, you remember every detail. He could still remember the scent of jasmine tea, cooling in the pot. The tea cup he had been using had a small crack. He'd felt it against his lips every time he took a sip. His mother's face had been grim and pale, but fierce. Rather like Jade's expression now. "No, I gathered that part. I mean, when did you have this conversation with Hannah?"

"When she read Lily's cards. It... sort of came up. In a related discussion."

"Related to what?" He couldn't possibly think of anything they could have discussed that would have turned them on the subject.

"The point is," Jade continued, drumming her finger into the duvet cover. It sunk down silently, dulling the ferociousness of her expression and tone. "There's no way a bunch of cards or the person who reads them can know the future. There are too many variables."

"After all you've learned since coming to the Coven, I'm surprised you're struggling with this. As a child, you died." He wished he could take the words back when her expression went flat and cold. But now that the words were out, he pressed on. "You were a living soul inside another human's body, and then you created your own body. You've learned magic. You can create and control fire. You've been to the demon landscape and faced the Gorgon."

"That doesn't mean telling the future through a bunch of cards is true."

"No, it does not. But you can see why certain weight is placed on those predictions."

"If you tell me what she said, I'll stop it."

He was stunned by her words. "You can't make that statement without knowing what it might entail."

"So tell me what it entails."

"Jade," he sighed. "It's four in the morning. We've been up all day-"

"If ever there was a reason to stay up at four in the morning, this is it. What did Hannah tell you?"

"I appreciate your vehemence and tenacity. But this is not the time nor the place."

"All those things you said about me are true. Apparently, I died as a kid and didn't have enough common sense to stay dead. I lurked in someone else's body for years until I ended up being the only one in there. Then, I learned how to use magic, joined a Coven, met a demon, got banished to the Dearth and came back after stopping in to play Hide and Seek with a Gorgon. If you think Hannah's reading is true, you've got zero to lose by telling me and pretty much everything to gain."

"I'm deeply touched you would make such an offer and perhaps, I will tell you someday what Hannah told me, but..." He sighed. "Again, I reiterate, it's four in the morning and rest assured nothing in her reading will come to pass in the next twenty-four hours."

"What about the next forty-eight?" she countered.

He laughed, he couldn't help it. Her face was so earnest and fierce. If she had a lasso long enough, she would capture the moon and bring it down to Earth if he so much as hinted it would help.

"The immediate future is safe."

Her eyes narrowed. "How immediate is immediate?"

"I can guarantee the next fortnight at least."

She looked suspicious. He shifted closer to her side of the bed and reached out. After pausing for a moment, he placed his hand on top of hers. She stared down at it, like she wasn't sure what to make of their hands in such close proximity. She looked back up at him.

"Are you now, finally, ready to go to sleep?"

She pursed her lips and nodded, shuffling back down into the bed without letting go of his hand. He used the same spell as before to put out the light of her nightstand.

"I don't even know what a fortnight is." Her voice carried through the dark.

He laughed again, squeezing her fingers slightly. "Two weeks. Fourteen nights."

"Oh. Okay. If you think I won't put it in my smartphone calendar to check in again in two weeks-"

"I would be sorely mistaken," he finished. "I'm sure."

#

Jade didn't think she would sleep well knowing she was sharing a bed with Paris, even though it was a king size and there was about a mile of space between them.

But she slept like a rock. A tired rock that had used a shit ton of magic. The feeling of falling asleep with Paris' hand holding hers had been odd for the two point six seconds it took for her to fall unconscious. Her last thoughts before sleep had been, *what if she had to move her hand? What if she wanted to turn over? Did she just pull it away and then roll over?*

And then she was asleep.

Unfortunately, falling asleep quickly and being exhausted didn't mean she slept dreamlessly. Her dreams were disjointed and confusing - a mishmash of the night she was assaulted, the day she split from Lily, and finally her trip to the Dearth. In her dreams, the Dearth had trees and they were on fire. Paris stood in the center of the forest, the area around him burned to a crisp, smoldering and hissing. His face was sunken in and hollow, like she'd seen him in the in-between when they were transported by the Fae. She reached for him and he turned away from her and started walking into the burnt out husk of the forest. The dead trees parted as he moved and closed behind him afterward, a curtain of death and destruction. She opened her mouth to scream, but no sound came out other than a high-pitched whine - like an injured stray dog on the side of the road.

Then she was falling. No, not falling. She was being pushed down, being *held* down and it was awful. There were hands against her shoulders and the weight of a body on top of her. She couldn't move and still no sound would come out of her mouth. But this time she had magic, didn't she? She reached for it, but there was nothing there. It felt like falling down the last unknown step of a stairway she thought had ended. A sickening gap, a void, where her magic should have been but wasn't.

"Jade."

She woke up like she was landing from her dream fall, her limbs jerking in chorus with each other. One moment she was asleep and the next she was awake. No peaceful, soporific wakening - just fear, panic, anxiety, consciousness.

"Jade."

It was Paris' voice. Paris saying her name. She looked around to get her bearings. Hotel room. Forest fire. Gym bag on a stand. She was magical support. Her dream collided with her memories from yesterday. There was a forest burning, but the forest wasn't entirely turned to ash yet. Paris wasn't walking away from her, being swallowed up by wreckage and ruination. She also wasn't in an apartment, fighting off a violation she couldn't stop. She was safe.

"I'm awake." Her mouth was dry. She swallowed and it felt sticky and thick.

"Are you?"

She looked at him. He was sitting up, turned toward her. The covers on her side were pulled and wrinkled. She was sitting on half of them, trapping herself. No wonder she'd dreamt of being restrained. She slowly untangled herself.

"Yes. Bad dream."

"You were struggling. I didn't want to..." He reached out, mimicking shaking her awake. At some point in her sleep, they must have let go of each other.

"No, that's... probably good that you didn't." Honestly, if she'd woken up with hands on her, she wasn't sure what she would have done. Tried to sock him in the face? Kick out with her feet? Shoot off some magic? Speaking of, she reached for her power and breathed a sigh of relief when she felt its resonating ping deep in her bones. "Sorry."

"For what?"

For being herself, she guessed. She shrugged. "I dunno." She rubbed her face, grateful she'd gotten all of yesterday's makeup off before she went to bed. "What time is it?"

"Nine. The alarm was set to go off at ten, so it's a bit earlier than I'd expected. You could probably still rest if you wanted."

She wanted. Getting out of bed always sucked. But she'd feel worse if she managed to doze and then had to wake up a second time. "Nope." She freed herself from the covers and swung her legs out of bed. "Is my phone around?"

"On the dresser."

She shuffled over and found six texts when she checked it. Five from Lily, one from Henri.

Lily: BTW, obviously have put off trip to see mom and dad. Will wait till you return.

Lily: Bruce is a bed hog.

Lily: AND A COFFEE STEALER. That was the last of the cream. WHY BRUCE WHY?? #ohthehumanity

Lily: Did you switch mascara? I can only find this pink and blue tube. Did they stop making the other one?

Lily: LMK how you slept. Or didn't sleep as the case may be ;) JK, I know you're working. OR ARE YOU?????

She texted Lily back quickly that she'd slept fine and yes, she was working. She smiled when she read Henri's text next.

Henri: *I hear you're firefighting! I also hear there are a lot of hot dudes (PUN INTENDED). Pics or it didn't happen.*

She texted back: *sry, too busy saving the world to take pics.*'

Henri must have his phone with him because he immediately answered.

Henri: *You're never too busy for pics of firefighters. Help a brother out.*

Jade snorted and saw Paris turn to her out of the corner of her eye. "Henri wants pics of hot firefighters. If I'm too busy, think you can help the cause?"

He frowned and looked like he was actually considering it. "What does Henri look for in a gentleman?"

"Oh my god, I'm texting him you're asked that and you might be on pic duty." Her fingers flew over the touch screen and she let the typos and incorrect auto-corrections stay, knowing Henri would understand.

Henri: *Hahahhahahhahhaha. A true leader! Well, anyone who looks like the BF. Tall. Dark. Handsome. Or short. Blond. Shirtless preferred. Rugged. If they're a bit dirty, that's good too. ;) And of course, they have to look like they have the soul of a poet. He spends all day fighting fires and chopping down trees, but at night he writes poetry and helps save puppies and kittens.*

"There's no way I can read this out loud with a straight face. I'm just going to leave this here," Jade said, putting her phone down, "and you can read it yourself while I'm in the bathroom."

Just before she shut the door to the bathroom, she saw him leaning over the dresser, reading Henri's text, a soft befuddlement on his face. She felt her cheeks heat up and didn't know why she was blushing.

She guessed she didn't need another shower since she'd had one before bed. She rooted around in her gym bag, glad she had doubles of all her makeup shit. She had switched mascaras when she found a new formula that worked better. She'd have to text Lily about it. Ah, the transfer of world-changing information that smartphones enabled - new mascaras and pics of hot firefighters. She couldn't help but laugh when she though out Paris trying to take photos. Would he be stealthy? Or would he just snap away? Or would he, dare she hope, *ask permission* to take photos? She suspected the last option. She laughed to herself as she put on some basic makeup and then cursed when she jammed the mascara wand under her eye by accident, leaving a large black smudge. It would look a little shitty all day.

She traded places with Paris. Him going into the bathroom as she exited and she took the time by herself to text Lily again, asking after Bruce and if she was at her new job at Supernatural Relations. She changed clothes and put her ghost busters fire suit on again as she did. It smelled heavily of smoke. The scent crawled up her nostrils and embedded itself in her soft palette.

Lily: *I am! New job! My own desk! But no coffee mug yet. Apparently, a lot of the older mugs were breaking so there's a safety policy you have to*

266 / UNCONTROLLABLE BURN

bring in your own mug? WTF? I'm going to get one made that says 'I joined a Coven and they still made me buy my own mug.'

Jade laughed but it set off a coughing spree. She had to clear her throat four times before the tickle in it was gone. Smoke inhalation, she guessed.

#ILeftMyLifeForThis,
#IThoughtMagicWasCooler, Jade texted.

Lily: *OMG YASSSSSSSSS*

Paris exited the bathroom just as her laughter set off another coughing spree.

"We should see if we can get you some PPE to guard against that."

"Is that like a shot or pill?"

"Personal Protection Equipment."

"So, do you, and like, all the other Coven Leaders sit around and make up new acronyms, or do they come to you as a *fait accompli* and you just have to approve them?"

"It's a well known acronym."

"If you say so." She pocketed her phone. Paris had also changed while in the bathroom and was again in his fireproof suit. She didn't know if he'd need it, but liked that they matched.

"C'mon, I'll buy you breakfast," she said.

"Breakfast is free." His tone and expression indicated he clearly understood she was joking and wanted to participate.

"Details." She waved a hand. "Oh my God, I hope they have baby cakes."

"What are baby cakes?" he asked, pulling the room door shut behind them.

"Manna from the gods. Deep-fried hash-brown manna." She got wistful just thinking about the possibility. Surely all this magical fire-stopping was burning some calories, right? She could afford some deep-fried goodness?

To Jade's delight, breakfast was a buffet and though there were many healthy and smart choices, she gravitated toward bacon and baby cakes. She and Paris took their takeaway containers to one of the long, banquet tables and Jade brandished her plastic cutlery like it was gifted to her from a king. She made a proprietary pile of salt and ketchup packages, eyeballing Paris when his gaze lingered too long.

"Get your own ketchup."

"I have no desire for ketchup; I'm simply intrigued at what you think you'll do with that much."

"No ketchup? Blasphemy." She looked at his tray which contained fresh fruit, what looked like some of the Greek yogurt and some muesli.

"Okay, it's not like I eat like this all the time," she gestured at her container of bacon and baby cakes, "but this is a magical emergency and we are magical support, so if ever a time deserved baby cakes, don't you think this is it?"

"In the grand scheme of things, I suppose if there is some kind of baby cakes worthiness scale," he said the words like they were strange and foreign, "then yes, this qualifies. However, they are simply unappealing to me."

"That's the saddest thing I've ever heard." She noticed that he had his customary cup of tea as well. "But since I can't vouch for the compatibility of baby cakes and tea, you might be better off." She shrugged, taking a sip of her coffee. Normally, she added two creams to get it the right shade of beige, but this cup had taken four of the little creamers and was still at tad too dark. She grimaced at the sip. She remembered something he'd once said to her, at the Coven Ball when she'd tried the whiskey he'd been drinking. It seemed appropriate. "That'll put hair on your chest," she said, referencing the coffee.

"Let's hope not."

It was exactly the same thing she'd said to him. She looked up, unable to stop her lips from breaking into a smile. He smiled back at her, his expression indicating he too remembered their exchange from the Coven Ball.

Jade didn't know what drew her attention from Paris to the door of the ballroom where other people had been coming and going, but something did. She looked up just in time to see Adam and Michael, two of the three witches helping, enter. Clay, the softer spoken one, wasn't with them. She didn't know if that was *de rigueur* or happenstance.

"Ugh, Tweedle-asshat and tweedle... more asshat." Okay, not her best word smithery, but whatever.

Paris looked over his shoulder. When they'd arrived, Jade had planted herself in a position to be able to see the door, as was her custom. Paris had easily taken the spot opposite her, leaving his back to the entrance.

As if summoned by her words, Adam and Michael caught their gaze and headed over.

"Oh, shit. We made eye contact." She didn't break that contact as she took another sip of her coffee, watching them over the rim of the cup.

Adam it seemed was also a member of the, *I will not look away first* club, holding Jade's gaze easily as he wove his way around people carrying a tray of food. Michael followed a little behind him, and Jade had the sudden image in her head of Batman and Robin - the lead superhero and the sidekick.

"You're going to need more protein than that for firefighting," Adam said as he sat down across from Jade. Michael came around and sat next to her.

Jade looked at Paris first, almost like he was a camera and this was a reality TV show. She hoped her expression conveyed the full force of how tedious she found them both.

"Wow. Thank god you're here. I've apparently only managed to stay alive and feed myself for the sum total of my entire adult life by happenstance and luck." She looked at his plate and of course it had egg whites and fruit with a piece of brown toast. She looked back at her baby cakes and bacon. Damn it. She was going to have to run a bunch of miles to work them off.

Adam exhaled, a wry twist to his lips. "Fair enough. So, what was it you were doing out there yesterday?"

His tone wasn't accusatory, but it was intensely inquisitive.

Again, Jade glanced at Paris, and he almost imperceptibly shrugged a shoulder. He had no idea what Adam meant either. "What do you mean?" She asked.

"With the fire. You didn't make it stop or turn back. You burnt it out."

She could be mean and rude, but she decided to be an adult and have a real conversation. Damn it again. "Is that bad?"

"I've never seen anyone do that. How did you do it?"

"I dunno. I just did."

"How long did you have to train before you were able to conjure your first fire?"

"Jade managed to create fire the first time she tried," Paris replied. "The Supernatural Council knew someone was performing magic outside a Coven and we found Jade. She did it her first try."

"Yeah, not including the things I was setting on fire by accident before that," Jade added, remembering her kitchen at home and at work.

"Holy shit," muttered Michael.

"So you had no formal training and you just… did it. How?" Adam's gaze was sharp as he questioned her.

"I don't know. It just happens."

Adam studied her for a moment longer and then nodded, directing his attention to his plate. "Well, you do good work."

Jade blinked a few times in surprise. "Uh, thanks."

"My first fire," offered Michael, "it took me a while to get the hang of it. They sent me out in the helicopter and the pilots pointed to where I was supposed to work and… nothing. We had to come back down and I had to go back up with Adam. I had to watch him work first, feel his magic, and then I could do it."

They were sharing personal stories. Was she bonding with them now? Had she passed some kind of test and they were peeps? Comrades in arms? While both Adam and Michael were focused on their food, she looked up at Paris and then tapped his foot under the table to get his attention. *What the fuck?* she mouthed. He shrugged and made some kind of gesture that she thought meant, *go with it*. Ugh. People-ing was hard.

Danvers approached their table and stood in front of them. "Good, you're all here. Except that other one."

"Clay," Paris offered.

"He's probably on his way. He's not a breakfast person," Michael said as he stabbed some fruit with his fork.

"He can catch up. You," Danvers pointed at Jade. "And you," he pointed at Adam. "I need you along the line of the highway."

"What part of the highway?" Adam asked, pulling out his phone and presumably looking at a map. He held it out and offered Paris to take a look since they were side by side.

"All of it."

Paris set his tea cup down. "That's too large of an area."

"How big is it compared to what I did yesterday?" Jade asked.

"Quadruple. At least," Paris answered.

Jade sagged back into her chair. Shit. That was big.

"And I was only able to do part of what you did yesterday," Adam said.

"If the fire jumps the highway, we might not be able to stop it before it hits town," Danvers said, hitting the table with his pointer finger.

"Are all of us in that area?" Adam asked.

Danvers shook his head. "No, we've got a natural gas pipeline running under another area that is in danger due to last night's wind shifts. I need the other two there."

Jade turned to Paris. "Can we get more witches?"

"I can ask. At this point, we may need to bring in people who aren't extraordinary proficient in fire. Perhaps anyone with a good control of their magic could work under direction."

"If you're going to do that, it needs to be done fast. I need all four of the witches out in thirty minutes. The pilots are prepping the helicopters. We can't let the fire jump the highway. We need it to evacuate, and secondly, there's nothing else to stop it after that."

The hash browns hadn't been a good idea. They were heavy in her stomach, and felt like they could climb back up her esophagus, slippery with too much grease.

Danvers opened his mouth to say more - a harsh pep talk, more bad news, or simply an order, Jade didn't know. Before he could, he was swarmed by four people all talking numbers, weather, and incident reports. He was sucked into their blob and moved away from the breakfast table toward the main command one.

Even if she felt like eating more, the rest of her baby cakes looked cold and unappetizing. She pushed her plate back. So much for breakfast. Duty called.

CHAPTER THIRTEEN

Paris wasn't able to accompany her to the helicopter site. He needed to contact the Supernatural Council and have them put out the request for more witches, but to do that, he had to find the Fae assigned to this incident. Though the Fae didn't actively help, they facilitated, and if Paris didn't go through proper channels, they could make things "quite unpleasant." His words exactly. Jade didn't know what that meant in the realm of the Fae, but thinking of the story Paris told her about the guy who'd suffered a work accident and was made rich, she didn't want it clarified.

Paris and Jade had shared an awkward goodbye. At least it felt awkward. She didn't know if it looked as awkward as it felt. As they stood from the table, Paris tugged at her hand and leaned in to kiss her quickly on the lips and again on the cheek. She'd stood there like some kind of stupid mannequin, not sure how to respond. Then he moved away from her, pulling out his phone and starting to dial. Michael walked away with him, off to get Clay or find Danvers or… something. Jade didn't know.

"So, you and your Coven Leader," Adam said.

Jade swiveled her head toward him, confident her gaze conveyed the full force of *you really want to go there?*

Adam held up his hands in defense. "No judgment. Just an observation." He gestured for her to lead the way out of the ballroom.

"Yeah. So?"

"Like I said, no judgment," Adam replied as they started walking. Jade guessed there'd be a car or something to take them to the helicopter site. Jeez, she hoped Adam knew since she'd forgotten to ask. "Is that why he came with you?"

"Yeah, I guess. I'm still pretty new to the magic thing." Jade shrugged.

"First witch born outside a Coven."

In her mind, Jade recalled her past conversation with Sakkara. Though it hadn't been too long ago, with everything that had happened since, it felt like a lifetime.

"I'm the first witch born outside the Coven. I'm different."

"You are different," Sakkara had agreed. *"I made you different. We made you different. But you were not born outside the Coven."*

"Yes, I was. I had a mother and a father and they were shitty parents, but they were ours, Lily's and mine. And we grew up away from here. We didn't have magic."

"You always had magic," Sakkara replied. *"Lily has it now too, but I think that is a side effect of*

being tangled with you for so long. In a sense, she *is the first witch born outside a Coven. As a result of her association with you."*

Jade swallowed and nodded at Adam's words. "Yeah. That's me. Born outside a Coven." It wasn't like she was about to dive into the truth.

"How did that happen?"

There was no malice in his tone. Only a genuine sense of curiosity and expectation. Like he assumed Jade had it all figured out. He just expected somehow she had made sense of it all.

And in a way, she supposed she had. But it wasn't the kind of story you shared with someone you'd just met. Or anyone really, and certainly not when you were already wearing a headset linked to one of the interested parties. She could only imagine Paris listening in as Jade tried to explain it.

Well, I don't know all the details for sure, but what I'm pretty sure happened is this: Paris had his cards read as a child and this old witch said he was going to die, die young. And his mom, who may have always been bat-shit crazy, was all like "hell no." So, she made some kind of a deal with a demon. Not clear on the details, haven't had the opportunity to ask, and my best source is the demon living in my pantry. He is kind of trustworthy, but not. Demons. What can you do? Anyyyyyywayyyyy. Paris' mom, the batshit one, drowned me as a child. That's what the pantry-demon tells me. And she did it to somehow protect Paris. Again, fuzzy on the details. So, I'm drowned, right? Only I don't stay dead. I somehow end up sharing a body with this woman named Lily, and if you thought you had bad roommates in your past, at least no one ever took over your body like I did to her. Talk about pushing boundaries. So we grow up together, get the shit beat out of us, and then get sexually assaulted, and then long story short (haha, at this point you think I'm kidding, but I'm not, there's actually more that I'm not sharing) we "separate"and I'm on my own. And then I find out, I'm magic. I decide to give it a shot and join a Coven. But then, another Coven member tried to kill me and steal my magic. I've got some demon living in my pantry, and I was stalked by Paris' mom and she acts like I owe her something and then! Then! She banished me to the demon landscape, the Dearth, to face the Gorgon, Medusa. Yes. That Medusa. No, I'm not making this up. I guess her demon mistress was part of all this shit and made me the way I am so I could face Medusa and not be turned to stone. Shrug. So after all that, when I saw an email that said, hey, can you help out with firefighting, I was like, what the fuck, why not?? Gotta be easier than what I've been doing, am I right, am I right???

She obviously paused too long because Adam's expression had gone past expectant and into the realm of, *shit. I wish I hadn't asked.*

"That... complicated."

Adam snorted a sound of agreement. "I bet."

At the helicopter, Adam made a move to help boost her into the craft and she flinched, slapping at his hand.

"Fine, get in on your own." He made it sound like he was offended, which irked her. She was the one he was reaching for without consent. It's not that he was a total asshole, but asshole did seem to be the primary building component. She squished herself in the corner of the helicopter, taking comfort in the cold press of metal and industrial-strength plastic against her body. Before she'd gotten in the helicopter last time, Paris said he would be listening. She figured he was now too. Should she ask? She glanced at the pilots (a different pair from yesterday) and Adam. They were already involved in some light chit chat - fires, firefighting, the weather. She'd have to interrupt them if she wanted to see if Paris was listening. Taking a chance, she pulled out her phone and saw she did have some service. She sent him a quick text.

You listening?

She felt a flush course through her at how quickly he responded.

Paris*: I am. Is everything all right?*

She sent back a thumbs up emoticon before realizing Adam was watching her on her phone. She slipped it back into her pocket. It amused her that Paris texted in full sentences. Jade couldn't be bothered. Maybe he used text to speech or maybe he was just like that.

She would get to find out, if she wanted. They were dating. She could ask him things or just observe him. She thought about the press of his lips against hers, warm and firm. Something in her stomach turned over, but in a pleasant and fanciful way.

But then, without warning, she recalled her dream from the night before. The feeling of being pressed down, of being held down against her will. Although she knew Paris wouldn't force her to do anything she didn't want, she probably wasn't going to be able to keep herself from drawing comparisons, or comparing being with Paris with the last time she'd dated. There hadn't been anyone else since her assault. The assault itself had left her absolutely unwilling to try, then the loss of Lily had consumed her like a black hole. Even if she'd wanted to pursue something (which she hadn't), there wasn't anything in her left to fuel that.

Before the rape (and god, she still struggled with that word. It wasn't like it was easier to use the words *assault, event, attack*, except for how it was), she hadn't really had a lot of interest in dating anyway. Jade understood the mechanics and biology of it, but it never appealed to her. She could see how and why it appealed to other people, but it mostly seemed like a shit ton of effort and frivolity.

But now, with Paris…

She liked him, obviously. She respected his opinion and she knew he respected hers. He recognized her boundaries and asked about them, instead of not seeing them or seeing them and not caring.

But sometimes, most times, when she thought about taking things to a more physical level, even when Lily tried to joke about it, Jade felt something in her seize and lock up. Like a wild rabbit in the forest that felt a predator's eyes upon it. She didn't want to, it just happened - a hind-brain reaction she didn't know how to stop.

"Are you listening?"

It took her a second to realize Adam was talking to her. "No," she said honestly. There was no point in lying. He could tell from her answers and expressions that she had no clue.

To his credit, he didn't roll his eyes or make a disparaging remark. "We're coming up on the highway. I don't know if I can combine my magic with yours, so I thought we could work separately and see how it goes."

"Okay." She didn't know if his plan was good or not, but it was a plan, and she could work with it.

The fire was hungrier today, if such a thing were possible. When she stretched out to touch it, she wanted to recoil, curl in on herself and let the pilots know they could drop her off or keep going, whatever. She would tap out.

Jade stole a glance a Adam. He looked like she felt and it gave her confidence. If misery loved company, so did unease and insecurity. Seeing him feel the same way dulled the sharp edges of her fear. She watched him work - he seemed to study a part of the fire for a moment, then his magic flared out and he burned the pathway the fire would have needed. It seemed like a small drop in the very big bucket of what they were here to accomplish, but it was something. She took a deep breath and started working on her own area - finding a patch of fire she could isolate and force to burn bright and suicidal. The familiar flame colors danced before her eyes, like yesterday, but there was an added element today, feeling Adam's magic working so closely to hers. It wasn't a bad element, it was just intrinsically there - another layer to her own power. His magic smelled like peanut butter and a hint of saltiness. Barbecue? She wasn't sure and didn't have time to think about it before they finished their spots. The helicopter swerved and they were working on new areas.

"I'll keep working on the south if you can keep working on the north."

Okay, truth be told, she was good with spaces, but had zero directional awareness at the moment.

She assumed he meant "I'll keep doing what I'm doing and you keep doing what you're doing, *capiche*?" That seemed fair enough so she nodded.

Time passed, but it was inconsequential. There was only this piece of fire, that piece of fire, the next and the next. The helicopter swerved and dipped, corkscrewing around an area. She'd didn't think she'd be sick, but her stomach violently protested the speed and maneuverability of the helicopter. A sharp burn of bile tickled the back of her throat and she coughed, trying to dislodge it. It set off a five minute coughing fit that left her feeling red in the face, her eyes watering profusely. She finally got it under control and went back to work, struggling with a section. She couldn't make it surrender. She couldn't bend it to her will. And she was tired. If her magic were a muscle it would be trembling and shaking, looking at her with accusatory eyes and asking *why are you still doing this to me?*

"I can't…"

She thought she voiced her problems out loud, but when the words were repeated she realized they were coming from Adam. "I need to get closer. I can't do this from here anymore."

God, Jade felt the same way. It had felt easy to work from the helicopter so she hadn't questioned it, but now, feeling fatigued and worn out, she felt too far away from the fire. When she and Lily were small, they used to play a game on merry-go-rounds at the park. The Shoe Game. They'd pull off their shoes, chucking them far away from the merry go round, just far enough they'd be almost out of reach. Then, they'd run, sock-feet, not caring as the gravel of the park dug into their heels. They'd hop on the merry-go-round and lie down, their chest and belly against the cold, pockmarked metal. They'd hang on with one arm, and both legs and reach their other hand out, trying to get their shoe. If they'd managed to make it too easy for themselves, the shoe easily within reach, they'd push it out with their fingers, trying to make it harder. Then they'd start again - pushing the old merry-go-round until it spun as fast as they could make it. They'd lie down on the metal, feeling the imprint of the raised-star pattern on their chest. It was probably a miracle she didn't have that permanently embedded in her flesh. The metal had been warm in the summer and cold the rest of the seasons, frigidly so in winter. Of course, everyone else's parents knew enough to keep their kids inside in the winter, but Lily and Jade's parents had been drunk and vacant the majority of the time and hadn't cared so long as Lily and Jade weren't there and asking for things like a sandwich or a cup of juice. So the playground it was, making up games to play by themselves. They would stretch, their shoulder joint and forearm burning, reaching out with nail-bitten fingers, all to grab their own shoe.

Reaching for her magic was starting to feel like that now. Effort, strain, pulling, slight pain. But it was there. It was *so close*.

"The only way to get closer is to dead drop you down there."

"Jade, I don't think that's a good idea." Paris' voice was in her ear at the same time that Adam turned to look at her, assessing.

"What's a dead drop?" Jade asked Adam.

"How is your magic holding up?" Paris asked; at the same time, Adam answered, "They drop us on the ground. Closer to the fire."

"How much closer?" Paris immediately asked.

"We'd be right on the ground, in the fire," Adam answered.

Jade frowned. "How do we get out if we need to?"

"Same as you get in," one of the pilots answered. "We drop you, and you have to hike the rest of the way in. If we need to get you, you have to hike back out. We can't get too close to the fire due to updraft."

"When you say hike..." Jade began, letting her words trail off.

"Three to four kilometers," Adam replied and the co-pilot nodded. "How's your fitness?"

"Okay, I guess. I run."

"What's your mileage?"

She kind of ran along to the playlists until she felt like stopping. When she started, she was diligent about tracking her distance, but now she just knew how long she needed. She tried to think about her runs with Daniel. "Uh, I do a couple 5Ks a week. And then maybe a 10K on the weekends. I'm not super fast, but my cardio's okay."

Adam nodded. "That'll do."

The co-pilot added, "We could send down a rescue basket if it gets sketchy, but if it were sketchy, there's usually too much wind resistance from the fire."

"What's the scientific definition and quantification of *sketchy*?" Jade deadpanned. This all sounded scary as fuck. But also a workable idea. She could do more from on the ground. It wasn't like she thought getting out of the helicopter was a good idea, but she couldn't imagine doing much more from where she was. It was too much stretching and reaching.

"How many times have you been dead-dropped?" she asked Adam. The words felt strange on her tongue, like she was some kind of hipster wannabe, using terminology she didn't know just to be cool.

"Once. I was down on the ground for a couple hours and then air-lifted out."

"And it worked?"

Adam paused and then nodded.

"There was a pause there. Why?" Jade demanded. She needed to know. Paris wasn't actively asking questions, but she could feel him listening, wanting the same answers.

"It's tough down there too. It's hot."

"No shit."

"Hotter than you think. Hotter than you're ready for. And the earth.... It cracks. The trees... scream." Adam took one look at her expression and hurried on. "You might not feel it. It depends on how good your Earth magic is. The Earth is burning. It's dying. And it's not going down happy or easy. It hurts. It's harder to concentrate, but easier to work fire magic being closer, if that makes sense."

Jade touched her radio, feeling more in touch with Paris as she did. "Did you catch that, English?"

"Adam's correct. Depending on how sensitive you are to Earth magic, it may very well be quite uncomfortable on the ground. And..." He hesitated. "I don't like the idea." Each word sounded like it was a full sentence - like they had been forcibly pulled from his mouth with a set of pliers.

"Do you think it could work?" Jade looked at Adam when she said it, but it was both Paris and Adam that answered.

Adam answered immediately. "Yes."

Paris took a fraction of a second longer. "Yes."

The pilots were staring at her. How she managed to be the ruling vote, she didn't know, but the weight of it was heavy and cumbersome. She was scared, but wanted to try. She thought of those maps spread out on Danvers' tables - houses, hospitals, convenience stores, parks. It was all in the path of the fire if they couldn't stop it. She wanted to try.

"Okay." Jade took a deep breath and exhaled. "Dead drop it is."

#

If the fire suit was unflattering before, it was downright criminal now.

The co-pilot helped Jade into some kind of a harness that pinched and cut across her body in intricate and uncomfortable ways. She hadn't asked the co-pilot's name before and now that he'd nearly had to grope her inappropriately to get her into the harness, it seemed a little late to ask. He'd handed her a bottle of water and she'd jammed it into a side leg pocket. It stood out horrendously, like an extra limb, pulling at the fabric.

Given how much access the co-pilot had to her body and how much he'd touched her, it had been a very methodical, clinical and logical process. Jade had frozen at first, when he reached out with the straps in his hand, but he gave off a professional *let's get this done* vibe. It was like at yoga, the few times she'd been dragged by Lily, Callie and Henri. The instructors there had a non-threatening vibe and although she'd probably sucker punch anyone else who stepped that close to her it was okay. The co-pilot was the same. He turned and went through the exact same process with Adam and his harness - clinical and logical.

Standing in a helicopter was kind of like being drunk on a boat, she guessed. She had to have a certain sway and bob to her knees to go with the motion, but not so far she'd tip over.

"Who wants to go first?" the co-pilot asked.

"I will," Adam replied. "You can watch me and then you'll know what to expect," he said to Jade.

"Thanks." She was pretty sure he couldn't hear her quiet response over the din of the aircraft, but he must have read her lips because he nodded.

"Will the radios still work down there?" asked Paris, his voice coming over the radio clearly.

The co-pilot nodded, as if forgetting that Paris couldn't see him. "Should do okay unless we get too much smoke interference."

"And if they need to be pulled out?" Again, Paris with the good questions. Jesus, she was glad he was asking them. Jade was too busy watching Adam get rigged up to some kind of pulley system. The co-pilot slid the door to the helicopter open and the cabin was flooded with more air, noise and an impossible amount of smoke. She hadn't thought more smoke was possible and she gagged on the smell. Adam was swung outside the helicopter. Outside where only birds should be. Her heart stuttered.

Unfazed by the wind, the noise and the smoke, the co-pilot was talking, answering Paris' question, Jade realized. "They tell us they need to be extracted. We come back here and send down the cables. They hook themselves up and we winch them in."

Jesus fuck. Was she supposed to have memorized how Adam got hooked up? Was there a manual she could take with her? This was a bad idea. She'd rather go back to the Dearth, hang out with Seth, and face Medusa. But it felt too late to change her mind. Adam gave the thumbs up gesture and then he was descending, dropping to the ground. Jade's stomach lurched in sympathetic response.

Shouldn't they be closer to the ground before they started dropping him? Shouldn't there be some kind of workshop for this? She lost sight of Adam once he descended about half way. Jade shuffled a step closer to the open door. Nearly all the cells in her body protested vehemently at her proximity to the door. She looked down her nose, unable to tip herself forward to see him. It was hard to tell from her angle how far from the ground he was. Suddenly, the cable went slack and she flinched before realizing that meant he was on the ground.

"I'm good. Unhooking. Okay, you can take it back up now." Adam sounded confident and calm. Just got dropped out of a helicopter. No big deal. Jade's stomach clenched tightly.

The co-pilot hit a switch and the cable came back up, too fast for Jade's liking.

"Are you sure you want to do this?"

It took her a moment to realize that wasn't her internal monologue, it was Paris.

"You don't have to," he continued. She wished he was next to her instead of only a voice over the radio.

"I know," she said, even though she felt like she did have to do this. She could say no and back out, but then what? Her magic couldn't reach and stretch for the fire anymore, so if she didn't go down and get closer, she'd just be done. What then? Go back to the hotel and face everyone and admit she couldn't do it? She was good with fire. She knew she could do more. She just couldn't do it from here.

"I know," she repeated, this time feeling more secure. "I want to. I can help."

The co-pilot knelt before her with his arms stretched out, waiting for her to step into his personal space so he could hook her up.

"If I get into trouble, I'll ask to be pulled out. I promise."

"I'll hold you to that."

"You better. You also better make sure there's wine tonight at the hotel. I'm not doing all this and not having a drink when I get back."

Paris laughed and it was blush-inducing. "What kind of wine do you like?"

Jade stepped closer to the co-pilot and he started clipping her to the pulley lines. She watched what he did as he did it. "Uh, I'm not choosy. But I don't like thin wines."

"Thin?"

"Yeah, you take a drink and it's like thin on your tongue. Like someone forgot half the taste."

"You mean you prefer something more robust."

"Uh, sure." The co-pilot seemed satisfied she was clipped in. Jade wanted to ask him to go over all the clips again, but it probably wouldn't help her feel any better. He gave her an inquisitive thumbs up and she tried to smile, but knew it was at best a loose approximation of a grimace.

He pulled the cables and hoisted her off her feet.

"Jesus!"

"Are you alright?" Paris asked immediately.

"Can you not ask any questions right now?" she blurted. "But keep talking. Something super English."

She swung outside the helicopter and there was nothing underneath her feet. Except maybe her baby cakes if they came back up. God, she didn't want to barf on herself. Okay, new metric: as long as she didn't barf on herself, this would be considered a success, no matter what else happened.

"Oh, um, of course. I assume you're looking for a distraction?"

"No questions," Jade replied, jaw tight so tight the muscles in her cheek spasmed.

"Right, yes. Um, do you know we have a witches camp? Unfortunately, you're too old for it, but it's quite the milestone for our younger witches. You can't attend until you've passed certain spell work, but once you do, it's open to all witches in their pre-teen and teen years. It's quite memorable for those that attend. I went for a few years as a camper and then a few more as a counselor."

"So help me god, if this is a story about hooking up at summer camp…" Jade stared to give Paris grief and then a strong gust of hot wind hit her and she swayed with it, clamping her lips shut. She didn't want to die like this. She looked up to where the co-pilot was still winching her down. He seemed unconcerned. She really should've asked his name. Her life was in his hands.

"What? Of course not. Parents send their children, Jade. Children."

She wanted to argue with him that he'd said teenagers, not children, but she was too busy hanging on for dear life. "What do you do at camp?" she managed.

"Oh, it's quite festive." Jesus, only Paris could use the word festive and not be ironic. "Each day there's an activity. We partner with some local farms and the witches get to ride horses or feed cattle. Gather eggs from a hen house. It's all very grounding; helps them realize the world is full of living things and they're a part of it. There's a rope course where they can work on their trust skills. You have to trust your fellow Coven members to assist you across the course or work as a team to solve a problem."

God this was all sounding more and more like shit she would fail. Team work? Problem solving? Maybe it was for the best that she never went to Witch Camp. The ground was getting closer, too fast and not fast enough all at once.

"We have arts and crafts and there's a hike out. We have to pack up all the supplies needed for a couple days and hike out with tents and such. Live off the land."

God, camp sounded worse. Everything was all outside. She liked being inside. Inside was where the sofas were and the coffee was hot and fresh. The ground was getting closer. Adam was there, looking up at her expectantly, like he would help her land. He was kind of an asshole, but he was turning out to be not all bad.

"At night, there's a campfire, magical of course, and everyone gathers. There are songs and stories. It's very heartwarming."

She might barf. Not from his stories about camp, but from how fast she was approaching the ground. And okay, a little from the camp stories. The ground rushed to meet her and she felt the jolt of landing in every joint of her body - toes to jaw. Maybe even in her skull. Tough to say. Adam's hands grabbed at her shoulders to steady her and she was grateful for the stability.

"I'm down. I'm on the ground." Her hands shook as she unclipped herself, completely missing one of the links. Adam got it for her and she managed a tight-lipped smile. She pat herself down, needing to check all her bits were still where they should be. She looked up and saw the lines that had carried her down disappearing back into the sky, toward the helicopter. It seemed so small from the ground.

"Do you have a preference?" Adam asked.

"Er, no? What?" Jade asked, not sure what he meant.

He pulled out a map. Why did he have a map? Jade didn't have a map. Goddamn, was she supposed to have gotten a map?

"I think we need to divide and conquer. I can take the west side if you can do the east." He pointed to vaguely west and east directions on the map. Jade looked up and then into the forest. She paused, wondering how close the fire would feel now.

Taking a deep breath, she unfurled her magic, letting it run loose in the forest. She knew the fire would feel stronger on the ground, or rather, she suspected. Like an archeologist, she scratched at the dirt.

It needed. It devoured. It wanted.

It was a black hole in front of her - endless, timeless, a wide open maw. Nothing except need and hunger. It lay waste to anything in its path.

Her magic reacted. She didn't mean to, but she pushed out against it. It pushed back - hard, angry, unyielding.

"What are you doing?"

Jade blinked, not recognizing Adam's question at first.

"Jade, what's happening?"

Paris' voice in her ear was a touchstone, a heavy anchor pulling her back.

"Nothing, I tried to reach out and I wasn't prepared." She squared her shoulders, pulling them back and away from her ears. "I'm okay. I'm ready. Yes, the east. I can do that."

Adam rolled the map back up and stuffed it in his back pocket. It would never survive the heat, Jade thought. "Okay, we'll stay in contact by radio. If you need extraction, you come back here or wherever the pilots tell you."

"I can do that."

"Good luck. May the Goddess be with you," Adam said.

"Uh, same to you. See you when we're done."

He nodded, a grim expression on his face, then turned his back to her, walking away and into the forest.

Jade swallowed, turning east. She didn't need to push her magic out to know where she needed to go. The fire was a pulsing heartbeat on the horizon. She could feel it lurking, looming, lying in wait. A ravenous, insatiable thing. She touched her radio, needing to know she still had it on, that Paris was at the other end.

"Can we switch to another channel? Just you and me?" she asked. She wanted to talk to him, but didn't want everyone else to hear.

"Yes, er, let me check." He was silent for a moment. "Channel six is free."

She switched the dials on her set. "You there?"

"Yes. This is a limited channel at the moment. No one but us."

Jade smiled. "Okay. So, tell me more about these camp songs," she said as she stepped into the forest.

CHAPTER FOURTEEN

Jade was glad they were on a semi-private channel. Not that anything Paris was saying was super secret, but she didn't have to worry they were hogging the main line or that everyone was listening in.

"Didn't you ever go to summer camp?" Paris asked.

She thought back to her summers as a child. They were interminable, endless stretches of trying to keep herself out of the house and away from her father and mother. Lily's father and mother, she guessed. All while still trying to keep herself fed and clean. She and Lily would get up early and pack some food and hop on their bike - a horrible clunky thing. Despite its looks, it functioned quite well. They'd done some chores around the neighborhood and bought a drink holder and padded handlebars. It had been red and white and they'd found some old silver nail polish and painted stripes on it. They'd bike around town and have lunch. Maybe hang out with some other kids (if Lily was in charge - Jade didn't like to socialize too much). Then they'd bike home, hoping Dad was already passed out drunk or out of the house and Mom… well, they didn't usually worry about Mom, actually. She was always there, but not really *there*.

"Uh, no. Didn't have the chance."

"Oh, I suppose not."

She could hear in Paris' tone he knew exactly why they hadn't had the opportunity to go to camp. Her fire suit itched and she pulled at the collar. "I guess I'll have to live vicariously through you. Arts and crafts? Songs? Camp outs? I feel like I'm listening to a 1980's feel-good comedy. Unless there was suddenly a freak with an axe who terrorized you and you've been left haunted and scarred all these years."

"Pardon me?"

"You know, 1980's slasher flicks? Kids at camp, making out and then whap! Death by axe."

"What sorts of movies have you seen?" he mused in her ear.

"What sorts have you missed out on? Late night cable was one of the only companions I had." When she said it like that, it was dismal and depressing. But she'd liked watching those films. She still did. Back then, late at night, when she'd been sure their dad was asleep or passed out, she could finally relax. It had been fun to be scared by the films, but not worry that fists were going to hit and bruise her. "You're telling me that not one person was murdered horrendously at your witches camp? Ever?"

"It's rather charming and quaint, I suppose." His tone was fond, warm. It made her happy. "I went for three years and then was a camp counselor for another three years."

"Oh my god, did you make out with all the girl camp counselors? Or boys," she hastily added. "No judgment."

"Hardly," Paris answered, his voice dry. Jade pushed some brush out of her way with her hands as she hiked, focusing on Paris' voice. "My mother was Coven Leader. I was expected to maintain a very high level of decorum and behavior, as befitting the future Coven Leader."

"Yeesh. That sounds really boring." She blinked her eyes. With the smoke, they were drying out something fierce. Not even the Dearth had been this bad.

"But... you and Veronica. You were a thing, right? Was that at camp?" Ugh, she didn't mean to ask it like that, but it had come out and now was out there.

"Yes, we were involved in a relationship some time ago, but it wasn't at camp."

Jade nodded, before she realized how absurd it was since he couldn't see her. She kept on hiking, farther into the forest, closer to the fire. She couldn't tell if it was getting hotter as she hiked or it was just exertion. Paris chatted more about camp - the rope course again, some kind of team exercise where they were set loose in the forest and had to capture a flag or something. Bad oatmeal at breakfast. Having to eat everything on your plate, even if you didn't want to.

Compared to her childhood of dodging beatings and trying to stay alive, she felt small and...

resentful? She didn't know. Shouldn't that have been her life? Witch camp? Coming home to a petite blonde mother who had eyes that matched her own? Maybe her mom would have made her hot chocolate or made sure her sheets were fresh and clean. Her eyes burned and she didn't know if it was the smoke or something else. She didn't have time or the energy for it to be something else.

"This is Adam, sorry to break into your channel, but I've gone as far as I can. About two klicks in. I'm starting my fire work now."

"Uh, okay," Jade responded. "I don't..." She looked around and carefully, gently, reached her magic out. The fire was close. Hungry, angry, and close. *But not quite where I want it be*, she thought. "I need to hike in a bit more."

"Are you sure?" Paris asked. "If Adam's in two kilometers, you likely are close to that as well."

"I am. I mean, I think I am. But I feel like I need to be closer."

"Check in when you get where you want to be," Adam said. "I'm getting back to work."

Did she say roger? Roger dodger? Was there appropriate radio lingo? "Uh, okay. Thanks. I'll let you know."

She pulled out her bottle of water and drank a couple mouthfuls. She was glad she was moderately fit or this would really suck, and she said as much over the radio.

"Not that I've been running a lot lately," she added.

"Well, you've had several intense experiences. And your leg was injured when you came back from the Dearth."

"Yeah," she murmured. It bothered her now. The wound was healed, but was an awful dark pink-purple color. She knew scars faded, but it would take years on her fair skin. Her hand drifted up to her neck, running over the marble patch of skin there. She didn't think that would ever fade. It was part of her now.

If she'd had physical scars from when she'd been assaulted, she wondered if they'd be like the scar on her leg - vicious-looking, but able to fade in time, or if they would have been like the patch on her neck - not as noticeable, but a permanent part of her, forever unable to be changed.

"Are you all right?" Paris asked.

"Yeah, why?"

"I wasn't sure if you had something to add or if you were thinking."

She wasn't able to articulate her thoughts, certainly not over a radio channel where anyone could listen if they chose. "Maybe I'm waiting for the next camp story, or for you to sing campfire songs?"

He laughed and she smiled at the sound.

"I'm afraid the only one I remember is about a randy aardvark."

"What?" She laughed. "You can't be serious."

"I am! He was lonely and found a lady aardvark and they had to spirit away somewhere private."

"Was there wine? Did he wine and dine her?"

He hummed a bit and she was confused until she realized he was singing the song in his head, recalling it. "I don't think so. I think it was more about them finding each other and being happy."

"That is so nerdy and precious. Was it a naughty song? Did you guys all blush?"

"We did!" he exclaimed. "It was horrible. As a camper, I hated it, but as a counselor, I relished making everyone blush."

"If you had to, so did they," she surmised.

"Just so."

She hiked for twenty more minutes while he told her more camp stories, including a time they played capture the flag and he was 'kidnapped' by the opposing team and made to wait in a small, badly-constructed, thatched house.

"English, that's so undignified. Did you sit on the dirt?" she teased, trying to imagine it.

"I did. I'm quite good at being outdoors." He sounded affronted and she stifled her laughter.

Just then, a zing of power plucked her magic, like a string instrument finding the right harmonic. She paused. *Here*. She was here.

"I think I'm where I need to be." She turned in a slow circle. It was like any other part of the forest in her sight, but when she reached out with her magic, it was like hitting the right pace on a hanging bridge and feeling it sway immediately, finding its natural resonance. "Yeah, this is good. I'm going to get back to work."

"Do you know where you are?"

"Not really, but I know where I need to focus, if that makes sense?" Her magic felt like it was waking up from a really satisfying nap - the kind where you sleep hard and deep, unaware its still day time. She started working with the fire again. It was different this time, not being able to see what she was doing. Being in the helicopter had enabled her to get visual feedback, but now, she only had the sense of her magic to go by. In her mind, the fire was a long line, undulating along the landscape, moving closer to the highway. It was easy enough to picture it and work on burning it out. She could sense Adam as well - and more distantly, Michael and Clay. Adam was like a medium-sized star - visible to her magic senses, but Michael and Clay were more like dark matter. She could sense their work, but couldn't pinpoint where they were; she was only able to sense the after-affects of their presence.

Like before, she lost her sense of time. There was a rhythm and roll to it. Feel the fire, feel how it burned, burn it hotter, eat all its fuel, crush it, and move on. Wash, rinse, repeat. Holy god, there was so much of it. At one point, she paused, stretching her magic along the length of the entire highway. It was demoralizing in its length. She didn't know how much they expected her to do, and she couldn't imagine quitting before she was done.

A stutter of magic from Adam made her pause. "Adam?" she asked, wondering if he was still on the private channel with her and Paris.

"What it is?" Paris asked.

Jade shook her head. "I don't know. I'm switching channels." She flipped her radio back to the main channel. Adam," she said again, "was that you?"

"I can't..." He was breathing hard, his inhalations and exhalations loud and ragged in her ear. It made Jade realize she was breathing hard as well. She swiped at her forehead. She was hot. Now that she took a break from magic, she realized she was drenched in sweat. Her ponytail clung to the back of her neck when she moved her head. The forest was deathly still and quiet around her. Her water bottle was empty, clutched in one of her hands. She had no memory of finishing it.

"You can't what?" she asked.

"I need an extract. I can't... I'm out. My magic isn't responding."

"We've got your coordinates, but we can't land," answered one of the pilots over the radio. "You're too deep in the forest, the fire's too close. Can you hike back out?"

"I don't... I don't...." His voice trailed off.

"Jesus, can you get him out?" Jade asked. "What about the basket? Can you lower it down and grab him?"

"He's too close to the fire."

Jade paused, sending her magic out again, looking for Adam. Instead of a medium-sized star, he was now like a dim bulb, flickering. Not even a regular light bulb. He was an old-time Edison bulb - dark yellow and hardly luminous. And the fire... the fire was approaching.

"Adam, can you cast a circle around yourself?" Jade didn't know if it would protect him. She only knew her own circles were protective in nature.

"I think so. But I can't... I waited too long. The fire is turning this way and I... I don't think I can stop it."

He was right. Jade could feel the fire moving toward him. He was a vacuum now that he wasn't actively casting, and the fire was a living, intelligent thing that sensed his weakness. "I think I can. Stop it," she clarified. "But you need to cast a circle so I know exactly where you are."

"Jade, you're taxing your own magic," Paris cautioned, back on the public channel.

"I know, but?" She didn't know how to finish. She knew Paris was right, but at the same time, what were her choices? Leave Adam in the forest? To burn?

There was a weak pulse of magic from Adam. In her mind, she saw a circle of blue rise up from her mental map of the forest. A lazy smoke ring.

"I see you now," she murmured. She rooted around, searching for the edge of the fire. It was approaching him. His magic was a residual echo overlaid on top. He'd been holding it back for some time. While Jade had been eating up the forest in the path of the fire, Adam had only been able to try to turn the fire from the highway. He didn't have the same power she had; he'd not been able to send his own magic out to preemptively devour the trees and deprive the fire of its fuel.

The fire had gotten far closer to Adam than she realized and she didn't think she could work the same magic near him. Her magic was too powerful and not controlled enough. If she had better control... ugh, she needed to be a laser, but she was a flashlight - sending out her magic in too wide of an arc. She'd burn him alive if she tried to chew up the fuel around him.

But...

But...

Adam had been pushing the fire away from the highway. He made his magic a rock the fire couldn't go past. She sent her magic out and tried to do the same thing. To be a stone in the path of the fire; a barrier the fire couldn't pass, couldn't go any further.

It wasn't working.

The blue circle of Adam's magic was fading. He was tired. The pilots were taking in her ear and she didn't understand them. Their chatter crowded her mind when all she wanted to focus on was the fire, and keeping it from Adam. Adam and the highway. Something in her neck felt like it snapped, sending a ping of power into her skull, wrapping around her eye. Like when she turned her neck too fast and had a pulled muscle. It hurt. It made her magic wobble. She couldn't *push* the fire anymore.

But maybe she could *pull* it. Jade imagined the fire was a large, heavy wool blanket, spread out across the forest and instead of pushing at the edge, she slung it over her shoulder and turned from it and *pulled*. Something else in her fractured. She pressed at her forehead. Sweat dripped down her face and her upper lip and she swiped at it, surprised when her hand came back covered in blood. Her nose was bleeding. She should stop. The precursor of a migraine pulsed at the base of her skull and when she looked to her surroundings, everything had a strange halo around it. Ocular rings of light encircled the trees, the grass, the sky.

The pilots' chatter was a din, but she made out they were close to Adam. They were lowering the harness and he was buckling himself in. When she looked up to the sky, she didn't see the sky in front of her, but instead saw the sky on top of Adam. She could sense a hot updraft of air about to hit the chopper, poised to knock it from its messy hover. She pulled at that too, reaching out with her hand and making a grabbing motion.

The fire, previously an insane, ravenous thing, took note of her. It *saw* her. It recognized in her a threat to its existence. She no longer had to actively pull it to her; it came of its own free will. The power in it recognizing the power in her and wanting more.

"Oh shit." She turned in a slow circle. Everywhere she looked, she saw blurred images and strange striations. Heat waves changed the landscape in front of her. Pain stabbed her grey matter and she shut her eyes.

"What's wrong?"

Jade clutched at her head. This migraine came on fast. It slithered into her grey matter and took hold with hooked barbs, digging deep into her skull. She heard distantly as the pilots' confirmed they had Adam. Suddenly, there was earth beneath her fingers, her palms. She was clutching at the ground, on her knees. She didn't know when it had happened. The fire was a roar in her ears and against her magic.

"I fucked up," she managed.

"You need to be extracted," Paris said, and she laughed, wetly, swiping at the blood from her nose.

"Yeah, yeah, I do." The earth was warm under her hands. The fire was coming, the heat of it a precursor.

"Cast a circle," Paris instructed her, just as she had Adam. She reached out with her magic and started the rudimentary arcs for a circle and... failed. Tendrils of her magic rose to the air flitted away. She thought of Bruce. If she had him here, he could have helped. But he was miles away. As if conjured by her magic, her phone buzzed in the pocket of her pants, a dull thud against her skin.

She tried to push to her feet, pressing her palms into the earth, but couldn't stand. She'd taxed her magic too much.

"I'm sorry, I'm sorry," she repeated. She'd promised she would be careful, and she had been, she was, but she was in the middle of a forest fire and her magic wasn't responding. She pulled at it again and felt something deep in herself tear. Something wet and heavy fell out of her nose and she stared dumbly at the blood clot in front of her. It hovered on the ground for a moment and then sunk into the earth.

"Cast a circle. I need you to try." Paris voice surprised her. Where was it coming from? Oh yes, the radio, around her neck.

She pulled at her magic and again found... nothing. She stretched out her hand and pressed her fingers into the ground, pulling her arm in an arc. Da Vinci's *Vitruvian Man* flashing before her eyes. A mathematical marvel. She was a child again, on a merry-go-round, the world spinning madly as she stretched and reached. Trees blurring, ground rushing past. She was stretching, reaching, trying, her fingertips so close, so close, and then nothing. She curled in on herself. She hurt. Everything hurt. She shouldn't have pulled so hard, she shouldn't have hiked so far. She shouldn't have, she shouldn't have....

Jade inhaled and tasted dirt. Grass, moss and earth. She wanted to spit it out. Someone was driving a spike through her brain she needed it to stop. And then, from behind her, the fire. Oh god, the fire. It was hot, hungry and angry. She curled up tighter. She was sorry, she was so sorry. Her fingers dug into the ground, dirt pressing uncomfortably against her nails. It hurt too, but it was real, it was there. And on top of everything was Paris' voice.

#

His phone was going wild in his pocket - vibrations, ring tones, text alerts. For all he knew, the entire Coven could be falling apart. He couldn't think about it. Jade's voice was all he focused on.

"I fucked up." Her voice wobbled as she spoke, betraying her exhaustion and panic.

"You need to be extracted." He scanned the room, looking for Danvers. If there was a way to get Jade out, he would know. Paris moved through the crowd, keeping his attention focused on his radio. She wasn't as clear any longer as she had been, as though she weren't wearing the gear correctly.

"Yeah, yeah, I do."

"Cast a circle." He wasn't sure how much protection it would offer, but it would be something. Danvers looked up from his table, listening to his own radio and Paris knew in that moment he was getting information about Adam's extraction, and Jade's situation.

"I'm sorry, I'm sorry."

He didn't know what she was apologizing for and he was afraid to ask. Her voice was thick and wet, slightly slurred. It didn't bode well for her state. He'd heard Adam on the radio, trapped by the fire, and he'd known Jade would respond; in that moment, he resented her for it. It was the right thing to do, and she'd done it. He wished she'd hadn't. Not that he wanted Adam to suffer, but she'd saved him at the cost of herself. Adam was safely extracted by the pilots and Jade....

"Cast a circle," he repeated. "I need you to try." Jade's magic was powerful when it was protecting her. He remembered when she'd used one to keep her safe from Dex. Though he also remembered she'd cast a circle to ward off his mother and it hadn't worked. This was different, he reminded himself. Jade wasn't facing someone intelligently malicious, like his mother. She was up against a force of nature. Perhaps nature would also protect her.

He reached out with his own magic, searching for hers. She was a small spark in the center of a maelstrom. Pulsing dimly. Getting dimmer.

"Jade needs to be extracted," he said, finally reaching Danvers.

"I know, I've got the pilots on the radio. But they can't get to her. The fire's moved too far."

"Then send people in on the ground. I'll go."

Danvers shook his head. "How would I get you there?"

"Fly me in. As close as you can."

Danvers shook his head again. "I don't think you realize the situation." He motioned with his hand for one of the data scientists to come over.

"No, I don't think *you* realize the situation." Paris gestured hotly toward the marshal. "We put her out there to help and now she's trapped. I don't think she has much magic left."

"I get that, but we can't get her out. We'd kill people trying."

The small data scientist with the spiky hair set her laptop down on the desk, pivoting it toward Paris and Danvers. "Um, so I don't know exactly what happened; we're still chunking and reviewing the data. But there was some kind of weather inversion and the fire was bolstered by the wind. That's where the one witch was caught." She pointed to an area of her screen where an animated fire was happily chomping up a swath of land next to the highway, where Adam had been. "And then the other witch-"

"Jade. Her name is Jade," Paris interrupted.

The woman nodded. "I mean, I don't know how magic works exactly, but Jade pulled that part of the fire toward her, I think. But there was already an increase headed her way. And now there are these two streams." She motioned with her hands, dove-tailing them together. "Coming toward her." Her eyes were wide and she looked back and forth from Danvers to Paris and back again. "I mean, can't she use more magic?"

"It's not like that," Paris began tersely. "She was already out there for hours and she's... she's mortal." He shook his head. "Even if she weren't, Adam is another example. He used too much and couldn't do anymore. And now Jade..."

"Oh." She looked back down at her screen. "I... I mean, the fire... we didn't know about the inversion. We get the best data we can, but... we didn't know. And then it takes time to process."

It wasn't her fault. It wasn't anyone's fault and he wanted to say that, but the words failed him. His palms tingled hot and cold. He wanted to ask again over the radio if Jade was all right, but she wasn't, and she wouldn't be. She was trapped in a forest fire with no extraction planned. His phone continued to buzz in his pocket and to give himself a moment to think, he reached for it and pulled it out.

It was Lily. Lily calling him, Lily texting him. An ending stream of messages about how she couldn't contact Jade and something felt wrong and one of them needed to call her right away. He put it face down on the table. He needed to think.

"I'm sorry," Danvers said. "But we can't get her out."

Paris stared at the map on the table in front of him. He could see where Danvers had marked with dry erase pen Adam's location and then Jade's. Further off to the side were the other two witches.

"Call them in," Paris said, gesturing to the other witches, Michael and Clay. "They may be able to contain the fire, keep it from reaching Jade."

Danvers nodded. "I have people moving them already."

"But they're exhausted too, aren't they?" Paris murmured, hearing the hesitation in Danvers' voice.

"Yeah. They are."

Paris ran his finger across the map, tracing the space from where Jade was to him - from the forest to the hotel in the city. He scratched at the map for a moment, a thought forming.

"How deep does a fire burn?" he asked.

"Pardon? I don't follow." Danvers shook his head.

"A forest fire, how deep does it burn?"

"Depends on the fire. Some crown fires actually burn more underground than above. And you heard the scientists the other day talking about waiting for next winter. Even if we get this under control, it can smolder in the earth, feeding off roots and moss."

Unbidden, he recalled his thought from earlier. That somewhere, near the Coven, Jade's mortal body was buried. Her mother'd had a funeral for her. There'd been a ceremony. She'd been interred in the earth, returning her back to Mother Nature.

"What are you thinking?" Danvers asked.

Paris ran his fingers across the map again, fingertips tracing the distance. He stood suddenly. "I need to be outside."

His body was further ahead in the plan than his mind. He felt like an automaton as he made his way through the large ballroom, the foyer of the lobby, past the concierge desk. He turned sideways to slip through the slow-moving sliding doors demarcating inside from outside. Once finally outside, he stared dumbfounded at the concrete surface of the parking lot. It would not do. Off to the side was a patch of earth. A small, sad garden in front of the hotel. Hardy perennials were embedded in the earth - the kind of flowers picked for sturdiness and strength, not beauty. He knelt and pressed his hand into the earth. Earth had always been his strongest power. He sent his magic out and felt the roots of the flowers, bland and lackluster. They would bloom, but only because there was no other option for them. Chemical additives fed them what was required and it was good enough. He pushed his magic out further, dimly aware Danvers was behind him, along with the young data scientist.

"What are you doing?"

"He's looking for her."

It was the Fae representative assigned to the fire who answered. Paris had found him earlier and asked for further assistance. He'd assured Paris he would contact the Council. Out of the corner of his eye, the Fae stood impassive. A stoic, strange presence.

"You could you get her out." Paris looked up at him. He still had the presence of mind not to ask a question of the Fae. He hoped his words didn't sound like an accusation either.

The Fae man inclined his head slightly in agreement. "Your kind do not enter into exchanges or requests with my kind often. I understand it's because you find our way of measuring and balancing cruel."

"You're more akin to being amoral than immoral, I suppose."

"We are as close to Nature as we can be. Nature is neither kind or benevolent. Nature is." He paused and Paris felt the words he wanted to say rising up in his throat, clawing their way to his lips. Demands. Pleas. Anything that would help Jade.

The Fae spoke again before Paris could. "Retrieval, in such a maelstrom as this, is difficult."

Paris' magic split in the ground, one tendril snaking upward to find the Fae who stood before him, even as the majority of his magic was searching for Jade. It was a strange void where the Fae stood. No, not quite a void. More like... he was in near perfect resonance with the Earth. Because of that, he was nearly indistinguishable from Earth herself. Paris sunk his fingers deeper into the ground, discarding the Fae and searching for Jade. He felt the Earth welcome him and his magic. He was a calm, static presence, one the Earth appreciated.

He felt the fire. Angry, harsh, destructive. The Earth cried out in response. The fire devoured life and the Earth didn't know how to stop it, couldn't stop it.

The fire *consumed*. The fire *annihilated*. It was a hot, ferocious thing, and it devastated anything in its wake.

Along the lines of the earth, he found her. Jade. He could see the soft, fragile bubble of her magic stretched out, thin and weak around her. The fire pressed against it. To it, she was fuel. More fodder for the mill. The fire would consume her and move on, always eating always destroying. Always hungry.

But with Earth... Paris could protect her. Earth was a nurturing magic. Strong and implacable at times, but inherently maternal and protective. With Earth, he could *save* her.

He could bury her.

Paris twisted his fingers in the small, sad garden of the hotel parking lot. His magic traveled through the dirt, under the concrete, down along the soil and clay, through the roots of the small grasses and mosses, thin trees and bushes in the city, and then onward to the larger timber and foliage of the outskirts.

Through his magic, he could see her - on the ground, curled into the fetal position, hands and arm protecting her face. He pushed more of his magic out, with the intent to protect her, and the earth responded, sending roots, branches, moss and lichen up to envelope her.

She resisted. She twisted on the ground, writhing against him, against his magic. She pushed at him with weak and tired tendrils of power.

"Please, let me. Let me help you," he murmured, sending his intent into the earth, willing it to travel along the roots in the soil and find her. "Please."

Jade pushed back at him, feeble and thin. It was nothing at all like her normal power, except for the faint taste of cloves at the back of his mouth. He tried to cocoon her with the Earth, sending more power through, focusing on his intent, hoping enough of it made the journey that she would recognize it.

"Here, can you she hear you?"

It was the woman scientist, grabbing at the radio on his chest, her short-bitten fingernails scraping the plastic. He'd forgotten it.

He spoke directly into the device. "Jade, you need to let me help you. I think I can protect you. From the fire. Do you understand?"

"I don't… It's trying to be all over me. You're holding me down. You're pushing me down."

"I am. The Earth will protect you if you let me help." He didn't understand why she was fighting him. Was she too tired to understand? Had she pushed herself too hard and was suffering a migraine?

"I don't like it." Her voice was weak and reedy. Though the Earth, through his hand, now sunk past his wrist, he could feel the fire coming closer to her. A lion at the gate.

He didn't know what to do. The thought of using his magic to overwhelm or overpower her without her consent made him ill. So did the thought of letting her burn to death in the forest.

"Please, let me help you." He repeated and waited for a response.

CHAPTER FIFTEEN

It was hot. And she was tired. Sometimes when she didn't feel good, she would think about how fucking glad she was she was an adult now and could do something about it. Find some Advil, drink some hot tea that people drank when they were sick. When she was sick a kid, no one gave a shit. She had lie there and figure out how she was going to get to school and home and back to school again. Staying at home sick wasn't an option. Not unless you wanted to get your ass kicked.

She was an adult now. Wasn't she? Except this was like being a kid. She couldn't move and she needed to, but her head hurt. Hurt wasn't even the right word for it. Hurt was stubbing your toe and hopping around cursing and hissing, *walk it off, walk it off!!*, feeling like as long as she kept moving the rest of the pain couldn't catch up. But now, it felt like the only thing that would make her head better would be for her to saw her skull open, take out all her cauliflower-shaped grey matter and set it aside on a shelf. Just find the fucking off switch. *Yes, thank you, Brain. I understand some deep and heavy shit has gone down and you're grievously unhappy. Message received. You can stop sending the pain right the fuck now.*

She curled in on herself. She raised her arms and draped them over her head. Her face was hot, her arms were hot. Everything was hot.

Because of the fire. Right. That was a problem. The fire loitered at the edge of her magic. Hungry, always hungry, but she didn't have anything left. She really fucked up. Paris told her; he told her to be careful and she had been. She'd been careful, but then Adam was trapped and and she thought she could help. She was wrong. Or not wrong. She did help, but now she was fucked. She was sorry. A fat lot of good it would do her charred corpse.

She'd probably die of smoke inhalation first, right? Isn't that what they said? She'd be dead long before she actually burned, wouldn't she?

Jesus, this was horrible. She curled in tighter. She missed Bruce. She missed Lily. She missed Paris even though she just saw him a few hours ago. This sucked. She thought she was moving on and making progress with her life. Maybe she was an idiot to think it in the first place. Maybe this was all there ever was going to be. A promise of something, someday, and then bam! Dead by fire. Goddamn it.

Something pulled at her. Everywhere. Something was yanking and pulling and Jesus! It was the ground. Trying to eat her alive! She pushed at it, feeling the wet-noodle ability of her power. She twisted and pulled, finding moss and grass wrapped around her wrists. Entwined around her legs as well. She kicked out, trying to scramble away. What the fuck was this? It wasn't bad enough she was going to burn, now she was going to be eaten by the forest?

A far off sound in her head sounded like Paris. She paused at his voice. He sounded… he sounded… like he was begging. Plaintive. Worried.

Okay, she thought, *step up. All for the helping right here.* Had she said anything out loud? She didn't know. More of the ground pawed at her. It pulled her down, pushing her into the earth. Her hind-brain revolted and she kicked out. She didn't want to go! She didn't want it. It was being held down, being *forced* down. She didn't like it. She didn't want it.

"Jade, you need to let me help you. I think I can protect you. From the fire. Do you understand?"

Her heartbeat was a runaway train in her ear, making it hard to hear Paris' voice. Adrenaline warred with her higher logic. Her heart thumped, her lungs panted, and overtop of both, Paris' voice.

"I don't… It's trying to be all over me. You're trying to hold me down." She kicked at the branches and the grass that wound up her legs. She leaned back on her hands, trying to scoot backwards, only to jerk her hands up when they sunk into the earth, moss, and lichen growing upward on her skin.

"I am," said Paris. "The Earth will protect you. If you let me help."

Jade shook her head. No. She didn't want to. She had to fight, she had to get to her feet if she could. If she lay down, if she got down on the ground, she was lost; she couldn't win.

"I don't like it."

"Please, let me help you."

Jade didn't know if she could. The fire was close. Any closer and it would be licking at her skin - burning, searing. She needed help. But when she thought about not trying to fight... the way the earth crept, slithered over her... Something in her panicked even more. She wanted to scream and cry, but her throat was too tight. God, there had to be another way; this couldn't be the only way to help.

"Stop it. I can't... I can't do this."

"Please, Jade. I don't... I won't force you. But I don't think I can help you any other way."

She glanced around her. The trees snapped and cracked a they started to burn. The fire was closer; the heat of it scalded her. Tree roots enveloping her ankles. Earth magic. Paris' magic. Trying to protect her. She didn't know what it would mean to surrender, to submit. She didn't know if she could. Something deep in her gut and chest urged her to keep struggling, keep fighting back. But... it would mean her death. The fire... a lion at the gate. She kicked her feet, watching them shuffle in the moss and grass.

She inhaled and caught the scent - mint and sandalwood. Paris' magic. Just underneath that, cedar chips and clean laundry. Her heart stuttered. She thought being in the kitchen with him, before the Fae came. How he'd stepped into her space, waiting for her to say no or push him away. The way his body gave off heat. The way his lips had pressed against her forehead. Then in the hotel, the way his magic washed over her as he dried her hair. She breathed in again. He wouldn't hurt her. He didn't want to hurt her. He wanted to help. If she wanted to live, she needed to let him help.

She breathed in this time, hearing a hitch in her breath. She wanted to cry and didn't know why. It wasn't that she was angry, or wanted to keep fighting... but she was scared.

"Okay."

Jade wasn't sure he heard her at first. There was such a long pause and then he repeated her word. "Okay?"

"Okay, I'll let you. Help. I need help." She swallowed and lay down on the ground, exhaling. The sky above her was grey with clouds and smoke. She blinked, hoping it wasn't the last thing she saw.

"Are you sure?"

"Yes? I think so, yes." Something slithered across her ankle and pulled it firmly to the ground. She made make a sound - a noise of distress or fear. Or both.

"Jade?" Paris asked.

"No, I'm okay. I trust you. It's just..." She exhaled again and blinked, tears blurring her vision. God, she was scared. Even though she didn't have much magic left, it was taking everything she had not to lash out with it, not to burn the roots around her legs to ash, even though it would just mean she'd leave herself to burn in the forest. "I trust you," she repeated.

"Close your eyes."

Jade squeezed them shut and felt all of the earth reach up and grab at her - a thousand strands of roots, grass, lichen, and moss. Pressure all over her, stretching up, around her, encompassing her whole. It squeezed her tight; she gasped in one last breath before then the earth swallowed her whole, sucking her into the ground.

#

Jade stood on the dock of the lake, squinting. The light was all wrong. The forest was on fire. The Nature Preserve at the Coven. But that was wrong. She wasn't there. Was she?

Something brushed against her back and she turned, finding Hannah there, holding a deck of cards.

One card, and I'll tell you the future.

Jade shook her head. Hannah threw the cards in the air and they scattered, some landing on the dock, some falling into the water and lazily bobbing and swaying with the surface tension.

You've such potential, but you squander it by being willful.

That was Sakkara's voice in her ear. As soon as Jade recognized it, she heard something else - the flapping of wings. Sparrows. A flock of them crossed over her head and she ducked, afraid she would be caught up in the rush. She couldn't tell if it was about to be night, about to be day, or some kind of Neverland in-between - a perpetual world of strange shadows.

I'll gladly take the title of monster. You should do the same. Monsters always win.

Medusa was at the other end of the dock, by the earth. She walked away from Jade and into the forest. Once there, she stretched her arms wide and tipped, falling backward. As she hit the ground, her hair turned to snakes that burrowed deep, dragging her down into the earth.

A sound on the lake drew Jade's attention. A boat, moving. Rowing away. She could hear the sound of the oars hitting the water, the swoosh of the paddles dragging before they rose up, went above the surface, and plunged back in again.

It was Paris rowing. Rowing away from her. Away from the dock. Away from the shore.

The lake stretched out further than she remembered and she couldn't see the end of the water and the start of the horizon on the other side. She took a step forward, her bare toes curling around the edge of the dock. It was cold. Cold and damp. She called out, called his name. She didn't hear the sound of her voice as it should be. Instead of being loud and clear, bolstered by the echo off the water, it was muffled and nearly mute, as though she were far away from even herself.

Paris didn't stop rowing. Swish, swoosh. The oars maintained their perfect rhythm.

Movement from the side made her turn. A woman stood on the bank of the shore. Sakkara again? Medusa? No, the shape was all wrong.

Yvonne? Jade blinked, confused.

Yvonne's eyes never left Paris as he rowed further and further out. She turned to Jade and their eyes met. Jade shuddered. Yvonne opened her mouth and from it, a crow emerged. Its black body sailed overtop of the lake before swopping down low to land on Paris' shoulder.

Yvonne stood there a moment, illuminated by the strange half- light. Then, she turned and disappeared into the forest.

Jade reached out, as though she could catch Paris and pull him back, but he was too far away. He became smaller and smaller as he rowed, turning into a speck on the horizon. Jade's cheeks were wet and when she touched them, her hands came away stained red with blood.

Sleep.

She slept.

#

His magic was a tether connected to her. One he couldn't let go of nor ignore. The moment she allowed his magic to consume her, to swallow her whole, he was inextricably linked to her. Her heartbeat was a steady, heavy rhythm against his flesh. The sound of her still existing. Of being alive. At the last moment, as she'd been consumed by the earth, he recalled the spell he'd used once when she had a migraine. A spell to put her to sleep. Though he didn't have the same ingredients now, he forced his magic out, used as much power against her as he dared, and willed her to sleep.

"Sleep."

He felt something else. A hand on his shoulder. It pulled his attention from where it wanted to be, six feet under the earth, cocooned with Jade. He turned toward the tactile sensation of his body.

It was the female data scientist, staring at him with large, wide eyes.

"What happened?"

"I buried her."

She was surprised by his answer, her body stiffening. "Is that metaphor, or do you mean you buried her alive?"

He flinched at her words. Jade wasn't buried alive. That implied she was trapped, that she suffered. "No, I buried her with magic."

Her eyes flickered to the earth, the soil of the small garden where his hand was still sunk down, up to the wrist.

"Holy shit," she said on an exhale.

"Can you move? Can you leave?"

That was Danvers' voice and Paris slowly moved his eyes from the data scientist to the fire marshal. It was difficult to focus on sounds. His ears were acutely attuned to the echo of Jade's heartbeat, slow, so slow, in his ears.

"No," he replied." He looked back down at his hand, flexing his fingers slightly in the dirt. He didn't know if he could move, but he knew he didn't want to. His magic surged at the thought. Miles away, he felt the Earth sigh and shift around Jade.

"He could, but he does not wish to."

It was the Fae. He regarded Paris with a strange look. Paris looked away, focusing back to the Earth, his connection to Jade. He didn't know if what the Fae said was true. Could he move? But, if he pulled his hand from this soil, would Jade's heart stop beating? Would she be unable to breathe, buried underneath the surface of a burning forest?

"What would happen if I move my hand?" Paris asked the Fae, ignoring the protocol of never asking them questions. He couldn't recall the last time he had to ask someone what his magic would do. For years, he'd just known. But now, uncertainty coursed through his veins.

"Your magic is strong. It will endure, even if you remove your hand."

Paris stared down at his arm, focusing on where his hand and soil met.

"What's wrong with him?" Danvers asked.

The Fae answered. "His interest, his focus, is miles away, entombed in Earth. He's focusing on her. On keeping her alive. Until the fire passes over her, it's drawing his energy, which is why he looks ill. Thin."

"Until it the fire burns over her, you mean," Danvers clarified.

"Yes."

"Well, should we move him?" Danvers asked. Every cell in Paris' body hunkered closer to the ground.

The Fae made a sound. The closest thing to laughter Paris had ever heard from their kind.

"You could try. I wouldn't."

The young data scientist set her water bottle down next to Paris and he stared at it for a moment, confused.

"In case you're thirsty. I mean, I can get you a fresh one if you want." She sat and set her laptop on her crossed legs. "I'll text someone to get you one right now. I'll stay. I can tell you when the fire's passed where she last was. Would that help? Or would you already know?"

Thump-thump-thump. Then the ghost of a magical inhalation and then exhalation. Jade's heart and her breathing, unconscious, underground, protected by his magic. Each sensation catalogued against his skin.

"That… would help." His voice sounded far away, even to him.

At some point, he moved from his crouch to sit on the ground, much like the data scientist, crossing his legs. His back protested at his outstretched arm, still submerged. It moved slightly, escaping part of the soil and his heart stuttered, wondering if it would affect Jade's well-being. Still, he felt the steady, slow beat of her heart. Carefully, thinking of the Fae's words, of how his magic would endure. He pulled his hand out of the earth slowly, so slowly, until it was free. He still had a tether of magic connected to Jade. He felt it in his entire being - connected to the Earth, connected to her.

The fire burned. It was a roaring sound, dull and distant in his ears, but there nonetheless. It was overtop of Jade. Burning the landscape while she slept. *Thump-thump-thump*. The sound of Jade's heart. Paris felt the earth expand and contract, rhythmically, mimicking Jade's breath.

The young scientist asked if he needed anything and when he didn't answer, she rattled off some statistics to him. Heat, wind speed, duration. His phone buzzed mercilessly in his pocket. He finally pulled it out, recognizing Lily's new Coven number. He wanted to ignore it. She would be frantic - unable to reach Jade, and likely feeling something was wrong or amiss. She'd want answers. She'd want comfort and he selfishly, awfully didn't think he had any to give.

"Hello?" he answered it before he could think on it any longer.

"Where is she? Where are you? Is she okay?"

"She's… in the forest. The fire… the fire had her trapped."

"Oh my god, is she… is she …"

"She's alive."

"Because Bruce collapsed and he won't wake up. He was sitting in front of the fireplace panting and I thought it was because he was hot, but there wasn't a fire going and then he fell over. I thought he was dead, I thought she was... she won't answer the phone."

"No, she can't. I had to... she's in the Earth."

Lily paused. "What?"

"There was no way to get her out. I've buried her. With magic."

"She's... underground." He heard Lily swallow over the phone and then exhale loudly. "Is she conscious?"

"No, I put her to sleep."

Again Lily paused. "Like Bruce."

"I believe so, yes."

The phone was silent between. He didn't know what else to say and apparently, neither did Lily.

"What do you feel from her?" he asked.

"Uh, I try not to dial in too much because it causes the migraines." Paris heart sunk at her words, but then Lily continued. "But I couldn't help it. She was panicking, and it was hot and she was scared. And then... then, it all went away and I didn't know what that meant."

"She knew what I was doing, what was happening. I asked her, and she agreed."

"I think... I think I felt that too." Based on Lily's voice, she was crying. He wondered if he should call or text Callie to go over and be with her. "Your magic," said Lily. "It smells like sandalwood to her. And laundry. And I was thinking of those things just before I... couldn't feel her anymore. She was thinking of you. She was glad to be thinking of you." Lily took a deep breath and exhaled.

"You should call Callie. She'll come sit with you and Bruce."

Lily laughed, somewhat wetly. "But will she bring wine?"

"I hope so." He tried to find levity in her words. Tried to supply it for her as well. "I'm supposed to find some. Jade told me this morning there'd better be wine waiting for her tonight. But I don't know what she likes."

Lily sighed. "We like Grenaches. Syrahs. Rich blends. And we pick by how the label looks, so even if you get the taste wrong, all will be forgiven for a really pretty label."

"Thank the goddess you've told me this. All she told me is she doesn't like thin wines."

"You should get her nachos too. Or appetizer food. We like small food. It's fun and easy. Mozza sticks. Chicken fingers." Lily paused again and then added in a rush, her voice cracking and wobbling, "And tell her to call me. Even if she thinks… even if she thinks I already know. When she's awake. Tell her to call."

"I will. But you should call Callie. Or Henri. Invite them over. If you can't, I can for you."

"Yeah." Lily's voice was thin and reedy. "How long?"

"I don't know," he replied, knowing exactly what she meant. He looked to the data scientist. As if sensing his eyes were on her, she looked up. "How long, do you think?" he asked her.

She looked at her computer, bit her lip and frowned. He should ask her name. He should already know it. It was awful of him not to know it. He was a

Coven Leader. His mother... he shut that line of thinking down.

"A couple hours. Maybe longer. She burned out the area around her, so there's nowhere it can go, but it's got to finish chewing up the fuel in the area. We get data dumps every hour, so I can tell you more as we get new info." Her eyes darted again to her computer and then back to Paris. "But I don't think it will cross the highway. I think she burned enough to stop that."

"Did you hear that?" Paris asked Lily.

"Mostly. Just... tell her to call me. I'll keep an eye on Bruce. And I'll Callie and Henri. They'd want to be here for news, you know?"

"Yes, they're fond of her. And she of them."

"You know she kind of wanted to paint her room, I think. Maybe we can pick something for her."

"Really?" he asked, just for something to say.

"Yeah. Blue. She likes blue. It reminds her of you."

"I wonder why."

Lily laughed again. "Take a look in the mirror. It's your eyes."

He was humbled and embarrassed by her words, and didn't know what to say.

Lily took another deep, long breath and then spoke again. "Okay, when... she's out, tell her to call me."

"I won't forget."

They hung up and he was left holding his phone, staring at it dumbly.

"Was that her sister or a friend?" the scientist asked.

He didn't know how to describe Lily. "Both."

"I got more water." She gestured to some bottles that had seemingly appeared without his notice. "And I can get food too, if you want."

He shook his head. He tuned into the rhythm that was Jade in the soil. *Thump-thump-thump.* It was a meditation drone.

Danvers left at one point and then came back, wordlessly watching Paris and before leaving again. He likely still had other areas of the fire to deal with. He could have them. Paris wasn't sure he cared at the moment. The Fae representative came back, peered curiously at Paris and then at the soil. He nodded once and left.

Through it all, he listened to, actively reached for, and felt the slow, rhythmic beat of Jade's heart and her strange, not-quite there inhalations and exhalations. Faint echoes of what he imagined they normally sounded like. He imagined her, entombed in the earth, chest moving slowly. Did the earth move through her mouth and lungs? Or was it only her body recalling the ghost of breathing while she was unconscious by magical force?

Someone else came by and spoke with the young woman. He left a couple more bottles of water and a tray of hot beverages and some protein bars. Paris eyed them with disinterest. The scientist slid a bottle of water toward him and he drank without thinking.

Thump-thump-thump. Paris was tempted to call Lily back and inquire after Bruce. If something were wrong with Jade, Bruce would know. But he supposed if there'd been any change, Lily would have called him.

"The area is no longer directly burning. The main intensity of the fire has passed and it's pushing toward the highway, but running out of fuel. There's also a wind from the east that's helping to block it."

He blinked, feeling as though he was arising from a stupor at the data scientist's words. "Could we get her out now?"

She wobbled her head - neither a yes or no movement. "I'm not a pilot, but I don't think so. I'll have Steve ping Danvers and find out."

"Who's Steve?"

She looked up at him. "One of the scientists."

"I don't even know your name."

She blinked. "I'm Lucy."

"I'm Paris."

"I know. And she's Jade." Lucy tipped her head to the small garden area.

"Yes. I apologize for not knowing your name."

"Dude." Her eyes were large and dark. "Understandable. And if you forget it, don't worry about it." Lucy went back to her computer, typing away.

An hour later, Danvers returned with the same two pilots who had taken Jade and Adam out earlier in the day.

"We got clearance to go out there. These guys can take you."

Paris stood up, his muscles stuff and sore from sitting in one place for so long. He stared down at the small patch of soil, sending a pulse magic through it and checking on Jade. He didn't know how many times he'd done it while sitting there, but each time there was a heart-stopping pause until his magic came back, like a sonar ping, and he felt her heart and the slow steady movement of her lungs. *Thump-thump-thump.*

"Can you not leave? Is that how your magic works?" Lucy asked, seeing him hesitate.

"No, I can leave. My magic is still protecting her. But... I won't be able to check in on her if I'm in the air."

"But you won't be able to get to her unless you fly."

Paris nodded. He took a step away from the small garden, and then another, toward the pilots and Danvers.

"All right, let's go."

CHAPTER SIXTEEN

Paris was surprised when Adam joined them. The dark circles under his eyes contrasted with the paleness of his skin.

"Are you all right?" Paris asked.

Adam nodded. "My magic's on hiatus, but I was, uh, hoping you'd let me come out with you. I don't think I can help magically, but she saved my life so I'd like to go. If that's okay."

Paris nodded and Adam joined him in the truck. It was a silent drive out, with no one speaking or offering conversation. Once they arrived, as soon as his feet were in contact with the earth again, he sent out another pulse of magic. It found Jade and came back again. She was still alive. Still asleep. He hesitated before getting in the helicopter.

"Do you not like flying?" Adam asked.

"No, I've no compunctions, but once we take off, I'll lose contact with the Earth."

Adam nodded. "You've been checking on her."

"Yes."

Adam didn't have anything to add other than a grim, knowing look. The pilots talked amongst themselves - flight arrangement items, statuses and work chatter. In only moments, they were off.

The landscape was stunning in a desolate, destroyed manner. It was as though someone had taken the natural scenery and decided to only sketch it out in black and grey, leaving out all the color. It was ruined, scorched. In some places, spindly, stark limbs shot straight up, like burned toothpicks jutting up to the sky. In other places, formerly more lush and billowy trees left behind only their curved, fractal branches; giving them the appearance of clawing their way out of the ground, trying to escape. The smoke was a living, moving thing, pushed across the landscape by the unseen hand of the wind. He noted it was moving away from the populated areas, but he didn't sense any magic about it. He wondered if the meteorologists and air and water witches ever managed to determine if they could affect the weather. Most likely not. The calculations were too complex. He longed to reach his magic out again and find Jade, but he was too far from the ground. He was also afraid. Though his magic had indicated she was alive when he'd checked on her, what if this time, it came back differently. Perhaps he'd been deluding himself this whole time and she couldn't possibly be alive. Looking down at the scorched earth, he wondered how it was possible.

They landed, the pilots indicating it was as close as they could get to where they dead-dropped

Jade. Once out of the craft, Paris sent out his magic, like a sonar, to find Jade. When it came back, the now-familiar beat of her heart and rhythm of her breathing washed over him, making him weak in the knees. It was "louder" out here, stronger. She was alive. Buried underground, but alive.

"You know where she is?" Adam asked and Paris nodded. They set off hiking in the forest.

It was hot. Though the fire had passed, the residual heat emanated from the earth, the trees, the very air. The ground beneath their feet cracked, crunched and splintered. Paris sent his magic out on a never-ending loop, reaching out for Jade and returning to him - both a way to find her and a way to remind himself she was still alive, despite the death and destruction around him. On each return of his magic he felt as though...

He frowned. If he could ascribe a word or feeling to the Earth, it would be whimpering. Weeping. The Earth cried at the destruction. Yet beneath all that was a glimmer and hope of life. Just as Jade was buried in the soil, so too were the roots of the trees, the moss, the grass. The Earth would rejuvenate. This was another horrendous tragedy in Her long life and She would recover.

Paris didn't know how long they'd been hiking when he stopped.

"What's wrong?" Adam asked.

"She's here. Somewhere. She's here." Paris crouched down, getting closer to the ground. As he had when he'd been back at the hotel, he sunk his hand into the soil and willed his magic outward. He extracted his hand and moved several feet to the left.

He did it three more times until he knew, he knew, Jade was beneath him. Buried.

"Here. This is where she is." His fingers hovered and hesitated, still afraid. Doubt clawed at him. What if he'd been wrong this whole time and when he buried her, he killed her? What if she'd been unable to be sustained in the soil with his magic? What if he raised her up and she was nothing but a corpse? Or what if she were alive, but horrendously burned? Damaged and unrecognizable?

"What are you waiting for?"

Paris shook his head, not sure how to answer Adam. He wondered if he should call Lily. She would know, wouldn't she, if Jade were injured or dead? Wouldn't he have already heard from her? Would Bruce still be alive if Jade were dead? If he pulled his phone out, would he see messages from Lily demanding he call her because Bruce had died? Could he bear to hear such things from her? Or would it be better, would he deserve, to find out directly from the Earth itself?

He knelt on the ground. The lingering heat of the fire was transmitted through the fireproof fabric of his suit, hot against his skin. He hovered his hand and then placed his palm flush on the soil. The Earth was hot. He wondered if his skin would blister from it.

Thump-thump-thump.

By his magic, he felt and heard her heartbeat. It was as though she were a radio transmitter on all frequencies.

"Can you hear her?" Paris murmured, wondering.

"What? No, I don't have any magic right now. I don't hear anything," Adam said.

Perhaps it was just for him. He reached with his magic and pulled. He pulled with everything he had. The earth buckled and shifted under his force, and he moved backward, unable to hold his current position. In one huge motion, the Earth expelled her, pushing her forth like the true mother it was. It birthed Jade, releasing her from the protective cocoon of soil and dirt.

Suddenly, she was there. In front of him, stretched out in the fetal position, her eyes closed. She was still and serene, as though she were sleeping. Or a corpse.

"Jade."

He was afraid to touch her. What if he reached out and her flesh was cold and stiff under his fingers? What if she'd died the moment she'd been swallowed by the Earth, and what he heard as her heartbeat was only an echo of his own?

"Jade," he repeated. She didn't move

Paris could bear it no longer and placed a hand on her shoulder. Her body was warm and pliant under his touch. He exhaled in relief.

"Wake up." He used not only his voice but his magic, sending a pulse of it out, through his hands into her body, into her flesh, and willed it to be so.

Her eyes opened, her irises the clear, stark grey he remembered so well. She gasped, mouth opening almost comically. Her body curled upward, like a bow, like some unknown force was pulling at her. She inhaled sharply again and then rolled immediately to her side, coughing. A large chunk of dirt fell from her lips. She spat, inelegantly, more dirt spilling from her mouth. She raised her head, her eyes wild until they fixed on him. She lurched forward and clutched at him, knocking him over with her weight and strength, her fingers sharp even through the fabric of his fire suit. He felt the tips of her nails, pressing into his flesh. He wrapped his arms around her and held her close, marveling at the sensation of the true motion of her lungs expanding and contracting as she breathed. It was no longer only the phantom mimicry of life while she was buried.

A sound of distress escaped her lips - a cry or a sob. He wasn't sure which. He pulled her closer.

"You're all right. You survived. It's all right."

Her grip tightened and he responded in the same, pulling her closer. She breathed as though she'd run a marathon, clinging to him like she was afraid he'd pull away and the earth would swallow her whole again.

"I've got you. You're all right," he repeated.

Jade coughed, the sound harsh and beautiful in his ear. She was saying something. He didn't understand her until he concentrated.

Thank you, thank you.

He pressed his lips against the flesh of her temple. He wanted to respond in the automatic fashion, saying she was welcome, but the words were cheap and inadequate. Again, another sound like a sob escaped her and she buried her face in his neck, breathing deep. He should stand. He should help her and they should leave this place of death and ruination, but he found he was unable to move. The solid weight of her against him was reminder she was alive and he was loathe to do anything at the moment. He inhaled and smelled the scent of her magic - linden blossom and cloves. Something in him released and unclenched.

"You're all right. We're all right."

#

Paris smelled of sandalwood and laundry, but also of earth and soil. Or maybe the smell of dirt was her, Jade didn't know. She should get up. They were laying on the ground, her face pressed into his neck and this had probably gone on for too long. It wasn't like she had some kind of yard stick to measure it by. When you'd been trapped by a forest fire, and the guy you were kind of dating buried you to save your life, how long were you allowed to lie there and be really fucking grateful it worked?

She could have kept pondering that question except for the migraine. She had two seconds of consciousness before pain descended on her brain, its spiked tentacles finding the entire thing made of soft, squishy parts it could sink deep into.

"Your nose is bleeding."

Jade flinched from Paris' voice, finding the volume of it too loud. She squeezed her eyes shut as well, trying to keep the sharp talons of daylight from her retinas.

"I'm sorry. Migraine?" Paris' whispered now, still too harsh and grainy against her ears, but softer than it had been before.

"Yes." It was hard to speak, but the idea of nodding her head made her want to vomit. Something felt like it was crawling on her neck and her fingers twitched to swat at it. She flexed her scapula, wondering if she was buggy and gross from being underground. As soon as she thought that, a thousand places on her started itching and tingling. She shifted in Paris' grip.

"I want to go."

Okay, so not the most poetic thing to say after her ordeal, but fucking truthful.

"All right, let me help you."

They were a tangle of limbs and though she understood intellectually that he had to move away from her to get to his feet then to help her up, she had to force herself to unclench her fingers from where they were wrapped in the fabric of his fire suit in order for him to move.

Someone else's hands were on her and she flinched, opening her eyes. She raised a hand to bat the person away. She managed to stop at the last moment when she saw it was Adam.

"I'm trying to help, but I can not." Adam held his hands up in surrender. He reached into his pocket and pulled out a wad of tissues, holding them out to Jade. "They're clean. Despite how they look."

Jade carefully took one and wiped at her nose. Her nose was still actively bleeding. That wasn't going to cut it. She ripped a corner of the tissue off and jammed it up her left nostril. It was the worst offender. Attractive, she was sure. She kind of gave a fuck, but mostly didn't.

Paris stood and reached down to help her. She felt like an epileptic colt as she struggled to get her legs underneath her and gain her balance, all while pulling on Paris' arms. Adam lurched forward. She really didn't want him touching her, but also couldn't figure out how to actually stand. One try of trying to get her legs and she realized she needed Adam's help too.

"Okay, I could use help," she managed. "To get up."

Adam nodded and between him and Paris, Jade was on her feet. The world swayed and she almost fell back down. Her thigh muscles wobbled and her tongue was thick and fuzzy. Her migraine stomped on her grey matter, in time with her heart. Each beat was a sharp spike. She dry heaved, managed to swallow, but could feel too much spit pooling in her mouth - a pre-cursor to tossing her cookies.

"Okay, perhaps you should lie down and we'll get a medical team out here," Paris said.

"No, I'm up now. That was the worst part, I think." *I hope.* "Just give me..." She trailed off, her eyes drawn to the pile of soil at their feet. It was uneven and loose. That was where she had been buried. Buried alive. But not. She felt the phantom sensation of the earth pressing against her flesh. How deep had she been? How had she survived? She remembered surrendering to Paris' magic and then.... Strange images flashed through her mind. A grave. She'd been thinking of a grave. But not her own. Fire. She'd dreamed of fire and tarot cards. Sakkara. Medusa had been there too, the snakes of her hair turning to worms in the Earth and god, Jade wanted a shower. Badly. She'd dreamt of Yvonne. She'd stood on the shore of the lake, watching a boat row away from the dock. A lighthouse on a stormy night.

"Jade, are you all right?"

She turned to Paris and meant to answer him, but found herself staring wordlessly at his face, his eyes. She was so fucking glad to see him. She inhaled, her whole body leaning toward him, sending her center off balance. Sandalwood and mint. Laundry. She was okay. He'd said so.

"All right. We'll sit you back down call for help."

"No, I don't want to stay here." She leaned against him, feeling the strong grip of his arm around her waist, holding her up. "I can walk." Then she added the hardest words she knew in the English language. "But I'll need help."

His lips pressed against her temple again and he tightened his grip, moving his center of gravity closer to her. "Okay."

"Uh, you're not going to sock me one if I try to help, are you?" Adam asked, holding out a bottle of water. He'd already screwed the cap off. She took it and hoped her expression conveyed some kind of thanks. The water was tepid and had the strange taste she associated with purchased water. Thousands of advertising claims indicated there was nothing to taste, but she knew different. Adam and Paris shared a look - probably trying to determine how to get her out of the forest without her face-planting, she guessed.

"Ready?" Paris asked, still keeping his voice low. God, this probably was a bad idea. But the alternative was to sit back down, next to her pseudo-grave, and wait for help. No, thank you. Paris' one arm was tight around her waist, the other held her hand. When he took a step, her body was obliged to follow. She supposed they looked like they were dancing in a way - if they weren't walking through a burnt out husk of nature. Adam fell in step on her other side, close enough if she fell, but not crowding her.

As they walked, she took in destruction. Everything was dead or dying. She knew forest fires happened, and the earth could and would recover, but all she felt was sadness. Sadness and guilt. Fire was easy for her magic, quick to respond. But fire was what had done this. It could keep people warm in the winter and be a cozy, friendly thing to curl up against, but just as easily, it could burn out of control and lay waste to everything it touched.

In that respect, Jade wondered how much she had in common with it.

Her existence became a measure of steps, resulting throbs in her head, and the sounds of their breathing. She thought about the hike in, wondering how long it had taken. She'd had Paris' voice in her ear, telling her about their witch camp, and hadn't kept track of time. She could ask him about it now, but the thought of hearing anything, of more assaulting her migraine made her cringe.

"When we get back, if you feel up to it, Lily would like you to call her."

Paris had whispered the words and Jade responded in kind. "Okay."

They broke the battered tree line and the pilots came forward, their faces somewhat recognizable to Jade even through her squinting. They whooped and hollered, happy to see her. The sound had her pulling away from Paris quickly and she vomited bile and water in the burnt, charcoaled grass. It put a damper on her victorious survival, she supposed.

The ride back was more of a blur. Paris asked if he could cast a spell around her to dampen sound and light and she'd wondered why he'd waited so long.

"I don't think you could have walked out under it. May I?" he asked.

"Yeah." She leaned back in her seat in the helicopter and closed her eyes. Seconds later, Paris' magic washed over her and for a split-second, she feared she was back in the forest, on the ground, waiting for the Earth to consume her. To bury her. She jerked upright, jamming her chin into Paris' shoulder, where he hovered over her. Her eyes watered from the onslaught of pain and that was it. That was the last straw. She was crying. The ugly cry and it was messy, wet, and awful. Paris settled in next to her and pulled her close to him. Finally, with her face pressed into his chest, it was quiet and dark. Whether it was his spell or just being close to him, she didn't know or care.

"Close your eyes. Sleep."

She felt his magic pulse at her, testing to see if it was allowed. She let it run over her. His words like a peppermint balm on a sore muscle. She sagged and let everything around her go fuzzy and grey.

#

She woke when the helicopter landed. They had to get out and into a car. Like a sleepy toddler on a road trip, she blinked and stumbled, leaning heavily against Paris. She stayed awake long enough to get into the back seat of an SUV; she turned her face into Paris' shoulder again, uncaring about the rest of the world around her. Her head hurt and her magic was gone. She knew it wasn't gone-gone. She could feel it coiled inside her like a fat slug, too cold to move in the winter months. But it wouldn't be coming back tonight. Paris rested a hand on the back of her head, right where the pulsations of her migraines were the worst. The pressure helped.

"Can you push harder? On my head?" she asked. He paused for a moment, whether because he wasn't sure what she meant or how hard to push, she didn't know. At any rate, he pressed down with his entire hand. The pressure made it easier to cope with the pain. Her shoulders relaxed and she pushed the front of her head against him, finding a counterbalance.

"Better?"

"Little bit."

"Is there a doctor available at the hotel?" She heard him ask, his voice quiet, but not directed at her.

"We've EMS. I don't know about actual medical doctors."

"I need to sleep this off. I'll see Gellar when we get back at the Coven," Jade said. She didn't want anyone she didn't know poking or prodding her. Bad enough when Gellar did it, at least Jade knew her now.

"Are you sure?" Paris asked.

"Yes." She didn't move her head to nod. There was a good balance between the pressure of Paris' shoulder and his hand at the back of her skull. She was thankful the car ride was mostly smooth. When she tried to picture the route they'd taken on the way from the hotel to the helicopters, she was surprised to have zero recollection of it. She'd been looking out the window. She'd been looking for the fire. She knew she had been. But when she tried to call up a memory of it, there was nothing. Just a blank space.

It was fine. She was tired, and used a shit ton of magic and nearly been buried alive. There were bound to be some glitches.

The hotel lights were bright. Jade wanted to close her eyes against them, but didn't like not being able to see where she was. She managed to squint as Paris moved them through the lobby to the elevator.

"I'll see what I can find out about a doctor," Adam said. "In case you change your mind."

She wouldn't, but just then they stepped in the elevator and it gave a weird lurch. She shut her mouth to keep from vomiting again.

A blissfully short amount of time later, they were back in the hotel room. She looked at the bed and sighed, not moving toward it.

"You should lie down."

"I'm filthy."

"You can shower when you wake up." Paris went to her side of the bed and pulled back the covers.

"I'm filthy," she repeated, "and hotel sheets are really white."

"They can bill me for the extra service." He looked up at her expectantly.

"I'm probably all buggy. If I get into bed, then it will be all buggy."

"I have a spell for that."

"Really?"

Paris nodded. "Yes, really. Can you stand for a moment longer?"

If it was to get rid of bugs, then yes. She closed her eyes and pressed her palm against her forehead. He moved into her space and murmured. She caught some of his words, but not all. Something about returning things to the earth that belonged to the earth. She opened her eyes and clutched at him.

"What if that means me?"

"Pardon?"

"I was buried. You buried me. And my body, my little body, is buried back at the Coven. What if your magic...?" She swallowed. "What if it gets confused?"

He pulled the ponytail out of her hair with far more care than she ever took, smoothing errant strands down. "It won't. And you don't belong to the earth. You belong here. With us. The Coven. With me."

Suspicion curled in her gut, but she wanted to trust him. "Okay."

He started his spell again and she couldn't tell if it was working. She felt blanketed by his power, but it wasn't like she had felt in the soil. This time was light and soft. Fluffy? She didn't know the right word.

"There you are," he said quietly. He ran his hands down her arms and grabbed her fingers. "Shoes off." He knelt at her feet and unlaced her boots, becoming a sturdy balance post when she leaned on him. "Into bed."

"I should take this jumper off."

"Do you want to take it off?"

Jade sat on the bed. "Maybe. It's gross."

He shuffled around the room and came back to her side holding out a bundle of fabric. Her yoga pants and t-shirt. "I can leave or turn my back..." He started, but she decided, fuck it, she'd been buried alive and lived to tell the tale. She couldn't be bothered. She unzipped the fire suit and peeled out of the top, slipping the t-shirt on over her bra. She picked her feet off the floor and shimmied out of the suit.

"Ugh, everything smells like smoke and dirt. Including me." She lay down, pressing the heel of her hands against her forehead again.

"A temporary problem. One I'll gratefully take if it means you're all right." She felt the bed dip at the edge and knew, without having to open her eyes. Paris was there, sitting carefully.

"Can you press my head again?"

At first, Jade wasn't sure she'd said the words aloud since Paris didn't answer. But then she felt him shift from where he sat and move to his side of the bed and crawl in. She turned toward him, eyes still closed, curled into the fetal position. One of his hands come to cradle her skull and the other come atop her own against her forehead. He squeezed. She exhaled. It didn't make the pain go away or lessen, but it somehow made it more bearable.

"Like that?" he asked.

She managed a low sound of agreement.

"I'll let Lily know you're back and that you'll call her when you're feeling better. Although she might know you're back already." He sounded far away, like Jade was at the bottom of an impossibly deep barrel and he was at the top, speaking at his normal volume.

"How?"

"She mentioned Bruce fell asleep. About the same time I imagine you did." He sounded further away, like she was drifting.

"But he's okay, right?"

"Yes. I think he's sleeping. Like you were. Like you are about to."

She wasn't sure how much time had passed, if any, when there was a knock at the door. His hands disappeared from her head and she curled in tighter on herself, like a caterpillar. The bed jiggled as he moved and she heard the door open and then she heard soft talking. Paris and someone else. The door closed and he came back to the bed, setting something down on the table.

"That was EMS. Adam sent them by. They brought some extra-strength ibuprofen. Are you up for taking it?"

Frankly, given how her head felt, that sounded like trying to hammer a nail into a two by four with a butter knife, but she'd give it a go if it was the only choice.

"Yeah."

He brought her a glass of water and helped her sit up and take two pills. He frowned at her when she motioned for two more.

"I survived being buried and you're worried about me OD'ing on over the counter meds?"

"I think you should see a doctor."

"I don't know these people." He frowned deeper, if that were possible. "Gimme two more and if it's still like this when I wake up, I'll go," Jade grudgingly replied.

He agreed, handing over two more small capsules. She supposed she could have taken the bottle from him, but Jesus, that felt like a lot of effort. She slowly, carefully, lay back down, trying not to jostle herself. She curled up again, pressing her hands against her head.

Paris settled next to her and settled his hands again on her head, pressing hard.

"I dreamt of things. When I was in the ground," Jade said suddenly, the images coming back to her. They were sharp in her brain, poking the soft edges of her migraine, making it bleed pain into the rest of her body.

"You're all right. I'm sorry you had to go through that."

"No, I…" She wanted to make him understand, but words were getting harder. Her tongue was thick and tired. "I don't think it was about me."

"You should sleep. We can talk about it in the morning."

His voice drifted away from the edge of the barrel, leaving her alone in the dark and quiet.

CHAPTER SEVENTEEN

Jade slept, but struggled to stay asleep. She had periods of unconsciousness interspersed with moments of being awake, when she realized, yes her head still fucking hurt, and yes, she was still curled up next to Paris. While the first thought was hard to ignore, it was the second one that occupied her mind. The room was quiet; she could hear her own breathing and Paris' as well. Quiet inhales and exhales. Overlaid was the sound of the A/C in the room. Quiet, but definitely mechanical. She thought she might also hear the muffled sounds of people walking above them, or in the hall. Mostly it was the sound of breathing - hers and his.

A buzzing sound broke the semi-quiet and she flinched. She automatically cursed the movement for jostling her grey matter disagreeably against her skull when she realized it didn't hurt as badly as it had. Either the ibuprofen or time, or both, had helped. She slit her eyes open as she felt Paris move. He reaching for his night-side table and grabbed his phone, the creator of the buzzing. He answered it, speaking quietly and turning further away from Jade.

"Yes? She's still sleeping."

"She's kind of not sleeping anymore," Jade said, wanting to let him know she was awake and listening.

"I'm sorry, I'll take this in... well." She heard the gears of his brain realize there was no other place to take a call but the bathroom.

"No, it's okay, I'm feeling better."

"It's Lily." He held the phone out at the same time Jade made *gimme* motions with her hands. "Hey," she said.

"I swear, I was trying to wait until you called me, but then Bruce woke up. He smacked his lips and went to the kitchen and drank a bowl of water. I thought, well, if he's up... but I didn't mean to wake you."

"No, I'm up. I mean, I was starting to wake up."

"How do you feel?"

Jade exhaled. "Migraine is better. I need a shower." It wasn't much of a status update, but it summed up how she felt and what her priorities were.

"How bad was your migraine?"

Jade flicked her gaze to Paris for a moment, who looked like he was trying hard to not eavesdrop. It was impossible for him not to hear while in the hotel room, and it's not like she had any secrets from him. Well, not about this, anyway. "It's better now," she said.

"I'll head downstairs and see if I can find you something to eat." Paris stood from the bed and gathered his keycard and his wallet. She wanted to tell him she didn't mind if he stayed, but before she could, he was already heading out the door. She watched it close behind him before turning her attention back to the phone.

"It was really bad, hey?" Lily asked. "And you don't want to say so because Paris can hear you. Okay, I won't push, but seriously. You need to see Gellar when you get back."

Jade opted not to tell Lily that Paris left the room since she really didn't want to get into her migraines. "So I've been told. How's Bruce?"

"I told you. Awake. Drinking water. And nosing around the garbage, but I think that's because there's, like, four filters worth of coffee grinds and some empty pizza boxes. It's been tough waiting for news from you."

"Sorry."

"Jesus, don't apologize. It's not your fault," Lily answered. "Unless you come back and tell me all about what happened and it turns out it is your fault in which case, yes, apologize away."

Jade laughed, careful not to keep it soft in case it caused her migraine to rebound. "Not my fault. I don't think. So you've been eating pizza?"

"Yeah, Callie and Henri are here. They're downstairs. I thought I would try checking in with you when I saw Bruce. I'll let them know you're okay." Lily paused. "You *are* okay, right?"

"Yeah, totally."

"Paris told me he buried you."

It was Jade's turn to pause, not sure what Lily wanted or needed in response. "He did."

"What… what was it like?"

Jade swallowed. "It was like being swallowed by the earth." She didn't know how else to explain it. "But also, being swallowed by his magic. It didn't hurt, but... it was hard." Hard to surrender. Hard to let go. She didn't think she could say those words out loud yet. "I don't think I could have done it if it hadn't been him. It was too much like submitting."

The sound of Lily's exhale had both a tone and a feeling to it, though Jade couldn't put either into words. But she knew Lily understood what she meant.

"I'm glad you're okay."

"Me too," Jade said, trying to add some levity to her voice. She needed to break the heaviness. She was still too tired to handle it.

"You're coming home right away?"

"Yeah, I mean, I think so. I don't think there's anything else I can do here. My magic is fried and I'm..." Tears welled up in her eyes and her throat went tight. "I'm tired. It's been a hard day."

"No shit." She heard sympathy tears in Lily's voice. "Well, I told Paris what kind of wine you like so maybe this trip won't be a total bust and you can have a nice dinner and a drink. If you feel up to it."

"That sounds pretty fucking fantastic right now. But first I need to shower. I smell like smoke, I feel like the forest floor. I need to drink a liter of mouthwash too."

"Okay, I'll let you go. But nachos with Callie and Henri when you get back. You can tell us all about how you saved the world. Again!"

"I hardly saved the world."

"The best stories are those that are embellished. Start selling it. I'm already telling people the whole world would've burned if not for you."

"I miss you."

"I miss you too. I'll see you soon."

She swiped at some errant tears racing down her cheeks as she hung up the phone. She stretched out across the king-sized bed, aiming for putting the phone back on Paris' nightstand. It suddenly fell from her grip and landed on the bed. She reached for it and paused. Her fingers were moving without her permission, trembling, like she was shivering or had a tremor. She stared them uncomprehendingly for a moment until she made a tight fist, stilling their motion. She held the fist, counting to ten and flexed her fingers open again. They were still for a moment before they started shaking again. She left the phone where it was and drew both hands into a fist.

It was probably stress. A temporary result of all the magic she used. Once she was better rested, had some food, and was back at the Coven, it would be fine.

#

Paris wasn't sure how long he should give Jade and Lily to speak. He ended up in the main lobby before making his way to the ballroom. It was still busy, but didn't have the same frantic level of energy as before. Danvers looked up and waved him over.

"How is Jade?" he asked.

"Resting. How is the fire?"

"Under control. We've got it contained now and there's no chance it will cross the highway into the city. Thank you for that."

"You can thank Jade."

"I will."

"How are the other witches? Clay and Michael?"

"Back in from the field. Tired as well. They'll be returning to their Covens tomorrow. Adam too. You guys?"

"Yes, we're going home."

Danvers glanced around, looking. "I don't know where our Fae representative went. They're cagey bastards."

Paris thought of the gut-wrenching portal transport and grimaced. "I'll arrange commercial transport. We used the Fae on the way here because of the time constraints, but I'd much prefer taking normal routes home." He didn't mention he didn't want to subject Jade to another portal trip given her migraines.

"Fair enough. In case I don't see you before you leave." He held out his hand. They shook and Paris took his leave, heading to the main desk.

With the help of the concierge, he set up their trip home and also ordered some food, directing it to be sent up to the room. Wondering if he'd given Jade enough time, he supposed he could head back up and always leave again if she was still on the phone.

The shower was running when he entered, so he took a moment to tidy the room, collecting their fire suits and folding them haphazardly. He left them on the dresser. He had no idea if they were to be returned or not. Jade would likely need to keep her boots for their trip home and he set them next to the door.

The shower turned off and a few minutes later, Jade exited in a cloud of steam and lightly scented soap and shampoo.

"Can you do the hair thing again?" she asked, waving her fingers around her head.

"Of course."

She pulled out the small desk chair and sat, turning her back to him.

"How's your migraine?" He ran his hands just above her wet head, sending pulses of magic out to dry her hair.

"Better. I no longer have a strong desire to be unconscious," she joked. She tucked her hands under her thighs. It was strange to hear her speak and not see them moving around at the same time.

"Tired?"

"Yeah."

"I have some food on the way."

"I hear there might be wine."

"There is, but I wasn't sure if you'd want to drink with your migraine."

"English, I can't think of a better reason *to* drink than a migraine." She shivered.

"Cold?"

"No, it's… your magic. And my hair. It's like getting a really good scalp massage."

He felt a surge of pride at her answer, his lips curling slightly in a smile. When her hair was dry, he carefully placed his hands on her shoulders, watching for any sign of discomfort. She turned slightly, tilting her head up, and smiled at him. He didn't think he'd ever seen her look so open and trusting. It wasn't a look he was accustomed to seeing on her.

"Thanks."

He leaned forward slowly, aware she could perceive him as looming over her. He trusted if she didn't like him encroaching on her space, she would say something. She didn't move except for her gaze, darting quickly to his lips and back to his eyes. When he kissed her, her lips were warm and he could taste the mint lip gloss she was perpetually applying. He slid one of his hands from her shoulder to cup her neck, keeping his grip loose and easy in case she moved away. She didn't.

He felt one of her hands rest against his, her fingers feeing like they were trembling slightly. Nerves, perhaps? She hadn't pulled away, so although she may be nervous, he took heart in that. He angled his head slightly and opened his mouth to kiss her deeper.

The knock at the door must have startled her because she flinched, knocking her teeth into his, then pulling back.

"Sorry, sorry." Her skin flushed red as she raised a hand to her lips, pressing her fingers against her mouth. His teeth tingled from the hit, but he was otherwise unscathed.

"It's all right," he replied with a smile. He went to the door, taking the cart with their food and drinks from the waitstaff. As he pushed it into the room, she rolled her eyes, seemingly at herself, shook her head and dropped her face in her hands.

"I'm, like, a total dork. This is horrible."

He set their food on the small, card table. "I find you charming."

"You were probably dropped on your head a lot as a child."

Paris laughed out loud and had to rest his hands on the table as he chuckled. He felt light and happy. Almost carefree.

"What did you order us?"

"I have some toast and eggs, a hamburger and fries, some pasta and some steamed veggies with steak."

Jade perused the plates he uncovered with a critical eye. "A little of everything?"

Paris nodded.

"Including wine and dessert?"

"There's a red blend and some fruit and whipped cream, as well as a chocolate cake." He uncovered the desserts as he talked and pointed at the bottle.

"Awesome sauce. Let's start with that."

"Dessert before dinner?" he asked, raising his eyebrows at her.

She shrugged. "Why not? You're Coven Leader. Break some rules."

She was flirting with him, he realized. Now that he studied her, she looked nervous about it. Her toes were pigeoned - pointing in at one another and she had a slightly hunched look about her. He smiled again and she seemed to relax a bit.

"Why not, indeed?"

CHAPTER EIGHTEEN

"God, it's good to see you." Lily hugged her like she was afraid Jade would leave again.

"We have the same face. You see me every time you look in a mirror."

Lily pulled back and socked Jade on the arm with her fist. "You know what I mean, you asshole."

Jade smiled. "Yeah. Yeah I do."

Coming back at the Coven felt like coming home. It had surprised Jade, in a happy, pleasant way. They took commercial transport home - a taxi, a plane, and another taxi. She'd been awkward and shy as Paris walked her to her front door and kissed her before leaving. She'd stupidly waved about four times as he got back in the taxi to go to his own house. Coming inside, having Bruce barrel over and nearly knock her over, followed by the same from Lily.... Her heart felt full. An odd sensation to her.

"Henri is dying to know if you got any pics of hot firefighters."

"Ugh," Jade said as she pulled off her boots. "No, but I might just go find some online and lie. I mean, there were dudes all around. It was guy-heavy event, but there was no time. I thought there'd be more women among the witches, but no."

"Really? That's so weird."

"That's what I said! I guess women tend to be good at Earth and Water." Jade shrugged, putting her hands on her hips. "I dunno." Bruce sniffed at the fire boots Jade had taken off and huffed before whacking them off to the side with his long tail.

"I know, buddy," Jade said sympathetically. "They stink like forest fire."

"Soooo," Lily began and Jade knew what was coming. "It's not like I'm spying, except for how I totally am." She raised her eyebrows and bounced on her toes.

"You saw Paris kiss me."

"Yes! And you didn't sock him one! This is great!" Lily grabbed at Jade's arms, pulling her into the living room where she pushed her down on the sofa, sitting to face her. She held Jade's hands in hers. "So things are happening."

Jade thought about it before she answered. "Yes. Things are happening. But slowly."

Lily waved a hand. "Rome was not built in a day. Slow progress I can handle, but no progress? Was killing me."

Jade laughed and without thinking lurched forward and hugged Lily. She still smelled familiar, but there was now the scent of her own magic - grapefruit and cinnamon - underneath. They used the same shampoo, the same shower gel, the same perfume, but their magic was different. She sniffed at

Lily a bit. At least, they used to wear the same perfume.

"New perfume?"

"You like? It's this maple lemon thing. I got a sample. I like it." She went back to holding Jade's hands.

Jade nodded, her throat tight. "I do." Lily looked excited about it. It was another new thing for her. Something different from Jade. Another way they were drifting apart. They weren't the same person anymore. They never had been, but it was still hard for Jade to accept.

Lily squeezed Jade's hands and frowned. "Your hands are shaking."

"Oh, um." Jade pulled her hands back, clasping them tightly together and holding them in her lap. "I'm still tired from the magic I did, and I had a bad migraine. They've been shaking a bit."

Lily eyed her dubiously. "You need to see Gellar, don't you?"

Jade swallowed. Bruce toddled into the living room and stretched out in front of the unlit fireplace. He flicked his tongue at Jade. She wasn't sure she had it in her to conjure him even a small fire. Like he'd heard her thoughts, he looked away, closing his eyes, seemingly content without a fire for the moment.

"Yeah. I think I do," Jade agreed.

"Does Paris know?"

Jade shook her head, pressing her lips together. "No. I might just be tired still. You know?"

"But…"

Goddamn, she loved that she and Lily knew each other so well, but it was also a pain in the ass. "But I don't think that's it. I don't know." Jade sighed. "I mean, I knew it was a problem for me to push my magic too far, but I thought... I thought it would all be temporary. I've got all this power. Surely I'm meant to use it, right?" She shook her head. "But the migraines are bad. I push it. I don't mean to, but I get in these situations and I know I can do something and the power is there. I can feel it. I can see it. So I use it." She tightened her ponytail. "If I tell Paris, he'll tell me not to use any magic at all. I think." She exhaled. "But I like it. Using magic." She met Lily's eyes, so green and clear. Lily waited for Jade to articulate her thoughts. Not prodding or rushing her - just waiting with an easy grace. "I like the power. I like being really good stuff. And I *am* good. The fire... I don't think anyone else could have done what I did. And I like that." She wished she could say she was totally altruistic about the whole thing, but she wasn't. She liked being powerful.

"But the migraines are bad," Lily finished. "Getting worse?"

Jade nodded. "Getting worse. This one... When I was in the forest, I had a bad nosebleed with the migraine. And as my nose was bleeding, I thought, well, that's it. There go my brains out my nose. This other witch, Adam, kind of a dick, but he needed help, and helping him fried me out. Buried the needle of my magic. But I saved his life. I'm glad I did it. He's a dick, but no more so than a lot of people. Mostly harmless, I think. But I used a lot of magic to do it. Maybe too much. I don't know."

"So Gellar for sure."

She hated to admit it, but yeah. Jade needed to see a doctor. "Gellar for sure. I don't know if she'll have to tell Paris."

"Why would she? Your health is private."

"Maybe outside a Coven, but when it has to do with magic, I don't know what the rules are. I feel like I've got a lot going on. Formerly a Coven member, being dead, and now I think Paris and I are dating."

"That's a good thing. I'm really happy for you." Lily squeezed Jade's knee and Jade put her hand on top of Lily's, needing to say another thing.

"I was uncomfortable at first, when you told me he knew about our assault, that you told him. But now even though it's fucking awkward, it's good that it's out there, because I don't think..." She sighed.

"You don't think you could do this if you didn't know you could tell him stop and he'd stop the world."

"Yeah. And when I was in the forest, when he had to bury me?" Jade waited for Lily to nod and give her a go-on gesture. She knew Paris had talked to Lily, but she wanted to check that Lily knew what had happened. "At first, it was too much like... like then. His magic was trying to push me down, pull me down. He was everywhere. His magic, his scent, his presence." Even now, Jade had a visceral knee-jerk reaction and wanted to get up and move around - just to prove she could. She forced herself to stay seated. She was fine. She wasn't in danger. She was safe. "But I knew he was trying help. I knew it."

"But it was hard to feel it."

"Yeah."

"You know, I did a lot of reading on this, and I'm still reading stuff on this," Lily started.

"You be careful with what you find on the internet. Some people there think the world is flat."

Lily swatted her on the thigh. "I'm serious."

"I know." Jade hadn't been ready for a long, long time to hear what things Lily might have learned. She stilled herself. "What have you read?"

Lily squared her shoulders. "When we're in that emotional state, that state of panic and fear and anxiety, our animal brains are fully in charge. Fight or flight. Anything that's not fighting or fleeing is just white noise. The lizard brain can't understand it."

Boy, that sounded about right. "So what do you do?" Jade asked. "What do I do?"

Lily squeezed her knee again. "You're doing it now. You're talking about it, and processing it, while you're in a calmer state. While you can reason through it."

"I hate talking about it."

"I know. Maybe there's something else you could do. I can Google that too. But what you've been doing, what we used to do, burying our head in the sand and pretending it didn't happen, or knowing it happened, but pretending we could get over it if we just didn't think about it… that definitely didn't work." Lily paused and Jade knew she was going to say something hard and ugly. "We were raped."

Even knowing it was coming, Jade flinched. She struggled with the words themselves, finding them hard to hear and say. She could only nod.

"But we're still here," Lily added.

"We're still here," Jade repeated, letting the words roll around in her mind. Still here.

#

Jade was looking forward to getting back to work on Monday even though she had an appointment with Gellar in the afternoon. She'd hoped after being home for two days and doing nothing but hanging out with Bruce, going for a run with Daniel, and eating nachos with Henri, Callie and Lily, the tremors in her hands and fingers would go away. They hadn't. An appointment with Gellar was necessary. Paris had also called to remind her about it. She thought about lying and saying she would go but not actually do it, but he followed with asking her out to dinner and she'd felt a burn of shame. She didn't want to lie to him. And it was important she go see Gellar. If she did, she wouldn't have to lie to Paris and say everything was fine when she didn't actually know.

But everything would be fine. She hoped.

Laundry in the machine and the coffee pot brewing a fresh pot for the afternoon, Jade turned her attention back to what she'd been working on before the fire. The resurrection-like rune in Sakkara's books. She currently had all of Sakkara's demon grimoires in her house. She usually only kept one and Paris had the other two, but he'd dropped both off in the morning, asking if she would mind keeping them safe for him. He didn't like the idea of them being in his house, which wasn't demon warded. She'd solemnly taken them and promised to keep them safe. After creating some extra warding for them, she'd tucked them under the sofa. Bruce huffed, as he was usually wont to do, spitting three times next to the couch. She guessed that meant they were safe.

She had one out now and still had about an hour before Paris came back to pick her up for dinner. Lily had helped her pick out some nice jeans, a brown sweater and some jewelry. She felt like the necklace and earrings were a bit busy, but Lily said it looked good and if Jade wore some knee high boots, the jewelry wouldn't feel so over the top. She'd deferred to Lily's opinion.

Jade snapped a quick picture of the rune and then called the number Paris had given her for Yvonne.

"This is Yvonne speaking. How can I help you?"

"Uh, hi. This is Jade. You... well, you found me on a street corner and brought me back to your hotel?"

"I remember, Jade," Yvonne answered, an amused tone to her voice. "How are you?"

"Good. I mean, better than when you last saw me."

"I'm glad to hear it."

"Uh, thanks for that, by the way." Jade stumbled through her gratitude. Yvonne had been really nice to her when she'd found Jade - gotten her clothes, gotten her a room, brought her toiletries. All without being intrusive or inquisitive. She'd been calm, clear and concise. "I was kind of a mess and you were really... nice." She winced at the word. It was so non-descriptive, but it fit.

"You're welcome. I'm glad I was able to help. How is Paris?"

"Good, he's good. Um, about that. So, you knew his mom, right? Sakkara?"

"Of course. She was Coven Leader for my entire life at the Coven."

"Yeah. Well, we've got some of her grimoires and there's a rune in one that Paris asked me to look into. I don't know how to say this except just to say it. I hear you're a necromancer."

There was a pause and Jade figured she'd fucked everything up by blurting it out like that, but then Yvonne spoke. "I was. I mean, I guess I could still be. I had some powers of necromancy when I was younger."

"But not now?"

"Well, I don't know."

"Not the kind of thing you bust out and use, I guess." She thought of what Paris told her - about how Yvonne's mother made her bring back her dead sister, Kira, over and over again. It would make anyone with that power hesitant to use it, she supposed.

Yvonne laughed, wryly and darkly in Jade's ear. "Pretty much. Sakkara, she helped me."

Jade felt something sink in her gut at Yvonne's tone. It was grateful and fond. She knew Sakkara had been a well-loved Coven Leader, but no matter how much Jade heard it, she couldn't reconcile it with what she'd experienced herself. In Jade's mind, Sakkara would always be the Sparrow Lady - haunting her dreams, forcing her to the Dearth, treating her like a tool to be used.

"How did she help?" Jade asked. "Can you tell me?"

"Did Paris tell you about me? About... what happened?"

"Yeah. Yeah, he did." Jade knew what it was to have something in your past you didn't want to explain or detail. If Yvonne wasn't going to offer specifics, Jade could work with that.

"After that..." Yvonne sighed. "I didn't want the power. I mean, I never wanted it, but especially after that. My mom. Kira. I asked Sakkara to break my magic. All of it. I was willing to give up all of it just so I wouldn't have the necromancy anymore."

"But she didn't," Jade mused out loud, looking down at the rune in front of her. She traced it with her fingers. "You still have magic. That's how you do your work at the casino. Checking for magic cheaters."

"Yeah, I still have most of my magic. But not my necromancy."

Jade traced the symbol on the page again, something locking in place in her mind. "She bound your power. Your necromancy only. That's what this symbol is."

"I don't know the symbol you mean. If you send it to me, I can take a look at it. But yeah, Sakkara bound my necromancy. I can't use it anymore."

"I'll email it to you." Jade quickly sent the symbol to Yvonne, hearing Yvonne's phone *ping* a second later as the email arrived.

"Yeah, that's the one. I remember."

Jade supposed when you were dealing with the power of raising the dead, shit like that got burned in your brain. She tapped her finger against Sakkara's grimoire. Something was still not quite right, but she didn't know what it was. Only that something was bothering her.

"So you have Sakkara's grimoires?" Yvonne asked. "I'm glad Paris has them. She was such a great Coven Leader. I miss her. Not that Paris isn't good. I'm sure he is. I just... I grew up with Sakkara and she helped me so much that summer."

"She... was something else, for sure. From what I hear." Jade was careful to speak of Sakkara in the past tense and not like she was alive and well, demon-dealing and causing havoc. Yvonne must think that Jade had Sakkara's regular grimoires - the ones she would have used for general magic. Hardly anyone knew about Sakkara's hidden grimoires. Her demon and dark magic ones. "Thanks for talking to me about this. Paris was... concerned when he saw the rune in Sakkara's books. I'd been looking into some other stuff for him, and I wanted to thank you for helping me, so I asked if I could talk to you about it. And ... thanks," she repeated, feeling lame and awkward. "For everything."

"I'm happy to help. Like I said, Sakkara was so kind to me. I don't know if I would have made it without her binding my power. It's a terrible thing. I couldn't live knowing I had it inside me. The power to bring things back from the dead, but not enough power to keep them alive. I still don't understand why nature would grant such a thing."

Jade thought of her own situation. Being drowned by Sakkara as a child, yet finding her way somehow to Lily and existing in her body. "Yeah, nature's kind of fucked up sometimes."

Yvonne laughed and this time it wasn't dry or sad, it was open and bright. "No shit."

"Okay, so take care?" Jesus, she hated ending phone calls.

"You too. Come by the hotel sometime, I'll get you some casino chips to play with."

"I just might. Goodbye." Jade hung up the phone, still scratching idly at Sakkara's grimoire with her left fingers. She traced the rune again, and on a whim, sent a pulse of her magic into it. It shimmered except for one small portion that stayed dark, like it was incomplete or...

"Able to be broken," she said out loud. She turned her head to the pantry, debating for a moment. "Seth," she called. She waited ten seconds and cleared her throat, making her voice louder. "Seth." She felt the tingle in her spine that indicated he was about to appear and she braced herself.

"Possum!" He appeared with his strange heat-shimmer before he solidified, leaning against the inside of her pantry, hands in his pocket. He was beautiful. Even with the horns and tail. "You rang?"

Jade made a face at him. "Hello, Seth."

"Long time no chat. Have any wine?"

Jade stood up from the kitchen table and checked her wine cupboard, pulling out a bottle and glass, and pouring a full one for Seth.

"Not joining me?" he asked as she slid it past the warding and into her pantry. He sniffed it and looked disappointed, but drank it anyway. "Is this that same screw-top from before?"

"Yes. Still on sale."

"It actually ages not too badly." He took another sip and smacked his lips. Then, his eyes travelled up and down her, as if examining her.

"What?"

"You've done something. Something... with a lot of magic."

She clenched her hand into a fist, feeling the strange sensation of it wanting to tremble and shake. "I'm a witch. I do magic."

"Yes, but this," his eyes roved over her once more, "this has cooked your noodle a bit."

"Awesome. I had no idea you were a doctor as well as a demon."

Seth shrugged. "I'm a Renaissance man. Now, what did you call me for?" He narrowed his eyes. "Heard from Sakkara? Or my sister?"

"Thankfully, no." God, that was all she needed. Another demon showing up. "Although this is kind of about Sakkara."

"Mother Dearest. You know, she's a piece of work, and considering the kind of mother I had-"

Jade held a hand up. Her left. It didn't tremble as bad as the right. "I don't think my brain can handle knowing anymore about you personally. I already know too much about you and Medusa."

Seth grinned lasciviously. "Oh, the stories I could tell you. I'm still working on getting back in Medusa's good graces. Any ideas on that?"

Jade couldn't help but answer honestly, thinking back to what she saw, or rather heard, of Seth and Medusa's interactions. "Try not being such a dick. She didn't kill you on the spot, but you're kind of... slick with her."

Seth looked like he was actually listening and considering Jade's words. "What do you mean, slick?"

"You're trying too hard to be charming. She's not charmed."

"I don't try to be charming, I *am* charming."

"Fine. Don't take my advice. Keep doing what you're doing. You let me know how that goes."

Seth's jaw worked for a moment. "Fine. I'll try it your way. I've only had thousands of years experience with her-"

"And look how well that worked out. You're still casting about for advice, so clearly you know what you're doing isn't working."

"I dislike your logic and intelligence intensely."

"Liar."

"Yes," he said simply. "I do rather like your brain. Which is why I'm somewhat concerned you seem to have done something to it."

Jade resisted the urge to reach up and touch her temples. She had some kind of muscle twitch there now as well. Well, she was seeing Gellar soon enough and would much rather her medical opinion than Seth's.

"Getting back to the item at hand. Sakkara." She grabbed the grimoire and held it up. "This rune. It's some kind of Binding Rune, but I think it's incomplete."

Seth tapped his finger on the door jamb. "Are you asking for my help, Possum? Because demon favors are not free."

"I'm exchanging knowledge."

"What are you offering?"

Jade smiled. "I already gave you help. You asked about Medusa."

"I did not."

"You did too," she shot back, feeling like a six year old and relishing it. "You wanted to know how to get back in her good graces, and I answered. Then you asked for additional clarification and I also answered." She ticked the items off on her fingers as she spoke.

He groaned, looking disgusted. "I can't believe I'm making rookie mistakes. All for the love of Medusa. That woman…"

"Have your existential love crisis on your own time." She tapped her finger on the book. "The Rune."

He beckoned her closer with a flap of his fingers. She moved in and held the book up closer.

"Yes, you're correct. Incomplete Binding Rune. Probably done to keep someone's necromancy in check."

"In check, but not bound forever?"

"No. This could be broken by anyone with sufficient demon rune knowledge. I could break it." He glanced at her. "You could break it."

"Me?"

"You've shown to be adept and you knew enough to recognize there was something wrong with it. You've also warded this pantry quite well. And…" He stretched his neck, peering past her. "Something in the living room. Your sofa. Nicely done. I admit, I've tried to break your wards and have been unsuccessful."

"When? I didn't feel that."

He waved a hand at her. "Please, as if I would let you know I'm pushing them. But, as I said, you're annoyingly good at what you do." He shot-gunned the rest of his wine and put the glass down, giving it a slight push to send it back through the warding. "More info I'm going to need more from you." Seth said more like it was a vulgar word. She wanted to shower from it.

"No, that's it," she said, closing the grimoire. So, Sakkara bound Yvonne's necromancy, but not permanently. But Yvonne didn't know that. Why?

"I do love watching your mind work. I swear I can see a little hamster in your brain, running on his wheel. It wears a little back leather jacket and black eyeliner. Guy-liner, I think they call it."

"As amusing as this is, we're done for today."

"No more wine?"

His tail swished back and forth behind him and she swore his horns perked up anxiously. Remembering her time in the Dearth, she stupidly, ridiculously, felt sorry for him. She poured him another glass and sent it through the ward. Her doorbell rang and caught her attention. It would be Paris, for their date.

"Are you blushing or having some kind of apoplectic attack? No, you really are blushing! Is it your Englishman? Have there been developments?"

"Goodbye, Seth." Jade grabbed the edge of the pantry door, getting read to slam it.

"Don't you want your wine glass back?"

"Keep it for next time." She shut the door in his face. She took a deep breath and smoothed her ponytail. By the time she got to the foyer, Bruce was at the front door, clawing at the wood.

"Oh my god, I'm getting it." She shooed at him. Once he realized she was opening the door, he scurried backward, his entire lower body wiggling.

Paris stood on her doorstep, looking calm, smiling, and - she blinked.

"Are you wearing jeans?"

"Yes." He looked down at himself. "Is that a problem?"

"No, I just…" He looked casual and relaxed. Comfortable. She could feel her face flush more. "You look…. Nice." Ugh, again, qualifier of non-qualifiers. She could try to fix her bland statement, or she could find her purse and get her coat and boots. She turned away and took a minute to get her boots on, wanting to curse when one of the zippers gave her trouble. Once done, she grabbed a medium-weight jacket and her purse, pausing pet Bruce on the head. "Be a good lizard. Nothing but, okay?" She stood up and found Paris still smiling, this time showing some teeth.

"You look lovely."

She laughed nervously and randomly wondered if she had anything stuck in her teeth. "It's okay? You didn't say where we're going."

"Have you ever had Peruvian food?"

"No. Do I have to eat anything weird?"

"No. Maybe spicy, is that all right?"

Jade nodded, pulling the door shut behind her as she exited. "A little spice might be nice."

Want More Covencraft?
Book #6 (untitled) coming June
2018

About the Author

Margarita loves the art, creativity and romanticism of storytelling. Sometimes, however, the act of putting pen to paper proves challenging. She works to develop genuine, relatable characters which grow in the hearts of her readers. From that foundation, the stories flourish into a warm friend.

She enjoys pursuits which blur the lines between the analytical and creative sides of her brain. She believes there is a place for both logic and imagination to work together. When they do, the results are magical.

The 'label' she identifies most with is 'storyteller.' According to Wikipedia, storytelling is the conveying of events in words, and images, often by improvisation or embellishment. It seems to fit pretty well with how she feels about her work.

At www.margaritagakis.com you can sign up for her newsletter to get updates on her current work and upcoming releases.

Also by the Author

Ravenwood (writing as Margaux Gillis)

The night of the full moon....
Still grieving the recent death of her parents, Elinore Reed is called to live with family she's never met at Ravenwood. A carriage accident leaves her alone, in the forest, on the night of the full moon, where something lurks in the trees.

A bite that will not heal...
After being bitten in the woods, Elinore fears for her sanity. The bite is turning black. She hears things she should not be able to and feels emotions strange and foreign to her. Unnerved by her new surroundings and by the disquieting behavior of her uncle, Hayter, Elinore takes comfort in the companionship she finds at Ravenwood, including her growing affection for Caleb, her cousin by marriage.

A deepening mystery...
Why is the bite on her arm turning black? Why does she dream of the forest, of wolves and of ravens? Why is she compelled by a wolf howling at night? As Elinore struggles to understand life at Ravenwood, what will happen when the truth is revealed?